THE PHOENIX ELITE

SACRED BLOOD

C.T. CLARK

QUARK LEGACY

ISBN-13: 978-1-962600-00-2

The Phoenix Elite: Sacred Blood

Book Cover designed by Miblart

Character Illustrations by Emmanuel Sylvester

http://www.ctclarkbooks.com

This is for MacKenzie.
We go to the ends of the Earth for each other.
Thank you for all of the inspiration.

C.C.

PROLOGUE

OFFICIAL MEMORANDUM

By the order of the United Nations Security Council, the PHOENIX ELITE INITIATIVE is terminated. Funds for our initiative have been reallocated to other programs, and we can no longer continue. All staff and administrators have seven days to discard any existing materials and pack equipment into the secure crates provided. All previously signed nondisclosure agreements will be enforced to the full force of the law, as the terms of imprisonment for any leaking of classified material have been communicated throughout your service. Any retention of classified material, willful or otherwise, carries a mandatory minimum thirty-year prison sentence for each charge.

We know you may be concerned about the well-being of the sensitive material in our custody. A special czar has been appointed to tend to these cases. The remaining funds in our account have been put into escrow for the czar to apply in these cases until exhausted.

Under no circumstances are you permitted to continue studies of existing material.

We appreciate your service in this project.

Justin Hodges

Justin Hodges
UN Security Council General Counsel

CHAPTER 1
BLOODBORNE

THE SUN SETS IN MONROVIA, LIBERIA, casting the last remnants of a scorching summer day. One could only assume the lush greens in the distance are beauties of the natural world that remain untouched by man or machine, but they are too far away to discern. All one can do is admire this paradise through a tiny tempered window. The window, no wider than a brick, was an inane touch to create an illusion of coziness. Instead, it serves as a reminder of the outside splendor that those inside rarely could embrace.

The green space wasn't what drew the United Nations Security Council to the old skyrise hotel three miles from the African coast. When it refurbished the aging facility decades ago, the ongoing civil conflict in Liberia was the central selling point. It kept the tourists away from their spaceship of a building.

Inside, the guts of the structure were reshaped from the highest grade of available steel, its form adorned with extravagant curves and arches that served no purpose beyond aesthetics. Hidden within these fussy walls, the top-secret science lab was assembled with a few spare billions of contributions from member states. In its prime, this space redefined *state of the art* every day. Today, on this depressing day in 2003, the once-gleaming steel loses its luster. The spacious tables that once buzzed with scientific fervor now stand desolate, stripped of equipment and experimentation. It's moving day.

Because of a bunch of sad-sack, visionless morons.

It's their fault that he'll have to do the unimaginable.

James Bricker hates being told what to do. But thanks to some government-puppet halfwit, there's this minuscule window to imagine his next step in life. It is not how he planned he'd start his fifties. He packs a clean flask into a custom-fit foam casing. The foam fits perfectly inside a steel container. Of course it does. The government wouldn't wish to see their eight-dollar flask damaged, so they needed to spend ten dollars on the custom foam to shield it from harm.

Bricker's eyes feel heavy, the product of decades of sleepless nights. He certainly hasn't caught any z's in the last seventy-two hours. How some penny-pinching paper-pusher could undo years of progress on the most important work of his life is not a topic to be broached. Today, his sole refuge is the generous pour of whiskey on ice patiently waiting for him in his apartment. It's his medicine for his laundry list of ailments, especially the recurring tremor in his right leg. Today, it'll be just because.

Over his shoulder, a pair of armed military officers stand guard at a reinforced titanium sliding door. Together, they are less than four hundred pounds, and their hard-earned whiskers hold fewer than forty years between them. His shoes are older than these basic-training bootlickers. They couldn't see nuance if it was spelled in bold letters on a piece of paper. By the look of their impatient scowls, they resent they haven't been relieved for a lunch break yet. Poor babies. Bricker is perfectly content to make them wait indefinitely.

Bricker snaps the steel container shut, its metallic clang punctuating his frustration. He places it on a pile next to dozens just like it. Each case bears a stamped mark, haphazardly placed, announcing Property of United Nations—Phoenix Elite Initiative Discontinued.

Over his thirty-year career, it was always the same story: scientists pour their souls into groundbreaking initiatives, only to have their efforts extinguished carelessly by the whims of government overlords. There's always a new shiny thing for them to pour their billions into, and the rest of the mere mortals obediently fall in line.

This time, it all hurts worse.

With the advancing precision of the genetic tools at his disposal, the art of cloning was nearing perfection. He knows he isn't perfect, but if given the chance to follow through on this work and nurture the children, he would have reshaped the world for the better. With the DNA they had in stock, he was sure of it. The Rolls-Royce-riding, big-gov lawyer who drew up his reassignment paperwork was clearly on a mission to close that door.

But that's not what hurts the most.

He was on the precipice of something genuinely earth-shaking. He never bothered to tell anyone else in the lab his little secret, not even Kebe.

Bricker's Liberian brother in science and long-time partner, Emmanuel Kebe, diligently scrubs the inside of a beaker, the bristles of a special brush dancing across the glass. More flecks of gray pepper his hair than when they first met. All that running and weightlifting he does doesn't stop time completely. Bricker muses on the peculiar synchronicity of their partnership—a universe seemingly intent on balancing his crotchety disposition with Kebe's unyielding optimism. Truth be told, Kebe stands among the world's most esteemed scientists and has always had his pick of opportunities, but for some reason he always opted to stay. Any chemistry they've developed has brought out the best of each other, though that's often been after colorful and articulate clashes.

"I'm not sure what I'll do without seeing your smiling—" Kebe says as Bricker glances over. "Well, your regular face."

A quiver shakes from Bricker's otherwise tight lips. Over the years, nobody has made his gruff exterior crack like Kebe. Bricker didn't get into this career to make friends, and he hasn't—with one exception.

"You finally gonna learn to sail?" Bricker asks.

Kebe stifles a laugh, the noise chiming through the sterile laboratory air. "Nah. First, I'm going to try your funny American game of golf."

"Keep your eye on the ball," Bricker says.

"I thought that was baseball."

Bricker checks over his shoulder again. The armed military officers grumble to each other, distracting them from their duty, just as he wants them. Calorie deprivation and dehydration can only serve him well today. It's as close as he can get to lulling these babies to sleep.

About ten feet away, tucked behind a glass storage unit labeled Authorized Personnel Only rests a case of hundreds of crimson vials. A queasy exhilaration overtakes him. The lab is kept at a chilly sixty-five degrees, but typically Bricker doesn't get goose bumps. Today, every fiber of his being drums with a vitality he hasn't felt in decades.

It's time.

Kebe's voice breaks through his charged headspace as he looks up from the clean beaker. Concern etches his features. "Are you okay, James?"

A pair of deep, labored breaths escape Bricker's lips, his long-practiced mindfulness techniques taking effect. He allows himself a moment of respite, a calmness settling within him. Meeting Kebe's brown eyes, he musters the strength to confront the inevitable. "I'm sorry I have to do this."

Without hesitation, Bricker reaches into his lab coat, prompting a raised eyebrow from Kebe. He pulls out a semiautomatic triple-barreled pistol cast in red brass. The custom black grip was designed to resemble the mythical basilisk, the serpentine enemy of the phoenix, a connection Bricker found all too fitting when he stumbled upon it. Though the center silver barrel points straight ahead, the two others angle outward, but are still poised to strike his target's chest.

With one swift pull, three bullets pierce Kebe's muscular chest. The bang of the three chambers is no louder than a typical handgun, but it's as if each chamber competes for dominance, their collective echoes bouncing off the wall. Kebe crumples to the floor, his frame collapsing into a lifeless heap. A pond of blood forms along his right collarbone, staining his once-pristine white lab coat.

A twinge of remorse stabs at Bricker's gut. He's gone down an irreversible path. If there were another way to go about this, he would have taken it.

Before the military officers can react, Bricker readjusts his aim. With one quick bang, the two officers collapse simultaneously, their weapons slipping from their grasp.

Bricker hurries to the glass storage unit. He forcefully strikes the fragile barrier, causing it to shatter into a myriad of sparkling fragments. Brushing away the shattered pieces, Bricker clutches the coveted case in his hands. For a moment, he revels in his prize—these paper-pushers gravely underestimated the lengths he was willing to go to protect his life's work. He cradles the precious cargo in the crook of his arm.

"Don't do this, James," Kebe says, his voice strained as he frantically searches for anything within reach to stem the bleeding from his chest. He drags himself over to his desk. Underneath is a red security button. Bricker and Kebe lock eyes in a brief yet poignant moment, eliciting an unexpected pang of care within Bricker's hardened heart—a gush of empathy that catches him off guard. Nevertheless, he aims his pistol at his old friend, resolve hardening him from the inside out.

"This will not end well for you," Kebe says.

Kebe triggers a screeching alarm. Gripping his pistol, Bricker turns from his old friend and hurdles the fallen officers. *Kebe did precisely what I knew he would do.* Bricker would have been foolish not to plan for it—and he's no fool. He flashes his ID across a scanner. The titanium doors open into a long, sleek metallic corridor.

He knows exactly where he's going—and has for months. He estimates he has a mere ten seconds until a swarm of armed guards converges on his location. They will likely deactivate his ID by then, so there will be no more easy passages. He kicks over a commercial-sized metal waste basket, causing it to clatter on the ground. Swiftly tearing away the lining, he unveils his large, military-style backpack. In one fluid motion, he slings the weighty backpack over his shoulder, carefully tucking the case of vials under his arm like a football.

The added burden strains his weary muscles, threatening to buckle his knees under the weight. Balance is his primary enemy today. The wobble in the legs will be his undoing. He presses forward, his mind locked in a delicate dance between the nervous and musculoskeletal systems, desperate for them to cooperate for a few more minutes.

Strobing lights flash all around, blinding him momentarily. Within moments, a group of military officers appears before him, their guns raised, closing in rapidly. "Freeze! Show us your hands!" yells one of the officers.

With a stumble, Bricker turns and sprints the other way. He reaches into the depths of his coat, retrieving a smoke bomb. He pulls the pin out with his teeth and tosses it behind him, releasing a billowing gray cloud that engulfs the officers, shrouding the walkway in a haze of disorienting smoke.

Bang!

A bullet pinches Bricker in the leg. A searing pain rips through his left hamstring, his better hamstring. His delicate balance quakes. All his concentration goes toward staying on his feet, and the case of vials slips from his grasp, tumbling through the air with wild abandon. Upon impact with the ground, the plastic lid springs open, sending the vials cascading to the tile floor, where they shatter upon impact, bursting into a million pieces, the sound of broken glass ringing in Bricker's ears. His mind races, desperate for a solution, but all he finds is panic.

"Oh God, no!" Bricker shouts. He hadn't planned for this. Frantically, he reaches for a large fragment of a shattered vial, his trembling hands attempting to capture the spilled blood. It's useless. Desperation grips him as he fumbles for another partial vial, inadvertently flicking it away down the hall into the billowing cloud of smoke. The blood from the separate vials swirls together into one massive puddle.

The last resort. Bricker dives chest first into the blood. He swirls his arms in the red lake, trying to soak up as much as possible. A stampede of footsteps closes in on him. Bricker emerges from the pool of blood with a desperate roll, his lab coat now a grotesque palette of crimson stains. He fires into a trio of officers who emerge through the smoke, and three more rounds into the fog.

Regaining his footing, he runs. He reaches an intersection. Behind him, rushing officers burst through the clouds and hurdle their fallen comrades. In front of him, another group turns the corner. Straight ahead, a window that overlooks Monrovia.

"I said freeze!" the lead officer yells. "If you have a clean shot, take it," she tells her team.

Bricker adjusts his backpack over his blood-soaked lab coat. He empties his magazine through the glass. Cracks spiderweb across the surface, splintering the window into a fractured mosaic. He dives headfirst through the cracked window and into the clear, empty skies, nine stories up. Glass particles erupt into a haze of dust, and the wind gusts through what's left of his gray hair. The crisp sunlight hits his battered body.

He rips a cord on the shoulder strap of his backpack. A parachute springs open. The violent jerk of the unfurled chute sends a shiver down Bricker's back.

At street level, a black SUV idles in the fire lane. Reaching the earth, Bricker dumps the backpack and limps toward the getaway ride. Clutching his balled-up lab coat, he stumbles into the passenger door. He has won.

CHAPTER 2
OFFICIALLY A DISASTER

TENSIONS BROIL in a packed lecture hall of the College of Chemistry. Multinational corporations of all stripes have flown in for this presentation. Some are here for the information; others are here to scout the talent. The only time you'd find these types in Switzerland at this time of year is for a luxury ski retreat. Yet, everyone's routine has been disrupted on this particular day at École Polytechnique Fédérale de Lausanne.

To say Adam Eberhardt is anxious for this moment is an understatement's understatement, surpassing any conventional measure of anxiety. Much like his unruly, unkempt hair, his anticipation points in every conceivable direction. Positioned at a lab bench surrounded by an array of liquid chemicals, the young German man prepares a demo, an endeavor no less unnerving than his previous gig.

Before the impending presentation, he diligently carried out his duties as the enforcer of name tags at the welcome table, a post that only intensified his unease. Titans of medicine, weapons manufacturing, and consumer electronics scribbled on the ultra-cheap name tags. His job was to ensure the guests slapped the stickers on their fancy-schmancy embroidered suits. It was a price of admission some of the head honchos did not enjoy paying. While his university had recently refurbished the wooden roof of the lecture hall, they opted against splurging on lanyards. It's a decision that feels incongruous on this momentous day that warrants greater prestige.

Within the sea of expectant faces, Adam spots a refined gentleman with blue eyes framed with mocha-colored bifocals. It is his mentor, Professor Louvet. If Louvet is nervous about his protégé's presentation, he isn't showing it as he sips from a thermos. He probably has good job security since he's been at the university for two decades and has brought in five hundred million dollars of grants. Louvet practically lives on campus. Adam has seen the pictures of his six grandkids on his desk, so they do exist. Adam has never understood why he'd spend so much on eyewear to look at photos when he could fly to see them. Or take a train. But one thing is for certain: Louvet would have known how to get those lanyards.

The bigwigs are not accustomed to the shoulder-bumping, standing-room-only crowd they find themselves in today. Approximately thirty percent have already peeled off their name stickers, and there's not enough time to compel them to put them back on. He'll have to devise a solution to address that problem in the future.

In the presence of all these fancy dressers, Adam can't help but think the twenty minutes he spent on the internet searching for "cool-looking man clothes" was a waste. He suspects the main concepts were lost somewhere between the inspiring images and his application. Perhaps if he had searched for clothing suitable for "gorilla-sized" people, it would have worked out better. Unfortunately, in his haste this morning, he forgot to wear socks. Though standing by this lab bench of beakers is quite a responsibility, it's not every day Adam has a front-row seat to witness the birth of a star.

Emerging from this nebula is a twenty-four-year-old wunderkind. Margot prepares her laptop on the nearby podium like any other day. However, the swirl of tension in Adam's gut defies any known description. He is far more anxious about Margot's presentation than Margot herself appears to be. Her title slide spans the giant projector screen: NUCLEAR MEDICINE APPLICATIONS FOR PATIENT CARE—MARGOT CZARNECKI MD–PHD—SEPTEMBER 13, 2024.

Though most of their college peers do not look like academics, Margot defies expectations. Some might be surprised to see someone so young captivate this crowd, but she's been waist-deep in this research for a while—eight years, to be precise. Adam has never seen her in the knee-length black dress or checkered blazer she's wearing today. She must have borrowed them from a friend, because there's no way she'd spend money on such clothes. Margot wears whatever practical things she can thrift. The lone exception is the elegant silver watch on her left wrist, part of her daily ensemble. After all, she says time is her most valuable asset.

Margot came to the university at fourteen, one year earlier than Adam. There has never been any confusion regarding their respective abilities, especially not in the eyes of Professor Louvet. That's all quite okay with Adam. Everyone knows she is special—except her. Adam is happy to just be near her. Academically, figuratively, and most certainly literally. Of course, she does not know that.

Margot's words flow confidently as she clicks to the next slide in her deck. "With greater use of integrated imaging, clinical nuclear medicine can reach into diagnostic radiology and oncology. Yet there are concerns before nuclear medicine becomes the quintessential modality. The financial advantages of diagnostic radiology and an insufficient pool of qualified nuclear clinicians handicap its present-day usefulness." With the bright lights on, Margot owns her moment.

Margot gestures to the lab bench Adam mans off to the side of the stage. She reminds him of an old silent-movie actress in a film he saw once, but he doesn't remember her name. Her blond hair has streaks of brown and glints of auburn like a warm log in a fire. Women budget so they can have streaks like that, but hers are natural. She might have done something to it today. It usually is wavier. And, of course, her legs. They'd be nice legs to have for walking, or standing, or other things legs are needed for.

"Adam?"

Adam snaps out of his daze, immediately aware of the weight of everyone's eyes upon him, including Margot's. *Oh God, what did I miss?* She's so totally staring at him. Three seconds is long, but six seconds is twice as long as three seconds. A vertical line carves between Margot's tense eyebrows. "Are you ready?"

"Oh . . . uh . . . yeah." Demonstrating potential synergies between proton therapy and boron neutron capture theory by incorporating boron into tumor cells. Yep, that's what we're doing.

Disoriented, Adam reaches for a beaker. On the way, his elbow nudges a graduated cylinder filled with liquid ammonia, teetering it precariously. Reacting swiftly, he lunges to catch it but inadvertently knocks over an entire row of flasks, triggering a symphony of shattering glass. The acoustics of the finely crafted wooden ceiling amplify the collective gasp that resonates in Adam's ears. The anxiety swirling in his stomach activates hyperspeed.

His muscles seize up, all but his eyes—they dart back and forth to capture the audience's reactions to his blunder. The enormity of his failure engulfs him, and he absorbs this massive defeat. "Uh . . . that's my bad."

Margot puts a hand to her temple because, well, where else is she supposed to put it? She turns to her audience. "I'm sorry, but it appears we will be unable to conduct the radiopharmaceuticals demo today. After this session, we will email links to those of you who opted in to our mailing list, and we will perform the demo live via web conference once we can reset. For now, I'll continue with the presentation."

On hands and knees, Adam scrambles to salvage the situation. With some rags and a random tissue he finds in his pocket, he hurries to soak up the chemicals. She can continue if he can keep the different substances separated.

The fluid cools his fingertips as the chemical pools slowly inch toward one another on the parquet floor. It's a futile pursuit, but he can't quit. Each dab of the rag flings particles from one pool into another. He's sure Margot won't ever look at him again, so his last three years of obsessing have likely been pointless.

Adam's thoughts are interrupted by wisps of smoke emanating from the pooled chemicals, drawing comments from the crowd and interrupting Margot's presentation again.

"Don't worry, that's just a little boron," Adam says, trying to calm the concerned audience. A pungent, malodorous gas invades his nostrils. Though overwhelming disgust flows through his nasopharynx, he does everything he can to keep it from showing on his face.

As billowing smoke fills the room, the shrill screech of the fire alarm jolts the room. The sprinkler system unleashes torrents of water, soaking everything in its indiscriminate path. The guests flood the exits, their heads shielded by an assortment of makeshift defenses, including file folders and purses.

The relentless downpour collides with the chemical concoction, rattling off a cacophony of firecracker-like snaps and pops. Each crackle feels like a piece of Adam's soul splintering away. This was her moment.

The sprinkler relentlessly showers Margot, transforming her from a poised and confident presenter to a drenched spectator, her clothes clinging to her form. She closes her eyes and takes a deep breath as if she can't bear watching her dream walk out the door.

"Margot," Adam says, his words tumbling forth. "I'm, you know, so, so very sorry. I know how hard you worked for all this."

Margot brings her fist to her mouth as if to censor herself, her hurt eyes holding back emotion. "Adam, I can't do this with you right now. Thank you for volunteering and offering to help." Margot shakes her head as she marches over to a nearby side exit. She flings open the creaky, weathered wooden doors, their hinges protesting against the force, causing them to crash against the wall. As she exits, the doors gradually swing shut behind her.

It's officially a disaster.

THE SIX HUNDRED GUESTS, now evacuated and annoyed, dry out hats, scarves, blazer jackets, and phones in the autumn air. Standing apart from the crowd with Professor Louvet, Adam is careful not to make eye contact with any of them. Surely, his hulk-sized body makes it impossible for anyone to mistake the bumbling fool for someone else. Three fire trucks have parked near the front of the steps of the towering chemistry lecture hall. Emergency workers navigate the area. Firefighters rope off a barrier around the building. Police officers stand guard around the new perimeter. Medics provide first aid to attendees with scraped knees and others who complain of smoke inhalation. Men in hazmat suits sweep the area with detectors.

A middle-aged man with slicked-back hair barks into his phone. "What do you mean my jet isn't ready? Look, it's just a couple of hours earlier than I had scheduled!"

Adam's heart rate has yet to slow as hazmat guys exit the building with bags of contaminated material. "I'm sorry, Professor . . . again. I, uh, got anxious. With all the people and . . ." Adam's voice trails off, blowing away with the autumn breeze.

"I don't think I'm the one you should be apologizing to," Professor Louvet says, gesturing toward the crowd gathered on the other side of the expansive lawn.

Adam's gaze follows the professor's hand to where Margot takes questions from a throng of eager academics, sopping hair and all. Without a demo, slides, screen, and notes, she delivers an impromptu version of the presentation they came for. She checks her trusty watch to ensure she isn't lingering too long on a point. They love her.

"I was finally able to get to your paper over breakfast," Professor Louvet tells Adam. "You make some rather bold assertions about the future of laser fusion energy."

Adam's mind races, unsure how to interpret the professor's statement. Having finally managed to stop sweating from his blunders, he'd rather not work up another stream. "Well, I wouldn't call them bold," he says, trying to downplay any potential impudence in his work. "I just . . . I guess I see burning plasma being particularly useful as a clean, carbon-free option, but, uh, I mean . . . I'm probably so far off the mark."

Louvet squints at him with his sharp blue eyes drilling into him. Adam has no idea what it means. If he had to guess whether the professor's gaze harbors approval or disapproval, he'd prefer to flip a coin than trust his judgment. "During all those hours you spend at the gym, do you recall anyone ever dropping a heavy weight on your head?" Louvet asks.

"No, sir. I don't go to the gym. I only do bodyweight exercises. Well, that's not necessarily true. I do have a few dumbbells and a kettlebell, but I'm actually borrowing that kettlebell—"

"Adam, I think you should apply for one of the doctoral programs in Britain. And I know there are plenty of opportunities in the States."

Huh. It's unexpectedly encouraging, Adam thinks, detecting a parental tone in Louvet. "I don't know if I'm cut out..." Adam's attention drifts to Margot. Two guys in gray suits sporting earpieces maneuver their way to the front of her crowd. Margot engages with them. If these guys attended her presentation, he would have noticed—*and they are not wearing any name tag stickers*. A tingle shoots down Adam's spine.

"And even if I were," Adam continues, "I don't think I could handle all that British weather."

"Regardless, for everyone's sake, we need to find someone capable of running your experiments. That way, we can keep our building on its foundation." Louvet says, gently patting Adam on the back. Clearly, Adam's propensity for the occasional whoops has not escaped him.

Towering over Margot, the mysterious men in expensive suits share some paper with her. She reads it and covers her mouth in shock. She rarely expresses herself that way. They nudge her away, and she obliges, concerned about whatever they have shown her. She offers goodbyes to the crowd.

It's probably nothing, Adam thinks. *Margot is brilliant. Perhaps she even knows these gentlemen.*

As they turn the corner of the building, one of the men reaches out to guide Margot by the wrist while the other scopes the crowd, which continues its activities obliviously. As they move away, she engages the man in conversation, but a few people walk in front of Adam, limiting his view to only glimpses. Pangs of nausea sweep through his gut. Leaning forward, he strains to see, desperate to catch a glance, but every angle is obstructed. For a fleeting moment, he finds a narrow window. From behind Margot, the second man reaches around, covers her mouth, and drags her out of view.

"Hey!" Adam yells from a distance. He sprints like he was shot from a cannon. In pursuit, he bumps into a bigwig in an expensive suit, sending the man tumbling gracelessly into the grass. Adam doesn't break stride.

He rounds the corner onto the École Polytechnique campus, but no Margot. The five acres never felt so imposing. He sees squished blades of grass still bearing the marks from their trampling moments earlier. The trail unfolds ahead, guiding him step by step. With each stride, fallen leaves emit a rhythmic, haunting crunch beneath his feet. There are more low-hanging branches on campus than he realized, their naked limbs jutting out like barbs. He ducks under one, feeling it scrape across his back.

He catches sight of Margot, a hundred meters away, being manhandled by the abductors, their grip tightening as she kicks and thrashes to free herself. Adam slams into a group of college students that crosses his path. With the power of a linebacker, he plows ahead, sending them sprawling. Locking eyes with one of the bewildered students he just trampled, he urgently instructs, "Get the police. They're all back there."

"On who? On you?" a student asks.

A realization strikes Adam like a meteorite. He's put the eyes of the entire campus and local law enforcement on the chemistry hall. He's Margot's first and last line of defense. He dashes ahead, disappearing into the labyrinth of trees, weaving through them with the precision of a tiger in its natural habitat. His mind is solely focused on the impending confrontation. He's ready to rumble.

In the alley between two campus buildings, Margot writhes, swinging her bound wrists like a club, but her strikes bounce off the men. She kicks, but one of the men catches her foot. The abductors spot Adam, and in a chillingly composed manner, they exchange hushed whispers. Swiftly, they force Margot into the back of a white utility van. She lunges to exit, but its doors slam shut with finality.

Adam closes in quickly. He clenches his fist. He's never pressed his fingers this deep into his palm. There's a new fire in his belly, one he hasn't felt before. All rational thought leaves his brain. His limbic system drives, and the accelerator is stuck to the floorboard. His ordinarily compassionate nature transforms into that of a vengeful mother grizzly. His weapon will be an overhand right, honed from his earlier days throwing baseballs. It should theoretically be a crushing force if he keeps his elbow locked tight. Theoretically.

Planting his back foot firmly, Adam unleashes the overhand right. A chin is directly in the trajectory of his incoming bomb. Yet, mere centimeters from his target, Adam's world abruptly turns dark—a sharp, disorienting thwack rings in his left ear. Pain floods his senses, robbing him of feeling in his legs. Helplessly, his body crumples to the unforgiving sidewalk, his skull colliding with the unyielding concrete surface.

Fragments of vision flicker back to existence, like scattered puzzle pieces desperate to interlock. Through the haze, a malevolent presence with long hair casts a shadow over him. A third man leers down, his face a canvas of twisted amusement. He kicks him in the stomach before hopping into the van.

Echoes of a screaming woman mix with the rhythm of a diesel engine. Cheek on the unforgiving pavement, Adam squints at a blurry world, a wasted mess. The white van gradually disappears down the road.

CHAPTER 3
COORDINATION

THE BANDAGE AROUND Adam's head loosens, allowing access to the sterile dressing beneath. Twelve arduous hours have passed since Nurse Genni took charge of his care, yet Adam hadn't uttered ten words in her presence. She's likely acutely aware his physical wounds are not his primary issue, but despite her friendly face, he isn't going to talk to her about it.

Scattered haphazardly around his hospital bed are crumpled scraps of paper, each scribbled with hastily scrawled diagrams, plans, and ideas. *Why did Margot go with them? What did they show her? What do they want her for?* To an outsider, the display could pass as the plot of a schizophrenic madman, but to delve into Adam's head is to navigate a hyperactive swarm of ideas, concepts, patterns, personal doubts, and interconnectedness. There are brainstorms, and then there are storms in the brain—depending on whether logic or emotions dominate his thought space. For now, he has put the pen down.

Perched at the edge of his hospital bed, Adam glues his entire being to the twenty-four-hour news network blaring from the flat screen across the room. The chyron flashes: BREAKING NEWS—COORDINATED SERIAL ABDUCTIONS.

Hospitals are supposed to be places for healing. It is not living up to this billing today. Being here has cranked Adam's anxiety from his ordinary discomforting 8 out of 10 up to a nearly unbearable 9.785. Not only did he lose Margot, but he also failed spectacularly. Had it been filmed, he'd have gotten clowned online. How had he not noticed the third guy? Of course someone was driving the van. The incessant self-doubt and self-recrimination are torturous, surpassing not just second-guessing but delving into the realms of twelfth- and thirteenth-guessing.

Equipped with replacement gauze and bandages, Nurse Genni delicately peels the padding back to inspect his twelve stitches. She freshens up his wrap. "Coming along quite nicely. Is there anything you require?" she asks.

"Thank you," Adam murmurs absentmindedly, his focus still captured by the broadcast, unable to tear himself away.

Nurse Genni can only offer a smile. "Oh, I forgot to mention," she says as she reaches the doorway, "there's someone here for you."

Adam furrows his brow. Who in the world would that be? On any other day, such an unexpected visitor would have piqued his curiosity, perhaps even sparked a glimmer of excitement. But not today, not amidst the swirling turmoil that consumes him.

"A gentleman has been waiting a few hours and would like to speak with you. Would now be a suitable time?" Genni continues.

"That's . . . yeah, that's a mistake. Tell them I'm . . ."

Who would be kidnapping all the scientists? Why would they target Margot specifically? True, she possessed an unsurpassed brilliance, but . . .

". . . not home," he finally manages to utter. His world returns to the TV.

Nurse Genni smiles with wide eyes and a deliberate nod of her head.

On the news, a seasoned broadcaster holds his hand to an earpiece, listening intently to the latest tidbit of info—the lower-third updates to Serial Abduction of 30 Science Prodigies around the World. The broadcaster composes himself, his gaze steady as he reads from his prompter. "This just in: Based on the profiles of the abductees, our exclusive sources indicate that many of these academics have recently published research in the field of nuclear energy." The screen splits to include a young reporter. "Live at Harvard University in Cambridge, Massachusetts, we have our correspondent, Anika Blackstone. Anika?"

A fresh face to the beat, Anika clutches her microphone as she keeps her hair from blowing in her face. "As of now, we have not been able to contact any of the victims," she says with urgency and professional composure. "Given they are all nuclear scientists, the intelligence sources I'm speaking to suggest it's likely the abductees are not in immediate danger. Their rationale is that since they were likely abducted for their knowledge, they can provide it only if they are alive. However, my sources readily admit that that can change at a moment's notice when dealing with criminal cases of this nature. Back to you."

The broadcast shows a collage of photos of the victims during happier times, among them Margot's radiant face. Adam, his heart heavy with anguish, instinctively shuts his eyes as if doing so might slow the crushing of his soul. It doesn't.

"And we've assembled these photos of the victims provided by the families," the broadcaster says, "If you see any of these victims, please contact your local authorities as soon as possible."

A deep, commanding male voice breaks through the disheartening news from the doorway of Adam's room. Reluctantly, Adam opens his eyes to see a man clad in a military uniform. Indeed, this has to be a mistake.

The medals on the soldier's burly chest gleam. Like many great military leaders of yesteryear, his chin is almost a perfect trapezoid.

"Adam Eberhardt?" the soldier asks, resolute and unwavering.

Adam's mind races, struggling to comprehend the purpose of this unexpected visit. Was it somehow about that rich guy he knocked onto the grass? Did the explosion injure anyone? Adam manages to stammer, "Oh . . . uh . . . yeah?"

The soldier strides robotically toward him. He presents an orange envelope in his tanned, calloused hands, the vibrant color contrasting against the soldier's navy blue uniform.

"Did I, uh, well, I guess, do something wrong?" Adam asks. He can't help but stare at the mysterious package before him.

"No sir."

"You're sure . . . ?" Adam asks. He looks like a very competent man—one you'd trust—but he must have the wrong information. The only conceivable explanation arrives on his tongue, "My nurse might know if there's another Adam Eberhardt in this hospital."

"No sir. I am in the right place," the soldier replies, his conviction unflinching.

Adam looks him up and down and notices the US flag patch sewn into his uniform. "You're an American?"

"Yes sir. That's affirmative. I'm Major General West from the US Army."

Was I somehow brought to America when I was asleep? Adam wonders. Glancing out the window, he feels compelled to point out the obvious. "This is Switzerland," he says.

"You are correct, sir. This is Switzerland."

With the orange envelope securely in his grasp, Adam's attention turns to its vivid hue. It is very orange, oranger than most orange things. *If something is more orange than something else, do you say it is oranger? Because I don't recall ever hearing that word.* He fumbles with the unique string-clasp that holds the envelope together. After unwrapping it, he peeks inside. "You are sure, like completely sure, that I'm supposed to open this?" Adam asks.

"Yes sir."

Adam carefully extracts the contents from the envelope. It's a slim tablet device akin to an iPad but lacks any official branding. A small sticky tag reading Thumbs Here points to two circles toward the bottom of the device. Simple enough. Adam regrips the tablet and lays both thumbs over the circular sensors. The device unlocks at his touch.

An image materializes on the screen—an intricately stylized phoenix rendered in shades of red and orange.

"What the . . . ?" Adam whispers as his breath snags in his throat. His eyes dart to the tiny spot on his right wrist. The spot would appear to be a freckle to most, but it has always looked like something more to Adam—something like, perhaps, a bird rising from gray flames.

It's the exact design displayed on this tablet.

Emotions surge through him as if riding an oscillating electromagnetic wave, while his heart pounds with escalating amplitude with each next beat. He locks eyes with Major General West. "Did you . . . tell me who sent you?"

There is a crack in West's facade of confidence, but he plays coy and doesn't respond.

At that moment, Adam's gray marking flickers orange before returning to its original color. This peculiar phenomenon has only happened at a handful of pivotal moments in his life, each seared in his memory not just because it is weird but because it followed instances of significant trauma—always acting like a guiding light, leading him back from the depths of despair. And a few hours after Margot is taken, it shows up again.

Major General West looks at his glowing wrist. "Mr. Eberhardt, I need you to come with me."

CHAPTER 4
FIND A FRIEND

AS ADAM CAUTIOUSLY STEPS out of a military jeep, his gaze sweeps over the unremarkable, remote, dew-covered, grassy Swiss terrain that stretches into the distance—and one conspicuous object that doesn't belong in the picture. Major General West escorts him toward a sleek, futuristic Aerion supersonic jet. He could be convinced the crisp-white tube was a missile.

Walking is Adam's preferred mode of transportation. It is one of the few activities that tethers his mind to the earth. Even the concept of obtaining a driver's license never interested him, for the simplicity of his two feet sufficed. But now, as he approaches this rocket to the unknown, he realizes he is about to embark on a journey that transcends more than mere distance. It was a voyage into a different stratosphere, where the boundaries of knowledge blur and the possibilities of the unknown whisper seductively in his ears.

A solitary figure is on the desolate runway. In the distance, a bearded vulture devours a carcass with savage hunger. The sight only reminds him of Margot's abductors. Though absent in physical form, they are somehow still devouring his innards.

He scratches his head absentmindedly as if the stitches were living entities gasping for breath in the open air. Otherwise, he's no worse for the wear. A mild concussion, they said. Adam matches the swift strides of Major General West, their rhythmic cadence echoing the urgency of the mission. "Can you tell me where we're going?"

"Confidential, sir," West replies. "All your questions will be answered when you arrive at the destination."

Major General West has no idea who he's talking to. Adam's life is a tapestry of innumerable inquiries. Still, they all seem to converge into a singular, overarching, ever-present question: *Is there a reason he is the way he is?* If someone at the end of this flight can answer *all* of his questions, they will watch the end of eternity together.

Anxiety rushes through him, a visceral warning pulsating through his intestines, urging him to stop walking and refuse to board the imposing aircraft. Adam grapples with a torrent of thoughts with each step. Was this related to the abducted scientists? The answer eludes him, drifting like hazy mist through his grasp. Yet a flicker of determination kindles within him. Uncertain as he may be, if boarding this plane has even a remote chance of bringing Margot home, he has to swallow his fear and forge ahead.

If he's being honest, the firebird intrigues him. It is the first time he's seen the symbol beyond the confines of his wrist. It reminds him of Baba.

As they approach the jet, a staircase unfolds from its side with a near-silent grace. Adam draws in a deep breath, summoning the courage to ascend the first few steps, but his progress abruptly stops. It is as if his mind has emptied itself, leaving him grappling with a sudden loss of understanding of how to propel his legs forward. How will he get up all these steps if he has forgotten how to walk? Uncertainty engulfs him as he remains oblivious to whatever is within the aircraft. Major General West waits on the asphalt runway, a silent sentinel.

"Aren't you coming with me?" Adam asks at the realization of this game-changing development.

"No sir," Major General West says. He executes a deliberate, perfect salute.

Adam can only stare. *Is this real? Last chance! Jump off the stairs! Why is he still saluting me? I really don't deserve that. Will he hold his hand there until I board this plane? How long can a person keep their hand like that?* Ten seconds transform into infinity, yet the Major General is unmoved by his delay. Summoning the remnants of his resolve, Adam musters the strength to ascend the remaining steps into the jet while the staircase folds behind him.

Within, silver trim outlines fancy white panels with faux wainscoting, resembling a fancy dining room more than any airplane Adam's ever ridden. He peeks to his left, peering through a thick pane of glass separating the passengers from the cockpit. However, no pilot occupies the space; there isn't even enough room for a child to sit.

"Please take your seat. We will be departing momentarily," a male voice says over a loudspeaker.

Suddenly, the plane surges forward, its acceleration jolting Adam back. He clutches onto an emergency handle attached to the ceiling. Buttons flicker in a frenzied light show within the cockpit. It dawns on him. This is no ordinary aircraft; it is a drone controlled by unseen hands.

Adam turns toward the fuselage. There are rows of oversize chairs and cutting-edge technological panels that adorn the flying command center. The interior resembles a lair curated by the minds of the US military's geek squad, boasting an onboard infotainment system that showcases global maps with thousands of tiny dots that move along it.

Adam cautiously maneuvers down the aisle, gripping the headrests of each leather seat. Surely, he can't be the only one on this jet. He presses ahead a little farther. Greasy blond hair rises above a headrest; their back is turned toward him.

Apprehensive, Adam raises his hands, ready to defend or attack. Slowly, he peeks over the seat, only to find a person engrossed in a tablet. On the screen, a man bludgeons a zombie with a baseball bat wrapped in barbed wire.

"Hey," Adam says.

Startled, the man rips out his earbuds, his eyes quivering with surprise. "Dang, dude. You kinda rolled up on me right there," the man says, pausing the video, freezing on a close-up of a zombie's grotesquely mangled face.

"I'm sorry," Adam quickly responds. He's petrified, only able to move his eyeballs. "I didn't mean to. Are you okay?"

The man lets out a deep, stabilizing breath. "Give me a sec. Holy goat! Let me boot up my heart monitor app." The man places his thumb on his iPhone, activating flashing lights. Nonchalantly, he flings his oily blond ponytail over his shoulder.

Adam's gaze lingers on the man, noting the thickness of the black glasses that frame his face. The man's unwieldy stubble suggests a disregard for conventional grooming, while his disheveled appearance hints at shared experiences of sleepless nights and restless curiosity. If Adam had to guess, they were about the same age. The man wears a Massachusetts Institute of Technology hoodie adorned with a cartoon beaver and a collection of sauce stains around the front pockets.

"Forgive me. Today's been a tad unusual," the man says as his iPhone emits an alert. "Oh God, the red zone. My goodness, I haven't been there since the last time I thought I was pregnant."

"Wait. What?"

The man chuckles, a mixture of amusement and reminiscence. "Well, not me, my engineering professor, but that's a long story. I ended up doing very well in that course," he says. "Is it just me, or is this whole thing kind of freaking you out?"

"Wait. So, are you . . . ?" Adam trails off as he tries to put his thoughts together. This couldn't possibly be the guy he's supposed to meet.

"Oh, how rude of me. Brandon Freeman," the man introduces himself, extending for a handshake. On his wrist is a small gray mark mirroring Adam's.

"I'm Adam," he replies, completing the shake, though confusion continues to ripple through him. As Brandon moves his bag to open a chair, Adam sits across from him, attempting to regain his composure amidst the whirlwind of perplexing events. His eyes involuntarily zero in on the splotches of sauce staining Brandon's hoodie; the majority of the blobs are indistinguishable, except for one that is undoubtedly ketchup.

"I'm sorry, did I . . . make you spill . . . ?" Adam asks, searching for an explanation for the stains. However, there isn't any food or drink in sight.

Brandon looks down as he ponders Adam's question. "Oh, this? No. Just haven't had time to get down to the campus laundry center. If they took crypto, good ol' Tim would've gotten a cleaning a few weeks ago. Who has time to find quarters nowadays?"

"Tim?" Adam asks, his voice laying bare his befuddlement.

"Yeah, Tim the Beaver. I didn't choose MIT because of him, but he probably was a nonzero factor, if I'm being honest. Better than a Quaker, am I right?"

Though his muscles have relaxed, Adam's confusion intensifies with each passing moment. "Do you know what's going on?" he finally asks, hoping Brandon might fill in a few gaps to his understanding.

"What's the easiest way to say this?" Brandon contemplates for a beat. He looks somewhere in the distance for the right words. "Uh . . . no. No, I don't," he says. Brandon leans in as if he's going to reveal a secret. "I'm thinking that maybe we should swap our phone numbers. Just in case we end up in a Nepalese labor camp and one of us can escape. There are a few lady friends I probably owe some closure to. You know what I mean?"

"You think the US military would take us to a Nepalese labor camp?"

"Nah, it's purely hypothetical," Brandon reassures, but his words only thicken the fog of confusion in Adam's mind. "The Nepalese, it's my understanding, are hospitable people. It's reckless of me to sully their reputation in that way. They don't deserve that. A British labor camp, how about that?

Anywho, that fact's not material. Just in case, I wrote up a simple Find a Friend app." He swiftly turns his iPad around, eager to demonstrate its functionality. "It's only in beta, but it's solid enough. If you download it, we can link our accounts—"

"I don't own a smartphone."

Brandon's eyes widen in horror, his jaw dropping as if gravity had suddenly betrayed him. The awkward silence hangs heavily between them, their gazes fumbling to find a connection point. Finally, Brandon manages to break the tension. "So, where'd they catch you?"

"Catch me?"

"Oh, you came on your own accord," Brandon says, a glimmer of understanding shining in his eyes. "I see."

Despite the fact that part of his brain has been replaying his day on a loop for eighteen hours, Adam is not in the mood to relive it. "I was in the hospital," he finally says.

"For the . . . laceration?" Brandon motions to the gash on his head.

Adam's core tightens, anticipating the familiar discomfort that accompanies his anxious moments. He braces for the gastric reflux as the burning sensation claws at his chest. He manages to utter, "Yeah."

"How'd that happen?" Brandon asks, a spark of anticipation flashing across his face. "Don't mind me. I like to ask a lot of questions."

"I can see that," Adam replies, noting the similarity, though Adam prefers to bottle most of his inquiries in perpetuity. Brandon gazes back with the penetrating eyes of the most unkempt counselor. The eye contact seems unyielding as if Brandon won't break it until Adam responds. "I fell."

Brandon feigns deep intrigue. "Oh, you fell," he says, as if pondering the profound significance of such an event. "Falling. That's a thing that happens. Even I've fallen twice or thrice." Adam's eyebrows knit together, his mind grappling with the unfamiliarity of Brandon's choice of vocabulary. Brandon's hands move in an attempt to dismiss his last words as if they can erase them from existence. "Sorry, that just means two or three times."

"Yeah, I get it. I just don't usually hear—"

"Yeah, some of us Americans rise to another level of sophistication," Brandon says, pausing to emphasize the point. "I'm just kidding. I don't even know why I said that. I don't think I've ever said it before, actually. But I do kind of like it. Maybe I should jot it down." Brandon swipes and scribbles on his iPad. "Yep, I should jot it down. It's a keeper."

Adam tries to decode this most unusual, scrawny, college-aged Hulk Hogan. "I'm sorry . . ." He trails off as he searches for words to express his confusion.

"Oh, I just like to keep my thoughts. Journal 'em. Never know when a golden nugget falls out of this dome, you know what I mean?" A quiet moment of weirdness passes between the two of them. Brandon raises an eyebrow a little bit. He waits pensively. "Was there anything you wanted to ask me?" he finally prompts.

Had Adam forgotten something? The answer is definitely not on the jet's roof, but there are soft blue lights segmented into rounded rectangles. "I . . . uh . . ."

"It was 3:10 p.m. Eastern Standard Time, and I had just woken up for my biochem lab and decided to get my fourth set of push-ups in for the day before I headed out."

At the sound of push-ups, Adam's eyes involuntarily trail along the contours of Brandon's veiny forearms. Though the hoodie makes it hard to tell, it's clear he wouldn't fill out a T-shirt like Adam, but maybe they have something else in common. "Oh, this how they—"

"This is the authoritarian takedown of Brandon Freeman. Buckle thy seatbelt." A quick examination reveals there are no seatbelts on this jet. "They started banging on my door." Brandon mimics the officer's deep voice. "Brandon Phineas Freeman, are you in there?"

Brandon reverts to his usual tone, squinting with one eye as he reenacts the scene with gusto. "I check the peephole. It doesn't look good: a pair of armed officers packing some weaponry. They know who they are dealing with. So I go through the shared bathroom and slip into my neighbor's room. They never, and I mean never, remember to lock their door. They started yelling at me, but I didn't think anyone would be there. It's Thursday!" Brandon throws up his hands in disbelief. "I know I have to make a run for it before they break down my door. It's a do-or-die situation. In moments like this, I regret not getting a room on the third floor or lower. An obvious miscalculation, an error in judgment I shall not make again. So I roll with my only option: I hightail it down the hallway completely and totally nude."

"Excuse me, you—"

"Yep, I usually hang out in my dorm naked. My roommate is never around," Brandon says as if it's the most ordinary thing in the world.

"That's probably because you walk around naked." Cause and effect have never seemed more straightforward.

"It could be. Could be." Brandon drifts off as if this is dawning on him for the first time.

"Well, then what happened?" Unexpectedly, Adam's curiosity is genuinely piqued.

"They had bolstered the lobby with additional officers, leaving me with scarce options for escape," Brandon says, his tone filling with bravado and nostalgia. "I tried to jump them. I was the Pennsylvania Division-One champion in hurdles, mind you. I springboarded myself off the wall and cleared the first officer with no problem. But alas, the second officer wasn't as easily evaded. But six more inches on my vertical and I would have been scot-free. Hurt my penis a little, but nothing a little ibuprofen can't handle. I'd consider it an abrasion," Brandon says. "But your story was cool too."

"Yeah, I'm sorry. I'm not really . . ." Adam sifts to find the words, any words. "Today's been . . . terrible. Crazy. And you . . . naked push-ups . . . it's been a lot of . . . something." The memory of Margot's anguished screams echoes through his mind, drowning out the peculiarities of their conversation.

Lost in his thoughts, Adam stares at the boundless sky beyond the window.

Brandon breaks the silence. "You wanna watch the second half of *Zombieland* with me?"

CHAPTER 5
GOODBYE, SITTO

UNDER A GOLDEN SUNSET and docile, fluffy clouds, the tires of a military Humvee tear across a vast expanse of sand. About a thousand kilometers west of Iraq, the machine navigates the terrain of the Sahara Desert, the towering Pyramids of Giza and the Great Sphinx in the distance. Passing these ancient relics, the Humvee closes in on a twenty-first-century city, a collision point between the past and present: Cairo, Egypt.

Bands of sweat and dust gather on the face of Hala as she maneuvers between clumps of grass among patches of dirt on the football pitch. Hala enjoys the art of movement. It's the same reason she enjoys fiddling with her mother's harp. Her peers try to convince her she's a natural, but she thinks otherwise.

The college-aged women bump shoulders as they compete for possession. The red team deflates as a midfield crossing pass makes it to Hala, streaking down the wing. She is careful not to get too far ahead of the play as the eagle-eyed referee watches for offsides. The ball has a magnetic relationship with her feet. She dribbles through the opposing team's defense, leaving them in her wake. *Where's her crosser?* Her instinct tells her to pull up to find a passing lane. Moments later, one opens. She threads a needle across the field. Her teammate veers left rather than pushing forward, and the play results in a turnover. Maybe next time.

As Hala turns back up the field, a contingent of US soldiers appears, joining the sparse crowd of spectating family and friends. The contingent offers little hello waves and smiles to ease any tension. Though the presence of foreign troops isn't all that uncommon, Hala's never seen them at a game like this.

As the opposing team retaliates, launching the ball back into Hala's attacking zone, she races along the sideline, her outstretched foot expertly retrieving the ball millimeters from the faded chalk line. The sound of chewing cleats alerts her to the imminent challenge from the opponent's fullback. Hala pulls the ball away from danger like magic with the tip of her toe, leaving the fullback sprawling on the ground. The goal beckons, a clear path before her. The center defender desperately tries to close the distance, but Hala remains composed. With plenty of time, she can pick her spot on the net. The goalie angles toward her. She plants her cleat into the dirt, her body poised for action. She deftly fakes a kick and slides a pass over to a teammate for a tap-in, but they flub it, and the goalie makes an easy save.

Along the sidelines, the audible thud of a father's hat hitting the ground coughs like a misfiring engine, stirring up a miniature dust storm. "Ah! All she does is pass! It sickens me!" the balding man mutters in Arabic.

Hala jogs past, her gaze focused forward, avoiding eye contact. A tender touch from the man's wife in a flowing purple dress attempts to pacify the situation, averting any potential embarrassment—but he persists, "She has the skill but never uses it to score!"

The final two whistles signal the end of the game. Hala merges with the handshake line, embracing familiar faces with warm hugs and exchanging polite words. The female football players in Cairo are a tight-knit community, and she's played with or against most of these girls throughout her life.

Hala gathers her water bottle and towel, almost entirely parched and ready to cool down. She delicately wipes her wrist, ensuring her intricate henna bracelet that encircles her gray birthmark remains intact. As the damp fabric caresses her face, removing the layers of mud that cling to her bronze skin, she notices a flash of light. Did her eyes deceive her, or did she see what she thought she saw? Did her glyph-like birthmark blink orange? Doubt tugs at her senses, prompting her to wipe her eyes. She watches, waiting to see if the flash returns.

Amidst her self-reflection, the US soldiers approach her. Their immaculate uniforms starkly contrast with her sweat-stained jersey. Her coach and a group of fathers swiftly intervene, forming a protective barrier to block their path.

"What do you want?" her coach says in Arabic. Coach Abdi leaves little unsaid, whether critiquing her performance or staking a claim to extra portions at their pregame meal.

A female soldier, her skin as smooth and white as porcelain, speaks in Arabic, gesturing toward Hala as she speaks,

"We need to speak with her. She hasn't done anything wrong. We come in peace."

Despite the soldier's plea, the men remain unified, dismissing the request with a wave. Hala, however, steps forward, locking eyes with the soldier, and forges an unspoken trust. "It's okay, Mr. Abdi," she says. With a gentle nudge, she urges the men to step aside. The men reluctantly assist the coach in bagging the balls, never fully taking their eyes off the soldiers.

A tall soldier, his jaw lined with a five o'clock shadow, addresses Hala in Farsi. "Are you Hala El-Mallawany?"

She did not expect the soldier to know Farsi. And how do they know *she* speaks it? Nervousness flutters around her. Nevertheless, she musters her composure and replies in Farsi, "Yes. I am Hala."

Suddenly, her elderly sitto, her beloved grandmother, embraces Hala tightly, showering her with affectionate kisses on both cheeks. Her wrinkled face beams with pride as she speaks in Arabic, "You were fantastic out there, habibti."

A warmth radiates from Hala's heart to her cheeks. She replies in the same language, "Ah, that's sweet. You know where I got my moves from. Thank you for coming." Even though Sitto is oblivious to much of the world around her, she is always a welcomed sight.

As Sitto releases the hug, she says, "It's my favorite thing. I wouldn't miss it, inshallah."

"Inshallah. I'm glad to hear it. Be well, Sitto," Hala says as Sitto gingerly returns to her large extended family waiting patiently for her. She blows a kiss to the rest. Her attention returns to the soldiers, but it's brief as she waves goodbye to another friend.

A female soldier with wraparound sunglasses speaks to her in French, asking, "Where do you live?"

Why were these people all speaking different languages to her? Her gaze turns westward, and with a nod, she responds in French, "Over that way, two kilometers or so."

A short soldier with large dimples hands her an orange envelope. Speaking to her in Mandarin, he says, "This is for you."

Hesitant, she accepts the envelope, her mind buzzing with curiosity. In Mandarin, she replies with tentative gratitude, "Thank you."

Her fingers trembling slightly, she carefully opens the envelope to discover a tablet inside. Fiddling with the device, she follows the instructions, watching as a red-and-orange icon loads on the screen. A sudden pressure throbs in her head. Though on solid footing, she's oddly off-balance. The image mirrors her amorphous glyph. In full color, she sees a bird that has lurked in her dreams and brought her great fortune.

In English, she musters the courage to ask, "What is this about?"

CHAPTER 6
GREAT KNIGHT

UNDER THE DANQING PAINTINGS of pagodas and the frozen grins of stone dragons, the onlookers of the largest chess tournament in Asia fill the ballroom of the Shanghai Hotel with quiet electricity. Guowei Zhang leans over his chessboard in anguish. This is one position he never anticipated occupying. He found chess long ago, and he's lucky that he did. Relocating from the city to a farming village twelve years ago did wonders for his mind and body. All those experiences, all of his parent's sacrifices, have led him to this very moment.

The timer between him and his opponent, the reigning world champion, Xun, displays their names. The numbers tick away relentlessly—seventeen hours, twenty-four minutes. Opposite him, Xun exudes confident composure with no sign of wearing down. The no-nonsense thirty-something wears a silk turtleneck with a floral pattern, her cup of tea cooling nearby. She hasn't touched it; she's too busy analyzing the pieces. She briefly interrupts her scrutiny to fix a penetrating gaze upon Guowei. He has yet to master the art of reading his opponent's eyes, so he averts his.

Guowei inhales in rhythm to keep his heart rate down and to avoid becoming her next victim. This behavior has been well practiced and now serves him well. He finds solace in chess, a sanctuary that helps him center his mind and move past the explosive outbursts of his youth. Now is a time for breathing. This tournament marks Guowei's debut on such a grand scale, and he certainly didn't expect to face off against the world's highest-ranked player.

With unwavering concentration, Guowei's mind ignites, envisioning his possible moves. The potential sequences flicker in his mind's eye—his options glowing red, Xun's shining blue. He mentally navigates hundreds of variations within mere moments. His fingers delicately grasp the smooth ivory headwear of his queen, his gray scar peeking out from beneath his shirtsleeve. Deliberately, he lifts the queen and captures her pawn.

The crowd inches closer, their whispers merging into a dull rumble.

"Check," Guowei says, releasing his piece. The move makes his queen an almost certain sacrifice—an audacious play he has observed but never executed. Internally, a wave of anticipation washes over him. Externally, he ensures that not even the slit of his mouth moves a millimeter.

A painful grimace overtakes Xun's face. A grandmaster like her saw this coming. She likely would've made the same move if she had been in his position. He's fortunate to have found this opportunity. Halfheartedly, she takes his queen with her rook.

The onlookers lean forward, their murmurs brimming with anticipation.

Guowei seizes her bishop with his knight. "Mate," he says.

The thrill of victory swirls behind his abs, and it stays there. The nerve endings along his legs stand up like troops in formation—tension releases from his broad shoulders. The days of wielding a steel plow on his parent's farm have led to this. Not a trace of excitement creeps onto his face, his composure obstinate.

The crowd is left speechless, stunned into silence. They did not expect their revered empress to be taken down, certainly not by a Uyghur kid from the outskirts of Xinjiang. Guowei rises from his seat, bowing respectfully to Xun, who, despite her tense jaw, returns the respect to him.

Towering over the crowd, Guowei bows to the onlookers as they offer him careful, controlled applause. As the crowd disperses, he takes a selfie with some new fans. It's a strange feeling.

Out of the corner of his eye, he catches sight of a patient Chinese soldier in full military regalia holding an orange envelope, awaiting him.

CHAPTER 7
NOT MISS UNIVERSE

J **ACKI SCHULTÉ KNOWS** military interior design when she sees it.

The gray room is furnished with seven mismatched chairs, obvious remnants of a surplus supply store. Positioned inconspicuously in a corner, a mostly empty top-load water cooler offers refreshment to the next few who want a drink. If it's anything like her French military, they'll have to lick every drop out of that barrel before a fresh one gets brought out. Adjacent is a table of shredded barbecue beef boxed lunches, some already consumed by her and her two companions. The chef is military too.

The only apparent exit is through the large steel garage door they came through—but they aren't alone. They're being watched. A single camera silently observes their every move up high in the corner.

It's been two hours and forty-three minutes in the chair so far. Having risen through the ranks of the Armée de l'Air, Jacki has grown accustomed to the perpetual state of *hur-*

ry up and wait. It's a formidable obstacle for someone with an unwavering desire to move. The best she can do is keep her shoulder and joints loose, ensuring she remains ready and agile. She's also become adept at keeping track of time without a watch. She has a cell phone in her pocket, but it's unnecessary to confirm what she already knows—it's been two hours and forty-four minutes.

She estimates she's about eight thousand kilometers away from home after flying here on a northeast route, but it's hard to say for sure. The top female pilot in her squadron, she is confident the drone jet that brought her was the fastest she had ever moved through the sky, possibly twice as fast as anything in the French fleet.

Under the watchful gaze of the camera in the corner three meters above, one of the men constructs a makeshift tower of chairs, desperate for a closer inspection. Her new friend Nigel appears to have reached his wit's end. She's honestly surprised it has taken him this long. He must hoard all his patience for his morning me time in the mirror. Sporting short dreads and a meticulously sculpted goatee, he looks like he's trying to land himself on the cover of *Vogue*. At long last, Jacki has found the true center of the universe.

Enduring the incessant grievances of a guy wearing a Giorgio Armani shirt and tie has worn on her. It's been a long two hours and forty-five minutes of theatrics with Nigel, certainly long enough to know who she's dealing with. She'd enjoy nothing more than watching his chair pile collapse underneath him and see his laceless luxury loafers fly off his feet. To her dismay, he keeps his balance and seizes hold of the camera, angling it down to focus on himself.

"You can't just hold me here! I demand to know what the hell is going on! Do you have any idea who I am?" Nigel yells at the invisible man hiding in the lens.

Jacki reserves her eye rolls for narcissists. As a fighter pilot, she hangs with many of them, so she gets plenty of practice. Nigel and his gold cuff links test her restraint. Nigel's accent sounds British, but she won't pretend to be a linguist. He could be from the mainland or one of the mother country's many conquered territories so that only rules out about half the world. One thing is sure: after two hours and forty-six minutes, he thinks he's persuasive and is accustomed to his tactics working. He doesn't follow orders regularly.

Jacki is fully aware that these circumstances suck. When Capitaine de Corvette, told her she had to do this, of course, she wanted more specifics. She believed him when he told her it was beyond his pay grade. Her commanding officer always shot straight with her. Trafficking in vagueness or hypotheticals isn't something Jacki likes to do, but here she is. It was an order.

"Relax. They'll inform us soon enough," Jacki says.

"Easy for you to say. Some of us are needed elsewhere." Nigel hops off his chair pile, landing on solid ground with ease, loafers and all, triggering an inward grimace in Jacki.

"What's that supposed to mean?" Jacki's jaw tightens, her penetrating gaze locking onto Nigel's eyes. Her intense *I'll destroy you* scowl is a weapon she has honed to perfection, and she locks it in effortlessly. It's muscle memory.

Nigel stares at her for a moment but ultimately averts his eyes. Jacki keeps up the pressure if he decides to look back for more. He doesn't. Perhaps Jacki didn't give him enough credit; this man isn't a complete fool.

Jacki glances over to Carlos, the other guy in the room. Leaning against the wall, he casually lights up a joint, seemingly amused by the dust-up. He cocks his oversize Los Angeles Dodgers cap to the side, no bend in his bill, over his messy black hair. Carlos effortlessly exudes swagger—swagger that Jacki presumes Nigel is trying to buy. Carlos wears a plain white tank top that draws attention to his sleeves of black-ink tattoos. The art looks tribal to her: a pyramid-like temple, a stylized sun, and a panther of some kind, as well as text she doesn't understand. Given the flow, she'd assume there's a rhyme and reason to this gallery that escapes her.

Carlos exhales a puff of smoke. "You gotta get back to watch your trust fund, Fingernails?" he taunts with a smirk.

Nigel examines his manicure, muttering, "All because of some stupid bird." He slams his fist against the wall. On his wrist, he has the same gray bird tattoo that Jacki has.

"You trust the bird, homie," Carlos says. In contrast to his tough exterior, he turns philosopher: "The bird flies out to the distant spaces, scouting the land. It can see the world like we wretched humans can't. Still, too, it falls. Burns. Only to rise again through its flames. The bird never dies." He strikes a poetic tone. "Nothing ye shall ever fly as wondrous as the phoenix in the sky."

Something in his words resonates with Jacki. If she was even in remote contact with her emotions, she might be able to pinpoint it. Though it was an order, the truth is she'd follow the bird on her wrist anywhere. When it popped up on that tablet, there wasn't a question of what she'd do. There is duty, and there is service; this is both.

"When everything else abandons you, the bird always comes. Now the bird needs me," Jacki says with conviction.

"That's the truth, sister." Carlos says. He and Jacki share a moment of understanding. Carlos gazes into the distance as though he can see secrets beyond the grey concrete walls. "I had a job in Caracas. Me and my cousin. No blood between us, nothing like that, but we rode together. We'd always do work together. If he had to take care of something, I'd bring my hammer. Whatever it'd call for. We didn't see it coming—we should've seen it coming, we always saw it coming—but we didn't see it coming. We were in a bad way. In a crossfire. All nonsense. No cap. The bird came."

Jacki senses a potential bond with him, though she's in no mood to sift through memories. Nigel slices the moment with a verbal knife. "Maybe I'm just not that needy."

A storm swirls inside Jacki. There's fire in Carlos's eye. After two hours and forty-eight minutes, it's nearly time to teach this man a lesson. Her respect for that glowing gray mark and the man associated with it gives her a responsibility to see what lies at the end of this mystery.

Just as she is about to leap across the room to choke Nigel, the steel garage door rolls open. Five pairs of shoes appear underneath, striding toward them.

The guard ushers four people inside—three men and a woman—each appearing to be of similar age. The four of them scope out Jacki and the others. The presence of the seven chairs in the room finally makes sense. The guard leaves as the steel door rolls closed behind them.

"Yo, what's up?" a man with long, greasy hair and glasses asks, cracking the silence wide open. The man wears a filthy sweatshirt with a giant cartoon rodent on it. It looks like we have a comedian on our hands, even though his attempt at humor falls flat on its face.

A hulking man with uncombable hair and a gnarly gash on his forehead leans over to the comedian, his voice low. "Maybe they don't speak English."

"Hey, Language Girl, you wanna let them know we aren't here to murder them?" the comedian asks.

Language Girl wears a flowery hijab, eyeliner, and lip gloss, done up for the occasion. She waves to them, speaking English. "Hi, I'm Hala. It's nice to meet all of you. If you speak another language, I can try my best to translate. Maybe we could go around and introduce ourselves. Get to know one another."

Eeesh. Something about the Language Girl's cheeriness immediately grates on Jacki's nerves. "This isn't a Miss Universe contest," Jacki regurgitates. She couldn't help it. Unfortunately, she won't be joined by more like-minded people today.

Language Girl's bubbly exterior melts off her face.

Nigel breaks the silence, voicing the question lingering in everyone's minds. "Do any of you all know what we are doing here?"

"We were hoping you would know," the comedian replies. He raises his right wrist to display it. "All we've figured out is we are gray-freckle bird buddies. Y'all got these too?" In response, everyone awkwardly exposes the inside of their wrists, confirming the shared mark.

"Well, there are only seven chairs, so maybe . . ." the hulking man says. "I'm Adam, by the way." Adam's humble nature serves as a better rallying point, sparking a chain reaction of name intros. Fond of the nickname, Jacki determines Hala will retain the title of Language Girl until Jacki decides otherwise.

Gears crank to life again, but the steel door remains firmly positioned. The sound becomes deafening, akin to the roar of an F-16 taking off. Language Girl says something, but her voice doesn't rise above the noise.

Carlos slides his hand along the wall to feel for any vibrations. Nigel scopes the perimeter with his sharp gaze.

Adam gestures to the center of the room. "It's coming from beneath."

Jacki rises from her chair, shaking her limbs, ready for action. Suddenly, a crack emerges in the floor like a clean, straight fault line. Amid this rupture, a concrete staircase beckons them into the darkness below.

Emerging from the abyss is a clean-shaven soldier clad in freshly pressed combat fatigues. The lantern attached to his tactical helmet casts an eerie glow, guiding his way. He carries an AR-15 confidently, suggesting a seasoned combat vet. "Follow me," the soldier says. Guowei, being closest, assumes the position of line leader. Jacki follows him in.

The cobbled walls of the passageway ooze moisture and bugs. A musty odor of mildew dirties the oxygen, and the temperature drops a degree with every step. Jacki thinks twice before touching the wall for balance, though she does anyway. A spider as big as her hand scurries by.

"I ain't got time for this," Nigel mutters.

Jacki teeters in her standard-issue military boots. As much as she would have liked to see Nigel tumble earlier, she doesn't want to be a domino now. His fancy loafers are ill-suited for a terrain of jagged and damp concrete.

Guided by the soldier's lantern, the group trudges forward, their footsteps clacking through the subterranean passage.

"Can someone ask G. I. Joe if he has a finished basement?" Brandon hollers toward the front of the line.

"Just shut up," Adam whispers to him.

Someone behind Jacki slips and scrambles, their shoes squeaking. She instinctively presses her palms into the damp walls, feeling the moisture trickle through her fingers and down her wrists. Bracing herself for a potential fall, she prepares to bear the weight of the impact, but there isn't one.

"Good lookin' out," Carlos says.

"Of course," Language Girl replies.

Finally, the soldier reaches the bottom of the staircase, leading them to a flat expanse covered in gravel. The surroundings, reminiscent of a fifteenth-century tunnel, clash with a state-of-the-art metal detector checkpoint illuminating the darkness.

The soldier turns to address the group. "Surrender all electronics on your person. No exceptions. Only then will you be granted entry."

It's not ideal for Jacki, but this is par for the course when dealing with classified information. After a jet ride and an arduous two hours and fifty-eight minutes of waiting, this isn't a deal-breaker. She removes her cell phone from her pocket, ready to comply.

Nigel, on the brink of his personal Waterloo, can no longer contain his frustration. "You haven't told us anything, and you expect us to give you our personal property just because you say so? What are we doing here?"

The soldier raises a rubber bucket. "You will receive all your answers on the other side of that door. Your electronics, please. They will be returned to you later." Though they splurged on the metal detector, the rubber bucket looks to have been salvaged from the secondhand store decades ago.

Brandon clutches his iPhone. "I'm sorry, but that's impossible. This little device pretty much holds my life. I have 329 apps. My crypto wallet . . ."

The soldier doesn't flinch. Jacki, Language Girl, Guowei, and Carlos fill the rubber bucket with their devices. Adam leans over to Brandon. "Just give him your stuff."

With a deep exhale, Brandon squirms, grudgingly dropping his iPhone in the bucket. He empties his pockets, depositing several other phones, headphones, and a couple of watches until the bucket is brimming with electronics.

Does this guy have a USB port installed in his ass?

The soldier accepts the surplus devices, including an iPad that doesn't fit. "If I find any of these on eBay later, I swear to God," Brandon says as he passes through the metal detector.

Nigel follows suit, but as he steps through, the metal detector blares a concussive screech, its blinding red light slicing Jacki's retinas. The soldier's glare intensifies. "What do you have, sir?"

"This is ludicrous," Nigel says. He hands over a phone and passes through it again.

Nigel is greeted on the other side by Carlos. "So, you think you're the exception, eh?" Carlos asks, but Nigel ignores him. "Don't worry, homie. Daddy will buy you another one."

"At least I have a daddy," Nigel replies. "Yours probably left you, right?"

Carlos lets out a huff, shooting lasers from his pupils. "I know people like you. They're all dead. Cowards are what we call them."

Nigel smiles arrogantly, obnoxiously inviting a smack.

"Relax. Save your energy for what's behind that door," Guowei says, nodding ahead.

The seven wait in a cramped bunch in front of a secure metal door—Jacki uncomfortably in the middle. It's way too close for comfort for her. It's been a long fifteen seconds. She has no need for everyone's excess body heat. She is perfectly capable of maintaining her own internal temperature in this cave.

"Anyone else feel like they need us to kill the Minotaur?" Brandon asks, breaking the uncomfortable tension, trying to catch Jacki's eye. Not today. "Maybe that's just me," he adds, his voice fading into the murky atmosphere.

At long last, the soldier steps forward, his thumbs pressing firmly into the scanner. The secure door slides open with a mechanical whir, folding seamlessly into the surrounding walls. An eerie anticipation hangs as he gestures for them to enter.

Jacki follows the others into a high-tech conference room, and her eyes are immediately drawn to the large video screens that dominate the walls. Surveillance cameras show the interior and exterior of the building. The exterior shots point straight down into the gravel around the building's foundation. There are no landforms, structures, or hint of the climate that could help her place where she is—likely by design. Matte-finished metal trim lines the floor, ceiling, and other doorways that connect to this room. Seven sleek ergonomic chairs sit at a table filled with creative holes and slices, a testament to material efficiency. *The interior designer is not military*, Jacki thinks as she takes a seat.

As the others settle into their chairs, Brandon makes a beeline for the open seat beside her. "Hey, I'm Brandon," he says, his enthusiasm palpable. "Do you mind if I—"

"Yes," Jacki interrupts. It catches him off guard. Brandon stops himself mid-squat. He slides smoothly over to the next empty chair.

Meanwhile, Guowei and Language Girl exchange timid smiles, their hushed greetings barely audible over the faint hum of warm air circulating through the HVAC vents. As Jacki observes their subtle interaction, it triggers a barrage of inquiries. She wonders about their backgrounds, qualifications, and what has brought them all together in this mysterious place. She senses a military operation afoot but can't shake the feeling that she's the only soldier in the group.

Everyone takes a chair except Carlos, who leans against the chevron-style upholstered wall. Jacki presumes his preference to be on his feet is something he's probably learned over time; to be the only one not doing what society wants him to do, he seems to come by naturally.

The automatic door at the center of the room stirs. Its bulletproof tempered glass panels split apart. It slowly reveals a high-tech corridor of carbon-fiber paneling leading deeper into the underground bunker, offering a tantalizing glimpse into the unknown.

A figure emerges from around a corner, and when he comes into focus, Jacki is stunned into silence. Confusion. Curiosity. Wonder. Disorientation. Disbelief. Bewilderment.

In absolute and complete astonishment, Jacki whispers, "The bird."

CHAPTER 8
THE BIRD

SHROUDED IN A VEIL OF SORROW, Jacki stood among the mourners that awful day three years ago. Her eyes went anywhere but where they were expected as she couldn't bear the sight. A mother hoopoe retreated to its cavity in a century-old oak tree. In its beak, a cricket, destined to be lunch for her defenseless fledgling. The vibrant orange-and-black plumage atop their heads had once captivated Jacki's youthful gaze during her idyllic days in the French countryside. But today, the world, drained of color and joy, was replaced by an oppressive, enveloping gloom.

As a young girl, Jacki had been the only one to dress up as a hoopoe during the La Toussaint festivities. Despite her parents' distaste for the imported American holiday, Jacki eagerly anticipated the annual candy collection ritual. She reminisced about her mother, who had painstakingly hand-crafted her hoopoe costume because they were sold out at the store. It wasn't until years later that Jacki realized this wasn't the reason; it was that nobody else on earth thought about dressing up as one. That was fine too.

But Jacki's eyes were crusted with dried tears on that somber spring day. Tracks of saline sorrow traced their way down her cheeks and converged at the golden crucifix that adorned her neck, steadfast faith unrewarded. From her nest above the cemetery, the mother hoopoe patiently fed the nourishment to her helpless baby. It pained her soul.

Overcome, Jacki headed anywhere but where she was. Her long black dress, attire she despised because she'd always tangle her feet in it, brushed against the ground. Another reminder of her missteps. She squeezed the crucifix with her hand. Her pleas were not heard. In one motion, she ripped the chain from her neck and threw it as far as she could. And then, as she released a primal scream from the depths of her being, she fell, her anguish consuming her.

Just before her body collided with the unforgiving earth, strong arms encircled her and cradled her against a broad chest. Though the man wore a nice suit, he must not have been concerned about the tears or grass stains.

"It'll be okay, my dear," he whispered.

His voice was a balm to her wounded soul. At that moment, overwhelming emotions burst forth as the realization set in: the biggest and best piece of her had died.

"It'll be okay," he repeated, his words a steady refrain.

Meanwhile, a couple meters away, the hoopoe descended onto the grass and bobbed through the greenery with its long curved bill, foraging for sustenance. As the bird's gaze met Jacki's, a glimmer of recognition sparked within her. The gray mark on Jacki's wrist, a subtle insignia, glowed orange.

And then, without warning, the hoopoe took flight, leaving Jacki behind.

Jacki turned her gaze to the man who held her. He is the same man standing in front of her in the command center of this underground bunker.

She definitely isn't ready to revisit these memories. Not today. Not tomorrow. Sadness intertwines with regret, hope mingles with comfort, and she battles to contain this volatile mix beneath her stoic facade. With one deep breath, she keeps them at bay.

A shadow of his former self, Master Kebe leans on a cane, every step an arduous task fraught with uncertainty. His short gray hair is peppered with black, and he carries heavy bags under his eyes.

Nigel, wearing a gobsmacked expression, breaks the silence. "Oom, what are you doing here?" he asks. His astonishment mirrors Jacki's confusion. *Do all these people know her judo sensei?* Clearly, she's not the only one with questions.

Kebe signals for Nigel to hold the thoughts, extending his other hand toward the empty seventh chair. "Would you like to join us?" he asks Carlos.

"I'm good, Papi," Carlos says with a smile.

"Very well, Carlos," Kebe says.

"Oom, perhaps I'm the only one," Nigel begins, glancing around at the others, "but I have important business matters that demand my attention. You are well aware of this. I'd appreciate it if you could first enlighten me as to why in the world you are here and, second, let me know how I can get back to work."

"Nigel, I assure you, if we are not successful, you will have no business to return to," Kebe says. "Or country. None of you will." The weight of his words causes a shiver to shoot through Jacki's neck. What in the world has she gotten herself into?

Nigel settles back in his seat, a resigned expression across his face.

"I understand many of you know me by a different name or in a different way," Kebe continues, his steady voice permeating the tense atmosphere. "I'm aware that seeing me here today, under these circumstances, will be shocking to each of you. Please know that I have taken the liberty to inform your loved ones that you are safe and are participating in what I've termed a 'special project.' As you will come to appreciate, I've known your parents for a very long time."

"How long are we going to be here?" Language Girl asks. "I have classes . . . I'm helping care for my grandmother."

Kebe clears his throat, his expression pensive. "I don't know. But rest assured, the needs of your families will be met. May I?"

Jacki feels an onslaught of questions building up within her, but she restrains herself, eager to hear the information Kebe is about to divulge. Silence reigns, and nobody else voices their concerns.

"My real name is Emmanuel Kebe," he says. "I was a geneticist in a previous life, but now I'm a special assistant to the United Nations Counter-Terrorism Task Force. Soon, you may discover answers to questions you have wondered about most of your lives."

CHAPTER 9
MORE QUESTIONS

DID HE SAY ANSWERS? The words pierce Adam's churning anxiety, rousing a desperate curiosity.

It's been at least five years since Adam last saw Baba. He certainly didn't expect the reunion to happen today.

"I sincerely thank you all for your time and cooperation," Kebe continues. "I know that these circumstances are far from ideal. However, understand you are here for a reason of only the gravest significance."

The sliding doors part again, revealing a group of four military leaders. Their uniforms, covered in ribbons and medals, bear flag patches indicating the United States, China, United Kingdom, and Russia are represented. They stand in formation behind Kebe, their presence commanding and unnerving.

Guowei stands. "Yi Ji Shang, it is an honor to be in your presence." He exchanges a bow with the Chinese general.

Leaning closer to Adam, Brandon whispers, "Do you know any of these guys?" Adam can only reply with a confused shrug. Even if there were a German or Swiss representative, he would be equally oblivious.

Kebe clears his throat. "You are here because there is an international security risk unlike any ever documented. And it's imminent."

"Who specifically is at risk?" Jacki asks with authority and a furrowed brow. Her tank top shows off her muscular back. The only thing tighter than her obliques is her ponytail, which secures every brown hair. There's an aura about her that, instinctively, Adam is not eager to tangle with.

Kebe squirms as if searching for the right words to deliver the news. "Everyone," he says. "Anyone that loves life on this planet." Jacki remains unmoved, furrowing her brow deeper. She isn't sold.

"You're probably aware of the recent abductions," Kebe continues. "These are clear indicators the endgame is near." With a click of a handheld device, a giant projector descends from the ceiling. The black of the projector screen suddenly pops with color. A private Facebook group of an organization loads—the ARK. The cover image is a stylized depiction from the story of Noah, a red ark braving treacherous ocean waves. It's a private group with fifteen thousand members listed, a handful of whom sit in circular icons at the top of the page.

"The strike was orchestrated by the terrorist group Allied Rebel Koalition," Kebe says. "The organization uses social media to disseminate information, issue threats, recruit disciples, and revel in victories."

With a click, the image on the screen shifts to a page that lists members of the group. Under the heading New to the Group is a diverse collection of people between the ages of thirty and sixty from all corners of the globe. Some look familiar, photos he's seen on the news. As the page scrolls down, his heart skips a beat—Margot. A burning trickle of vomit flies up his esophagus and falls slowly back to his stomach.

Margot's abduction replays in Adam's mind. Her screams echo as she is pulled into that white van. His instincts were correct. He set foot on the jet, hoping he might be able to bring her home. And now, Kebe is here to help. Adam's sliver of hope expands by fractions of a percent, a fragile ember in the darkness.

The screen changes to a haunting pinned post dated yesterday. Kebe reads, "The ARK understands that the world is on the verge of self-destruction. To preserve life as we know it, we must be willing to exercise our God-given right to defend ourselves and build anew atop the ashes of any that oppose us. #betterworld." Hundreds of people responded to the post with hearts and likes.

"How do they think they can do something like this?" Hala asks.

And how in the world do five hundred people love this post? Adam thinks.

"We may soon witness the largest mobilization and deployment of nuclear weapons ever imagined," Kebe says, his voice heavy and foreboding. "The eve of a nuclear holocaust is upon us. Though the world doesn't know it yet, we are facing the first nuclear-capable radical terrorist organization. And we have to stop them."

A shiver zaps Adam's spine, his entire body gripped by a sudden chill. Did he just say *we*? His blood can't decide if it needs to hurry to his muscles or brain.

"Abducting the scientists serves two purposes," Kebe says. "First, it allows the ARK to increase the destructive capacity of their current nuclear inventory, which, based on our shared intelligence, is substantial." Kebe gestures to the stone-faced military leaders before continuing, "While we lack specifics, they intend to destroy urban centers they deem problematic to their cause and to alleviate the need for limited natural resources. Second, once they've reduced the population to what they believe is a manageable level, they aim to rebuild the world with a preferred population of talented, genetically superior beings."

"Eugenics?" Guowei asks.

"Indeed," Kebe says. "Combined with a very selective culling, we have never faced a threat like this before."

Jacki's voice slices through the tense air. "And how did we not know about this group?"

Kebe takes a deep breath. "Though they've been on the radar of intelligence operatives for years, the ARK hadn't made much effort to publicize its efforts until two weeks ago when it opened some of its social media channels. There is no mainstream attention at this point. And"—he gestures to the military leaders again—"the folks in the know haven't been interested in alarming the world."

"Because?" Jacki asks.

"That's complicated," Kebe replies, providing no further elaboration.

A question gnaws on Adam's mind. "But, yes . . . uh, I see the situation," he finally says, unable to cloak the trepidation in his voice, "but what do you need us for?"

Kebe swiftly clicks a button, displaying a social media post on the screen. Adam's eyes widen as he reads the chilling

words: ANY COUNTRY THAT THREATENS US WILL BE THE FIRST WE TURN
TO ASH. EVERY MAN, WOMAN, AND CHILD. #BETTERWORLD #REVOLU-
TION.

"No individual country can be seen as an aggressor in this
matter, or they risk the decimation of their own people,"
Kebe says. "At this point, the whereabouts of the ARK base
is unclear, and world powers have determined that any re-
connaissance risks being perceived as an escalation. When
we can pinpoint the threat's whereabouts, that calculus will
change, but that's not the moment we are in. Nobody wants
to be the first target. There is too much at stake. Hence, the
nation-states of the UN Security Council have elected to in-
volve a small special-operations initiative from an international coalition."

Carlos scratches his chin thoughtfully with his knuckles.
"So, you're looking for schlubs to do the dirty work so you or
your people don't get hit. Got it," he says. "And they picked
young ones so they can write us off as freelancing radicals
when things go sideways."

Adam's eyes dart around the room. The candor jars the
already tense atmosphere.

Carlos gestures to the military leaders. "By the looks of
this, I don't think I'm down to fight your battle." To Kebe,
he's direct and sincere. "Papi, I respect all you've done for
me and my people. I know I have that debt, but they won't
be the ones collecting on it. You're backed by conquerors,
strongmen. These folks step on the necks of my people. Until
they learn words like equality, reparations, and voting rights,
we don't play for the same team."

"I have no training," Hala says, her eyes examining the
faces at the table. "I don't know about any of you; maybe

you do." He might look like a college athlete, but Adam can't imagine what qualifies him for such a responsibility. Hala's voice quivers as she continues, "I just left my parents' house. I—"

Brandon picks up her thought, "I play a lot of *Etherborne Legends*, but I don't think those skills will translate here." He might as well be speaking Klingon to the military leaders, but he finishes earnestly, "I'm sorry to let you down."

Kebe clicks a button. A faint smile emerges across his face as the screen goes black. "You aren't here because you are kids," he says. "You are here because you are *my* kids, and I know you can do what we will need you to do."

At that moment, Adam's gray mark pulsates with an orange glow. It's not just him; it's happening to everyone. A cloud of silent contemplation descends over all.

"Oom, have my parents known about this all along?" Nigel asks. Kebe only offers a subtle nod in response, leaving Nigel to process it. "And they've kept it from me?" he continues, his voice cracking.

"There will be more to discover, Nigel," Kebe says, his cryptic tease jarring Adam.

"Sir, it doesn't make sense," Guowei says. "I have parents. I have a brother." He collects his thoughts. "And you are not Chinese."

"Your parents are great friends of mine," Kebe says with a sympathetic grin. "And the best lab technicians I've ever had the pleasure of working with. You are my kid in one sense; their's in another." Guowei looks toward the ceiling, deep in thought.

Adam gnaws off what's left of his thumbnail. How could this be possible? The revelation doesn't disrupt his picturesque childhood because he was a kid nobody ever wanted. Suddenly, the light bulb turns on. "You said you were a geneticist?"

Kebe's grin widens at Adam's comment. "Some say that ordinary soldiers are appropriate for a mission of this nature. We disagree. You may not yet realize it, but you are prepared to do what is needed. Since before the day you could walk, your bodies and minds were developed under strict supervision to reach your maximum potential. You might have noticed you were always stronger and smarter than your peers. You've been put into situations and prepared with certain skills because you were meant to be something greater than a soldier. For a day like this—a day I had hoped would never come." In a state of wonder, Adam flexes his bulging, veiny forearm.

Kebe clicks, and the logo of the familiar bird appears emblazoned on the screen. It fades away, and the words THE PHOENIX ELITE INITIATIVE fly in.

Kebe clears his throat, his gaze sweeping across the room, locking eyes with each individual. "But what's most important is what is inside you. You can tone a body; you can sharpen a mind. What is inside each of you is something you can't teach, train, or learn. It is irreplaceable. And it was put there on purpose. Everything inside you was put there on purpose. *I* put it there on purpose."

"Okay, okay, where's the camera? Are you a YouTuber?" Brandon asks, his eyes dart around the room, searching for any sign of a secret entrance. He springs to his feet, casually gesturing at the military leaders, "And these big, tough, serious guys—where did you get actors that can stand so still? I admit those uniforms look legit. You must have a budget for this. Did you make them in-house or get them on Etsy? You got me, Kebe! Ha ha ha. Funny! I'm laughing so hard my ass is literally falling off."

Kebe stares at him, waiting to make sure he's finished. "I assure you that I'm not a YouTuber," he says, "and this is just the beginning. I promise there's much more you'll learn about yourselves, my children. Let's get started."

CHAPTER 10
IN THE CAGE

A **DAM STEPS INTO** the expansive training facility, and his senses are immediately overwhelmed by the futuristic marvels surrounding him. Someone's whistle joins with the soft hum of the new-age technology. The walls, constructed from floor-to-ceiling carbon-fiber panels, serve as canvases for various displays—luminous words, intricate numbers, and dynamic maps that dance across the surfaces.

At the heart of the room, a holographic projection of a city hovers above a sleek table seamlessly integrated with gesture technology. The table responds to the slightest movements of Adam's hand, offering a complete 360-degree view of the cityscape. Adjacent to this digital spectacle, prototypes of state-of-the-art suits, futuristic armor, and advanced weapons float in midair, suspended from a sleek spherical station.

The facility unfolds into adjoining rooms, a juxtaposition of spaces. In one room, the ambiance mirrors a traditional classroom, complete with interactive whiteboards and traditional desks. In another, a fully equipped gym with cardio machines, free weights, and exercise equipment.

However, the centerpiece of this extraordinary facility commands attention—an imposing eight-sided MMA steel cage, its presence hinting at intense physical training and combat simulations on the horizon that Adam isn't remotely ready for.

Adam strolls through the space. Louvet has built outstanding facilities at École Polytechnique, but it is a preschool compared to this. Kebe leads the seven on a tour. Everyone else is utterly slack-jawed. Brandon waves at a giant mirrored panel orchestrating a map in the center. Despite having just walked into the room with tech Adam's never seen before, it's as if Brandon intuitively gets it. A maestro at work, he zooms the map into École Polytechnique and says to Adam, "Is that where you go to school?"

"Don't touch anything!" Adam whispers urgently.

Brandon waves again as he brings in a real-time video feed from outside Adam's chemistry hall. "I'm not," Brandon says with the zeal of a six-year-old twerp.

As Kebe walks them around, he informs the group, "In three days, you will be equipped with the most elite military training in the world."

Guowei is at the front of the pack, taking it all in. "I'm sorry, but help me understand why trained soldiers are not a better option."

Kebe leads the group over to a steel alloy vault. "You can't reprogram a soldier. We've tried. You need to be programmed differently. You need to be super soldiers. And you have to be able to use these." He places his two thumbs on a scanner. A panel within the door slides open.

Adam peers through the reinforced glass, spotting a laser grid resembling a cage guarding the contents. The cache is brimming with an array of crazy-looking gadgets, complementing the advanced technology in the training facility. The booty earns a whistle from Carlos.

Inside is a small handheld electric gun, another device that resembles a crossbow, and what appears to be a jetpack, among other items. The equipment has Adam's imagination running wild, especially with regard to the large gun in a black carbon-fiber shell. "Is that a plasma laser?" he asks.

"Not a laser," Kebe replies with a wry smile. "A bazooka. We'll talk about these later."

Behind a glass pane flanked by speakers, the military leaders observe from their meeting room, backlit by televised camera feeds. They must have eyes and ears on every square centimeter of the facility.

Ten minutes later, the seven join Kebe near the entrance to the steel cage. Adam adjusts the padded fingerless gloves he's been issued. They must have just come out of the package because they aren't broken in. Unlike the others, who easily slip into their gloves, sliding his sausage-link fingers through the leather takes some maneuvering. He struggles to fasten the chin strap on his leather boxing headgear, realizing too late that he should have completed these tasks in reverse order for better finger dexterity.

"Before we strap the world's most advanced technology to you," Kebe says, gesturing to the weapons cache, "we need to find out if you can handle yourself."

Inside the cage is a behemoth, his shaved head glistening under the bright lights. Towering about two meters tall and weighing a rock-solid hundred kilograms, he needs little else to intimidate. Through the honeycomb-style cage, Adam watches the fighter warm up, practicing various vicious-looking punches, elbows, and knees that exude raw power. In the fighter's corner, his training partners huddle together, exchanging muttered words.

"The men you will be taking on are here for one reason and one reason only," Kebe says, letting his words hang, leaning into the suspense. "To pull you into deep waters—and see if you can swim."

Adam feels an impending sense of drowning. He has never successfully punched another human. He's not optimistic. A tingly sensation runs through his extremities. "Dr. Kebe, I . . . uh, maybe I'm the only one . . . but I've never . . . I'm just not sure I understand the purpose of fighting a guy who . . . uh . . . he clearly knows what he's doing. And I . . ."

"You'll be all right," Carlos says, slapping him on the back. "Just go hard."

"Yeah, but . . . okay . . . I . . ." Absent skill, ability, and experience, *going hard* can't end well.

"You aren't the only one," Hala interjects. "Is this completely necessary?"

Kebe nods slowly. "I understand your concern. I do. This is an integral part of your preparation. Trust yourself. In our short time here, we will not build a world champion, but there are basic skills that will help you immediately. And you have to experience it. If it goes very, very badly, I assure you I will jump into that cage myself." The comment elicits a few snickers from the group but does little to alleviate Adam's mounting anxiety. The mental image of the seventy-year-old hopping over the walls of the cage like an Olympian does nothing to quell his unease. Not one iota.

"Once you complete your round," Kebe continues, "one of our assistants will escort you to your sleeping quarters. I'm sure day one has been a lot to take in. You all have done well. I'm proud of you." Kebe surveys the crowd. "Who wants to go first?"

Without hesitation, Jacki pops in her mouthguard, pounds her palms together, and almost dances into the cage like she's going to a party.

"Good luck, Lieutenant," Kebe says with a smile.

The cage door slams shut, sealing Jacki from the outside world, leaving her alone with the bald behemoth awaiting her. Everyone finds a spot around the cage for a good view. Nigel leans over to Guowei. "That dude's going to kill her." Guowei's gaze drops to the floor, his lip nervously caught between his teeth.

As Adam surveys the scene, a disconcerting realization settles in: there are no medical professionals on standby and no referee in sight. If things do go badly, who really will step in?

Across from the behemoth, Jacki nimbly bounces around, shaking out her arms and loosening her muscles, her every motion exuding a confidence Adam could only imagine having. The balls of her feet slide across the canvas with practiced ease, as if she's been here countless times before. With her hands up, she angles for an opening.

The behemoth lunges with a left-jab, right-hook combination that finds nothing but air. Adam flinches as the air whistles into his ears. The power behind the strikes draws a few gasps from the onlookers as if they just got hit with a gust of wind too. The collective anxiety grows palpable.

Jacki bobs and weaves along the cage's perimeter, her movements a mesmerizing display of feigned strikes. Then, in a split second, the behemoth dives for a takedown. Time stands still as Jacki's knee collides with his forehead, a thunderous impact that also sends a shockwave through Adam.

Seizing the opportunity with ruthless efficiency, Jacki grabs the behemoth around the neck, ramming his skull into her patella again. The combined gasp from the crowd blends with the sickening sound of bone meeting bone. The behemoth is sent crashing to the mat, the ground trembling beneath him.

Jacki secures a hold around his head and arm. With a quick rotation of her hips, her upper back muscles swelling, she executes a textbook judo throw, and the behemoth slams back-first onto the mat, sending a violent ripple of force through the cage. Adam takes an involuntary step back as if he can feel the *whoa* zip around the cage.

As Jacki releases the behemoth's head, he scrambles to get up. He doesn't. In a flash, Jacki trades her head-and-arm lock for one firm grasp of his wrist. From a seated position, she wraps her legs around his face and chest as tight as an anaconda wrapped around its next meal. Like a rower, she leans back, hyperextending his arm against the fulcrum of her pelvis.

"Tap," Jacki says through her mouthpiece. But the fighter refuses to yield, attempting to roll and escape her grasp. "Tap!" she yells.

Pop!

Moans cascade around the cage like dominos, disrupted only by a guttural "Oh God" from Brandon. Game over. The behemoth's arm is bent ninety degrees the wrong way. The fighter's training partners hop into the cage in a hurry, ready to perform triage. Adam suddenly feels like he's going to throw up.

"Damn," Carlos says, taking it all in.

The door to the cage opens, and Jacki exits the battleground. She nonchalantly unfastens the velcro on her gloves, a casual gesture given the violence she just unleashed. Adam follows her movements with a mix of admiration and apprehension swirling. "He should have tapped," she murmurs to herself.

The fighter's training partners stabilize his arm. They help him out of the cage and into the heavy silence enveloping the room.

"Who's next?" Kebe asks. His question hangs like an ominous cloud, ready to pop with lightning.

Guowei dodges strikes from his opponent, a shorter man with dangling curly hair overflowing from his headgear. In a southpaw stance, Guowei moves like an unoiled robot. A sigh of relief escapes Adam's lips—at least he isn't the only one that isn't a trained assassin. Guowei lunges with a jab but misses his mark, leaving him vulnerable. His opponent lands a resounding punch squarely on Guowei's jaw. He crumples onto the unforgiving canvas. As his opponent pins him down, all Guowei can do is stare at the lights.

Brandon bends over in a stance reminiscent of an Olympic wrestler, angling to grab his opponent's leg. His target, a skinny guy covered in tattoos, seems up for the challenge. Adam's no expert, but Brandon at least looks like he knows what he's doing. As Brandon's long hair flops around, trying to free itself from its ponytail, he buries his head into his opponent's chest and thrusts forward with his powerful quads, ramming the man into the cage centimeters away from Adam's face.

"Buttocks muscles activate," Brandon mutters as he presses the man firmly into the steel. A low rumble emanates from the audience as if they are surprised he's having any success. Drawing strength from his fans, Brandon delivers a couple of short punches to his opponent's ear.

Wham! Brandon's back slams the canvas as his opponent executes a perfect trip. Brandon tries to scramble back to his feet, but he barely gets to his knees before a crushing pressure sends him back to the mat again, and he doesn't get back up.

Hala evades her opponent, a bearded combatant with braided facial hair. The man dives in for a takedown, just missing her. Hala is no fighter; she will keep dodging until the clock runs out. Adam can only wish to be so nimble when it's his turn.

Hala throws a feeble punch, little more than an elongated stretch of her arm. Her opponent assumes a threatening stance and fakes a punch, but she leaps well beyond his reach. An amused smile spreads across her opponent's lips as he toys with her. With her left foot planted firmly, Hala unleashes a soccer-style kick. Her bare foot smacks her opponent's hairy calf, leaving a welt. That was undoubtedly an actual strike. Surprise flashes across her opponent's face, and he shakes his head in disbelief. Determined, he closes the distance between them, clenches her around her shoulders, and slams her to the ground. Hala's head bounces off the canvas.

"Doctor?" Adam calls out.

Guowei rattles the steel cage in futile desperation. Kebe, his expression pleading for patience, raises a commanding hand, silently urging the onlookers to allow the unfolding brutality to run its course, even as Hala is crushed beneath the weight of her opponent.

Nigel coolly rolls his shoulders, preparing himself at the cage entrance.

"Let's see what you got, Fingernails," Carlos chirps.

Nigel smiles, savoring his thoughts. "They do look good, don't they?" Another casual roll of his shoulder follows, loosening his muscles. "You don't want your grimy nails scaring off someone about to give you half a mil, know what I mean?" Nigel says. He looks Carlos up and down, then mutters, "Maybe you don't," before slipping in his mouthguard.

Nearby, Adam studies the face-off between the two men, wondering whether the fight will occur inside or outside the cage. It's only a momentary distraction from his impending fate; his number is about to be called. There aren't many of them left.

Nigel floats like he's riding a unicycle as the cage door closes behind him. His opponent, the skinny tattooed fighter, tries to keep up with Nigel's agile footwork, but where Guowei was four steps behind, Nigel is four steps ahead. In an orthodox stance, Nigel mixes his punches—jab, cross, hook, uppercut—hitting whatever part of the man's jaw he pleases.

Suddenly, his opponent dives for his legs. Nigel spreads his legs wide and evades the takedown attempt, forcing his opponent's forehead to the mat. He lets his opponent back up to his feet but greets him with a right-cross-and-left-hook combo. Lowering his hands, Nigel baits his opponent, goading him to strike. All the man can do is swing and miss. Nigel switches to a southpaw stance and deftly slips by his opponent's jab to land a right hook, crushing his jaw with pinpoint accuracy. The opponent crumbles, unconscious before his body bounces off the canvas.

Exiting the cage, Nigel grins and locks eyes with Carlos, who turns away in disappointment. Unfazed, Nigel traces his fingers along the untouched contours of his jawline. "Does my face look all right?" he chuckles. "South African Golden Gloves welterweight champion four years in a row."

It's Carlos's turn in the cage. He hops around on one foot, trying to wrench his other leg from the grasp of his curly-haired opponent. Despite the unfavorable position, Carlos exudes a cool composure. His opponent pushes to take him down, but Carlos backs into the metal cage for better leverage. Planting his palms firmly on his opponent's chest, he explodes with strength, forcing his opponent away to create some breathing room. Carlos lands a thunderous kick to his opponent's calf. The man's face contorts in pain, and he shifts his weight, a subtle hobble in his step. With a twist of his hips, Carlos launches a powerful spinning kick, digging his heel into his opponent's liver. The man puffs out a groan and stumbles backward.

Like a predator after its prey, Carlos charges forward with a flurry of strikes. Accuracy is an afterthought. He knocks his opponent to the mat with a haymaker, then hovers over his fallen adversary, a fierce determination carved on his face.

It's a position Adam can only dream about—who is he kidding? Even in his dreams, he's the man lying on his back.

Carlos hurls himself toward the downed man with a crushing right hand and sends him to Neverland.

"*Nos vemos,*" Carlos says as he rises to his feet.

And then there was no one left except Adam.

Adam takes a pair of timid barefoot steps onto the canvas, never missing his socks more. He looks up to see the skinny tattooed fighter on the other side. His apprehension threatens to swallow him. He's spent years adding bulk to deter these types of confrontations from happening in the first place. It's not as if his body can't take a punch, but there's never been this many witnesses to watch him embarrass himself. The metallic clang of the door seals his fate.

In the blink of an eye, the tattooed man closes in on him. Punches swarm like they are coming from multiple people, pummeling Adam's head and neck. He holds his hands up to shield himself, but the barrage continues, each blow landing with a resounding thud. He must be doing something wrong—of course he is. What might be advice from his corner never reaches his ears; it is all drowned out by his flesh being struck again and again like a tambourine.

As the barrage momentarily subsides, Adam steps back, desperately attempting to assess the situation. But when his hands drop, a powerful punch lands squarely on his battered chin. Blood trickles from the stitches on his forehead. His head jerks up as an uppercut finds his jaw, a strike he never saw coming. Every part of his face throbs. How does he seem to see everything in some situations, and in others he can't see anything? The enigma gnaws at him, intensifying the torment. Today, it hurts. One thing is sure: the art of combat is a foreign language to him.

Darkness engulfs him, his mind wandering. His cheek pressed against the cold pavement. The haunting screech of a white van fades from his sight. Margot's spine-tingling scream. From the depths of his despair, an upswell of raw power runs through him. He launches into a desperate tackle. He pushes and pushes, driving his shoulder into the opponent's midsection until they rebound off the metal cage. Dizziness envelops him, and his senses spin in disarray.

Amid the turbulence, he thinks he hears Carlos say, "This guy doesn't quit, eh?"

His opponent yields. Adam drags him to the ground; his opponent's legs coil tightly around his back. Perched atop his foe, Adam seizes a precious moment to draw breath into his beleaguered lungs. His thoughts drift back to campus; the elbow from the third abductor is coming toward him. This time, he evades.

On the mat, a blast of vigor flashes through him like a supernova, revitalizing his weary body. He rises, straightening his posture, and unleashes persistent heavy punches upon his fallen adversary.

His mind, again, goes elsewhere. This time to the distant past.

CHAPTER 11
BABA

ADAM WILL NEVER FORGET the worn-out grout lines that scarred his elementary school bathroom's tile floor. Lying prone on the ground, he found himself alone amidst scattered crumpled paper and small puddles of liquid, helpless with no aid in sight. There was no father, mother, or friend coming to his rescue.

An extension cord recoiled with a menacing crack across Adam's back. Agony shook through his body, yet he remained silent, refusing to grant his tormentors the satisfaction of his anguish. The relentless lashing had stretched on for five torturous minutes and felt like it would last forever.

The fifth graders wielding the cords taunted him. "Do something about it, you loser."

Another bully's voice overflowing with hate added, "You think you're so smart. How about you figure your way out of this?" The next blow landed across his back, igniting fresh waves of pain that burned from side to side.

The bathroom door rattled, but nobody was getting in. A wooden triangular block was wedged between the floor and the door, a crude barrier fashioned by the bullies imprisoning him within this chamber. "What's going on in there?" an older man asked through the door, a distant beacon of hope.

The older kids chucked their weapons into the stall and nimbly vanished through the window. It was routine.

Hours later, Adam was escorted into an office, a place filled with wooden shelves, books, and preferential treatment for his bullies. Inside were two men: the father of one of the boys who whipped him—the one who never listened to him, the one some called the headmaster—and Baba. Baba's countenance twisted with simmering anger. He towered above the headmaster, who greeted Adam with a nervous smile.

It wasn't long before Baba and Adam were in the car, a soothing plastic bag of melty ice on Adam's neck. "I've found a better school for you, Adam. You won't have to see those boys anymore," he said. A glimmer flickered within Adam's weary heart, but it mingled with a shadow of doubt. What would make the next school any different?

"And I'm still looking for a family who will take you in full-time," Baba continued. "I know that's what you really want. It's been hard given the world's economy, and since you're nine, it's harder to find permanent—" Baba stopped himself.

Adam gazed up at him. "Baba, why don't you adopt me?"

The stillness wrapped around them. A silence so profound Adam felt like he could almost touch it. "I can't," Baba said, his voice laced with sorrow, "but I'd love to."

"Why can't you?"

Another pause. Perhaps it was the hum of passing traffic that interrupted their connection.

"I won't stop working until I find a good person who can," Baba finally answered. "You will like the new school. They focus on science, technology, engineering, and math. Actually, I think you will love it."

"Okay."

EACH LASH OF THE EXTENSION CORD, rips through Adam's consciousness, eliciting an involuntary flinch. A powerful blow lands squarely on his battered chin from the fist of his tattooed mixed martial arts opponent. The crushing force of an elbow strike, dealt by the third abductor, resurfaces to meld in the traumatic mixtape. Margot's screams from the depths of the van serve as the agonizing soundtrack, an audible manifestation of his torment.

Sitting at the edge of the cot, hunched over, Adam's body heaves with each labored breath. Despite his stillness, sweat beads on his forehead and trickles down his back. Several hours have passed since his turn in the cage, but the cage in his mind offers no such end.

Within the private quarters, surrounded by cinder-block walls and a cold cement floor, the room resembles something between a college dorm and a prison. A sink, a toilet, and meager amenities underscore the spartan landscape. The empty boxes that once held the grilled chicken and mashed sweet potatoes he demolished upon arrival are the room's only decorations. The sole light source, a feeble lamp, casts haunting shadows.

If Adam were to lie down, the nausea and flank pain would be too intense to bear. The tumultuous day has been nothing short of madness, but this isn't unusual. Sleep, though cherished, is elusive. The process of getting there is treachery. How do you slow down a racing mind that refuses to decelerate on the open highway? How does one silence the anxiety that parades through veins like a demonic marching band? He would willingly solve thousands of calculus questions if he could unlock solutions to those two problems. Alas, he's awake.

At least he's dressed like someone who wants to sleep. He is clad in a white tank top borrowed from Kebe after he sweat through the shirt he arrived in. He rarely wears such things. These garments unveil the intricate network of gnarly scar tissue that runs up his back to his neck, silent reminders of his past thrashings.

The creak of a door hinge interrupts the silence. A thin crack of light seeps in. Paranoia tenses Adam's weary muscles until a familiar silhouette materializes.

"How did you know I was awake?" Adam asks.

"We have cameras everywhere," Kebe says. "But I didn't need to check them to know that." Kebe just stands there; his eyes are alert, present in the moment. Whatever purpose brought him here, he isn't rushing to reveal it, letting the silence linger between them.

"I . . . don't, I heard what you said . . . I—uh, I don't think I'm cut out to do this, Baba." Kebe moves to sit beside him on the cot, offering a silent presence. Leaning closer, he listens attentively as Adam gets his words out, "I don't know what . . . I can . . ."

Kebe pats Adam's knee and looks him dead in the eye. "Adam, you will be the heart of this team. Without you, there is no team. No mission," he says, unwaveringly resolute. The old man's gaze drops to the concrete floor. "Before we get too far into training," Kebe says. There's an uneasy shake in his voice that Adam hasn't heard today—or ever. "I need to tell you something. We tried very hard to find good homes for each of you growing up, and I understand that in your regard, we . . . I failed." Kebe's voice cracks, his eyes glistening with unshed tears. "Bouncing around, enduring what you did. I know it means little now, but . . ."

Adam's brow tightens, the muscles around his eyes straining. He swore off crying years ago but knowing that someone out there understood the depths of his pain offers a strange sense of comfort. "No . . . it made me . . . *me*."

"I had no idea how bad it was until it was too late. And that is my greatest regret. You've turned out to be an extraordinary young man." Tears well up in Kebe's eyes, his emotions laid bare.

"Well, I don't know about that . . ."

"I do," Kebe says, full of conviction. "I know what's inside you. Now, please try to get some rest."

"Okay, Baba."

As Kebe rises, he places a smaller orange envelope on Adam's cot, its exterior adorned with the symbol of a phoenix. "I want you to have this first."

"Why me?"

Kebe pauses in the doorway and smiles. "Because you're the oldest," he replies cryptically, savoring the mystery. "And I think you'll enjoy the reading," he adds before leaving

Adam with a torrent of unanswered questions as he closes the door.

A deep exhale. Adam twists his body, settling into the narrow confines of his cot. This is what rest is supposed to look like. Yet the moment he closes his eyes, his heart rate quickens. Without the distractions from the outside world, he's alone with his restless stream of thoughts.

What is in the envelope?

If I open the envelope and see what's inside, will I be able to sleep after? If I don't open it, will I wonder what's inside and then be unable to sleep? What comes first, the envelope or the sleep? Why is it always orange? Did they buy them in bulk from an envelope manufacturer? Does Baba like envelopes, or would he prefer a different kind of package? Would that new package be orange?

Why couldn't Baba adopt me? Why didn't anyone want me?

How could he think I'm the heart of a team? Does he mean the metaphorical center or a blood-pumping organ? Or both? Neither seems fitting. Octopuses have three hearts. What would it mean to be the heart of the team of octopuses? Which heart would you be referring to? Octopuses is correct, correct? I think octopi and octopuses are both acceptable.

Margot would know. I hope Margot is okay. It'd be great to talk to Margot about anything, even octopuses. But I have to save her first. Remember that one time when you tried to save her, and you failed?

Adam surrenders, popping back to life. He shifts to a sitting position.

The orange envelope stares back at him. Since he can't sleep, he might as well indulge in some nocturnal reading. He opens the envelope. Inside is a small tablet device, a scaled-down version of the one he had encountered before.

Its sleek design fits comfortably in his palm. As before, he rests his two thumbs on the sensors and activates it.

The tablet emits a three-dimensional hologram that hovers in the air. Adam passes a hand through the ethereal light, feeling like a Neanderthal becoming accustomed to his first wheelbarrow.

The holographic display bears his name in bold letters and a cascade of images and text floating in space. Amidst it all, a three-dimensional model resembling him stands at the center. They must have scanned him sometime today. Intrigued, he touches the model, and it spins around.

To his left are icons—BACKGROUND, LIFE STORY, TRAINING PROGRESS, and MODIFICATIONS.

Background is a loaded word. Painful. Though Adam doesn't fashion himself an envious person, it's the one thing his peers have that he wishes for himself. Whether his anxiety or pain came first is yet another wonder that travels through his mind regularly. Kebe was clear they would find answers, and "background" is the source of many of his questions.

Unsure how this tech works, he points his index finger like a magic wand at the BACKGROUND folder. He moves his finger forward and touches it. A faint click emanates from the tablet as the folder turns gray.

The display changes. The rotating model in the center disappears, replaced by new icons along the right side—PHYSICS, RELATIVITY, QUANTUM THEORY—but Adam's eyes linger on a hovering folder labeled PLASMA WEAPONS.

A text block appears in the center: CREATIVE | ECCENTRIC | GENIUS.

Then, a familiar image of the acclaimed German scientist Albert Einstein loads.

CHAPTER 12
TRUTH

BEHIND SECURE GLASS, the world military leaders should have a look at the entire training facility, but Carlos stands in front of them, obscuring their view. With a mischievous smirk, he's content to stare them down—or just troll them. The military leaders mutter to one another. Kebe walks by and redirects Carlos to the rest of the group. He obliges, but not before casting the leaders a parting *I'm watching you* gesture.

Day two dawns, and the seven have returned to the training facility. No coffee is necessary; the gravity of the moment is enough to bring the dead back to life.

In Adam's grasp is a gray shirt, its fabric reminding him of nylon. He stretches it out; it's a polymer of some kind. Whatever it is, he can tell putting it on will be a tight squeeze.

Jacki effortlessly pulls the skintight long-sleeved shirt over her head. The others adjust the formfitting garments.

Adam nudges Brandon's shoulder. "What did you think of the documents?" he whispers.

Brandon stares back at him. He's clueless. "I don't follow," he says. "What was in them?"

Had Kebe not provided Brandon with another envelope? If so, why was Adam the only one entrusted with such top-secret information? Pondering the weight of the responsibility, he seeks an easy resolution. "Never mind," he replies dismissively, eager to conclude the discussion. "I was just curious."

Kebe steps forward, holding a sample of the gray fabric used for their shirts, and addresses the group. "Sweat resistant, frictionless. These shirts make for ideal undergarments."

"Ah, so you do commercials now?" Carlos says, drawing a stifled laugh from the crowd and earning a smile from Kebe.

Chuckling softly, Kebe replies, "What can I say? I'm a man of many talents."

Hala adjusts the fabric around her neck. "What is it made of?"

Kebe reaches behind his back, producing a pistol from a concealed holster. In one swift motion, he aims the weapon directly at Brandon.

Bang!

Brandon's body flails backward, propelled by the impact.

Gasps reverberate off the walls, mingling with the palpable shock permeating the room.

The moment comes in a flash but lasts forever, cheating the space-time continuum somehow. Each of Adam's nerve endings freezes in place as if they are paralyzed.

"What did you do?" Nigel yells.

Knocked backward a meter, Brandon is still on his feet and miraculously appears unscathed. The bullet pings off the ground.

"Boron carbide," Kebe says, calm and composed. "With some nanoparticles."

Brandon's expression morphs through all seven stages of grief before finally settling on disbelief. "You shot me," he says finally.

"Indeed," Kebe says, a wry smile playing at the corners of his lips.

"What if I blocked the bullet with my hand?" Brandon asks, holding up his bare palm.

"Then you would have a bullet wound in your hand," Kebe says. "Don't you go to MIT?" A spurt of laughter punctures the tension as Jacki, Carlos, and Nigel enjoy the shared moment of dark humor. "And I recommend wearing the gloves," Kebe adds.

Kebe strides past the group, leading them into a space adjacent to the main area—the gym. Upon close inspection, it is a meticulously stocked sanctuary of cutting-edge exercise equipment and magnetic weights. Among the state-of-the-art machines, Adam spots the familiar tried-and-true staples: free weights, squat racks, and stationary bikes. The range of kettlebell weights goes up to two hundred pounds, the largest he's ever seen.

Kebe leads the group through the expansive gym to a bare wall. "We are starting simple and will get more complex as the day moves on—this I can promise you. In a mission, your physical and mental strength work in tandem," he says. "One does not work without the other. The best way to push these to the limit is one simple test: a wall squat."

"And who do you think's out first?" Carlos asks Nigel.

"I'm gonna put a big, tall stack of my daddy's money on you," Nigel says.

"Bet. Bet." Carlos puts his hand out to seal the deal.

"Can we get on with it?" Jacki asks.

Adam doesn't speak machismo; nothing in the linguistic sphere makes him less comfortable. It's clear to him Jacki has no appetite for the bravado either.

"I'm not touching that hand. Who knows where it's been," Nigel says.

"Been putting people like you to sleep," Carlos replies.

"Oh, you didn't see what I did to that man yesterday? I barely touched him."

"Enough, boys," Kebe says. His gravitas brings the commotion to a halt. "You will notice that the boron carbide under armor is not only flexible, but it will repel moisture. It chafes a little more than I would prefer. Get used to it."

Lined up in a row, their backs flat against the bare wall, knees bent at a ninety-degree angle, Adam closes his eyes. Unlike many other gym rats, on principle, he refuses to skip leg day. He's done plenty of wall squats, but never one that lasts this long. The ticking of the stopwatch is hypnotizing. He can feel the subtle tremor in his calves, his legs burning from heel to hip, with a persistent twinge in his lower back.

His fellow teammates emit grunts and groans of discomfort. Nigel adjusts his back and winces before succumbing, rising to his feet.

"Easy money," Carlos chirps. Ignoring him, Nigel shakes his leg to get the burn out.

Minutes tick by, and the grimaces spread like a contagion. Brandon goes down, followed by Carlos and then Jacki, their faces contorting in discomfort.

A bolt of lightning rides up Adam's back. He casts a glance at his remaining competitors, weighing his options. It's time to bow out. He straightens his legs, allowing his butt to slide to the rubberized floor. The relief is instantaneous.

Minutes drag by, and it is down to Hala and Guowei. Hala exudes an aura of tranquility, unshaken, relishing her moment of Zen. In contrast, Guowei writhes and moans, his bulging quads quivering, beads of sweat pouring off his brow. Hala extends her left leg and continues her wall squat with one leg, smiling playfully at him. It's a ruthless display.

Guowei relents and slides to the floor. All he can do is muster a smile in response.

Kebe raises an eyebrow at the unexpected outcome while the group applauds Hala and her remarkable feat of endurance.

An hour later, Adam's boxed tuna fish lunch begins to settle. Blinking and squinting, the group gets accustomed to the fit of their new tech-infused eyewear. It's as if, with each passing hour, they are moving further along the spectrum of innovation.

Adam uses the reflective metallic edge of a table as a mirror to slip a contact lens into place. He pulls at his eyelid to make a large enough opening. The geometry of it all doesn't seem to make sense. It's a peculiar sensation, as his vision has always been good. With a triumphant sigh, he finally manages to slip the lens into place.

Kebe pops the lens out of his eye to demonstrate. "The iGlasses are controlled by blinks and eye-muscle movement. They're connected to our secure satellite system, so you'll always have information at your fingertips. Well, in this case, the edge of your cornea."

As Adam peers around the room, an augmented reality of tiny white numbers and text pop up on the people and objects: names, dimensions, and ages. It's as if a Wolfram Alpha–style data explosion surrounds his field of vision. With a twitch of his left eye, the information turns into distances and angles, how far objects are from him. With a twitch of his right eye muscles, everything changes to the material composition of objects—the walls, reinforced steel and concrete, and the individuals labeled with percentages of oxygen, carbon, hydrogen, nitrogen, and calcium.

"This is incredible," Jacki says as she experiments.

"If you mean intrusive, then I agree," Carlos says. He gestures to the military leaders. "Don't let those guys have this."

Adam focuses on Nigel: NIGEL DILLON, 6'2", 195 LB. VICE PRESIDENT OF SALES AT DILLON EXOTICS. Small buttons hover on him: EXPAND, MESSAGE, LOCATION, VITALS. Curiosity piqued, Adam hones in on VITALS. To his surprise, the button unlocks to show Nigel's heart rate (75 beats per minute), body temperature (98.4 degrees Fahrenheit), and oxidation level (98 percent). Beneath the readout is STABLE.

"It won't take long for you to become accustomed to the eye-muscle movements and their actions," Kebe says. "It's best if you experiment, but if you'd like to turn off your display, blink twice."

Everyone clumsily experiments with the novel interface.

"They will serve as sunglasses in the daytime, but the AI will shift them to night-vision goggles in the dark," Kebe continues, "You'll have full access to the internet, full GPS integration among one another, the ability to review events each of you saw in the recent past, and perhaps most importantly closed-frequency capacity for chats typed through your thoughts. Simply look at the letters and words to build sentences. Our autocomplete feature isn't perfect, but it's close—and it will get better as you use it."

A blip of text in a comment bubble pops up on Adam's display—I'M STILL HUNGRY. THE TUNA FISH WAS MID.—next to a circular profile picture of Brandon.

"How did you figure it out already?" Hala asks.

"Uh . . . wait a sec . . . just need to make sure my Xbox status is offline," Brandon says. "Got it. What did you ask?"

Fifteen minutes pass, and the group reconvenes in the cutting-edge conference room where they first met Kebe. Adam notices for the first time a Greek-style meander pattern lightly embossed around the door frames and along the baseboard.

Across the giant projector screen, Kebe points a laser at the ARK logo. "The ARK is under the command of American geneticist James Bricker." Kebe clicks to open a profile of James Bricker. An expressionless Bricker clad in a lab coat stands before an American flag for his standard government-issued ID. "Eloquent, persuasive, disturbed. Bricker molds his followers like putty. Including his number two."

With another click, Kebe opens a profile of Zed. In contrast to Bricker's professional portrait, the photo of Zed is zoomed in and grainy. He appears to be somewhere outside an office building. He's a tall man in a long black hooded raincoat, oversize ski glasses, and a ski cap. Other photos load, all with the same distinctive accessories.

"Zed . . . his son. He'll follow him to hell. He might even carry him there," Kebe says. "They will not let their vision die. At any cost."

"Looks like he's ready to hit the slopes," Brandon says, misreading the mood. Jacki stares forward, not even acknowledging he's said anything. "Because of his hat and glasses," Brandon mutters to himself.

"Dr. Bricker and this Zed . . . this is the entire leadership group?" Guowei asks.

"Based on the intelligence we have today, it's just the two in leadership," Kebe replies.

"The head of the snake," Carlos says.

"Excuse me," Adam says. The connection seems obvious to him. "You may have answered this already, but maybe I just don't recall it. I believe you said you were a geneticist. Bricker is a geneticist. Is, or maybe it'd be more correct to say *was*, but . . . is there something we should know?"

"Very astute, Adam," Kebe says. "Bricker and I were colleagues for many years. Friends. Until he tried to kill me." With those words, Kebe pulls down his collar, revealing three scarred-over bullet wounds along his collarbone. "I regret I did not see the warning signs of his radicalization. He no longer resembles the man I once knew."

"Dr. Kebe, it's not clear to me how civilian terrorists were able to become nuclear capable," Guowei says.

"Genetic enhancement consulting services have been an under-the-table multibillion-dollar operation for decades," Kebe says. "They've been financed by nations looking for a competitive advantage in an ever-changing global landscape. Only a handful of scientists are at the forefront of this research, and only one of them was willing to cross the ethical lines required for these sorts of entanglements. It turns out he was also deranged." Kebe clears his throat. "A terrorist organization has never independently had billions of dollars at its disposal, nor has it had this level of scientific expertise, until today. And there may have been instances where arms technology was traded for certain premium services. Bricker is not a technologist, and we are unaware of one in his organization, so we cannot rule out the possibility of government or corporate bad actors aiding and abetting him. Unfortunately, our intelligence is limited, and we cannot know for sure unless we see their weapons in action—and we really don't want that."

Carlos points to the screen displaying the military leaders. "So you're saying those guys," now gesturing to the image of Bricker, "paid that guy to make them superhumans so they can . . . win."

"Maximum human performance . . ." Kebe says under his breath.

"Now it makes sense," Carlos says. "It's not just that they want the young schlubs so they don't get hit; they want this guy out so they don't get put out. No cap." Carlos strides purposely toward the screen with the military leaders. "You tell the world about the monster you made. You put your genie back in your bottle." Carlos turns back to the group. "It's always the same with these people! Greed makes a mess, and they find peasants to clean it up for them."

Kebe stands to meet Carlos eye to eye. It takes work. He winces as he straightens up. "Regardless of how we got here, we're here, and we are running out of time."

"We do the job, and they get away with it so they can think up their next mess. Is that how this works?" Carlos asks.

"I trust you more than I trust them," Kebe replies. "This is my call. The leverage you speak of is the leverage I've used to be able to make this call. That leverage has brought us all these bells and whistles." Kebe gestures to the high-tech command center.

Carlos's hostile demeanor cools. He slumps back against his wall, lowering the temperature a couple of degrees.

"When I send you out, you will have the absolute best those countries can offer on your back." Kebe points to the military leaders. "Those people report to me right now." His wry smile flickers across his face. "Having ethics, conviction, and evidence is a powerful thing, my children."

"Now, it's time to know the truth. The whole truth about yourselves." Kebe says, retrieving a stack of seven smaller orange envelopes emblazoned with the Phoenix Elite logo. "Among you are some of the brightest minds in the history of our world. You are clones."

CHAPTER 13
HISTORY LESSON

NINETY-EIGHT, NINETY-NINE, ONE HUNDRED.

Last night, Adam polished off his twelfth set of push-ups. Exercise was always food for his soul and the best weapon against his inner demons, but that night, he needed the extra fuel to keep up a relentless pace of study.

Like an angel of the night, Kebe came to quell a storm inside him. While the clouds may have cleared, Kebe didn't leave quietly. He left him with an earthquake that rocked Adam's world.

It was a long night alone in the drab concrete sleeping quarters. Adam scoured the file that Kebe had left him a few hours before. Inside were scores of photos taken that chronicled his childhood. What a way to cap off day one of secret military training.

Unbeknownst to him, he had been a carefully monitored test subject since his first memory. Was it possible that it was all true? How many people know about this? Were his professors in on it? Was that why nobody had been willing to take him in?

Am I really a clone of Albert Einstein?

A brain that sprints from thought to thought. A constant awareness of patterns woven throughout the universe around him. His fair share of idiosyncrasies and quirks. A prodigious cranium adorned with hair that refused to cooperate with any comb that could be found in this galaxy. It was not inconceivable.

But certainly he hasn't measured up to the billing.

Surely something had gone wrong along the way.

Many things had gone wrong along the way.

Within the Life Story folder displayed on the holographic interface, he delved into a log of events throughout his life. The entries were biweekly summaries accompanied by notes from an unknown author:

June 12, 2006: Parents Hans and Mia deemed unsuitable for Adam after secret engagements with Bricker. // Removal from home and country for his safety and future development.

January 2, 2007: Adam suffers physical and emotional abuse from replacement parents. // Removal from home for his safety; evaluating all options. Boarding school is likely.

September 4, 2008: Adam has encountered bullies at Rosenheim Boarding School. // Permit to instill toughness. Monitor closely.

April 13, 2009: Adam enrolls in Galileo STEM Academy. // Allow reprieve from bullying and reengage with his intellectual interests.

July 19, 2010: Adam is introduced to weight training. // Maximize muscle development modifications.

Though his nausea simmered on the back burner, he feverishly digested the material. It was a rare state of lucid focus, a play space he'd loved to live in forever. For that moment, he reveled in his time on the monkey bars. Adam backed out of the folder; his curiosity led him to click on one labeled MODIFICATIONS.

He has 99.95 percent Einstein DNA. Additional features include enhanced muscle development, increased bone density, improved cardiovascular function, and the firebird package.

A knock on his dorm room door jerked him out of his trance—just in time to receive a new orange envelope from Kebe, who also bestows upon him a knowing grin.

Shaking off the lingering haze of last night's memories, Adam scans the room, his gaze landing on his colleagues, their faces frozen in various positions of silent disbelief. They are all clones?

If I'm Einstein, who else is sitting here with me?

Kebe finishes passing out the envelopes. "My hands, with help from others, created you in a lab, and you were carried by surrogate volunteers. Once you were born, we worked to find you ideal adoptive families that agreed to carry out your specialized upbringings and training in environments that would best accommodate it. And I've followed along closely ever since. You are as much a child of your family as any adopted child in the world. The love you felt was real." Kebe's gaze meets Adam's, acknowledging him directly.

So that's why he gave him a head start on that information. *Love* was a foreign concept to any childhood he experienced.

"The love wasn't written in the manual," Kebe continues. "Do not doubt that. Most of you've had some of the world's most exceptional parents, but I'm biased. I'm sure you have a few questions."

"Do you have any extra pants?" Brandon asks. It's unclear whether it's a joke or he actually wet himself.

"Any other questions?" Kebe asks, yet the room remains silent, the weight of the revelation immobilizing their tongues.

Carlos lights up a joint, drawing the attention of everyone.

"Really?" Jacki asks before turning to Kebe, "Do you allow smoking in here?"

"Sorry, Papi, but I'm gonna need this one. You're talking crazy. Any of y'all want one?" Carlos offers, but he has no takers.

Kebe only demurs with a shrug before continuing. "Though you've lived your own lives in your own way, what is inside of you represents some of the greatest human potential Earth has ever seen," he says. He gestures to the tablets. "These devices will reveal your call signs and perhaps more about yourselves than you ever expected to know."

Kebe holds his arm out. "Adam, I made you first. You may have the honors."

Adam fumbles to open the envelope. He pulls out the familiar tablet, activating the 3D hologram display he studied tirelessly last night. On the left breast of his gray suit, nanoparticles dance into place, meticulously forming a patch with the name Einstein.

"Wait!" Brandon says. "Wait!"

"Is this for real?" Hala whispers.

"Welcome to the table the creative, eccentric genius Albert Einstein," Kebe says.

"Are you saying this is Albert Einstein?" Jacki asks.

"I don't think Einstein had those triceps," Nigel says. "Or back. Or neck. Or quads. I mean, have you seen that man's quads?"

Kebe smiles. "Yes, it's true we've made some subtle enhancements. Some changes are the byproduct of personal choice and hard work. The old nature-versus-nurture paradox. Other changes are from designed training, but what is before you is 99.95 percent pure Einstein."

Brandon reaches toward Adam's head and rustles his hair. He pinches and pulls wild clumps in opposite directions, tugging on his scalp. He then probes his face at a distance that is both awkward and inappropriate in any circumstance, like he is performing forensic analysis on an oil painting.

Taking a puff on his joint, Carlos squints at Adam before finally remarking, "I can see it."

"Are you saying that governments do this? That we are living among clones?" Guowei asks, quivering with incredulity.

Kebe corrects him gently. "Did this. Our program was shut down more than twenty years ago. The initiative spent the decade prior collecting DNA samples, employing various methods to do so—and we studied them. The ethics of our initiative were brought into question, and the cost of the program could no longer be justified. But at that point, you were already here."

"And Bricker?" Jacki asks.

The mention of Bricker triggers a palpable pause. Adam's eyes dart back and forth between Kebe and Jacki. He recognizes that the implication she raises has a new significance.

"Bricker has most likely attempted to continue this work independently. But to be honest, this is unclear. I'm not sure he would have gone through the trouble of kidnapping nuclear scientists if his homegrown ones had come of age already." Kebe nods to Adam. "This is why he was after you long ago."

All eyes turn toward Adam as if he might share a detailed, elaborate story, but he's got nothing to offer. He recalls the day Kebe refers to vividly, but Bricker's face is only a blur in that memory. Adam wrestles with the notion. Though it's clear someone has tried to hide him, he's never felt like anyone was chasing him all these years. And if someone were after him, why wouldn't they have taken him at the university?

"Something has spurred him to act now," Kebe continues, "and we have no idea what it is."

"How many of us are there?" Hala asks.

"Seven," Kebe replies, rubbing his wrist to emphasize the phoenix symbol. "If I had a hand in making you, you would have what I called the firebird package." Kebe gestures to Jacki to go next. "Lieutenant, if you please."

Jacki takes a deep breath, hesitating. With two thumbs in place, her hologram emerges from the tablet. In the center is a watercolor painting of a young girl in armor. Other images surrounding this centerpiece transport Adam to a different time and place.

"Ladies and gentlemen," Kebe says, "I'm proud to introduce one of the bravest leaders the world has ever seen. The devoutly religious teenage soldier Joan of Arc."

Color fleeing her face, Jacki watches silently as her patch forms the name: d'Arc.

"I think you've already lived more years than your predecessor," Hala says, but Jacki pays her no mind. Her eyes remain fixated on the display before her as if peering into a world beyond their own.

In the artwork next to the holographic centerpiece, Joan of Arc rides triumphantly into the English forces of the Hundred Years' War, a flag in one hand and a sword in the other. She is so young. Jacki whispers, her tone filled with reverence, "She is my hero."

"Well, this is meta," Brandon says.

Adam's mind races, trying to grasp the significance of this revelation. If he's kind of like Einstein, what parallels exist between Jacki and Joan of Arc?

"If you are a young French girl who likes to do boy things, this is who you imagined yourself to be," Jacki says slowly. She turns to Kebe, "Are you sure?" she asks. "I'm not worthy of this."

Another painting materializes within the hologram. It depicts Joan of Arc bound to a stake, a thick crucifix hanging from her neck as flames engulf her. Adam catches a glimmer of a tear in the corner of Jacki's eye, a tear that she valiantly holds in its place. He can sense her inner turmoil, the doubts that threaten to overshadow her admiration.

"You are, my dear," Kebe says with steadfast resolve.

"What drove her has abandoned me," she says, her vulnerability bare. Jacki swiftly regains her composure, holding her emotions in check and refusing to let them consume her.

"I know, my dear." Kebe gestures to Hala. "Are you ready?"

Hala takes a moment to collect herself, exhaling deeply. Adam suspects someone from Egyptian history based on the trend unfolding before him. *Could she be Cleopatra?*

Hala positions her thumbs and closes her eyes. As the holographic display springs to life, Adam faces a sarcophagus and an intricately carved artifact.

Kebe's voice fills the room, "All the way from the fourteenth century BCE, it's a pleasure to welcome the groundbreaking leader from Ancient Egypt and likely a linguist herself, Queen Hatshepsut." Surrounding the central image are modern-day photos of a majestic temple labeled Dayr al-Bahrī and towering obelisks that evoke a sense of grandeur and ancient majesty.

Guowei leans over to Hala. "You're an old lady," he says.

"I guess I am," Hala says. Her eyes lighten, soaking it all in as the nanoparticles etch the name Hatshepsut onto her shirt. "I'm ashamed to say I don't know her very well."

"Well, that is not without reason," Kebe replies. "Much of her life was erased from history. You will have plenty of time to get to know each other."

"Can we call her Hattie?" Brandon asks. "Shepster?"

"Hat-shep-soot," Kebe says, "I'd have imagined you would have heard of the first female pharaoh in Egypt in that prestigious American school you attended."

"Somehow, and this might be hard to believe, I don't recall it coming up," Brandon says.

Kebe redirects his attention to the table. "Carlos, are you ready?"

After one long drag from his joint, Carlos activates his hologram. It loads a familiar iconic photo of a mustachioed man wearing a beret. Carlos can't help but smirk, nostalgia flickering as he glances at the Mesoamerican art on his forearms.

"Joining us today is the controversial revolutionary guerrilla Ernesto 'Che' Guevara," says Kebe.

"Ah, well, that makes sense!" Nigel interjects.

"I didn't know we'd do villains too," Brandon says.

"A villain to whom?" Carlos asks. "One man's hero is another man's villain. That's the way this world works." He looks to the ground, "Some mistakes were made. A lot of mistakes were made. Terrible mistakes were made. He brought us Latin folks authoritarians in the name of socialism. He lost his way. And I've made mistakes, too." Carlos takes a drag off his joint, "Now maybe I'll get it right for the both of us."

Curiosity getting the better of him, Adam conducts a quick search about Guevara on his iGlasses, surfacing an article titled "What Was Che Guevara's Role in Firing Squads?"

"But if it's in him, it is all in him," Guowei says. "How can he be sure he won't, in his words, lose his way? I'm sorry," he says to Carlos, "I mean no offense." Carlos shrugs.

"A fair and relevant question," Kebe says. "Just because Mr. Guevara may have lost his way in one life doesn't mean it will happen again. But what can't be denied is that what is in him is exceedingly unique. We were confident in our ability to guide it, hence why he was a candidate for the initiative." Kebe looks to Carlos. "I think we did a good job. Did we?"

"Maybe," Carlos says with a mischievous grin that hints at a profound connection between him and Kebe beyond Adam's understanding.

"You're going to make me wait for last, aren't you?" Brandon asks.

"It's been part of my master plan, yes," Kebe says.

"You're savage."

"It gives you more time to think about it. Nigel, you are up."

Nigel positions his thumbs on the tablet, and a raised black fist projects from it. "Oh my," he utters, his eyes widening.

Kebe brims with pride. "The most recent among us is a peacemaking activist. He led a life of sacrifice and became the epitome of triumph. One of my personal favorites, President Nelson Mandela." Kebe raises his right hand. "From one African to another, I'm proud to say I collected his DNA sample myself."

The reveal draws a huff from Carlos. "I think you got this one wrong, Papi." Mesmerized by the information, Nigel ignores the verbal jab. But Carlos persists, "He probably doesn't even know who that man is."

Around the jubilant center photo emerge images of Mandela's stoic gaze from within a prison cell and his inauguration. "Oh, I know who he is. I don't have what I have without him," Nigel says.

Carlos points directly at Nigel like an arrow. "That man is not inside that," he says, intensifying the tension in the room. Nigel doesn't take the bait, avoiding eye contact, but his lips wrestle the words that want to come out.

"It's in there. I put it there," Kebe says. "Guowei, if you please."

Guowei holds the tablet in his hand.

"Confucius! Buddha!" Brandon blurts out, drawing everyone's eyes toward him.

"Are those the only Asian historical figures you know?" Adam asks him.

After a few moments of thought, Brandon says, "Possibly."

Guowei activates the tablet and the next historical figure loads. Everyone gasps. Guowei's eyes immediately drop to the floor, overwhelmed by the revelation.

"Well, that's some irony," Carlos says, clearly not forgetting what Guowei said to him moments before.

"Joining us today, we have one of the greatest military strategists in history, the conqueror Genghis Khan," Kebe says.

"Oh, now that's a real villain," Brandon says.

Hala's delicate hand touches Guowei's shoulder, but he doesn't respond, remaining distant. He can only make glancing eye contact with Kebe and nods. The atmosphere in the room shifts, becoming heavy and somber, akin to a funeral.

"And we have one more," Kebe gestures to Brandon.

"Wooooo baby!" Brandon rotates his shoulders and wiggles his fingers, unable to contain himself. He places his thumbs on the device, eagerly waiting for the revelation . . . and nothing happens. The initial euphoria that painted his face melts away. "Thumbprints might be a little sweaty." Brandon pushes them on the sensors more vigorously. Still nothing happens.

"Does this mean . . . ?" Jacki says, giving voice to the uncertainty in the room.

"A spy?" Nigel whispers.

Adam's mind spins, searching for an explanation to help his new friend, but he comes up empty-handed.

Brandon, though crestfallen, refuses to let his spirits be crushed entirely. He brings his wrist to his eyes for a very close inspection. "No, I'm one of the Bird Buddies. I'm a Phoenician. I'm a Firehawk. Whatever awesome name we are going to call ourselves. I know it. I can feel it in my bones. My famous bones."

"Maybe just wipe your hands," Kebe says.

Brandon hastily uses the bottom of his shirt to scrub down the device, beads of sweat forming along his hairline. "Oof, did someone turn up the thermostat in here?" With a deep breath, Brandon aligns his thumbs with the utmost precision, resembling a surgeon delicately operating on a brain. But once again, nothing happens. He looks to Kebe, silently pleading for a solution.

Kebe guffaws. "I'm just messing with you." He points a small handheld device at Brandon's tablet and clicks. "You can try it now." Uproarious laughter fills the room. Even the distraught Guowei can't help but smile.

"You sly old dog," Brandon says, shaking his head, but it does nothing to dispel the crimson blush.

"I've been looking forward to this all day," Kebe says, breaking into another robust laugh that feels like it might stop his heart.

Taking no chances, Brandon aims his thumbs, his eyes locked on the targets like an eagle in flight. Finally, he activates the device, and a triumphant yell escapes his lips. "Boom! That's what I'm talking about!"

"And a man who needs no introduction: the inventor, the statesman, the scholar, the one and only Benjamin Franklin. How does that feel?" Kebe asks.

The familiar face of the hundred-dollar bill, the recognizable Founding Father, hovers above the device. Brandon cycles through paintings of Franklin's famous kite experiment, his work on the Declaration of Independence, and his reading with bifocals.

"I suddenly feel like I've accomplished literally nothing with my life. I mean, getting to level 120 on *Etherborne Legends* isn't nothing; that's when you're permitted to learn the language of the Aetherium city-state. It's pretty exclusive . . . but . . . if I were gonna put words to it, mostly I have a large, gaping feeling of inadequacy."

"That's to be expected, my boy," Kebe says.

Brandon's eyes inspect the screen, a sudden realization hitting him like a jolt of electricity. "I can't believe I didn't go to Penn."

"I was quite surprised myself," Kebe says with a grin, leaning back in his chair, relishing the moment as if gravity is suddenly lighter.

Kebe clicks a button, and the presentation screen shows a model of chromosome pairs within a strand of DNA. "Each of you enjoys at least 99.92 percent similarity with your clone. In all cases, changes were made to optimize your abilities or reduce known genetic risk factors, but inside each of you, at this place"—Kebe clicks to zoom in on a single chromosome—"I put a small piece of myself. This doesn't truly make you my children, but I like to tell myself it does. And it connects all of you. Forgive me for being forward, but I've yearned to share all this with you for a very, very long time."

His speech stirs something deep within Adam, evoking an odd sense of belonging and interconnectedness. He has spent many nights longing for a family that never materialized, one he came to believe he didn't deserve. Eventually, only two words emerge amidst his spinning thoughts. "Thank you," he says. "Thank you for letting us know and for looking out for us." The others nod in agreement, echoing his sentiment.

All eyes remain locked on Kebe. Anticipation and curiosity about what's next hover around him. It's evident that he has more to say. Finally, he breaks the silence. "I understand this is a lot. Too much. This concludes day two of your training. Please do keep your devices and review your files at your leisure."

CHAPTER 14
BREAKING POINTS

GUOWEI WAS OUT FOR BLOOD. His first middle school basketball game had quickly gone off the rails. His teammate was slammed to the parquet floor after a lay-up attempt by a lanky opponent. The flagrant foul made something in Guowei snap. With their team down twenty points and only seconds left before the final buzzer, the foul was unnecessary and unwise in Guowei's eyes. After sharing some words with the opponent, the foolish boy pushed him in the chest.

In that frenzied moment, distinctions between friend and foe, brother and mother, blurred into insignificance, replaced by only animal instincts. Young bodies are scattered on the ground in his wake. In the eye of the storm, Guowei transformed into a whirling dervish, swinging elbows like katanas. Blood stained his jersey.

When the referee attempted to restrain him, Guowei's flailing fist shattered the fragile barrier of the man's teeth. A tooth flew across the gym, a casualty of his havoc. Squeezed in a bearlike grip from behind, Guowei was dragged away from the melee as he struggled to break free.

Guowei recognized the silver ring on the hand—his father's hand. It was only then his eyes looked into the small crowd. That Shanghai gym was unsure what to make of this show. Shame and embarrassment washed over him as he was paraded across the gym. His mother and brother trailed behind, apologizing to everyone in their path.

This and other memories haunt him still. Now, with hands wrapped in MMA gloves, Guowei watches the action inside the cage along with Jacki and Hala. Brandon wrestles with a training partner, executing a single-leg takedown and securing a dominant position.

"So, when we are in a side position like that . . . ?" Guowei asks Jacki, angling for a lesson.

"You want to control the head. Where the head goes, the body follows. But if you want to finish the fight, you can do this." With both hands, she grabs his wrist behind his back and wrenches it, shooting pain from his elbow to his neck. "This is a kimura. You are big enough. That's all you would need. Break the arm if you need to."

Guowei enters the cage as Brandon exits. Brandon yells, "That's why they call me Benjamin 'Big Balls' Franklin!" Jacki and Hala pucker as if they've swallowed mouthfuls of lemons.

A few meters from the cage, Guowei takes note of the military leaders within their glass chamber. The Chinese, US, and Russian leaders have already arrived this morning, attentively watching the fights from their front-row seats. Kebe watches from afar. Will Guowei redeem himself in their eyes?

Guowei squares off with his opponent, the man with a long, braided beard. Like potential moves on a chess board, he visualizes his opponent's potential attacks as blue streaks of light. They clinch, and the pressure in his chest builds. With a quarter turn of his hips and a lunge forward, he angles for leverage. His opponent stumbles, and a red streak of light guides Guowei's eyes to his adversary's leg. It's the first move he's seen for himself in this arena. Guowei charges, grabbing hold of the leg. His biceps engage as they wrap around the sweaty thigh. His opponent crashes to the mat, and gravity carries Guowei on top of him. He finds himself in total control, in the same side position he just rehearsed.

Jacki's urgent instructions find him through the chaotic symphony of battle. "Loosen him up. Hammer fist!" she yells.

Guowei obeys, delivering three thunderous hammer fists, clubbing his opponent's ear, causing him to wince and shield himself.

"It's there. Take it!" Jacki says.

Guowei grips his opponent's arm firmly with a double wrist lock. He torques the kimura. It feels right. The pressure builds on the arm. The bone groans under the stress test, threatening to fracture.

But as Guowei's dominance reaches its zenith, a profound darkness consumes him. Memories, like specters from the past, swarm through his mind with relentless speed. The sound of swinging elbows from a distant basketball court. The thud of his left fist knocking out a kid on his doorstep. A blur of him throwing another in the air at a bus stop.

Suddenly, his reality shifts, hallucinations transporting him to another world, a medieval battlefield. Guowei rides an armored horse alongside a fierce horde of Mongols. Steel clashes. Fallen soldiers cry. Guowei wields a formidable sword, cleaving through the enemy ranks. He leaps from his horse, his sword extended toward a helpless foe, poised to deliver the decisive blow that will end their life.

But before the fatal strike can be unleashed, a feminine voice slices through the illusion, jolting Guowei back to the present.

"It's over. That's enough," Jacki says.

The trance is broken. His opponent taps his leg wildly in surrender. He relinquishes his hold on the man's arm, letting him fall to the mat. Guowei leaves the cage in a fog, his emotions and senses turned off. Passing by Jacki, he musters a brief expression of gratitude. Hala offers a smile, but he isn't hanging around.

Guowei makes a beeline down a corridor to an office, a makeshift space filled with more books than shelf space and just as many dirty coffee mugs. He sits in the padded rolling chair, doubling over. He traces the intricate lines etched upon his palm. What have these hands done? His emotions have returned, bursting a levee, flooding his mind from all directions. Seeking solace, he uses the phone feature on his iGlasses. The text display reads Hai—Location: Shanghai, China.

"Guowei! Where are you?" Hai asks in Mandarin, his voice filling him with comfort and guilt.

"It's nice to hear you, little brother," he says. "Please tell Mom and Dad I am okay."

"When are you coming home? You know Mom isn't well. We had to take her to the city."

"I don't know when, but tell her not to worry too much. Tell them I love them, and I'm sorry I've disappointed them."

Regardless of what Kebe reveals, he is not confused about who his real family is. There is nothing more important.

Interrupting his thoughts, the sound of a plodding cane approaches, and Kebe hobbles in.

"I have to go," Guowei says quickly. With two blinks, he disconnects the call. "I'm terribly sorry," he says to Kebe. "This is the only room without cameras. I shouldn't use the devices for personal calls. I just needed—"

"It's fine. I understand," Kebe says, surprisingly calm. "Are you okay with what you are being asked to do, my son?"

"Why me?" Guowei asks. "You know who I am."

Kebe's prolonged silence feels like he, too, is grappling with the question. Finally, his gaze shifts upward, seeking guidance from the unseen forces above before speaking with measured caution. "You . . . you are an exemplar of what this initiative was intended to be."

Guowei had never noticed the deep lines and cracks in his palms before. "These hands are responsible for the ruthless killings of thousands of my ancestors, my people. I'm not sure *exemplar* is a word I would choose."

Kebe gently rests his hand on Guowei's shoulder as if trying to ground him in the moment. "Those hands are your hands. They can make a new history. We need them to."

Silence descends on the room as Guowei grapples with the weight of Kebe's statement. He finds himself at a cross-roads. He is torn between the desire for redemption and the haunting fear of what lies within him. He's always known a monster lived inside him, but now that monster has a name. "I never understood until now, but in my weak moments, I"—his voice cracks—"snap. I think I am too much like him."

He hopes this doctor can heal a wounded soul. "I'm afraid of what I might be capable of doing."

Kebe leans forward, his gaze piercing Guowei's. "We may need him too."

CHAPTER 15
INEXACT SCIENCE

KEBE RETURNS to the main training facility, his footsteps heavy with anticipation.

In the cage, Nigel moves with the fluidity of a seasoned boxer, his muscles loosening up in a display of controlled power.

Carlos takes the opposite corner, dismissing the curly-haired opponent from the cage to claim his spot for the fight. He gestures to Nigel. "You want this, Fingernails?" he says as he bites down on his mouthguard.

Nigel removes his mouthguard, a defiant gleam in his eyes. "Oh, you looking to make another mistake, eh?" he fires back. "You must be good at that. It's in your blood."

The two meet in the center of the cage, squaring off, the atmosphere charged with animosity.

Team building is an inexact science. Kebe watches the unscheduled confrontation unfold. He quickens his pace to join the rest cage-side, feeling the tension in the room rise like an invisible veil. Despite the real Mandela's admiration for the real Guevara, it's quite obviously not going to mirror that dynamic here.

Jacki notices his arrival. "Is this part of the program, Doctor?"

Kebe tacitly responds yes. It's wait-and-see mode. The unavoidable truth is he needs all seven on this mission, and perhaps sparring might be necessary to bring the team together.

Nigel bounces around the perimeter in an orthodox stance, circling Carlos with deft footwork. He jabs Carlos in the chin, then combos to take a clean shot of his ribs. Nigel is feeling it.

Undeterred, Carlos has his arms up, ready to fire. He spits out his mouthpiece and along with it verbal arrows lacquered in poison. "You are no Mandela."

Carlos charges, slamming Nigel into the cage. Launching into an assault, Carlos unleashes a barrage of strikes—face, abs, face. The close-quarter combat puts Nigel out of his comfort zone. There's no referee here to move the fight off the ropes, only a cold metal cage to hold him up.

Nigel grabs Carlos's head and rolls him to the ground. He scrambles to better position his body as he holds Carlos down, all while delivering elbows and short punches. Carlos, pinned beneath Nigel's weight, fires his own strikes.

Nigel wedges his forearm under Carlos's chin, his eyes momentarily shifting toward the onlookers. "Look at this tough guy now!"

Adam and Brandon race to open the cage door, but Kebe swiftly slams the door shut with a resolute thud. "This needs to happen," he says.

As Nigel winds up for a big blow, Carlos kicks him away. Both scramble back to their feet and square off again. Nigel wipes blood from his nose and flicks it away. They batter each other with hooks and crosses, looking for the elusive knockout blow.

This dance goes on for several minutes.

In complete exhaustion, Nigel and Carlos throw rubber-armed, harmless punches, but neither man breaks. Eventually, Kebe allows Adam and Brandon to step between them.

Carlos and Nigel share a moment. Is it admiration? Is it respect? Is it the end of their hostility? Yet they do not exchange a single word. It's as if an invisible knot has tied their tongues, leaving the room pinned under the weight of their unspoken thoughts. In that silence, all Kebe can do is pray.

CHAPTER 16
UNLOCKED

THE NEXT MORNING, the team explores their new uniforms while waiting outside the secure weapons vault. Adam zips up the black tactical suit, a red-and-orange phoenix logo embroidered on the shoulder, Einstein's name on the breast. The fabric is tough, but allows for a full range of motion. The real Einstein might have some ingenious ideas to enhance the gear, but the best Adam can do is wear it.

"This feels pretty official now," Hala says, checking out the patches on her suit.

Adam inspects his pockets, and there are many of them. In one pocket, he locates a compact tablet and in another a three-hub USB, an unexpected addition to their assortment of tools. His exploration takes an unexpected turn as he undoes a snap along his right hip pocket, causing the pocket to detach intriguingly. Interesting. Upon closer inspection, he discovers a holstered pistol nestled inside.

He hasn't shot a gun before, but it's beginning to feel inevitable. He hasn't envisioned a situation where he rescues Margot without going far outside his comfort zone.

"What about the Orange Force?" Brandon asks. He remains preoccupied with their team name. "I'm partial to Bird Buddies, but it doesn't have a lot of bite." Adam senses that the team has already learned to block out Brandon.

Kebe exits the military leaders' glass meeting room. Three military leaders stand at attention, clearly interested in watching their treasured prototype weapons get handled for the first time.

"My children," Kebe says, "I know I don't need to say it, but I'm compelled to. Please be careful with what I'm about to give you." After placing his two thumbs on the scanner, he inserts a special key, opens the vault, and deactivates the protective laser security grid.

Inside, Kebe unlocks and unwraps a chain securing a modern-looking crossbow to its stand. After carefully retrieving it, he demonstrates the weapon's touch screen with a pattern-lock interface reminiscent of a phone and uses his custom pattern to unlock it. "You have several attempts to complete the pattern. The device will lock if too many failed attempts are made, making it inoperable. It's a necessary safeguard. How many attempts, you ask? I don't know for sure. I haven't pushed my luck."

A couple of minutes later, the secure weapons vault is now empty—and so far, it remains blood-free.

Adam soaks in the details of how each of the weapons works. He might not be Einstein enough to dream these ideas into existence, but the science of it all sure is fascinating. Kebe hands Adam all twenty kilograms of his plasma bazooka and shoulder harness. He completes the pattern on the weapon's screen, and the display confirms a successful unlocking.

"Now, your device, I'm afraid, is one we will not be able to test," Kebe says. "But I trust you can imagine what a plasma bazooka might do when you pull the trigger."

Adam tries to think through assembling this powerhouse in the lab. The entire weapon is wrapped in a black carbon-fiber shell, carefully rounded, likely a product of injection molding. Inside, there must be canisters of helium awaiting superheated deployment. This part is simple. The real mystery is the pressure cooker that must bake to at least six thousand kelvins to produce plasma. Packing that punch into this tight space to a magnitude that classifies it as a bazooka, if it actually works, is a remarkable engineering feat. With the shoulder harness on, Adam locks it into place.

Kebe walks around as the group acquaints themselves to their devices. "Prototypes commissioned by the greatest militaries in the world. In your hands are the only operable versions of these weapons that exist. They are yours. Learn them. I've done my best to handpick tools that best fit each of you."

Meanwhile, Brandon fiddles with his pair of wireless lightning-rod tasers with stylized yellow lightning bolts on their cases. They're the same size as a traditional taser, but their barrels extend much further. Brandon takes aim at a concrete wall. A zap of white light zigzags from the weapon into the wall; metallic elements in the mixture crackle with life.

"These tasers interact with the metals in the target's body and blood and cause temporary paralysis from the inside out," Kebe says. "Be careful where you point them."

"Very cool. But Dr. Kebe, help me with one thing . . ." Brandon fiddles with his screen lock. "Screen locks are so passe. Why not thumbprint, face ID—something more, you know, modern? I thought we were getting the best of the best of the best. How are we connecting to the internet? Dialing up with AOL?"

Kebe smiles. "Ah, yes, Brandon. Good question," he says, his eyes twinkling with amusement. "It's so the enemy can't cut off your fingers or your face and use your weapon. Hypothetically." After two fatherly pats on the shoulder, Kebe moves on, leaving behind a chorus of amused snickers.

"Oh. Good idea," Brandon says. "You're always a step ahead, old man."

Jacki grips the two control rods for her solar-powered jetpack. She pushes one of their many buttons, and wings blast out from her back. With another button push, the thrusters activate, and she levitates.

"Whoa there! Careful!" Nigel yells, narrowly avoiding being clipped by the expansive wings, his voice drowned out by the roar of the jetpack's exhaust.

Nigel adjusts the nanoparticles in his matte-black gloves by pressing small copper buttons along their cuffs. He presses his right palm against a nearby wall. It's stuck there. Unable to get it off, he looks to Kebe. "A little help, boss?"

Amused by the situation, Kebe tells him, "Pull back with just your middle finger. Do the same with your index finger if you need to toggle to solid mode."

Nigel deactivates his right glove, releasing it from the wall. He lightly jabs the wall with the left glove, creating a disproportionately large crater sending dust flying. "Oops, my bad."

Over her hijab, Hala wears an ornate golden crown with geometric engravings. Decorative beads and diamond-shaped jewels dangle from its sides, which camouflage its lock screen. Hala tugs a jewel like a pull-cord light switch. Suddenly, a cloak flutters from the crown. Once it covers her entire body, she disappears.

The stunning illusion catches Guowei's eye. "Whoa."

As the cloak gracefully folds back into the crown, Hala releases her dangling beads.

Kebe addresses the group. "Should these devices fall into the wrong hands, under no circumstances should you unlock them. The ARK will covet this technology." He lowers Guowei's weapon toward the ground as he passes him. "And be very careful where you point them. Like our friend Genghis, it will leave an indelible mark."

Guowei adjusts the grip on his crossbow. He takes a test shot at one of Kebe's dirty coffee mugs on a table. A slender white arrow shaft strikes the mug and ruptures into a sticky white foam, engulfing it and adhering it to the wall like a gigantic marshmallow mishap.

Kebe taps Guowei on the shoulder. "We do not yet have a prototype that dissolves that foam," he says. Guowei gulps. "It takes two seconds to fully harden and up to two weeks to soften on its own." As Kebe leaves him, he reviews the work. "Nice shot, but that was my favorite mug."

Carlos slips on a pair of armored leather biker gloves. Affixed to the metal backpack he wears are two tires folded against his back, awaiting their moment. He completes the pattern on the lock screen on the back of his right glove, and a full-size motorbike unfolds from the metal case and slides beneath him perfectly. The handlebars rise, meeting his outstretched hands as if recognizing their master.

A low whistle escapes Carlos's lips as he takes it in. "That's what I'm talking about." He revs the motorbike and takes note of the rocket launchers on its side.

"Did I do well for you, my boy?" Kebe asks.

Carlos smiles. "Always."

"The miracles of modern engineering. In this case, the lightweight carbon-fiber frame and fully electric power source weigh far less than what you'd find on a standard motorbike."

"As long as it goes fast," Carlos smirks.

"Indeed it does," Kebe replies.

Adam practices aiming the bulky plasma bazooka on his shoulder. He discovers a small screen that pops out of the side of the device and provides an optical aim. Despite Kebe's assumptions to the contrary, Adam can't fathom the amount of power the weapon can generate. He studies the potential of laser fusion, but to this point his research is merely theoretical.

"It has eight charges," Kebe says. "No more, no less."

"How many will I need?" Adam asks.

"Ideally zero. But based on how my days have been going lately, probably nine. Choose wisely." As Kebe's words sink in, Adam feels the weight of a hundred more bazookas settle upon his shoulders. Though he trusts his judgment, decisions sometimes take days, weeks, or even years. The decision to fire his weapon will likely need to be made in seconds.

Carefully detaching the bazooka from his harness, he lifts it off his shoulder. As Adam sets it on the table next to him, he loses his grip. He bobbles the weapon, and the barrel spins wildly, pointing at the others, making them scramble like a pack of spooked deer.

He catches it in a bear hug, stabilizing it. He draws a deep breath. As he feels the rush of relief wash over him, he releases a slow exhale, the pressure dissipating from his body like steam from a teapot.

Adam sets the bazooka on the table with the utmost care. "I got it. Sorry about that."

Pink superheated light glows at the barrel of the bazooka. *What did he do?*

Kaboom!

Moments after the loudest sound he's ever heard, a gigantic circular stream of blinding energy flashes across the room. Voices cry out in alarm. Panic ensues. Adam's heart plummets into the depths of his pelvis. Everything inside him stops moving. *Was that real?*

A cloud of dust erupts, obscuring the once-clear space. A drink on a nearby table teeters before crashing to the floor. As the haze settles, the full extent of the destruction becomes apparent—an enormous and gaping hole through the wall, through unyielding steel, through the solid concrete, and ten meters into the earth's unforgiving crust. An acrid odor of charring plant matter permeates the room.

"Seven charges," Kebe says flatly.

"Oh. My. God." Hala whispers.

"Smooth move, Einstein," Nigel says.

Adam's face flushes with embarrassment. "Uh . . . my bad. Is there a safety on this thing?" His ordinary swirl of nausea churns into a tornado. Being prone to the occasional gaffe is certainly one quirk he would have loved to have left behind at École Polytechnique. If only Kebe had tweaked his DNA to enhance his coordination instead of his tricep strength.

"Should we be worried about radiation, Doc?" Carlos asks Kebe.

"Not with plasma," Kebe says. "I don't think . . . I'm not that kind of scientist."

"He can't have that weapon," Jacki says to Kebe. "It will jeopardize anything we try to do." She isn't making eye contact with Adam. He's glad she isn't. "Don't you have something less dangerous? Like a whip?"

The words hurt Adam, but he can't disagree in good conscience. As cool as the bazooka is, a whip would suit him better. Unless he lashes the wrong person—a possibility he can't ignore. There's no way Kebe will let him continue on in this mission.

"Adam will be fine," Kebe says. "He's the least of my concerns."

The *least* of his concerns?! What are his other concerns? Perhaps Kebe hadn't read the reports on him, or he'd be aware that this isn't his first monumental whoopsie.

"We need all seven of you," Kebe continues. "That's not up for debate."

Brandon inspects the colossal hole up close. "Good news is you can probably start a hyperloop track here. The hole might be too big, though. Wait, let me check. The iGlasses measure eighteen feet in diameter. According to *Popular*

Science, they are boring for twelve feet. So, yep . . . a little . . . too . . . big."

"Adam, get one of those chains." Kebe points to a pile of heavy-duty metal chains near the weapon's vault without looking at it. His attention is locked on something else, a stone-cold seriousness overtaking him. Only his eyes twitch as if he's using his iGlasses. Adam attempts to trace the direction of his gaze.

The military leaders throw their hands up in exasperation, likely unleashing a flurry of profanities in various languages. The three men from earlier are accompanied by a charismatic, red-haired man in his forties—a newcomer unfamiliar to Adam. He engages in handshakes and introductions.

"Get everyone to the conference room," Kebe tells Carlos, beads of sweat swelling at his hairline. "Bring the weapons. Be discreet. Do it right now."

"Is everything okay, Papi?" Carlos asks.

"We are out of time," Kebe says. "We've been compromised."

CHAPTER 17
GO

ADAM TRUDGES DOWN the dimly lit corridor, straining under the weight of a massive metal chain. The chain, easily surpassing fifty kilograms, threatens to tear his muscles off his bone. Though lifting fifty kilograms is routine for him, carrying it over a distance like this adds a new, painful dimension. He also undertakes this feat with a plasma bazooka strapped to his back.

Kebe's instructions echo in his mind, clear and urgent: retrieve the weapons and get out. Dread tightens its grip around Adam's heart. Whatever is going on, he sure is not ready for it. As he passes a doorway, Kebe yanks a lever, disabling the automatic door and making it manual.

The sight that greets Adam within the conference room does nothing to allay his growing fear. His comrades stand in various degrees of petrification, their faces engraved with shock as if the ground beneath them has given way. While Kebe has pulled a few jokes on them, it is clear this is not a drill. A frantic mess, Kebe trips into the room. A pillar of strength has been shaken to his core. Something is very wrong. Adam has never seen Kebe's eyes like this.

Kebe scrambles to his feet. "Chain that door," he says. Adam wraps the chain around the door's handles, his hands shaking from exertion and apprehension. Guowei hurries to assist him, and together they strain to tighten it. They have nothing to lock the chain with, so the best they can do is tie it in knots. The voice in his head tells him their makeshift barrier will prove woefully inadequate. With this door chained, they are leaving only one exit as an option—the old, earthen staircase from which they first came.

With the door secure, Kebe directs the others to stack the chairs, creating an additional barricade in front of the entryway. Panic swirls, suffocating the room as questions hang in the air, the unknown looming over them all.

"Who is here? What do they want?" Jacki's voice emerges, her words fighting for air between the stacking and screeching of the metal chairs and tables.

Kebe scrambles to grab the wireless keyboard, typing at a frenetic pace. "They are not here for us," he finally manages to say, his voice barely above a whisper. "We are in the way."

"In the way of what?" Jacki asks, seeking a glimmer of comprehension amid the chaos.

Straining to keep pace with the escalating madness, Adam's eyes dart anxiously between the flickering screen, the fortified door, and the palpable tension in the room. Many clueless faces look around for what's next, but the only man who might know can't stop to answer questions.

"Watch close," Kebe whispers, locking eyes with Brandon, communicating an unspoken gravity.

With a series of swift keystrokes, a prompt appears, and Kebe types in a complicated code. It is a code you'd only remember if your life depended on it. The text DESTROY DATABASE: CONFIRM? materializes on the screen.

"Who are they?" Jacki asks, but he isn't answering her.

Rather than click CONFIRM, Kebe performs another mind-bending series of keystrokes, gibberish to Adam, but Brandon follows along intently. He's the only one who speaks this language. After an avalanche of numbers, the entire system shuts down. Still plugging away at the keys, Kebe says, "I don't know. They're listening to us right now."

"Who's listening?" Nigel asks, his voice filled with an urgency that mirrors Adam's mounting unease.

In response, Kebe changes the presentation screen to display security monitors capturing various areas within the facility.

What are we supposed to do?

Adam can usually keep up when things move quickly, but now everything transpires at an overwhelming pace. His eyes, brain, heart, stomach, and lungs move asynchronously, each overpowering the next in a seemingly infinite chain reaction.

Carlos and Guowei glue themselves to one of the monitors. Screams and gunfire resound in the hallway outside the room. On the monitor, they see three bodies drop in the military leaders' room.

"Three dead," Carlos says. His words stab Adam like an icy blade.

Urgently, Kebe limps across the room and clutches Hala's trembling hands. He utters something to her in a language foreign to Adam's ears. Hala's eyes go wide. "What's going on?" she asks, teetering on the brink of a panic attack.

"My child," he says, "listen very carefully," and then slips back into the unknown language, saying as much as he can as fast as he can.

Across the monitors, a legion of soldiers armed with AR-15s, their faces obscured by armored tactical helmets, flood the hallway outside the military leaders' room. Clad in gray jumpsuits, they converge around the red-haired man in a formal suit—the leader among them.

"They've got an army," Carlos says, capturing everyone's attention. He pulls out his handgun and checks to see whether it's loaded.

Kebe wields a handgun of his own. Their time is running out. Adam's firearm rests securely in his holster, tucked away on his right side. He regrets that this is how he will learn how to use it.

Something slams against the conference room door like a medieval battering ram. The chains rattle, and the barricade of chairs wobbles.

"I am so proud of you, my children." Kebe's voice trembles with emotion, tears welling in his eyes. "Only trust one another." Hobbling to the exit, Kebe presses his thumbs to sensors, activating the door that opens to the passageway. "Go! Go! Go!"

Nigel leads the way into the darkness while Adam picks up the rear. But after reaching the dimly visible steps, he stops. There are no footsteps behind him. Kebe isn't following.

"Wait!" Adam desperately calls out to the others.

Kebe fires his handgun back into the conference room. His eyes meet Adam and the others who have stopped. "Go! That's an order!"

With his attention diverted, Kebe is bombarded by a swarm of bullets.

Collapsing into a puddle of his blood, facing the incoming onslaught, he fires another magazine at the door. "You will get nothing out of me! I will tell you nothing!" Kebe yells. "Twenty years of pain, I can take no more. If there is a God, may I rise from my ashes. Please forgive me of my transgressions."

He puts his gun to his chin and pulls the trigger.

"No!" Hala's anguished cry pierces the air.

A wave of crushing sorrow grips Adam's chest, stifling his breath. He instinctively covers his mouth in desperation and grief. The mysterious benefactor who slipped in and out of his life is gone. Without Baba, Adam can only fathom the catastrophic path his life would have taken. Through years of torment and trauma, he knew there was at least one person out there who cared about him and would fight for him, and while he didn't understand why he couldn't see him more growing up, Adam now understood Kebe was that watchful guardian for everyone else here. What Kebe had asked of him was far beyond anything he could imagine taking on. The only reason Adam had any optimism about this mission was because Kebe was here.

And now he's not.

Footsteps thump from below, snapping Adam out of his trance. Someone grabs hold of him, propelling him forward. Brandon pushes him up the stairs. "They need you in front!" he says.

Adam works his way to the front of the pack, each step bringing him deeper into the consuming darkness. The jagged concrete steps leave no margin for error. He collides with someone and utters a hasty apology, his balance teetering on the edge of uncertainty. Desperately, he grabs the earthen wall, breaking a chunk away. Finally reaching the front, he discerns the feeble glow from the screen on Jacki's jetpack. Adam locks his plasma bazooka into place. "Where do you want to go?"

Jacki points to the summit of the staircase. "Straight ahead," she says. "You need to blast our way out of here. We can't unlock it." Adam assumes the lead up the stairs.

But the ground beneath them quakes, a cacophony of noise assaulting their senses. "They're coming!" Carlos yells.

Adam fumbles with the pattern to unlock his bazooka. Sweat drips off his hand. His fingers are twitchy. *Come on. Come on. Come on.* The first attempt fails. He's sure he remembers the pattern, but he's just not doing it right. The second attempt fails, as does the third. Drops of vomit fly up his esophagus. Did he forget it?

On the fourth attempt, he unlocks the device. Relief. Adam steadies the bazooka into the darkness and pulls the trigger.

Kaboom!

A hot pink glow illuminates the void, the dirt overhead crumbling and permeating the passageway, burning eyes and throats. The dust settles to reveal a decimated wall and the stairway up to the drab, gray concrete room where they all first met.

A giant metallic crash from below is followed by a stampede of footsteps.

"It would be best to seal the tunnel," Guowei says.

Adam allows others to pass him so he can take another shot.

Rebels reach the staircase. Shots are fired. The bullets deflect off Brandon's boron carbide, centimeters from his head and neck, knocking him forward onto the steps.

Lined up in a row, the seven make for simple target practice. Adam can't wait any longer. He aims over Hala and Brandon and blasts the earth with his bazooka.

Kaboom!

As the earth shudders, the ceiling gives way, and an onslaught of dirt cascades down the stairs. Brandon loses his footing and tumbles backward. The rebels vanish behind the mountain of crust.

"It's falling!" Hala says.

Fueled by adrenaline, they sprint up the stairs and hurl themselves into the refuge of the gray concrete waiting area. They have all made it.

Except Brandon.

About fifteen steps from the top, Brandon is caught in the avalanche. Petrified, he flails and reaches for his teammates. He struggles to swim through the deluge of dirt but can't. It's too heavy. They can't reach him safely.

"Don't quit!" Adam shouts, his eyes frantically searching for a lifeline, finding none.

Brandon sinks beneath the mountain of dirt and clay. He takes a final frantic breath of air, his hand extended.

Knee-deep in the dirt, Guowei grabs Brandon's hand. As the relentless tide of dirt engulfs them further, Guowei pulls with all he has. Gripping Guowei firmly around the waist, Nigel lends his power to the Herculean task. Guowei loses his balance but not Brandon's hand. Dirt fills the cavity surrounding them, threatening to entomb them all.

The concrete floor begins to bow under Adam's feet. The foundation is compromised, teetering on the brink of collapse. Kebe said they needed everyone to succeed on this mission. They've already lost him; they can't lose anyone else.

With no better idea, Adam dives into the dirt, sinking instantly to his knees. He grabs Guowei's straining forearm with both hands, summoning every ounce of strength to aid in the rescue. Centimeter by agonizing centimeter, Brandon's clay-covered head emerges from the soil, gasping for breath and coughing out dust.

An unknown force envelops Adam from behind, a viselike grip that adds to the collective pulling strength. Every newton counts.

Hala positions herself on her stomach, aligning her gaze with Brandon's, her voice ringing out urgently. "You're almost there!" she extends her arm desperately to grasp Brandon's other hand.

The metal supports in the building's walls creak under the strain. Now thigh-deep in the dirt, Guowei pulls like a champion rower, bellowing with obstinate determination. The combined force breaks through, freeing Brandon from his earthen prison. Hala swiftly grabs his other arm, and Guowei and Adam pull him by the elbow and tug his lower half out completely.

Adam gasps as if he was the one suffocating. They all stumble back onto the concrete floor as the entire corridor succumbs to an unrelenting torrent of dirt. A gigantic fracture severs the floor and swallows two meters of the landing.

They've reached the top. Their arrival is met with a grim and haunting sight—bloodstained guards, lifeless and abandoned. These sentries must have defied the rebels and paid the ultimate price.

Silence reigns. Nobody knows which direction to step. Adam grasps for something simpler. "Are you okay?" he asks Brandon.

Brandon exhales a cloudy puff, his face caked with dirt. "You know, thanks for asking. To be honest, I've been better." He takes stock of the grime clinging to his body. "But this isn't the worst I've needed a shower this month."

Jacki moves toward a glimmer of daylight shining into the building, a fissure wrought by the implosion of the bunker. "We have to keep moving," she says.

CHAPTER 18
BEARINGS

UNTAMED FORESTS and a slumbering volcano dominate the horizon. Adam and the group move cautiously through the trees, his breath laboring in the biting mountain air. The altitude weighs on him, an ever-present reminder that he cannot formulate any theories about where they are or where they're headed.

Adam stoops under a low-hanging branch of a deciduous tree, his senses on high alert. The forest overflows with foliage. Adam half expects to find an assassin hiding behind each trunk. Though he hasn't discovered any danger among the first ten thousand trees, the nagging question persists—what about the ten thousand and first?

After thirty minutes, they have run about five kilometers, but it's hard to tell because of the circuitous route they've taken from the destroyed training facility.

Where Kebe was buried under the wreckage.

Adam shouldn't have let him stay behind to face the enemy alone. He should have picked him up and carried him out of the danger, just as Kebe did for him countless times. It would have been the least he could do to return the favor. What are these people after? Kebe had made it clear—it's not them. They are just in the way. But what are they in the way of? It's a puzzle Adam can't solve. He would turn to Margot or Kebe in times like these, bouncing ideas off their brilliant minds. But that's not an option.

Adam scopes out the wilderness. He's not a geographer. A hypothesis of where they are would only be a wild guess. It's about five degrees Celsius, ruling out tropical climates. It's eerily quiet; the crunch of leaves under his feet interrupts his thoughts for a moment, but they aren't any leaves he recognizes. If only he had dedicated more time paying attention to the nuances of the leaves of different trees. Any wildlife silently monitoring the situation is not interested in introducing themselves, but it would be a clue should a species decide to.

"I think we are clear," Jacki says, glancing cautiously over her shoulder.

"Uh . . . where in the hell are we?" Nigel's bewilderment echoes the sentiments of the group.

Guowei squints, scanning the unfamiliar landscape. "It is a terrain I am not familiar with. Perhaps Northern Canada?"

Adam's eyes drift to the calm lake below. "I don't see any geese."

Carlos taps the bark of a coniferous tree. "Not South American trees."

Although Brandon attempted to wash off the dirt, mud still mars his face. "I'd be willing to bet my American education on this," he says, with the zeal of an experienced professor, "That is Titila—a shield volcano located in the northern part of Kamchatka Peninsula, Russia. Last eruption unknown."

"How could you possibly know that?" Hala asks him, gawking with disbelief.

Brandon grins, his confidence unwavering. "Because unlike you all, I remember we're wearing supercomputers on our eyeballs. You should use these things. I haven't turned mine off."

"For the past two days?" Hala asks.

"No. Why would you?"

"Because I don't want to see numbers and letters flying over everything I look at all the time."

Brandon nods, acknowledging she might have a point. "Well then, it's good for y'all that Benjamin Franklin didn't die in that dirt avalanche that Einstein caused."

"Whoa, whoa," Adam says, taken aback by the unexpected friendly fire. Brandon's reassuring smile signals to him that it's all in good fun, a momentary respite from the mounting tension. "I guess, yeah. Okay."

"Kamchatka is north of Japan," Guowei says, "A couple thousand kilometers north of Korea."

Carlos gazes into the crisp blue sky. "Makes you wonder what else they do out here that they don't want you to know about, doesn't it?"

Jacki grabs Hala by the elbow. "What did Kebe say to you?"

Adam had forgotten about that. Perhaps Kebe left them something after all.

Hala's brow knits in concern. Deliberately selecting her words, she finally speaks, her voice strained with the weight of interpretation. "He spoke Swahili, not one of my strongest languages. I think he said . . ." She pauses, closing her eyes in concentration. "'This is only for you.'"

Hala reaches into her pocket, her hand tightly clenched. Gradually, she unfurls her fingers, showing a USB flash drive with a cracked case inside.

"'Countries cannot know. They will disregard the consequences. ARK will tear cities to the ground, but they won't until they get this. You must protect it. If you fail, cities will fall . . . ,'" Hala recites, trembling with the gravity of Kebe's message, tacking on, ". . . or something like that."

Nigel snatches the flash drive from her hand, his frustration bubbling to the surface. "Great. I'll go ahead and stick it in my laptop. This is ridiculous."

Jacki puts her finger in his chest. "You heard what Kebe said."

"Yep. Right before he shot himself."

"He was defending us. He *has always* defended us," Jacki says, refusing to let his comment slide.

Adam shifts weight to his toes in case he has to break up an impromptu clash.

Nigel throws his arms up. "Bringing us in for secret Power Ranger school, and then he goes and leaves us with a flash drive. Shoooot, I ain't got time. It's not like I volunteered for this nonsense."

"I thought he was your oom," Jacki says, her gaze penetrating Nigel's defenses.

"Now he's my dead oom," Nigel replies.

Jacki's stare sharpens. It's the type of expression that would haunt the nightmares of well-balanced souls. "Well, for some reason, he thought we needed you, Mandela," she says.

"For what? Why are we going to do this? I don't owe a dead man anything."

Carlos interjects, his voice calm yet resolute. "That's not how that works. The dead get their debts paid too."

"Really? And I'm gonna put my life on the line because I feel like I owe a dead man something? Shooooot."

"If that's what it takes," Carlos says. "I pay up. That's what a man's word means. But I get it. You don't know about that."

"And that part about the global nuclear holocaust," Brandon says. "It kinda would affect me on a personal level. You know, because of all the people dying and stuff. I know what Ben Franklin would be doing. He'd run into a nuke balls-first if it meant saving the world. You can't convince me otherwise. And you know what Genghis Khan would be, uh, well . . ."

"Hopefully, he'd try to make amends for the monstrosities he unleashed on this world," Guowei replies.

"You can't know what we know and not try to help," Hala says. "We are here for a reason. Made for a reason. Together for a reason."

Sure, a nuclear holocaust sounds awful, but amid the weight of their shared mission, Adam's thoughts remain aligned on a singular track. His reason is named Margot.

"And y'all are gonna just take his word for it? That's what's gonna happen?" Nigel asks.

"His word? Yes," Guowei says.

"This might be hard for you to understand, but some people feel obliged to serve the greater good rather than just themselves," Jacki says.

Nigel's snark only grows. "You out here trying to be like Joan? Your hero, right? Since when were you put in charge?

Did I miss the meeting? Was it before or after you found out Kebe was your daddy?"

Jacki takes a step toward him, locking eyes. The wrath of her stare reaches its apex. "I was the youngest *sous-lieutenant* in the history of *le Aéronavale*, but if anyone feels more qualified, I'll gladly step back," she says, gesturing to the group.

"You're doing a great job," Brandon says.

"Shut up!"

"Excellent idea, captain," Brandon says, falling silent, straightening his posture.

Carlos holds his hand out to Nigel. "Give us the flash drive, homie. Or are you playing for the other team?"

"Are *you*?" Nigel asks. "Don't think I didn't see you chillin' when we were all in the dirt." They stare at each other, neither willing to back down.

"Someone's gotta keep a lookout on the horizon, ya feel me?" Carlos says. "Heat might come from more than one angle. You're new to this life, huh?"

"This guy . . . ," Nigel mutters, shaking his head. He flicks the flash drive into Carlos's chest like a toothpick and marches deeper into the forest, stomping his message into the leaves beneath his boots. Guowei moves to follow him.

"Let him go," Carlos says. "We don't need him."

"Seven of us were asked to save the world," Guowei says resolutely. "I think we'll need all seven."

Out of nowhere, a sudden memory jolts Adam. "A pocket!" he blurts out. He starts patting himself down like a maniac.

"Uh, buddy," Brandon says. "Are you okay? Buddy?"

With relief and excitement, Adam flips open a small pocket on his chest—a USB port embedded inside.

"Oh! Good lookin' out, Einstein," Brandon says, "Never doubted you for a second." He reaches for the flash drive, and Carlos passes it to him. He plugs it into his suit.

"Turn your iGlasses on. I'll share the view," Brandon says. "To see my documents, it's left twitch, left twitch, left blink." Brandon demonstrates with the speed of a sandwich artist during a lunch rush, then, at their behest, walks them through it all again, this time slowly.

Adam follows the directions. Suddenly, a document folder from Brandon's screen appears on his. "This is weird," he says.

"Everyone ready?" Brandon asks.

"Yup. Do it, boss," Carlos says.

With a decisive click, a document opens, but it is password-encrypted. The instructional text is a message in a non-alphabetic language.

"What's the password?" Brandon asks.

"Kebe didn't give me a password," Hala says.

Brandon inputs a password eleven characters long. An error message pops up in English. The password isn't correct, and he lets out a groan. A prompt notes there are two more incorrect attempts before the folder locks.

"Well, that's bad," Adam says.

"It turns out 'Bird Buddies' is not the password," Brandon says.

"You wasted one of our attempts on 'Bird Buddies'?!" Jacki says.

"Regrettably," Brandon replies, "But in fairness, I thought we would have infinite attempts." He zooms in on the text. "Language Girl, what does that say?"

"Hatshepsut," Jacki interjects. "Or Hala . . ."

"Oh yes, for sure. Queen Hala."

Scrutinizing the message, Hala translates, "I believe that says 'Ask Carlos' in Arabic."

Carlos scratches his neck. "*Yolia*," he says without hesitation.

"Yolia?" Brandon asks.

"That's it. That's the word." Carlos is adamant.

"Is that with a *y* or a soft *j*?" Brandon asks.

"*Y-O-L-I-A*. It's the Nahuatl word for spirit."

Brandon inputs the five-digit code. "Is that what we are going with?" he asks the group.

Though Adam hasn't seen a butterfly in this wilderness, chrysalises may have hatched in his stomach. It doesn't take an Einstein to figure out they only have one chance left if this isn't right, and they are using this attempt on a word he's never heard before.

"Yes sir," Carlos says.

"On a scale of one to ten, where ten is the surest you could possibly be—"

"Ten."

"Are you rounding to ten, or is it a true ten?"

"Just do it," Jacki says.

"I'm submitting the password," Brandon says, ". . . momentarily . . . unless anyone tells me to stop . . . okay. Entered."

To their relief, the password is accepted, granting them access to an encrypted file. A smile lights up Carlos's face. "My man," he whispers to himself.

"Good work," Adam says. Carlos never showed one ounce of doubt.

The file opens, displaying a profile of an adorable four-year-old boy named Yusef, with olive skin and black hair. Underneath his photo is a map of Italy with a digital pushpin and a set of coordinates for an address directly in the heart of Rome.

"Bricker will tear the world to the ground," Hala repeats the ominous warning. "But he won't until he gets this. If you fail, the world will fall."

"I guess we are going to Rome," Jacki says.

Did Adam miss something? He looks around. Trees, trees, and more trees. He can't help but voice his confusion. "Yeah, uh, how?"

"I can get us a plane." Outside the circle, Nigel waits alongside Guowei. "Where's the nearest airport?" he asks.

CHAPTER 19
A NEW DAY DAWNING

AN ONYX-FRAMED CASCADE of screens sits before an advanced telepresence robot perched on the passenger seat of a jeep. The robot's neck, a titanium rod, extends from a four-wheeled base, while its head, a screen broadcasting Bricker's live video stream, periscopes toward the driver like a bird of prey. Bricker, unable to conceal his weariness, his voice barely a whisper amidst the engine's thrum, murmurs, "I take for granted how reliable you are, my son." An eerie stillness hangs. Failure was not an option.

"Yes, you do," Zed replies from the driver's seat, clad in his trademark black attire and ski glasses, a large gold crucifix hanging from his neck, and a triangular soul patch covering his chin. He's growing into a man before his father's eyes. "You ready?"

"Turn it on," Bricker says, his anticipation pressing.

Stories of abductions around the world stream in through the dashboard display. One screen shows the ARK Facebook page. It's all good news—with one exception. Bricker already knows that Etherington botched the invasion of Kebe's base but has yet to hear his version of events from his trembling lips.

On the primary screen, Etherington squirms in discomfort. Once dripping with confidence, the man has been reduced to a stagnant puddle. Even his fiery red hair now appears pale. Zed unmutes him.

"We infiltrated the base," Etherington says in monotone. "Dr. Kebe is dead."

Kebe is dead. Long ago, Bricker might have gotten emotional about this, but his years of meditation have paid off. Though the two had their differences, he focuses on the positives in his grief—perhaps Kebe rubbed off on him after all. But Kebe isn't Bricker's concern today. He just happened to be in the way.

Bricker leans his robot forward. "And the boy?" he asks, replacing Etherington as the center square.

"No sign of him," Etherington says, "and no data could be recovered. Kebe assembled a team. There are seven of them. I presume he aims to counter us. They were given weapons. Forgive me, but they escaped."

Bricker's silence stretches out like a taut thread in the atmosphere. "Seven, you say?" he finally responds, his voice betraying a hunger that threatens to consume him whole. His life's work could be salvageable after all. "I might want these seven."

A chat box on his video call opens and becomes the center screen. Text flies across the screen as he types: @BRUTUS515 ET TU 515 #APITY.

"Did you say weapons?" Zed interjects.

"Yes sir," Etherington nods. "Powerful weapons I've never seen before—prototypes from UN countries. They can only be unlocked by them and them alone. I saw what one could do. It blasted a crater thirty feet into the earth."

Zed turns Bricker's robotic screen toward himself. "Father, I know what I want for Christmas this year."

"Have you been a good boy?" Bricker replies. "Bring me the seven, and you can have their toys."

"No problem."

"I've directed the rebels to follow," Etherington continues, but now with desperate determination. "I will not disappoint you again."

"No, you won't," Bricker says, muting his video feed.

An exit wound silently bursts through Etherington's forehead, and his body falls forward.

With a couple of fumbling clicks, Bricker boots Etherington from the video call and terminates the feed. "I miss being with you every day," Bricker says. It's a genuinely heartfelt expression.

"A few more days," Zed replies.

"It can't come soon enough."

Zed smiles as he veers down a long gravel drive cloaked by ancient bald cypresses and chestnut oaks. After a quarter mile, he reaches the gate with a sign that reads EMPLOYEES ONLY.

Zed lowers his window, and a computer monitor scans his face. The gates groan open. The nondescript building looms behind the foliage. Its industrial garage yawns wide as the jeep enters onto a freight elevator and descends into darkness.

Years ago, the settlers that happened upon the region's abundant salt domes couldn't have guessed what would be happening there today. Digging a mine shaft was expensive speculative work at that time, but one that could return riches. Like its creator, the new owner has grand ambitions for the property—and they are hoping for a life-changing result. Bricker loves a good history lesson. The winners get to write them, and his favorite fountain pen is full of ink.

As the jeep emerges from the freight elevator, it drives between the rows of shelves stacked with bombs. Each one is encased in sleek matte-black metal. The streamlined aerodynamic design conceals the seething inferno dormant within. At a mere three feet in length, an observer could underestimate the catastrophic power at their own peril. Once the cataclysmic trigger of reactions is pulled, all confusion would be put to rest. In fact, it'll be a day they'll never forget.

Bricker periscopes his screen around to admire the arsenal. "A new day dawning," he whispers. The assembly line enhancing the thermonuclear warheads is a terrifying and glorious sight, each bearing a scribble of white paint like fighter planes of the past, with names like London, Beijing, Tokyo, and NYC. Hopefully, the citizens will see the artwork before they detonate.

Overhead, an aquarium holds a million fish but isn't large enough for half that many. A marvelous sight. Especially the thousands of chewed-up carcasses drifting along the bottom. It's an installation he couldn't have designed more perfectly. Everything is coming together.

Rocky walls line the underground silo, dimly lit by welding sparks and the headlights of construction equipment hauling beams of composite metal. Scientists and engineers scurry like the industrious insects they are. Patrolling head-set-clad rebels armed with assault rifles ensure everything stays on task.

Zed gestures to a group of scientists ahead, their forms bathed in flickering illumination. "These are the problem children."

"My favorite kind," Bricker says. "What was the one troublemaker's name?"

"Margot Czarnecki."

CHAPTER 20
PROBLEM CHILDREN

WHILE HER FIVE TEAMMATES line up, Margot doesn't budge from her folding chair. She is not anxious to impress, having already taken a blowtorch to any inkling of compliance. It has been days since her last shower. The enthusiastic go-getter from presentation day has long since perished on her journey to this creepy underground weapon silo.

The embodiment of toxic masculinity steps from the jeep, wielding a semiautomatic triple-barreled pistol equipped with an extended magazine. At over two meters tall, he dwarfs everyone. The man takes slow, menacing steps around to the passenger door and seizes hold of the metal spine of a machine with a tablet for a face. Margot has never seen anything like it. Large, expensive, unnecessary, and weird—exactly the vibe of this twisted operation.

With great care, the tall man sets the million-dollar device on the ground, its neck rod elongating to mimic the presence of a person. The bizarre robot pivots and glides smoothly on four wheels, fixing its gaze upon the row of scientists assembled before it.

"Do any of you sail?" asks the old man on the robot screen, cutting through the pregnant silence, the sound emitting from speakers somewhere in its base.

The robot glides alongside the group, scoping them out. Not a single word is uttered in response. The scientist standing nearest to Margot trembles; his fear lies bare.

"A dear friend of mine dreamed of sailing," the robot continues. "It's a complicated thing, you see. Especially when you're trying to get somewhere. A direction. A destination. The winds are strong. The waters are rough. Everyone has to work together. In the storm, some work the rudder, some adjust the sails. Teamwork. When I see other teams augmenting at a rate of three warheads a day, and this particular team hasn't yet enhanced a single nuke, I see a directionless ship. So here I am, the captain."

Dalip, a middle-aged scientist, clears his throat. The best he can muster is a stammer. "Most . . . of the team works well, but . . . there's an individual—"

"I don't build bombs," Margot interjects. "I won't build bombs."

The robot rotates to the tall man. "Brains, beauty, and boldness. Too valuable to kill, wouldn't you say?"

"She doesn't seem that smart," the tall man says, scrutinizing her form as though he's appraising livestock.

"Miss Czarnecki, or may I call you Margot?" the robot asks, attempting to establish some semblance of congeniality. He will be alone in the effort.

As she prepares her response, a fire ignites within Margot's chest. "I don't care what you call me. I will not under any circumstances aid in the construction of any tool for mass murder."

"Sweetheart, these are not tools of death," the robot says. "They are tools of life. You, of all people, should appreciate that. You might have to eliminate certain cells so others can thrive. So life can thrive. You see that aquarium?"

The group's attention shifts to the overcrowded fish tank above. Margot doesn't bother. She saw it when she was first brought here. No need to look again. And the stench of the decaying fish is among the many things here giving her a headache.

"What happens when that tank exceeds its carrying capacity?" the robot asks. "A battle for resources. Disease. Starvation. Cannibalism. Extinction. It's simple, really. Would you want that to happen to us? Because it is. Immorality is winning the day. We build these gargantuan cities, and they rot. Their leaders guide them right into a burning pit of sulfur. Good souls are going extinct. There are even countries building designer babies rather than using their God-given DNA just to keep up. Like it's a burger joint. Can you believe that?"

The robot moves closer to Margot, squinting to get a better look at her. "What do you think is next? They are destroying our way of life, but we will defend it. We are not cowards. We are the bold. We are willing to make the necessary sacrifices for the greater good. You probably assume I want to rule the world. Nothing could be further from the truth. I'm not built for that job. You can apply if you're interested. I'm simply a fisherman trying to save the fish."

"Kill me," Margot says, the words flowing effortlessly from her lips. She's thought them through many times in her confinement. Frankly, she doesn't see this ending any other way. There's no other way out.

The robot turns to the tall man. "Perhaps a bit moody," he says with derision. "She may be too high maintenance for you." Returning his focus to Margot, he points up to the fish tank. "If most of those fish have to die, wouldn't it be great if we could keep the useful ones?"

"I'm not interested in your sermon," she replies. "You are a radical, narcissistic, sociopathic nutjob. Kill me." That felt good. Her teammates are startled by her audacity.

A menacing scowl rises and spreads across the robot's screen. She's struck a nerve. "Sweetheart, understand that when an individual steps out of line, we aren't going to shoot them because they tell us to. You're not the captain of this ship. We shoot your team."

The tall man aims the three-barreled gun at Dalip, his finger poised on the trigger. Fear engulfs the room as Dalip pleads for mercy, invoking his family and children in his effort.

"So, who's the captain, sweetheart?" the robot asks. "Stand up and get in line."

Shit. Not what she had in mind. The collective tremble of her team hits her in her heart.

"Just do it," another scientist whispers to her.

Margot swallows hard. She was numb after the first few days here, but now she is overwhelmed with a surge of life. Pangs of fear rattle her. She won't compromise her morals, but is there a middle path?

Margot opens her mouth to speak, but before she can utter a word, the gun fires—an involuntary gasp from her soul follows.

Dalip crumples to the ground, writhing in pain as blood pools around his abdomen. The tall man moves on to the next target, cocking his gun while everyone else in the room covers their mouths, stifling their despair.

"Zed has less patience than I do," the robot sighs.

A whisper reaches Margot's ears, a fellow scientist urging her to act. Tears well up in her eyes as she realizes the gravity of the situation.

It was supposed to be her.

With a faltering balance, Margot stands and takes her place in line.

The robot tilts his screen down to see her, wearing a sympathetic grin. "Go team," he says. The robot spins around and exits the room, leaving behind a haunting sense of terror. After a moment of staring them down, the tall man follows suit.

The other scientists scurry to Dalip's aid, scrambling to stop the bleeding and save his life. Her knees weak, Margot crumples to the ground, tears streaming down her face.

CHAPTER 21
CODE RED

EMMANUEL KEBE HAD A JOB TO DO. Most days weren't pleasant. That day four years ago was no exception. The syringe hidden in the pommel of his cane was prescribed as the antidote to tame the world's ills. The waiting room chairs in the small community hospital might as well have been stuffed with needles. A screaming infant did nothing to quell the collective discomfort of those waiting. Dressed in a suit and a surgical face mask, Kebe locked in on his target.

Peering through his shades, Bricker's son Zed stared at his phone. Irritated, he cranked up the volume, hoping to drown out the cries. It hurt Kebe's heart to see what became of the young man. The intimidating-looking long rain jacket and ski cap were only coverings, but they indicated the man underneath was long gone, a victim of his festering father.

Zed was so distracted he hadn't even noticed Kebe's wooden cane clacking against the floor on his walk over to him. "Sir," Kebe said, "your baby probably wants to be held."

Zed glanced down at the shrieking, blue-faced child in the car seat, dressed in generic hospital attire they long overgrew. Zed absentmindedly rocked the car seat with his foot.

"Hello, I'm Emmanuel," Kebe continues. "I was an old friend of your father's. Is he seeing anyone?"

Zed didn't bother to look, seemingly annoyed that Kebe was still standing there. He pointed down the hall. "Two twelve," he muttered dismissively.

Kebe noticed the video playing on Zed's screen—an old pro-wrestling clip featuring a man getting smashed in the face with a steel chair. Kebe delved into his pop culture knowledge to extend an olive branch. "I'd wager you're an Undertaker fan."

Zed grinned, momentarily breaking through his gruff exterior. "You'd win that bet."

Finding his way down the hall, Kebe peered into the room. Bricker rested in his hospital bed. He had seen better days. Machines monitored his oxygen levels and heart rate while IV-administered fluids ran into his frail body. Thirteen long years had passed since he had been in the genetics lab of the Phoenix Elite Initiative, but by the looks of him, he had aged twice that. The tremors in his right arm had intensified, and a state-of-the-art electronic wheelchair sat beside his bed. Bricker read a Bible in his bed, a pen poised in his left hand—his nondominant hand.

"How are you doing, my old friend?"

Surprised to see him, Bricker sat up straight. "Why is a globe-trotting paper-pusher like yourself stopping by Podunk hospitals looking for me?" He closed his Bible and set it aside. A deep-throated cough crashed from his lungs.

"I was just passing through," Kebe said. "You wouldn't believe how much data the United Nations collects."

The comment drew a smirk from Bricker, just as intended. "Oh, I believe it."

"For what it's worth, I try my best to stop the paper-pushers from pushing too much paper, my old friend," Kebe said.

"I believe it."

Despite their many years apart, it was as if they hadn't missed a beat, but Kebe knew they were playing different songs. Kebe steeled his resolve. "Are you well? I've been worried about you." He wore a straight face, but today's visit was far from serendipitous. The intel he had collected about his old friend's ambitions had shaken him to his core.

"Apparently, I have too many comorbidities," Bricker replied. "At least that's what they told me. My son wanted me to get it checked out. I'm fine, but he didn't want me to chance it."

Kebe nodded toward the Bible. "You found religion? Good for you."

"I'm looking for it," Bricker replied, smiling. "After all these years of playing God, I thought I'd better acquaint myself with him."

"You mind if I . . . ?" Kebe gestured to the book.

"Yeah, go ahead," Bricker said.

Bricker had scribbled an illegible screed all over the margins and even onto the text. The annotations in the book of Revelations were a mix of words and symbols. Were they codes? Because they looked like the blathering of a cult leader. Kebe had spent years trying to convince Bricker to pick up the Good Book, but this wasn't what he had in mind.

Kebe's breath caught as he landed on an image of a missile drawn in the margin beside the passage about the Tower of Babel—with an emphatically circled *destroy* accompanying it. A few pages later, more missiles were drawn next to the header for Sodom and Gomorrah—the word *wickedness* underlined.

Years underground hiding from international authorities had turned his old friend into a recluse. Only Bricker's elaborate dossier of incriminating evidence against various countries protected him from prosecution and prison. For the better part of a decade, his willingness to sell his ethically questionable expertise had built himself an unrivaled blackmail feedback loop in the highest reaches of government. It was great for his pocketbook, which only enabled more blackmail.

"I'm . . . sorry about . . ." Bricker trailed off.

Kebe didn't need Bricker to apologize or open up old wounds, especially when his friend was in such a condition, and Kebe needed to avert a global crisis. Time was of the essence, and Kebe had only minutes to make a gut-wrenching decision. He flipped the Bible open to the book of James and dog-eared the page. "James is my favorite book. Surprised they named a whole book after you?"

Bricker was lost.

"What have you done, James?" Kebe asked. If the immoral scientific genius had lost his grip on reality, the world would pay the consequences. Despite significant evidence to the contrary, every time there had been a global pandemic, a historic wildfire, or an international security crisis, Kebe couldn't help but think about his old lost friend and wonder whether it had been his handiwork. "We can fix it" he said.

"I did it," Bricker said.

"You did what?"

"It," Bricker whispered. "I think I did *it*."

The words swept through Kebe. Before the visit that day, he strongly suspected what *it* was. What he saw confirmed it.

"I'm not sure what you are referring to, old friend," Kebe said.

"Maybe you can come work with me again one day," Bricker replied.

"I like my job."

A dour expression crossed Bricker's face. "I was afraid of that."

The gut decision was made. It wasn't pretty.

Adrenaline rushed through Kebe's body as he unscrewed the pommel of his cane. Syringe in hand, he jammed into Bricker's thigh, injecting the serum. Bricker's protest was cut short by a lung-choking coughing fit.

"Get well, James," Kebe said, glancing back, knowing that was the last time he would ever speak to him.

Without wasting a moment, Kebe pressed the red emergency call button on Bricker's wall and hurried out of the room. He hustled to the waiting room as nurses and doctors responded to the lights and dull siren with hollered orders.

Spotting Zed in the commotion, Kebe hurried over to him, his speech urgent and exuding concern. "It's your father. His oxygen suddenly dropped. They may be intubating him. They need to see you immediately. There's no time." Zed didn't budge, so Kebe kept spitting words with as much urgency as he could muster. This couldn't fail. Frazzled, Zed put his phone away and grabbed the car seat carrier, but Kebe stopped him. "I'll watch him. Hurry."

Zed eyed him momentarily, but he relented and ran around the corner into the bedlam.

Kebe unfastened the baby from the carrier, cradling their chest in the palm of his hand. With the waiting room distracted by his orchestrated chaos, he tucked the baby inside his suit jacket and made for the exit.

A minute later, Kebe ditched his suit in a bathroom for shorts and the infant chest carrier he stowed there. He hastened to leave the hospital and jumped into the back of an ambulance idling in the fire lane.

Inside, he was greeted by special operations forces.

As the ambulance pulled away, Kebe was at peace with his decision. But today was not a victory. If the doctors performed the lifesaving work they tended to do, it was likely just a roadblock.

CHAPTER 22
TAKEOFF

THE KAMCHATKA MOUNTAINS stretch before her, their majestic peaks reaching the moonlit sky. Standing on the abandoned Soviet airstrip, Jacki squints, momentarily envisioning the familiar silhouette of the Alps. The crisp scent of pine offers her the solace she needs to catch up to her racing thoughts.

Weeds pop from the asphalt; nature is slowly reclaiming what once belonged to it. After a twelve-hour wait, a gleaming white private jet lands on the jagged asphalt, its fuselage adorned with decorative script that reads DILLON & SON EXOTICS: BEST AND NOTHING LESS.

Carlos turns to Nigel, "You Dillon? Or are you Son?"

"I got you a plane. What more do you want?" Nigel replies.

"Snacks?" Hala interjects.

"Yeah, I got those too," Nigel says.

Jacki would've happily strangled Nigel days ago, but if she's being honest, she doesn't mind the jet. Perhaps that's why Kebe insisted they'd need him.

Though not one to eulogize, Jacki appreciates how Kebe helped her through her darkest days. Losing him is like losing another piece of herself—a good piece. The man who moonlighted as her judo coach always believed in her and made her feel powerful. If he thought he needed to sacrifice himself so they could escape, she trusts his decision, however unpleasant. Soldiers like her understand unpleasant decisions.

As she gazes at the towering peaks, their summits glistening with snow, it's what she doesn't understand that bothers her. What is she to do with being the second coming of Joan of Arc? They say never meet your heroes but never mention what to do when you become them. Jacki lost the faith that fueled Joan's courage, and now, somewhere in Italy, a young boy needs their protection. That's all they know. What would Joan do?

Her train of thought is abruptly interrupted as a file pops up on her iGlasses display—a link from Brandon. She deletes it without hesitation. Getting rid of his nonsense is the one part of the iGlasses she's mastered.

"So, are we the Dragonhawks?" Brandon asks. "Nobody has responded to my Google Form. Here, I'll send out a second link in case you all didn't get the first one."

If Jacki had to choose between the pompous ass Nigel and the juvenile ignoramus Brandon, it would be a two-way tie for last place. Besides, Jacki had already decided on the perfect name yesterday.

"We are the Phoenix Elite," Jacki says, drawing everyone's attention. "That's what Kebe started. That's what we are."

"That's a very impressive executive decision, if I may say so," Brandon says in his ongoing effort to schmooze her.

Against her better judgment, there's a nonzero chance his efforts amuse her.

"Cool, Captain d'Arc. I can feel that," Carlos says.

"You all had your chance to step up. You didn't," Jacki says, a faint smile gracing her lips, the first she's let out of the cage in a long while.

The thirty-something pilot strolls down the plane's airstairs to greet them, casually sipping an energy drink. His wavy hair sloppily spills out of his backward baseball cap. Clad in a cut-off T-shirt, checkered Bermuda shorts, and a pair of casual slip-on shoes, he is a frat boy who never grew up.

The Phoenix Elite walks over to greet him. Nigel connects with an elaborate handshake followed by a bro-hug, affirming that Jacki's read was spot on. "I owe you big time, Jimmy. Thanks for coming," Nigel says.

Jimmy soaks in the landscape. "Yeah, you do," he says, his gaze sweeping over their attire and weaponry. "What the hell d'you get yourself into?"

"We can't really—" Nigel says.

"It's top secret," Jacki blurts out.

Jimmy notes the hulking man beside her with the gigantic gun. "Is that a bazooka?"

"Yep," Adam says.

"Welp, where are we headin'? Or is that top secret too?"

"Rome," Nigel replies.

Every English profanity Jacki knows runs to the tip of her tongue. She understands that this is the first time in the trenches for most of her teammates, but even the greenest recruit should know that casually dishing intel isn't how to conduct themselves.

"You tryin' to set a record, Lindbergh?" Jimmy says. "Let's get on with it. I told the wife I'd bring home breakfast."

With haste, Jimmy stumbles up the airstairs, followed by Nigel, but Jacki grabs his arm before he can leave. "You're not serious," she says.

"What are you talking about?" Nigel says incredulously.

"That guy," Jacki says. She's baffled that Nigel doesn't get it. "He's not coming with us."

"Jimmy? Oh, come on, he's the pilot. He flew for hours at a moment's notice as a favor. Do you know what clearances he had to pull to get here in the first place?" Nigel's gaze sweeps across the group. "Any of y'all got your own plane we can use then?"

"Only trust one another," Hala says, echoing Kebe's words.

"We don't know him," Guowei adds.

"He's not the only one who knows how to file a flight plan," Jacki says.

Nigel looks around. "Puhh-lease. I've known Jimmy since prep school. I asked the man to fly halfway around the world. I'm not about to leave him stranded on a runway in the middle of friggin' Nowhereville, Russia."

Yet five minutes later, smack in the middle of friggin' Nowhereville, Russia, Jimmy stands on the runway as the jet flies away, shrinking into the distance.

Jacki can't help but smile—a complete smile. Settling into the cockpit, she tinkers with knobs and wipes off a dirty screen. Any day in the pilot's seat is a good day.

"Hey, bad news," Brandon hollers from the cabin. "I looked into getting Jimmy an Uber, but the closest option is four and a half hours away. Best bet is he grabs this two-star

Airbnb from this guy named Fedor. If he doesn't mind sharing a room with his pet wolverines, it might work out. Kinda cozy. Lots of natural wood."

Nigel stands over her shoulder, shaking his head. "If anything happens to the plane, I swear to God."

"I'm sure we'd be in better hands with Jimmy," Jacki says, handing Nigel Jimmy's swimsuit magazine and empty beer bottles.

With her cockpit clear of rubbish, Jacki punches in the coordinates for Rome.

CHAPTER 23
CHECK

FROM THE COMFORT of a plush green leather chair in the dining area, Guowei arranges chess pieces on a polished wooden board. He drinks in the lavender-scented recycled air, grateful for this brief respite. Instead of sitting opposite him, Hala gracefully slides in beside him. *This is nice.*

"But don't you have to be really smart?" Hala asks. "I mean, you have to remember all the moves, think so far ahead."

"My intellect pales in comparison to anyone fluent in eleven languages," Guowei says.

Hala's face flushes with a hint of embarrassment. "Well, no, that's different. Once you learn a second language, it's much easier to learn more. But this? This is like pure randomness."

"Your admiration is misplaced, old lady," he says. Flirting has never come naturally to him. This is the best he's got. "You think a chess player remembers all these patterns, but that's just how the game appears to you. The chess player is merely speaking the language of chess, one with which he is familiar and whose patterns he has seen many times and knows by heart."

"Okay," Hala says, her eyes gleaming with curiosity. "What's your favorite piece?"

"The knight," Guowei replies. "They're easy to overlook. Deceptive. With the knight, I can often attack multiple pieces simultaneously to force a capture—a fork. I achieve most of my forks with the knight."

Hala smiles. Her straight white teeth on full display. "Fascinating."

Just as Guowei demonstrates a knight fork to Hala, Carlos casually passes by, perusing the game board. He plops himself unceremoniously in the seat across from Guowei, an uninvited guest here to interrupt his subtle mojo. Carlos leads a pawn out two spaces. "Don't fill her head with that garbage," he says. "The knight is a coward. In and out, attack, retreat."

Excuse me? Unbeknownst to Carlos, he is treading dangerous ground. Guowei maintains his composure, preparing a countermove. Leading his own pawn out, he quietly counters Carlos's remark. "So, fighting an intelligent fight—"

Carlos interrupts him, confidently leading another pawn out. "An intelligent fight is a fight you win."

Taken aback by Carlos's audacity, Guowei collects his thoughts. When he slows down his mind enough, great inspiration can strike. He reaches for his knight. "So why don't we go find the biggest rock and beat each other over the head with it? See who dies first," Guowei says sarcastically.

Carlos's playful smile widens, his eyes sparkling impishly. "Sounds a little brutal to me," he says. "But you'd probably dig that, eh, Genghis?"

"Would you prefer I line them up, give them no trial, no due process, and execute them all, Che?"

Carlos can't help but smile at his comeback. "Not something I'm proud of. I'd like to think I've overcome some of my prior shortcomings."

"I as well," Guowei says. As Carlos's moves become fast and relentless, Guowei matches his pace without a second thought. He's not about to let his brash opponent make him appear weaker. Carlos has played before, but never with someone on his level.

Carlos leads out another pawn, his gaze shifting toward Hala. "You win with the pawns."

In a bid to compete for Hala's focus, Guowei gestures toward his pawns. "The pawns are primarily for forging your defense. Their structure must—"

"Your move."

Who does this guy think he is? Guowei moves his other knight.

"Pawns have balls," Carlos says to Hala. "They don't move backward. No fear. They die for the cause, guns blazing. Proud." He slams a pawn forward, a certain sacrifice.

Guowei captures the pawn, but it leaves his king vulnerable. "While the pawns have value, you cannot win a match with them alone."

"You're right," Carlos says, his voice tinged with amusement. "It's usually some idiot in a goofy hat that gets all the credit." Carlos slams down a piece and walks away.

Carlos's bishop has Guowei in checkmate.

His mind races to analyze the board. He attempts to replay the match in his mind, but his memory fails him. He wasn't paying attention to the game.

"Does that mean he won?" Hala asks.

CHAPTER 24
UP IN THE AIR

ON HIS iGLASSES, Adam scrolls through Margot's Instagram photos—laughing with friends, delivering a lecture, exploring the streets of Istanbul.

He pauses at one particular photo, where Margot stands beside Professor Louvet, her radiant smile captivating the frame. And there, on her other side, is Adam, beaming with pride. It's an innocent photo to any outsider, but not to him. This one means more. This picture was taken just after Margot successfully defended her dissertation. He can't recall how many hundreds of times he combed through her work. To his delight, she found the feedback she solicited from him helpful. After this photo, Margot had asked him to join her for coffee and a cookie to celebrate and formally thank him, but out of fear, nausea, or a frozen brain, he clumsily concocted a lame excuse for why he couldn't go. It's a mistake he hopes he'll have a chance to correct one day, but it's becoming less likely with each passing hour.

Adam closes his iGlasses with two deliberate blinks, escaping the world of social media.

Brandon flops into the vacant chair across from him. "I know the look," he says, his voice laden with understanding. "I, Benjamin Franklin, hath suffered heartbreak. Even though guys like us receive plenty of attention from the fairer sex, it's often the lady who isn't interested whom we are fondest for."

The insight baffles Adam. "Uh, what? How do you—"

Brandon gestures to his eyes. "These things are rather intrusive. I can't wait for them to go to market."

"Oh, I was just . . . practicing," Adam says, attempting to use his voice's most typical tone. Where exactly is his tongue supposed to go?

"Riiiight. Your heart rate is elevated. You're engaged in what you're looking at but clearly not reading, because your pupils aren't moving side to side. And of all of us, you are the only one who is Facebook friends with one of the abducted scientists—a girl who tagged you in two Instagram photos, including one from a couple months ago. I invented the telegraph. I can practically read your thoughts. You have good taste, for what it's worth. This might be hard to believe, but she might actually be out of my league."

"Ben Franklin didn't invent the telegraph."

"Oh, really?" Brandon twitches his eye muscles to use his iGlasses. "Bifocals, lightning rod, stove, odometer, glass armonica . . . huh, I would have sworn—"

"If you can, uh, keep this between, you know, us?"

"So you want me to go tell everyone?" Brandon replies. A tsunami of panic splashes down on Adam. "Relax," he continues, his tone pulling Adam back from the brink. "Your secret's safe with me. As I always say, he who lieth down with dogs shall rise up with fleas."

"I don't think that applies here."

"Yeah, but it makes you think," Brandon replies. "And he who thinks is a penny earned."

Adam doesn't have the heart to correct him. A friend checking in on him should not be taken for granted.

CHAPTER 25
THE ITCH

HOURS INTO THEIR FLIGHT, Carlos reclines for some sleep. He's comfy, but as always he's alert. If his neck starts itching, it's not the type that a scratch can remedy—it's the universe telling him it's time to pay attention. In this dangerous game they're playing, the rules can change in a millisecond. A student of history, the whispers from the Aztec, Maya, and Olmec symbols that decorate his arms remind him of this every day. Vigilance or death.

He could tell Kebe was the same way. Though they didn't share many words in this life, the mutual understanding between him and Kebe was unshakeable. It was a trust forged in the crucible of past trials. Carlos will never forget he was there for him when the real stuff went down. Kebe went out the right way, the way Carlos would script it for himself. He faced down his threat and went out on his own terms. No surprises there. In the next life, they'll share a few words about it.

There's only one move that Kebe made that has surprised Carlos: *Nigel*.

With a cell phone pressed to his ear, Nigel emerges from the restroom and strides purposefully into the cockpit. Carlos doesn't trust anyone very much, but there's something about Nigel that hasn't settled in him since the moment they met. Kebe brought Nigel here, but Carlos can't help but wonder if the old man got played. If ARK has the cash to buy nukes and can infiltrate Kebe's base, why couldn't they plant a snitch on this team?

In the cockpit, Jacki mans the controls. "It's about time," she announces to the back.

Carlos sits up, compelled to take in the panorama. The jet descends over the timeless cityscape of Rome. The patchwork of ancient structures pulsates with vitality even from this height. He can't help but marvel at the magnificence of the architecture below, each stone-crafted structure telling a story of a bygone era—an enduring testament to the craftsmanship of civilizations long past. They don't make them like this anymore.

The Colosseum, a monumental colossus, asserts its dominance over the skyline. The iconic structure basks in a gentle glow that accentuates its cracks. Though the same spirit runs through many cultures, Carlos can't deny some legit warriors worked that place.

Nigel stuffs the cell phone in his pocket before reaching Jacki. "You just missed the runway!" he says. "If anything happens to this plane, I swear—"

"Relax," Jacki says. "Please take a seat. We will be on the ground shortly."

"You better know what you are doing."

"You should Facetime Jimmy so he can teach me how to land."

The jet glides down and executes the landing flawlessly.

Upon arrival at the Rome-Centocelle Airport, a silence engulfs the desolate landscape. Abandoned beside the runway, an ancient biplane stands as a relic of the past, its decomposing frame veiled in a cloak of moss. Surrounding the landing strip, overgrown bushes and a handful of dilapidated mobile homes paint a picture of neglect. Rats scavenge through the brush. It's 5:00 a.m. local time, and Carlos is the last to leave the jet, the crisp night air hitting his lungs with an electric chill.

Brandon raises a skeptical eyebrow as the team gathers on the barren tarmac. "Rome has been oversold."

"There has to be a runway closer to the city," Guowei says.

Jacki points to the bazooka strapped to Adam's back. "Yeah, making an unannounced landing in the largest airport in Italy with giant laser weapons is not what I'd consider a good idea."

"Uh, good thinking," Adam says.

Carlos feels an uneasy itch crawl across his neck. He prowls away from the group. His teammates distract easily, and distractions are what get you killed. He creeps to a line of towering hedges, their emerald leaves teeming with the symphony of chirping crickets. The air carries a lingering scent of exhaust, though it fails to conjure the familiar aroma of jet fuel, which is more akin to kerosene. Suddenly, grass crunches in the distance—or is it? His itchy neck says otherwise.

"Someone's here," he says.

"No. Literally, nothing is here," Brandon says.

Carlos's hand hovers over the grip of his pistol, and he takes a few more steps toward a hedge, primed for a confrontation.

"Watch out!"

CHAPTER 26
IGNITION

FROM THE DEPTHS of the surrounding bushes, a gray sedan bursts forth, hurling splintered greenery in its wake. The engine roars, thunderously proclaiming that its accelerator is pressed against the floorboard—and speeds directly at Nigel.

In an instant, Adam's instincts kick into overdrive.

He sprints toward Nigel and dives, propelling him out of harm's way just as the car whizzes past a hair's breadth of their bodies. The heat emanating from the passing vehicle toasts his skin. A shot of pain pulses down his arm from the shoulder that broke his fall. Powered by urgency, Adam hurries back to his feet.

The sedan rips patches of grass from the earth and screeches to a stop. A bald middle-aged man in a long coat emerges from the driver's seat, erupting in a torrent of rapid-fire Italian. He gestures aggressively as if his hands are dancing to the rhythm of his words, a small object glinting in his palm.

Hala steps forward, replying to him in his native tongue.

"What is he saying?" Jacki asks, her hand reaching for her pistol.

As the man inches toward them, kicking dirt and jabbering angrily, Adam detects the jingling of metallic objects reminiscent of a pocket full of change.

"He says this isn't our airfield," Hala translates.

Jacki draws her gun, tension thickening.

Hala addresses the man again. She rubs her fingers together as if implying we can offer some money. Yet the man gets closer and closer. The jingling grows. The man's bulging pockets are filled to the brim, but with what?

"Tell him to stop moving," Jacki says.

"Watch your step, Andretti," Carlos says.

In response, the man gestures at him. "*Io sono solo polvere*," he says.

"'I am but dust'?" Hala whispers to herself, and a sudden comprehension flickers across her face. "No!"

With a sinister grin, the man says in perfect English, "And to dust I shall return." He raises his arm to reveal what lies beneath his raincoat. The dim light glimmers along a skinny wire that snakes its way down his body. "Long live ARK."

The truth crystallizes in Adam's mind. "A bomber!"

Carlos hurls himself at the man in a blur of motion, their bodies colliding just as his thumb hovers perilously close to the ominous red button. A fierce struggle ensues. Carlos clutches desperately at the man's wrist and pries at his fingers, his grip taut and unyielding. Suddenly, the man is haloed in a flash of white light.

The man shrieks, and Carlos finally wrenches open his fingers. The device falls from his grasp. The man's hands drop to his sides, his body incapacitated like a puppet with severed strings.

Brandon, hovering over them, lowers his lightning-rod taser. "Mine works," he says.

As they inspect the defeated assailant, they discover sticks of dynamite duct-taped to a silver vest, like one a waiter at a fancy restaurant might wear. The fuses converge into one strand and run up his sleeve to the trigger. The man's pockets are full of screws and nails. He was loaded to the max with shrapnel. At that distance, a detonation of even an amateur improvised explosive device would have ended them.

Guowei glues the bomber to the runway with his sticky-foam crossbow, spreading his arms wide like a misshapen snow angel.

While Jacki, Carlos, and Guowei hunt for a suitable set of wheels in the nearby neighborhood, Adam, Brandon, Hala, and Nigel scour the man's car for clues. The ten-year-old gray Fiat with manual transmission has fast-food wrappers strewn along the floorboard.

"Dude is grimy," Nigel says as he searches the backseat.

"Were you expecting the suicide bomber to have gotten his car detailed this afternoon?" Brandon asks.

Amidst the clutter, Adam spots a phone mounted magnetically to the driver-side air vent. With a swipe, he brings it back to life. "That's it," he whispers.

On its screen is an ordinary map app with coordinates ending in the airfield. Brandon leans in, pulling down the notifications. The top notification, written in Italian, is a text message from someone named Z.

"Hala, would you take a look at this?" Adam asks.

She stands behind the open trunk, her eyes aimed at the heavens, wearing a countenance Adam recognizes all too well. She's here but not here—a coping mechanism he has employed against overpowering and distressing reality.

"Yeah, sure," she says, turning the device toward her. "It says, 'Your family will be rewarded with a seat in the ark, good soldier.'"

"They know exactly where we are," Adam says, the implications slamming into him with the force the car nearly did. They were tracked from Russia to an obscure airstrip in Rome, and now they are leading ARK to Yusef, a target they are meant to protect.

With the first light of a new day creeping over the horizon, a beat-up white utility van speeds toward them. Tension ripples through Adam's muscles, every instinct urging him to brace for the unexpected. Logic and reason have flown out the window in the past seventy-two hours.

The van creaks to a stop with Carlos at the wheel. They have a ride to Rome.

CHAPTER 27
NAVIGATION

IF CARLOS DRIVES LIKE HE FIGHTS, argues, or steals cars, they are in for a wild ride. But somehow, after tackling the suicide bomber and stealing a van, Carlos has, according to Adam's iGlasses, a heart rate of just sixty beats per minute.

As Carlos accelerates, the stripped casing from the steering column rattles against the dash. Jacki rides shotgun, leaving Adam and the rest in the cargo area, devoid of seats and seat belts. The dilapidated van groans under its weight, its worn-out suspension protesting each bump and turn. The van may need a date with a welder, but it isn't a time to be picky. It rolls, and it can carry seven people and their equipment.

Nigel leans in, breaking him from his thoughts. "Hey, thanks for . . . you know."

Adam nods. "Yeah, uh . . . yeah, sure." That's not what's on top of Adam's mind; there's a teammate in distress.

Hala can't stop shaking. Her heart rate is more than double Carlos's, and even higher than his. Guowei attempts to calm her with a reassuring grip of her hand, but it does nothing to still the rest of her body. Kebe's words echo in his mind—they need all seven. Hala's translation abilities have been critical so far. If she descends into a panic attack, they won't just be undermanned but under-resourced. Adam takes a series of deep breaths, trying to steady his racing pulse as if it somehow might bring her down too.

Carlos cruises down the highway. "Keep your eyes peeled. They could be anywhere," he says.

"Baddies willing to nuke themselves are definitely not a great sign," Brandon says. "At least that's my experience . . . in gaming."

But how? ARK found them near instantaneously. Adam's voice quivers as he tries to make sense of their perilous situation. "How could . . . I mean, that place is out there, like *out there* out there, and they found us so fast? Even if they tracked the jet—which they might've, I get that—the likelihood they could dispatch a bomber to that tiny airstrip is inconceivable. It feels impossible."

"Unless one of us told them," Carlos says. The words send a seismic wave through the entire van. Carlos glares at Nigel in the rearview mirror, and an unspoken accusation hangs in the air like the stench of raw meat.

"Carlos, you damn well better know something if you're going to call one of us out like that," Jacki says.

"Who'd you call last night, homie?" Carlos asks.

"Who are you to put me on blast?" Nigel says. "Wasn't I the one almost run over by a car?"

"I never said you were smart."

"This is some nonsense," Nigel says. "I ain't got time. You come at me like that. I got us the plane, for chrissake."

A solution seems easy. Too easy. "Who'd you call?" Adam asks.

"What difference does that make?" Nigel replies.

"Uh . . . just about every difference," Adam says. Where was the friendly Nigel from a few moments ago? "It'd be useful to know if they're tracking us right now. Or if there might be, uh, other people willing to blow themselves up to stop us."

"I called my CFO. Y'all gotta problem with that?" Nigel asks. "Some of us actually had jobs and stuff before we got dragged into this mess."

"This ain't no Mandela," Carlos says, his words blending with bumps in the road.

"And you're Guava . . . Guerrilla . . . what's that executioner's name?"

"Ah, you tried to read something. Good for you."

"Oh, I know about you."

"I'm my own man, Fingernails. I call them as I see them," Carlos says. "You'd do better to learn about yourself and figure out whatever it was that went so wrong. Don't need to spend your brain cells thinking about me. You don't have many of them."

"Gentlemen, excuse me," Brandon says. "I don't know how to break it to you all, but there's a thing called the internet, and it isn't that hard to track a plane. I've set up numerous bots to track my least favorite celebrities."

"Especially one leaving Kamchatka, Russia," Guowei adds.

"It's a left here," Jacki says as they speed toward an intersection.

Carlos swerves sharply into the turn. The inertia flings Adam into the rusty steel of the van. Outside, a pack of runners jogs out in front of them.

"Watch out!" Jacki screams. Adam braces for impact. He shuts his eyes tightly, awaiting the sounds of bones crashing into metal and smashing against pavement. The van swerves again, releasing a horrifying screech of metal rubbing metal. Adam grabs hold of the door handle, desperate for stability. Carlos rubs paint with a parked car and straightens out the van. But the collision Adam feared never comes.

Outside, the joggers help one another up from the pavement, and to Adam's relief, there is no blood as far as he can see. A most fortunate miss and potential catastrophe narrowly averted.

Glancing back through the rearview mirror, Carlos takes in the aftermath of the close call. Nigel stares into space, shaking his head.

As Adam regroups, the glories of ancient Rome unfold before his eyes. The tapestry of architectural marvels paints a breathtaking backdrop where majestic medieval buildings and magnificent Renaissance structures coexist harmoniously. Each street reveals a new wonder. Intricately carved fountains dot the landscape, their sculpted cherubs frozen in eternal play, gracefully spewing arcs of water into the sunlit air. The aroma of freshly grilled sausages and wood-fired flatbreads wafts from food trucks that line the cobblestone sidewalks, enticing passersby with their sizzling delicacies. Locals and visitors navigate the bustling streets, searching for a coveted spot to sit for a morning meal.

A star on Adam's iGlasses display blinks, summoning his attention. It illuminates the next right turn, leading them toward their destination: ST. JOSEPH'S COMMUNITY HOUSE.

They have arrived.

CHAPTER 28
BOOTS ON THE GROUND

JACKI LEADS Brandon, Hala, Nigel, and Guowei up the worn concrete steps to the St. Joseph's Community House entrance. Tucked away from the main street, the building still attracts a moderate traffic flow. A sense of unease settles over Jacki as she considers the countless watchful eyes and prying ears.

The smooth, salmon-colored exterior of the building has uniquely rounded windows and doors. Time has taken its toll, leaving deep cracks in the mortar filled with invasive plants. Several stone pieces on the facade have gone AWOL. Who knows what the building used to be in its prime, but they've slapped a coat of paint on top of it. The marquee advertises a community rendition of *The Sound of Music* in three languages. There is a hustle and bustle to the building. People exit with yoga mats, and others enter with gym bags.

The Phoenix Elite split into three groups: Jacki, Brandon, and Hala will look for a supervisor to help locate Yusef in an expeditious, nonviolent way. Guowei and Nigel will scour the building themselves to find the boy. If the nonviolent approach doesn't work, they will be ready to take him. Carlos and Adam remain in the van, parked in the lot, monitoring for any signs of ARK threats and serving as a rendezvous point for a quick getaway.

"These places usually have safeguards to ensure children don't get kidnapped," Brandon says.

"We follow the plan," Jacki says. "If we have to take him, so be it. He's going to be taken. We just have to do it first."

"There are probably a hundred people in there," Hala says, her voice shaking with trepidation. "We can't just take the kid in front of everyone."

"Ideally, no," Jacki says. Hala's eyes widen at her cold reply.

Jacki would prefer searching the building, but Brandon and Hala would be useless without her. Being the de facto leader of this team means taking on assignments she isn't thrilled with. And though her homeland shares a border with Italy, she never bothered to learn any Italian because, frankly, what self-respecting French woman would?

"Whatever we do, we gotta do it quick," Nigel says, "or they're all gonna be blastin' our faces all over the internet."

Welcoming their arrival is an elegant archway entrance adorned with community artwork, each with a small price tag. A large wooden crucifix towers as the lobby's focal point. Underfoot, the floor unfolds into a stunning mosaic of tiny stone tiles in black, gold, and white hues, meticulously arranged to resemble a floral pattern. It is likely a relic of the building's better days.

A sign for reception points left. Jacki, Hala, and Brandon turn that way.

"Good luck," Guowei says. He and Nigel go right.

Navigating through the corridors, Jacki, Hala, and Brandon enter the main office. The air is heavy with the scent of potpourri, threatening to overwhelm their senses. Behind a large oak reception counter, a receptionist types away at her computer desk amid filing cabinets, a copy machine, and the vibrant presence of children's artwork decorating every centimeter of available space.

Jacki stops Brandon at the threshold. "We follow the plan," she says. "No jokes. No asides. No observations. No talking. No noises. You got it?"

Brandon purses his lips and offers her an enthusiastic thumbs-up.

Jacki's eyes narrow. "And none of that. That's just so weird."

The receptionist, a woman in her sixties wearing yoga attire, glances up from her work and addresses them in rapid Italian. Hala replies promptly. The receptionist calmly raises a finger as if signaling her to hold that thought before heading to the copy machine with a file folder in hand. While awaiting her copies, she scrutinizes them from head to toe. Retrieving something from a filing cabinet, she gathers it with her files.

"I'm Alice. What do you need?" she asks in English. The woman carefully cradles the folder to her chest, securing it with both hands.

Jacki needs no further information: this lady is now armed and dangerous.

CHAPTER 29
LOOKOUT

IN THE VAN'S SIDE MIRROR, Adam scans the surroundings in full-blown paranoia mode. A black car stops two blocks behind them, its worn exterior bearing the marks of time—a patchwork of paint blemishes and a dent on the fender.

A mother and son get out. Nothing to see there.

Carlos is staring elsewhere. "Yo, Einstein, what you think about Nigel? He working us from the inside?"

With his iGlasses on, Adam zooms in, peering into the windows of the building, desperate for any glimpse of valuable information. He's not seeing much. "I dunno," he replies. "I mean, it's possible, I guess, but I . . ."

"But what?"

"I, uh, I think . . ." Having always preferred to put his thoughts down on paper, Adam's never comfortable in the hot seat, a place where Carlos seems to thrive. "Your scrutiny seems a little . . . harsh," he finally manages to articulate.

Carlos offers a subtle nod.

"And if you trust Kebe," Adam continues, his palms drenched in flop sweat, "and I don't know if you trust Kebe, but if you do—I mean, did. And it seemed to me like you and Kebe did trust one another. So, well, he's the one who brought him in. Just like he brought you in. I don't think he would've, uh, made a mistake like that." Adam hopes his word salad reaches him.

"Word," Carlos says. "You're a smart guy, Einstein."

"Maybe in very certain, very specific ways."

Carlos adjusts his hat. "Don't sell yourself short, *mijo*." Adam forces a smile, unsure of what a *mijo* is, but from the context it sounds like Carlos is being friendly.

A black SUV comes to a halt across the street, right in front of the building. Carlos stares down the vehicle. "That one."

Adam's iGlasses show that the SUV is a rental with 5,361 miles and a gas mileage of twenty-one miles per gallon. Not particularly useful information. "It's a rental," he says.

"I know," Carlos says.

Adam strains to follow Carlos's line of sight, his gaze settling on a double-decker tour bus parked a short distance away. Dozens of people get off, touristy types who admire the architecture, but many are wearing matching gray jumpsuits—just like the rebels who invaded Kebe's base.

As the gray-clad figures gather around the black SUV, each carrying their distinctive helmet, Carlos straightens up and retrieves the pistol from his pocket.

This wasn't in the plan.

Three men step out of the black SUV. Adam cannot believe his eyes. Visions flash through his mind of running after Margot, throwing a haymaker, and getting crushed with an elbow.

It's unmistakable. Those are her abductors.

"Oh God, they're here," Adam whispers. On his iGlasses, he sends a message to the others: THEY'RE HERE!! GET OUT NOW.

Suddenly, the temperature in the van spikes—or at least it feels like it does around Adam's collar. His breaths come in short, shallow bursts, each inhalation a struggle to quell the rising panic. His heart pounds in his temples.

Carlos reaches into his boot for a second pistol, promptly handing it to Adam. "You need a backup?"

"Yeah, I, uh, probably yeah," Adam says. Carlos reaches behind his back for a third pistol. How many weapons can one guy carry at once?

"You know how to use it?" Carlos asks, his voice steady.

"You . . . pull the trigger?"

"You pull the trigger."

As Adam takes the gun from Carlos, he's immediately aware of how heavy it is; he expected it to be much lighter. He turns it over, examining as much as he can take in. He never wants to feel this oblivious about firearms again.

"Only point it at something you intend to kill," Carlos says, pushing the barrel away from his face. "Not me."

The army of gray jumpsuits descends on the community house from all angles, their synchronized movements and visored eyes creating an unsettling, otherworldly presence.

"We have to move," Carlos says, vacating the driver's seat and heading to the back of the van.

"We have to stick to the plan," Adam says as his partner suits up for war. "They are counting on us."

Carlos looks at him with a determined gaze, the steely resolve in his eyes leaving no room for doubt. "We didn't plan for this," he says. "Drive." Adam accepts that he needs to listen to him. The man exudes confidence, while Adam has never been further out of his depth. Clearly, Carlos has been in sticky situations before.

Adam slides into the driver's seat. Carlos moves to the sliding door, locked and loaded.

"Where?" Adam asks.

"Right at them," Carlos says with unwavering certainty.

Definitely not in the plan.

Adam floors it, expecting to be launched forward at the speed of light. The engine revs, but the van doesn't move.

"Hey, Einstein, you know how to drive stick, right?" Carlos asks.

Maybe he should have mentioned to Carlos that he's never driven a car. On his iGlasses, Adam executes a flurry of eye twitches, pulling up a list of thirty-two thousand YouTube videos for "driving stick." Eight minutes, six minutes . . . there is not a thirty-second video to be found. He settles on the shortest he can find.

"I, uh, just have to remember." Adam plays the video at quadruple speed, hoping to absorb the necessary knowledge in mere moments.

"You sure you know?"

Adam depresses the clutch and pulls the shifter into reverse with a sweaty palm. The van sputters in protest as he acquaints himself with the sensitivity of the accelerator, clumsily maneuvering backward before abruptly slamming on the brake with unnecessary force. As he shifts into first gear, his lack of finesse causes the van to emit a wretched grinding noise.

Carlos scratches his chin with his gun. "You gotta—"

"Yep, I got it," Adam says, his anxiety intensifying. He pushes in the clutch and shifts into fifth gear, wincing as the van scrapes the paint off the car next to him. He frees himself and maneuvers the van out of the parking lot.

"Anytime now," Carlos says.

Adam slams the accelerator. A deafening whir emanates from the engine. Is that the sound it's supposed to make? The van ramps the curb and hurtles straight for the crowd. Fortunately, the objective is running over people.

Many of the gray jumpsuits dodge the van. However, they fall into the path of Carlos. He opens the van's sliding door, brandishing two pistols with deadly intent.

"*Nos vemos.*" Carlos empties his magazine with a staccato eruption of gunfire. In one smooth motion, he retrieves another pistol from his waistband. Three men fire at the van, their bullets ricocheting off the metal.

Something snaps inside Adam. Minutes ago, he couldn't imagine taking a life. But staring down the three men who abducted Margot, now a piece of him is looking forward to it.

Adam grips the wheel and swerves in their direction. They aim their weapons. He stands on the pedal, zeroing in on the bearded one in the middle. Bullets whiz through the windshield and into his chest. It stings, but they'll have to hit him in the face to stop him. He presses harder, willing the van to its velocity limit.

The three abductors dive into their SUV as Adam hurtles past, careening the van down a stony road. Navigating through a spiderweb fracture on his windshield increases the difficulty of an already challenging ordeal, not to mention all the parked cars and pedestrians diving out of the way. Behind him, the SUV follows his winding path.

This is far from how Adam imagined his first experience behind the wheel.

Carlos flings the back hatch of the van open and sprays bullets. The windshield of the SUV shatters under the assault.

Momentarily distracted by the action in his rearview mirror, Adam's attention snaps back to a congested intersection ahead. He barrels into a sharp right turn, and the back hatch swings wildly, creaking on its hinges. The van's suspension groans like a tortured bedspring. Pedestrians scramble to avoid the oncoming metal beast, their cries mixing with the cacophony of destruction. A street food stand becomes an unwitting casualty, its contents—soups, sauces, and condiments—erupting into colorful ruin.

A wooden caution barrier blocks the path ahead. Adam accelerates. The barrier splinters as the van rockets through it like a projectile.

Before him, the awe-inspiring Colosseum towers. This wonder of the ancient world was no stranger to a battle—and it's about to witness another. Adam dashes toward it at 120 kilometers per hour.

"We have to go back! What if they found the boy?"

Carlos fires off two more shots. "To hell with the plan. This is war!"

Thinking quickly, Adam jumps the curb and drives onto an empty park in the shadow of the Colosseum. The SUV follows, hot on their trail. Police sirens howl in the distance.

They have to end this now.

Adam slams on the brakes, the screeching tires skidding the van to a forceful stop. For a moment, he relishes the stillness.

Carlos combat-rolls from the van's side door and fires through the shattered window of the SUV. One shot finds its mark, tearing through the target.

Adam hurries out of the van, using it as cover. His finger tightens around his pistol's trigger. There's no way he will hit his target—and he has to hit three. With no other options, he scrambles to unlock his bazooka.

The abductors hop out of the SUV, using its hood as a shield. Carlos retreats to the van, but he's hit in the back, hurling him forward onto the grass.

The bearded abductor aims for another shot, ready to deliver a fatal blow.

Kaboom!

The abductors are swallowed by an exploding pink fireball of plasma energy, an eruption as loud as a sonic boom. The SUV disintegrates into nothingness, and the men transform into particles of drifting dust.

A smoking bazooka sits on Adam's shoulder. Any hopes that revenge would make him feel better evaporate into thin air, vanishing as swiftly as the abductors' bodies. Taking the lives of three people leaves him queasy, but most importantly he hasn't gotten back what they took from him.

Adam rushes to Carlos's side, panic consuming him. The fabric of his armor is torn, but nothing penetrated. There's no sign of blood. But why is he still? Adam turns him over.

"Safe to get up?" Carlos asks.

"I, uh . . . ," Adam says, glancing around to double-check. "Yeah, those guys are gone."

"I ain't worried about them. I'm talking about your pink whatever the hell that is."

"Oh, uh, yeah . . . that's gone too."

Carlos pops up to his feet, no worse for the wear. "Let's roll."

The lingering smoke from a gigantic crater spoils their view of the Colosseum. Amidst the smolder, a passing bicyclist halts to survey the aftermath, their eyes widening in astonishment. They pull out their phone to capture the moment.

CHAPTER 30
ROLLING THE DICE

THE BOY HAS TO BE HERE SOMEWHERE. Nigel's eyes dart around a room full of spinning exercise bikes and along a mirrored wall. He searches the seas of sweaty faces, primarily women but all adults. Quick and discreet, Nigel and Guowei glimpse in each room. In a brick hallway of the community center, class is in session: aerobics for seniors, oil painting for beginners, and piano lessons for the tone-deaf.

Nigel never liked these places much. Having grown up on Johannesburg's wealthier, whiter side, if he hung out in a spot like this, he'd be stared at until he left—worse if he opened his mouth. It doesn't matter who your daddy is if you're living that brown life. Moving quickly and discreetly is second nature.

There's no kid in sight, let alone the one they're after. Nigel's nerves coil like a rattlesnake ready to strike. They turn a corner and find a grizzled janitor emptying a trash can, headphones on, oblivious to their presence. Across the hall is a set of recessed double doors with windows. Guowei slinks across, finding refuge in the nook. He signals Nigel to join him.

A concert of joyful shrieks is on the other side of the door—a gymnasium full of kids. Toddlers zip around on tricycles, their laughter echoing with unrestrained glee. But the main event is basketball bedlam supervised by an elderly volunteer. Dozens of children, ranging in ages and sizes, converge on the court with an eagerness that borders on controlled mayhem. Multiple rubber balls fly toward the hoop simultaneously, each knocking the others away. Amid the basketball frenzy, a big kid swats a smaller one's shot to take one himself. The smaller kid punches the ball from his grip as he prepares to shoot, and the two race for the loose ball.

In a quiet corner away from the action, a young girl in a wheelchair with vibrant red hair is absorbed in a spirited dice game at a nearby table. Her opponent is a little boy. *The* little boy.

Yusef scampers to retrieve a fallen die, ensuring it doesn't disrupt the basketball players, and gently returns it to the girl. He sports a *Paw Patrol* shirt and shorts, the familiar characters adorned with Italian text. His untied shoelaces flop around as he runs.

"That's got to be the kid," Guowei says.

"Yup." The ordinary sight before Nigel somehow defies his expectation as if the kid was supposed to have a third arm or something. "Why in the world do they want him?"

"*Cosa fate?*" a voice says.

Fear hijacks his thoughts. It's not like he hasn't been caught sneaking around a place like this before, but not as a full-grown man decked in a tactical suit. The janitor stands behind them. He's not happy. Nigel's heart races, his mind quickly assesses the situation, and his instincts set in. *Sell. Sell. Sell.* Though he speaks no Italian, and the janitor speaks no English, Nigel knows he can sell him a car with his eyes and smile.

"Yeah, we're just electricians," Nigel begins smoothly, harnessing every ounce of his charm. "We're filling in for . . . Mookie. They wanted us to reroute the Wi-Fi . . . to make the whole building . . . energy efficient."

Guowei remains expressionless.

As the janitor ponders his asinine story, Nigel is careful not to shift his weight or betray the slightest hint of insincerity. He calms his nerves and waits to close the deal. Any inkling of doubt could cost him the sale.

An uncomfortable silence looms until it is shattered by a flurry of gunfire. The janitor's eyes roll to the back of his head, and his body collapses lifelessly to the ground.

A crew of eight men in helmets and body armor invades the building, armed to the teeth.

"We have to take the boy," Guowei says.

The sound of gunfire transforms the ordinary basketball bedlam into full-fledged pandemonium. A loudspeaker erupts overhead with a woman speaking in Italian. Children scream in terror.

Nigel races across the gymnasium with his hands raised. "Hide! Fast!" he shouts to the confused adult volunteer. "Uh . . . *rapido!*" But where can they hide?

Meanwhile, Guowei seals the wooden gym doors with his sticky foam gun. He pulls the door to test it—it isn't moving. He adds a couple of diagonal lines for additional support to bolster their barricade.

Nigel opens an equipment closet. It's about fifteen square meters of space. With the volunteer's assistance, he ushers the children inside, their eyes wide with horror. Emerging from behind the group, Yusef struggles to push the girl in the wheelchair toward them, so Guowei scoops him up and rolls the girl in the wheelchair into the cramped closet.

Outside, the gym doors shake like there's an earthquake. Bullets fly through the old wood as it tries to withstand the relentless battering.

The volunteer reaches for Yusef, who reciprocates, but Guowei holds on. Desperation floods the volunteer, her eyes pleading for understanding.

"The boy has to come with us," Nigel says as the volunteer desperately yammers something in Italian. Clear that there's no time to communicate with the volunteer, Nigel pushes her into the closet. She lets out a blood-curdling yell of pure agony that drowns out the thunderous booms against the gym door. "Stay quiet," he says to her, closing her in.

Guowei nods to a nearby door. "This way," he says, clutching Yusef to his chest.

Nigel throws his shoulder into the door, but it's locked. A searing pain shoots down his arm, but undeterred, he takes a step back and delivers a forceful front kick to the doorknob. The door rattles, giving way slightly under the impact, but remains obstinately closed.

"Do you need me to try?" Guowei asks.

It dawns on Nigel that he's wearing a pair of souped-up gloves from Power Ranger school. Activating the security pattern, he flexes his index finger, causing the nano-gloves to harden. He strikes the wooden door with a crisp left hook, splinters exploding and scattering in all directions. "Whoa."

Shaking off the momentary distraction, Nigel reaches through the newly created orifice to unlock the door. It swings open, revealing an empty locker room. They scramble through the dimly lit space, where water trickles from above, and their footsteps slap against the damp concrete floor. Mold-laden gym clothes are strewn across puddles of stagnant, smelly water. Rows upon rows of dented metal lockers are silent witnesses to the room's abandonment. They might be the first people to enter this room in years.

Yet, amid their search, their hope dwindles. There is no exit. They navigate to the far side of the room, as far from the door as possible, against the concrete back wall.

Nigel's eyes narrow as he assesses their limited options. Sizing up the wall, Nigel's right hook sends shards of debris flying. A small crater forms, and he takes another swing at it. The hole opens a few more centimeters, but he runs into earth. The realization strikes a disheartening blow—this section of the building must be underground. This isn't going to work.

They've reached a dead end.

CHAPTER 31
LOCKDOWN

JACKI'S PATIENCE IS WANING. The woman before her, her intentions veiled behind a facade of bureaucracy, seems intent on drawing out this encounter, slyly exhausting their precious time. Every second feels like a minute.

Given the woman's efforts to cunningly detain them in her office, Jacki suspects Alice may have already silently contacted the police or, worse, alerted a subordinate to whisk Yusef away. Little does this woman comprehend the futility of the concealed handgun she clutches so tightly; it will prove utterly ineffective against the imminent onslaught that awaits just beyond her doorstep.

"I assure you that that child has never been in our custody," Alice says firmly. "We do not provide such services."

Jacki counters with authority. "Actually, we know he's in your gymnasium right now."

A wave of fear crashes over Alice, causing her grip on the gun to slacken. "You must be mistaken," she says, unable to disguise her distress.

"We have eyes all around, and we know he's here," Jacki says. "For the safety of everyone in this building, it's critical that you cooperate with us and tell us everything you know. Terrorists are coming for him as we speak. We have to take him with us."

Alice's gaze flickers toward the red-and-orange Phoenix Elite Initiative shoulder patch on their uniforms, and recognition dances in her eyes. "It's a phoenix," Jacki says. "You recognize it?"

Alice's breath catches in her throat, her chest seizing as if subjected to a sudden jolt of defibrillation. "A member of the United Nations brought him here," she finally manages to stammer.

"Kebe?" Hala asks.

"Yes, Kebe. How do you know—?"

"He's dead," Jacki says. "We are his team."

"We need to know why they want this boy?" Hala asks.

"I don't know," Alice murmurs. "I only promised Kebe that I would take care of him."

"Jacki, do you see that message?" Brandon's voice quivers with unease. Jacki diverts her attention back to her iGlasses display, and her gaze locks onto Adam's urgent message blinking at the corner of her vision: THEY'RE HERE!! GET OUT NOW. She isn't playing games anymore.

"Do you have a lockdown plan?" Jacki demands, propelled by urgency.

"What? Why?"

Without hesitation, Jacki pushes her way behind the imposing oak reception counter. "Get your people to safety now!"

Alice speaks into a microphone, making an announcement in Italian over the intercom system. Jacki, Hala, and Brandon take cover behind the wooden reception counter.

"They've stopped," Brandon says.

Jacki notices the static KHAN dot on her iGlasses map, but MANDELA is nowhere to be found. A sinking feeling overtakes her. They've either run into a dead end, or they're dead. In either event, if the boy is alive, they have to get to them.

Alice sets the intercom microphone back into its cradle and suddenly freezes. Her eyes drop to Jacki, Hala, and Brandon, hiding before her.

"Where's the boy?" says a voice, gruff and unmistakably American.

Instantly, Alice discards her file folder, drawing her concealed gun with lightning speed. A shot is fired, only to be met with the resounding ping of the bullet bouncing off something. Return fire echoes through the room, causing Alice to stagger backward, a trail of blood seeping from her chest. Her eyes lock onto Jacki as she falls to the ground.

A tactical military boot steps behind the counter, accompanied by the barrel of an assault rifle. Jacki seizes the gun barrel and yanks it, throwing the armored rebel off-balance. She snatches his wrist, and with a quarter turn, she strips his gun from him. She traps him in a standing wrist lock and kicks him. The rebel meets the wooden floor in a devastating face-plant.

"We have to go," Jacki says. She swiftly retrieves the rebel's gun and eliminates him with a single shot.

Her gaze lingers briefly on Alice. Alice waves them on, a green light to go savage.

Jacki hurries out of the office. The KHAN dot still hasn't moved. Walking in lockstep, Brandon unlocks his taser. But halfway down the hall, a sudden realization freezes them in their tracks.

Hala isn't with them.

Frozen in fear, Hala stands motionless behind the counter. Her gaze is fixed into the middle distance, leaving her exposed and vulnerable—an easy target for any lurking rebels.

"We can't wait for her," Jacki says.

Brandon can't take his eyes off his petrified teammate. He follows Jacki around a corner but glances back. A bullet whizzes past them, vaporizing into the mortar in the brick wall. The shooter crouches behind a water fountain thirty meters away. Jacki tucks herself behind the corner and grips the assault rifle. It's not her standard-issue FAMAS, but it'll do.

As she prepares to engage the shooter, Brandon dashes back to Hala. Jacki takes a deep breath and holds it. Her instincts were right, but she damn sure isn't happy about it. Jacki could shoot flames out of her nose. She should have sucked it up and learned some basic Italian years ago so Hala could've stayed where she belonged—in the van.

Peeking around the corner, she fires at the shooter and then swiftly retreats to cover. Another shot from Jacki finds its mark, and the rebel shooter crumples.

In the office, Brandon extends a reassuring hand toward Hala, but she is thoroughly disoriented. He grabs her by the waist to guide and stabilize her, helping her along as if she's been mortally wounded. His eyes meet Jacki's briefly, conveying helplessness.

Her team of three is now down to one.

Jacki wields her assault rifle down a vacant hallway lined with still-life oil paintings and watercolor landscapes. Brandon fleeing with Hala leaves her with just one primary focus: to not die. Babysitting others would only distract from that focus. Head on a constant swivel, Jacki closes the distance between herself and the KHAN marker on her iGlasses.

Reaching a corner, Jacki presses her cheek against the inside wall, peering cautiously around the bend: a hallway of open doors. Not ideal. She veers toward the dark room on her left and enters silently. Inside, it looks unoccupied, but a faint squeak breaks the silence. Sneakers tuck themselves under tables on the far wall, probably a dozen feet in all. The kids are much older than their target—not what she's looking for.

As she moves to the next room, a figure materializes from the darkness and presses a barrel into her skull.

Dammit. She should have checked the room on the right first. Maybe a three-person team would have been better after all.

"Click, click, boom," Zed murmurs. He's even uglier in person than in Kebe's picture.

Jacki drops her weapon. Opting for a pistol would've given her better versatility for this exact scenario, but now her options are limited. As she raises her hands in surrender, she flings an elbow and attempts to disarm him. Her grip on his wrist is brief. Zed seizes her throat with his left hand, powerfully pinning her against the wall. She's never felt strength like this.

"Where's my boy?" Zed asks. His mouth, bloody with gingivitis, reeks like a dog's. Crooked bottom teeth compete for space, and all of them are losing.

"He's not here," Jacki gasps, cycling through her escape options while her fingertips grow numb. Pain radiates along her neck. There are no good opportunities against this giant strongman. She tries to knock his hand away again, but his towering stature grants him formidable leverage.

What would Joan do?

"Wrong answer," Zed says. "I value honesty, Jacki."

Her mind trembles, her focus interrupted by his use of her name. "How do you . . . ?"

Zed leans in as if to tell her a secret. "I've known you since before you knew you," he whispers. His dog breath is even more wretched up close. "Before you knew Hugo."

Hugo.

Dormant embers ignite within Jacki's heart. Her muscles tense with newfound strength. Any remnant of humanity she had left leaves her. She would fillet this man if given the chance. With a jolt of power, she swings her arms and knocks Zed's hand off her throat. Finally free, she delivers a crushing elbow to his jaw, but he shakes it off. Zed drives his forearm under her chin and slams her back into the wall, pinning her in place.

"Keep that name out of your disgusting mouth," Jacki says. She squirms but can't break free.

Zed digs his forearm deeper into her trachea. "Seems like we have trouble with closure, do we?" He aims his three-barreled pistol right between her eyes. "My father would prefer that you join us; you mean a lot to him. But if you don't cooperate, you'll force me to make a difficult decision. Where's my boy?"

Kaboom!

The thunderous explosion rips through the building, causing the tile to shake underfoot. Frames along the hallway plummet. Fragments from the ceiling above crumble, cascading like an avalanche onto Zed and distracting him.

That can only be one thing.

Seizing the opportunity, Jacki sinks her teeth into Zed's fingers with all her might. Her bite hits bone, and then she clenches down even harder. All his pressure releases from her. Blood spews from his hand. Jacki kicks his gun away, sending it clattering to the floor.

Adam sprints down the long, empty hallway, his bazooka locked and loaded. Zed retrieves his gun and scampers away, leaving behind Jacki and a trail of blood.

As Adam reaches Jacki, he kneels and aims his bazooka.

"Don't!" Jacki says as she spits blood and wipes her chin. Civilians are hiding all over. As badly as she wants to watch Zed's body turn to ash, a shot would risk significant collateral damage. Zed turns a corner and disappears.

"Are you okay?" Adam asks, concern for her etched on his face.

Jacki resents being the recipient of that look. A sore throat and perhaps bruised vocal cords, but it's all unimportant. "This way," she says.

CHAPTER 32
OUT OF TIME

NIGEL POSITIONS HIS NANO-GLOVES against the cold concrete wall of the dimly lit locker room. With a deep breath, he jumps and slaps the wall. The gloves hold. His feet dangle precariously in midair until he puts them, spiderlike, against the wall. His mind spins with bewilderment; the body isn't supposed to work like this.

He wall-crawls up the concrete, about four meters off the ground. He clears cobwebs away with his right hand and holds himself up with his left. He can't make sense of the wild sensation, but he doesn't have time to think about it. He tries to line up a punch, but it's an awkward position for generating power. With all his might, he smashes through the concrete.

A glimmer of light shines through the newly formed hole, illuminating the desperation on their faces. "That's it," Guowei says. "Do it again."

Nigel widens the hole with another punch, but it's not even close to large enough.

There is a thunderous stampede of rebels beyond the locker room door. They have breached the gym and are closing in on their position.

Nigel readies for another swing. It'll have to be a big one. The punch doubles the hole. It's not large enough for him, but his little friend should fit.

Nigel clings to the wall and hoists Yusef to the tiny makeshift window he's made. His shoulders scrape the sides as the boy passes through, his feet dangling and flailing.

"We will come back for you. Don't worry. I promise," Nigel tells him. His years in sales have taught him how to make a promise even when he's not sure he can keep it.

Meanwhile, Guowei strains to hold the door to the locker room closed. The fireworks on the other side are deafening, and his sticky foam seals are giving way. They are down to seconds, not minutes. Bullets pierce the door, deflecting off Guowei, but he doesn't let the shots move him even one centimeter backward.

Yusef's feet kick against the wall. He must be unable to grab hold of anything on the outside.

"Hurry!" Guowei yells. His foot slips, and the door bows inward, the breach widening. Though he regains his balance, he struggles to regain lost ground. Nigel can't help. With the boy on the verge of falling, he has to stay glued to the wall. The sound of gunfire beyond the door escalates and intensifies.

Kaboom! A blast of energy propels Guowei and the door across the room, hurtling him into a locker with metal-denting force. The room rocks, shaking dust and debris from the ceiling, and smoke fills the space.

In the aftershock, Nigel's grip on Yusef falters, and Yusef plummets from the window. Nigel desperately reaches out, his hand snatching a handful of shirt, pulling the boy to his chest. With a firm grasp on Yusef, Nigel lets go of the wall, surrendering to gravity and dropping into the cloud of smoke and dust.

They are officially out of time.

Just as despair overwhelms them, Adam and Jacki burst into the room. The knots in Nigel's stomach slowly start to unravel.

"My bad, I should've checked my map," Adam says, rushing to assist Guowei, who lies prone. "That one got away from me."

"Maybe next time," Guowei says as he regains his balance.

Adam sets his sights on a solid concrete wall. "Stand back."

Nigel grabs Yusef and guides him to safety behind Adam. For the first time in this ordeal, optimism creeps inside Nigel.

Kaboom!

Adam unleashes his power upon the cement, blasting through its formidable facade. Five meters of earth is torn away, carving a makeshift egress wide enough to accommodate a Hummer. Sewer gas contaminates the air. Adam must have hit a pipe.

"Come on," Jacki says, her voice knifing through the lingering smoke. She leads them into the gaping pit. As they step inside, the settling dust allows a glimpse of the outside world.

An engine roars from above.

Nigel hardens his nano-gloves. "Is that us?" he asks the others. He's not going to be caught flat-footed.

"That's us," Jacki says.

"You should turn on your glasses," Adam says, reminding Nigel of the tool he had forgotten amidst the anarchy. Nigel activates them, and a digital map materializes, displaying their individual call signs. *That would have been useful.*

"We thought you died," Jacki says.

The van shudders to a stop, looking nothing like what they rode in on. The headlights are shattered, sections of the fender torn away, and deep scratches and bullet holes scar the metal surface. The once-white exterior is now a canvas of borrowed paint streaks from a multitude of vehicles.

The van's side door is open, and Brandon and Hala wait inside. The door itself dangles crookedly on its hinges, a mangled limb of metal—there's no way that door will shut again.

Carlos smiles from the driver's seat. "What's up?"

CHAPTER 33
REVOLUTION IS COMING

ZED SWAGGERS THROUGH THE BUILDING, his three-barreled gun swaying with each step. He lets the blood drip off his hand, unconcerned where it falls. Bodies are piled up around him, his own men. He doesn't care. *They're losers.*

He steps through the splintered remains of the gymnasium door, pausing momentarily to run his hand along the intriguing white foam. With a forceful kick, the equipment closet door swings open, illuminating the huddled figures within with a stark crack of light.

Zed peruses the children bunched together in the cramped space. They seek shelter behind a girl in a wheelchair. A sea of cowardly, powerless little monsters. None is the boy he came for.

He has come up short.

An elderly hag lunges at him, but Zed knocks her away like the loose-skinned ragdoll she is. Raising his boot high, he ruthlessly stomps on her outstretched hands. The crunch of her bones beneath his heel brings him satisfaction. He crouches on both knees and speaks softly in the hag's ear. "Teach these children the power of a revolution."

With that, he rises to his full height and casts a final glance at the huddled children.

"And kids," he continues before walking away, "listen to your teacher."

CHAPTER 34
ROAD TO NOWHERE

A LUXURY SATIN-STEEL-METALLIC SUV cruises down the curvy highway, tracing the contours of the land like a slalom skier expertly carving through an alpine slope. Towering trees conceal hidden sixteenth-century villas and luscious green hills striped with gold.

Jacki occupies the shotgun seat, pinching the decorative edge of the brand-new leather interior, while Carlos assumes his position behind the wheel. Most importantly, Yusef rests in the back.

Nigel's credit line has come in handy. In his honor, Brandon insisted they christen the SUV the Mandela Wagon, shortened to the Wagon by everyone else.

Jacki's eyes remain cast downward, her gaze lost in the depths of her troubled thoughts, a place she dreads to traverse. Her leg bounces restlessly, mirroring her inner turmoil. They got the boy, didn't they? They won, right? But it sure doesn't feel like it. It feels like a mirage dancing on the fringes of her consciousness that she fights to put back in the center rather than the shadowy memories that taunt her. A fight she's losing.

She looks for something, anything, to pull her thoughts in a different direction. Her weary eyes glimpse Yusef in the mirror of her sun visor. He peacefully rests his head on Hala's chest in the back row.

At least she makes a good pillow.

Hala didn't ask to do this. None of them did. Even though they are about the same age, Jacki knows she was prepared differently. The arduous journey to the apex of her military career was paved with obstacles, many of which felled her well-qualified, able-bodied peers. What can she expect from a girl who just left her parents' house?

But that's not why her leg is bouncing and her chest is tightening. Despite her fervent attempts to think about other things, her mind returns to Zed's penetrating words. Jacki has erected fortresses around specific memories, shielding herself from the overwhelming tide of emotions. Zed's words crashed against the ramparts, shattering the foundations she had relied upon to become the resilient woman she is.

Somewhere along her journey back to humanity from the community house, her emotions turned back on and are now overwhelming her. Emotions won't serve her well on a mission of this ilk, so if she can't rebuild her fortress, she must bury the memories the best she can.

Movement has always been her antidote, her most effective treatment. Martial arts training is her ideal release, yet even a simple run could distance her from her problems. For now, however, she remains trapped within the confinements of this stifling car.

Hala single-handedly jeopardized the entire mission. Jacki should put her energy into fixing that.

"You alright?" Carlos asks, cutting through her train of thought.

His perceptiveness is a wonderful asset, but it is pretty annoying right now. Jacki snaps back as if it were an insult. "I'm fine."

"You know Joan of Arc didn't actually fight?" Carlos says, unbothered by her sharp response. "She testified to that. She wielded her sword to inspire. A leader when women didn't lead men. She had a temper, was in the fray, and was injured, but she didn't fight. But you do. Damn, you do."

Jacki's not in the mood to dissect truth and fairy tales, nor does she wish to pick apart the seams of her hero's legacy. "I said I'm fine," she says, hardening her tone, determined to shut down any further conversation.

"Never meet your heroes, eh?" Carlos says. "Where we headin', boss?"

Jacki shakes her head, a weary gesture born from the absence of clear answers. "Drive until we can figure out something. Until we know where their base is, we just need to put more space between us and them."

"Copy."

CHAPTER 35
HERE FOR EINSTEIN

A **CRIMINAL WANTED INTERNATIONALLY**, Bricker rarely came out of hiding. When he did, it was because he wanted something very badly.

Sitting in the family recliner, he listened with rapt attention as Adam's adoptive parents, Hans and Mia, were in the middle of a struggle for the ages.

Once a military man, Hans found a second life navigating the endless maze of government bureaucracy, serving as the lead counsel for the Phoenix Elite Initiative. He had also been Bricker's most reliable golfing buddy. Mia had initially offered unwavering support for his career ambitions, but as the years progressed, her priorities shifted toward her role at the Italian Embassy and raising Adam. Two high-powered careers and two large personalities, they had had their share of spats, but that day it reached a precipice. A precipice at the tops of their lungs.

Bricker spent his time in the bunker exploring the far corners of the internet. Kebe, his daily dose of optimism, was long gone, and his sense of purpose had been stripped away by a paper-pusher trimming the budget. Within the recesses of the dark web, he had found an escape, an avenue to taste the elixir of life and descend down labyrinthine rabbit holes. In his mind, the only hope he had of getting off the United Nations terror watch list was through extortion, and the dark web was his last bastion of hope. Day by day, it changed him, but he was reluctant to acknowledge that to anyone.

With nuclear fantasies dancing in his head, Bricker saw a booming vision for the future. Resurrecting his laboratory seemed an insurmountable task, his ambitious life's work suspended indefinitely. But he was willing to cut corners to get back on track.

He was there for Einstein, the special key to unlock his Pandora's box.

"Honey," Hans said, trying to reason with Mia, "I don't see the difference between sending Adam to boarding school and—"

Mia wasn't buying what he was selling. "Full stop. Who are you to apply a false equivalence like that? It's the yammering of a maniac!" She thrust an accusatory finger at Bricker.

Bricker's eyes narrowed. He bristled at the audacious words directed his way. Though he had encountered countless lunatics in the depths of the dark web, he resented being labeled as one. "Hans," he said with controlled indignation, "tell your wife she should refer to me with more respect."

"How much money has this man paid you?" Mia asked.

Hans found himself at a loss for words, caught in the clutches of an uncomfortable truth. The answer was in the thousands, with plenty more zeroes to follow if he could persuade Mia to sign off on letting Bricker homeschool Adam six months out of the year.

"Don't think I haven't noticed the new shoes, the extravagant watches . . . the gambling," Mia said.

Not one to miss an opportunity, Bricker was thrilled to find out that baby Einstein was entrusted to a man with a closeted gambling addiction. He was honestly surprised that Mister Due Diligence Kebe hadn't discovered it.

But before Bricker could fully bask in his near triumph, the front door flew open, and Kebe strode into the room.

"Emmanuel!" Bricker said, caught in the throes of his transgressions. Kebe possessed an array of physical and legal options at his disposal. Bricker had nowhere to go, and he knew it.

CHAPTER 36
NO WAY HOME

ADAM'S BED WAS CENTERED in the room under the window. No sunlight entered that cloudy day. The space appeared empty, but Kebe knew better. Little Einstein always kept his room cleaner than Kebe would have predicted. The room's perimeter was outlined in Lego creations. Kebe had been spending a lot of time here working on those, but those days were over. He approached the bed, certain where Adam was.

Dust bunnies clung to the sweatpants of the young boy under his bed. Kebe had witnessed this scene too many times. Kneeling down and sweeping aside the toys, Kebe lowered his head to find the poor child underneath. "Hey, Adam."

"Hey, Baba," Adam said, smiling. How could he not smile at the guy who always brought him new Lego sets? Kebe reached out and offered a steady hand to the young boy.

Out at the car, Kebe assisted Adam in buckling his seatbelt. The click of the latch reminded him of how close he had come to losing this precious child. Six years ago, when Kebe had asked Hans and Mia if they would take on a burgeoning Einstein, they had jumped at the opportunity. Unable to conceive a child, they became parents with great anticipation. Kebe saw it as a dream pairing for the young man, but that dream quickly devolved into a nightmare—one he regretted failing to foresee.

Kebe placed an overflowing cardboard box of Lego beside Adam and glanced at Mia, who was wiping her tear-streaked face on her porch. Hans was nowhere to be found.

Bricker lingered, just like Kebe had told him to. Kebe was happy to make him wait. He knew his unbalanced former colleague could head down a treacherous path, but he had never fathomed he would go this far. It was a red line for Kebe, a line Bricker had knowingly and brazenly crossed, aware of the consequences.

"Stay away from my kids," Kebe said, packing bone-chilling intensity into every syllable. "Every. Last. One of them."

"Emmanuel, I'm very sorry. I truly am," Bricker replied. Kebe walked to him and looked him in the eye. There was no fight to be found in this broken, miserable person.

"My brother," Kebe said, compassion stirring in his heart. "Consider this my last act of mercy." He held Bricker's wrinkled face with his hands. "Stay out of the darkness, James. Don't make me regret this."

But as Kebe gazed into Bricker's eyes, what looked back at him was a soul he no longer recognized, a mere husk. It struck Kebe with an ache of loss, for he had been the pillar of balance that Bricker had depended on. Though this truth stared Kebe in the face, he clung to the dim hope that this transformation was not irreversible. "I'll give you a five-minute head start on the authorities." With that, Bricker stumbled into his black rental car and drove away.

Kebe offered a parting glance to Mia but had to look away. She didn't deserve what was about to happen to her. She held up her end of the bargain; she was a good mother.

As Kebe pulled away with Adam in the car, Mia ran, desperation propelling her forward until she faltered and tumbled into the grass. Kebe gripped the steering wheel, his knuckles white with the strain of his choice—it was the only option.

CHAPTER 37
LOST BOYS

IN THE BACK ROW of the Wagon, Adam sits beside Hala, with Yusef curled in the fetal position on her lap. She hums a soothing melody, her delicate fingers gently caressing his disheveled hair.

Adam wasn't much older than Yusef when he was taken from his first home—when he watched his mother chase Kebe's car until she couldn't anymore. It is a day etched into his soul, forever reminding him of the fragility of life. It is the day he learned that life as he knew it could end in a second. Any second. At least he knew Kebe a little, but he still recalls the torture he felt. His stomach twisted into knots, threatening to rupture through his skin. That same nausea remains with him, an unwelcome companion to his every waking moment. He can't imagine what this little boy is going through or will go through as a result. Whatever sorrows the young boy harbors within, it seems Hala possesses an extraordinary ability to assuage his pain.

Guowei offers the boy a drink of water. "Are you thirsty?"

Yusef responds with a distant gaze but offers a subtle nod of acknowledgment.

"Do you speak English?" Guowei asks. "Can you understand me?"

Another subtle nod.

With careful consideration, Guowei proceeds, "Okay, Yusef, do you know why bad guys are after you?"

"Don't scare him," Hala says.

"He may know something," Guowei says. "It makes sense to ask the question. If ARK wants him before it starts nuking the world, there must be a reason why."

Yusef nuzzles his face into the shelter of Hala's shoulder.

"He's not going to know that," Nigel says. "Leave the kid alone."

"So no ideas? Commit genocide. Rebuild with eugenics. Need this boy. It doesn't make sense to me," Guowei says.

The Wagon falls silent. Adam waits for someone else's brainstorm to spark his own. He has no idea how it all adds up. If only the real Einstein were here . . .

Brandon twists to face Yusef. "I know it might feel like we've kidnapped you. We pretty much did, but trust us. The other kidnappers were much, much worse."

"Will you shut up?" Nigel says.

"Sure." Brandon turns back around.

As Yusef's gaze wanders, his eyes inadvertently meet Adam's, kindling a silent connection, so Adam speaks to him like he's a younger version of himself. "I know you're scared, but we're the good guys. We'll protect you," he says. He tugs gently at Yusef's torn and dirty shirt. "Just like the *Paw Patrol*."

Nigel and Brandon exchange quizzical glances. "Did Einstein just say we're like the *Paw Patrol*?" Nigel asks.

"We are the Phoenix Elite," Brandon declares with conviction. "Isn't that right, Captain d'Arc?"

Jacki shakes her head. "You have to be the dumbest Ben Franklin."

"That's plausible," Brandon says before returning his attention to Nigel. "If we are going to be the *Paw Patrol*, I get dibs on Marshall. I invented fire departments. Captain d'Arc, you can be Skye. That's the girl dog. She can fly."

Jacki can't help but chuckle. She looks to Carlos for moral support. "*Loco*," he whispers to her.

Adam turns back to Yusef, whose eyes brim with uncertainty. "If you can answer some questions, that would really help us. Is that okay?"

Deep in Yusef's penetrating brown eyes is an old soul in the body of a preschooler. His fragile gaze remains fixed on Adam.

It's not a no.

Adam takes a deep breath, trying to quell the rising tide within him. He struggles to form the words. "Do you know where your mommy and daddy are right now?" he asks, every syllable a burden.

Yusef shakes his head.

"Do you know your . . . mommy and daddy?" Adam's speech teeters on the verge of failure. The moisture evaporates from his throat like his body is trying to get him to stop talking.

Once again, Yusef's response is a resolute shake of the head. However, this time, his eyes widen ever so slightly. Perhaps a bit of trust is beginning to blossom within.

Life without parents affects people in wildly different ways. Adam observed that some coped better with this reality while others grappled with it less successfully than he did. He always felt different from his peers and preferred to do unconventional things. Rather than subjecting himself to the chaos of sports, which his bullies would typically overrun, he'd make up his own game to play by himself—hoopball, for instance. Watching animals at the zoo was more interesting than the playground. Helping an adult clean up a mess was more satisfying than making one. Though his peers scurry about as if they are the center of the universe, kids like Adam know they're a small pebble floating around the sun, held there only by gravity, a valence electron waiting for a bond that never comes. Adults might be tickled at the sight of a boy with such appreciation and manners, but they don't realize that it's at the expense of the magical elements that make childhood, childhood. This four-year-old has grown up in ways he shouldn't have had to. But he doesn't get those penetrating brown eyes without it.

"And would anybody"—Adam's voice fractures completely, breaking under the strain of his vulnerability—"want to do anything bad to you?"

Yusef nods his small head.

Adam never understood why Kebe took him from his first parents or why that strange old man Bricker was in his house that day, but given the past week's revelations, he is beginning to understand his chilling intentions.

Now, Yusef is Bricker's only target.

Why?

"Has . . . anybody . . . ever tried to take you before?" Adam already knows the answer, and his heart breaks for the boy.

Yusef stares back, his gaze profound and filled with an overwhelming sense of hopelessness. He nods.

Hala squeezes him, cradling his head to her shoulder as she wipes a tear from her eye with her sleeve.

With Margot unreachable and Kebe deceased, only one man in Adam's limited Rolodex can uncover the mystery around this kid. Lucky for them, he's only about six hours away.

"I know someone who can help us," he says. "You just have to trust me."

CHAPTER 38
IN YOUR BLOOD

THE NIGHTLIFE at the School of Life Science and Engineering at École Polytechnique is as dead as the cadavers in the medical wing. Apparently, people have found more exciting places to be. Gray brick hallways, adorned with plaques and research projects, form a dual narrative—one part marketing, one part pride. After all, the university boasts accomplishments in scientific research that few others can.

Adam, a regular visitor to these corridors for the past five years, has memorized forward and backward the names and faces of the deans of medicine immortalized in portraiture. Though the golden baseboard that runs through the public-facing parts of the building always shines, Adam notices that the decorative stamped concrete floor gleams from a fresh coat of wax.

Professor Louvet, wearing his trademark navy suit, waves his badge, coaxing a pair of double doors to open. This is where the golden baseboard ends and the flat white paint begins. These halls, too, are devoid of life; not a person is in sight. It's so late that even the graduate students grinding away at their dissertations have retired for the night. But, as expected, Adam knew one man would still be at work.

Louvet takes the lead, ushering the group through the winding halls. Hala guides Yusef by the hand. Carlos scopes out the dark corners of the hallways.

"I was beginning to wonder if I'd see you again," Louvet tells Adam. "We haven't had an accident in a while. Frankly, it was getting boring."

"Thank you for understanding these unusual circumstances, Professor," Adam says. "I'd like to share more, but—"

"Adam, I've worked on top-secret projects more often than I've seen my grandkids. I don't ask questions." Louvet replies, smiling. "They keep sending me checks this way."

"Oh, of course, sir." Being swatted away by his mentor is a refreshing return to normalcy.

Professor Louvet presses his ID card onto a sensor next to a secure entrance of the DNA profiling laboratory. Adam holds the door to let everyone in like guests at his house. There's something awfully comfortable about the familiar surroundings.

The DNA profiling lab has all the fixings—their last ten-million-dollar grant ensured that. Its sophistication might not be immediately apparent to a casual observer. The room is furnished with standard lab tables, topped with commonplace items such as microscopes and flasks. Along the back wall, inconspicuous equipment, which might be mistaken for ordinary appliances like microwaves, dishwashers, and refrigerators, conceal a powerful ensemble of plasma treatment systems, flow cytometers, and high-speed ultracentrifuges. These unassuming elements are the heroes embodying the lab's technological prowess.

Brandon peruses the equipment and picks up an unused Petri dish. "Is it just me, or is being born on the same dish as fungus a touch on the weird side?" Even though nobody seems interested, he continues, "I wonder if we were all made on the same one."

Louvet moves through his drawers and devices with aplomb. He dons a pair of latex gloves and unwraps a long cotton swab. "Okay, young man," he says to Yusef, who sits on Hala's lap. "I'm going to need you to give me some of your haplotypes so I can closely examine your alleles. Then, hopefully, I'll figure out what's so special about you."

"What did he say?" Brandon asks Adam.

"Well, he's just going to, uh," Adam says, "use the swab and . . . I'm not sure."

Louvet playfully presents Yusef with the swab like he's an orchestra conductor. "Now, I'm gonna stick this through your nose, tickle your brain, and pull it out your ear," he says. Yusef's eyes bulge.

"He's just kidding," Hala whispers to him.

Louvet, maintaining his playful demeanor, issues a command to Yusef. "Open up."

Reluctantly, Yusef opens his mouth. Louvet slides his swab in and brushes the inside of his cheek. "All done. Not so bad, eh?"

Confused, Yusef looks to Hala.

"It'll take a couple hours before I have any definitive results," Louvet says to the group. "In the meantime, Mr. Eberhardt, perhaps you can do the cleaning you've neglected. It's your turn on the schedule, after all."

Mountains of loose, disorganized papers cascade over broken science apparatuses. The remnants of pizza and half-empty cans of energy drinks are strewn around the third-hand couches, and new crumbs mingle with old crumbs under a cloud of Axe Body Spray.

Welcome to the graduate student lounge.

Adam surveils the post-apocalyptic landscape with an industrial-sized trash bag at the ready. Brandon and Carlos poke their heads in and pull them out just ask quickly. Carlos slaps Adam on the arm. "All you, boss," he says.

"Oh boy, eesh. I almost died in that dirt avalanche, so I can't . . . you know . . ." Brandon says. He sniffs under his arm and recoils at the odor. "Oof . . . I've always wanted to try out one of those safety showers. Is there any soap around here?"

Adam begins loading in the piles of garbage. After the week's whirlwind, he welcomes the mundane activity of throwing out soiled paper plates. Among the mess, his eyes catch a glimpse of a familiar sight—a draft of Margot's dissertation.

Thumbing through the document, he revisits his notes, thoughts, and words of encouragement written in blue ink: LOOKS AWESOME! ELABORATE ON A FEW OF YOUR CONCLUSIONS! LET ME KNOW IF YOU NEED EYES ON THE NEXT DRAFT. ADAM. Emotions swirl in his gut. He knows what he really meant. It would have been easier to just ask her out on a date like other guys do, but in Adam's way, he's never written a love letter more clearly.

He only hopes he'll have the chance to provide feedback on her next big paper.

CHAPTER 39
STUDY SESSION

THE SOFT GLOW OF A SINGLE MONITOR envelops Nigel and the computer lab down the hall with its pale light. He is lost in the words of a Nelson Mandela biography sprawled across the screen.

FOUGHT FOR RACIAL EQUALITY DURING APARTHEID.

ARRESTED FOR AND CONVICTED OF SABOTAGE.

SERVED TWENTY-SEVEN YEARS IN PRISON.

FOLLOWING HIS RELEASE FROM PRISON, HE LED HIS PARTY IN THE NEGOTIATIONS FOR DEMOCRACY.

INAUGURATED AS PRESIDENT ON MAY 10, 1994.

Nigel soaks it all in. It is impossible to grow up in South Africa and not know the name Mandela. Still, while he projected otherwise, Nigel, the adult, didn't know anything more about Mandela than the typical South African fifth grader—a shameful and embarrassing realization. Mandela's face is on every rand banknote that Nigel coaxes from his customers, but beyond those financial transactions, he has given little thought to the man.

Nigel listened intently to the stories his teammates shared about Kebe's intimate involvement in shaping their destinies in concrete ways. But to Nigel, Kebe was a distant uncle he barely knew. If the goal was to become like Nelson Mandela, Nigel can't help but wonder why Kebe would let him become so different.

Suddenly, a voice shatters Nigel's reverie. "Anything interesting?" He hastily minimizes the biography window on the screen and turns to see Carlos looking over him.

"Just checking my email," Nigel says.

Carlos drifts toward a nearby window, a joint loosely between his fingers. It's a cloudless night, and the stars are shining. He smirks as he speaks. "See how far we slaves have come? We can drink out of the same water fountain. The US had a Black president. You and your daddy are allowed to run your own car dealership."

The smirk falls off his face. "But that's not the end of the story. If one teen from the suburbs goes missing, sound the alarm, man the battle stations. But if a dictator starves 10,000 kids in Sudan, in Colombia, those folks don't bat an eye. Some lives are worth more than others, you feel me? They might look if it moves their economy the wrong way—then they have to make a business decision. We don't get to make those. You might wear a suit, but if people like us speak truth and it's bad for business, all bets are off. They *allow* you to wear that suit. They want you to forget what's underneath. But rest assured they won't. Only a few of the real ones don't forget. Mandela was one of those."

Carlos takes a long drag from his joint, the smoke swirling around him. "And here we are, asked to save the world. Whose world are we saving? Theirs? We slaves have more work to do. But if there's one thing we're good for, we sure as shit know how to fight."

Nigel feigns annoyance. "You done?" he asks. "I really have to finish these requisitions."

Carlos plays along with a knowing nod. "Yeah, you go do that," he says before slinking out of the room.

Alone again, Nigel mulls it all over. Despite his disdain for the man, Carlos regularly leaves him with a lot to think about. Tonight is no different.

CHAPTER 40
QUEENS

HER HIJAB CAST ASIDE, Hala's shoulder-length black hair hangs listlessly around her face. Nestled on her shoulder, Yusef slumbers peacefully as she reads her Quran. She needs the solace on its sacred pages now more than ever. Like many of the chemical reactions discussed in the classroom she's borrowing, she's trying to make sense of what's been broken apart, each verse a potential catalyst to bring herself back together.

Merely weeks ago, she moved out of her family home, her sights set on pinning down a field of graduate studies—or at least narrowing down her twelve favorite options. Moving out was a giant step for her. Countless cherished memories had been made around the dinner table, where laughter, abundance, and her sitto's mouthwatering baba ghanoush held court, a memory all to itself. Her mother would pluck enchanting melodies from the strings of her antique harp, passed down to her by her grandmother. Though she knew she would need to spread her wings, the comforting embrace of home lingered over her spirit.

Jet-setting around the world, fleeing an armed invasion, negotiating with a suicide bomber, and abducting a child—she wasn't ready for any of these things, regardless of what Kebe thought. The man she once knew as her language instructor seemed to have an uncanny ability to push her out of her comfort zone. Though she recognizes her translation skills have played a critical role on the team so far, she can't help but think Kebe was wrong about her.

As she tries to still her shivering body, Hala certainly doesn't see the resemblance between her and Queen Hatshepsut, this bold Egyptian pharaoh lost to the annals of history and equally adrift within her.

Suddenly, the door swings open, and a figure stands in the doorway. Startled, Hala hastily places her Quran on the desk and hurries to fix her hijab. "Oh, I wasn't expecting—"

"I'm sorry, I didn't realize . . ." Jacki says as she averts her eyes.

Hala applies the finishing touches on her head wrap. "Do you need something?"

"I was just looking for the boy," Jacki replies. "I wanted to make sure he was safe."

"He is."

An awkward silence envelops them. Hala imagined that the two ladies on the team might have a kinship, but that's not the case, and it's been apparent from the start.

"We can't afford for you to be a liability," Jacki says.

And there it is. Any pretense is clearly a masquerade for Jacki to express this sentiment. Hala has been stewing in the shame of her inaction for hours. She doesn't need anyone to remind her. But she respects why Jacki is doing it. "Yeah, I know. At the community center, I don't know what happened. I just—"

Jacki's eyes fall upon her Quran. "I used to believe in fairy tales," she says.

Hala forces a smile. It's yet another reminder they won't see eye to eye. "When did you stop?"

Jacki wasn't expecting to spark a conversation. She takes a moment, contemplating the question as the seconds tick by. "No god's going to protect you out here." Her tone is biting. "The sooner you realize that, the better. You're going to need to get your hands dirty if we're all going to survive this."

Hala stays calm in the face of Jacki's incoming fire. She can only pray that she will be this calm in the face of the next enemy. "God is still with you," she says.

Jacki rubs the corner of her eye with her index finger and turns to leave the room.

"Can I ask you something?" Hala asks.

Jacki pauses at the threshold and hesitantly takes a step back in. "Sure."

"You are so good at this. The blood of a warrior. But I don't think that is in me. Everyone is counting on me, and all I can do is shake." Hala hangs her head, shame overrunning her senses. "How do you . . . not do that?"

Jacki nods the head atop her muscular shoulders ever so slightly. "Queens shake, but queens don't break."

Hala swallows hard as if Jacki's words lodge in her throat. She let Jacki down at a crucial moment. But Jacki's still here. Others could have easily written her off.

Hala looks Jacki in the eye. "Thank you."

Suddenly, a freshly showered Brandon barges in, munching on a bag of potato chips. "They're about done."

CHAPTER 41
THE RESULTS ARE IN

IN THE DNA PROFILING LAB, Adam, Guowei, Nigel, and Carlos perch over Professor Louvet's shoulder, watching the master at work. Hala carries Yusef like a mother chimpanzee as she, Brandon, and Jacki join the rest. A three-dimensional model of Yusef's DNA strand spins on the computer screen, captivating their attention.

"Most of the reporting is complete," Louvet says, addressing the group. "Your boy's chromosomes are completely and totally unremarkable." Adam's excitement deflates, crushed under a feeling of dread. The words hang heavy, leaving no room for optimism.

Louvet turns back to the report on the screen. "There are no abnormalities that would raise a flag on any genetics test, and our test's sensitivity is far beyond the capabilities of most labs. If there was anything to see, we'd see it." He dons a faux frown as he locks eyes with Yusef. "Sorry, but you aren't a superhero. Maybe you need to be bitten by a spider."

Dejection settles over the group. They are left with no answers or direction, only the looming threat of an impending nuclear holocaust—and Adam has wasted everyone's time.

"If he's just a boy, why would Bricker want him so badly?" Hala asks.

"Maybe he's his clone?" Brandon says.

"A clone, you say?" Louvet says.

As everyone leers at Brandon, he realizes his error. "Yeah, but people don't do things like that."

"You'd be surprised," Louvet says, an eyebrow raised in intrigue. "Well, we might be able to rule some things out. Let me see."

As far as Adam can discern, Yusef's curly black hair and olive skin are not similar to the pasty-white Bricker in any way. But he's not exactly a perfect facsimile of Einstein either.

Louvet clicks into a DNA ancestry database. "Some traits are known to belong primarily to certain populations. This database intends to match the DNA of living people with similarly recorded ancestors." Louvet positions the cursor over SUBMIT QUERY.

The database loads, and tension mounts in the room. "Well, that's something," Louvet says, his jovial disposition suddenly uneasy. He drifts into deep thought, leaving the room in an intense silence. Complete astonishment washes over Adam and grips him like a vise. His extremities go numb, and he clutches the back of a nearby chair for balance.

"Oh my God," Hala says.

On Louvet's screen, there's a list of potential relatives based on Yusef's DNA. Adam blinks again and again in case his eyes are playing tricks on him. It's not often his mind goes blank, but here he remains, awaiting a reboot.

The majority of the list is from Nazareth, Israel.

"'Oh my God' does appear to be a very appropriate phrase right now," Brandon says.

"The Messiah?" Carlos asks.

Eyes in the room gravitate to Yusef. Is he? Could he be? Really? Is it possible?

"There's no way," Hala says.

"Populations have migrated for many generations," Guowei says. "We can't make presumptions with this information."

"Look, a lot of people, so many people are from Nazareth," Brandon says sarcastically, his eyes wide, feigning certainty.

"Like John the Baptist?" Guowei replies. "Or Josephus? Or even a soldier from the First Jewish-Roman War?"

"Or . . ." Hala says.

"I don't know about you," Brandon says, scratching his chin, "but I'm going to go out on a limb here. I don't think the terrorists would be sending suicide bombers after us and hunting down a kid because he is a genetic match with a big-time player in the First Jewish-Roman War. But hey, I've been wrong before."

"That's . . . a valid point," Guowei says.

"How is it possible? There was no body, right? Don't you need that to get his DNA?" Nigel asks, mirroring everyone's bewilderment. Like most of the others, Adam is still digesting this idea. *Could Yusef be a clone of Jesus?*

"The shroud, homie," Carlos says cryptically.

"Care to enlighten me?" Nigel asks.

"After being taken from the cross by Joseph of Arimathea, the Lord Jesus was wrapped in clean fine linen," he says. "The shroud."

As Adam's brain kicks into gear again, he realizes he has no clue what Carlos is referring to. On his iGlasses he googles "Shroud of Jesus." An image depicts Jesus after being taken from the cross, a sheet covering his body.

"Stains in the fabric resemble a man who'd been crucified," Guowei says, demonstrating his familiarity with the information. "Researchers suggest it may be the blood of Jesus Christ, although there's no way to know for sure."

Jacki stares at Yusef in disbelief.

Louvet stands from his chair, disoriented. "If you can excuse me for a minute, I . . ." Constantly brimming with confidence, he's in a state Adam has not seen him in before. He leaves the lab frazzled.

"So y'all think this little kid is Jesus?" Nigel asks. "Are you out of your mind? He's just a kid. The guy said it himself: there was nothing remarkable about him. Wouldn't you think there'd be something strange about his genes since his daddy's a ghost?"

As Adam's thoughts settle, any potential divinity in the child seems irrelevant. ARK wants him. That's the only point that matters. "Well, uh . . . if he is or isn't, what difference does it make so long as ARK thinks he is?"

"How would we know if he's a clone or not?" Hala asks.

"Three days ago, I didn't think I was Genghis Khan. I don't know what's possible," Guowei says.

"I mean, he's incredibly well behaved," Brandon says. "Anyone seen him sin yet? Sins? Sins?" He looks around, soliciting suggestions. "Someone give me some good sins."

"Let me get this straight, boss. You think tempting the Son of God to sin will turn out well for you?" Carlos asks.

Brandon thinks about it for a few seconds. "Well, now that you put it that way, I formally retract the idea." He looks Yusef directly in the eye. "I'm sorry for saying that. Please forgive me."

"Good call," Carlos says.

Adam isn't familiar with the expectations or inner workings of Christianity, but he's confident Brandon is doing something wrong. Suddenly, a new message from the ARK flashes across his iGlasses, startling him: SHOWTIME. #WATCHITBURN.

After the potential Yusef revelation, his anxiety, bloodstream, and brain waves all slowed, but the post pumps everything back to life. Adam hurries to turn on a TV atop a cabinet and flips it to a news broadcast: BREAKING NEWS: TERRORIST THREAT GOES VIRAL. The anchor with short blond hair and glasses reads from her teleprompter, her tone grave. "The post linking to the video was originally made by user The Real Noah. You should be warned: what you are about to see is graphic."

A grainy webcam video shows a dimly lit room where a pixelated figure adjusts a tea bag in his drink. "Today, I lost my youngest son. And my son lost a brother," he says. "The wickedness of mankind knows no boundaries, one of the many reasons for its demise. A flood is coming, brothers and sisters. Only those deemed worthy will float. And to the seven of you . . . you take from my family?"

A rebel stands nearby, brandishing a gun. "I will obliterate yours." As the man steps aside, the camera focuses. Margot is tied to a chair. *No!*

Adam trembles uncontrollably, his heart thudding relentlessly within his chest. He's out of time. He doesn't want to watch, but he can't not watch. If he hadn't messed up her presentation. If he had expected that third abductor.

The pixelated man steps in front of the camera to obstruct the view.

Bang!

Smashed in the guts with a sledgehammer, Adam doubles over. They didn't show it. He didn't see it.

Someone puts his hand on his back.

They didn't show it. It didn't happen. They didn't show it because it didn't happen.

"The great conqueror Genghis Khan would flatten a city if it resisted his demands," the man in the video says. "You've resisted me. I will tear your worlds down until my boy comes home."

The camera pulls back, and the figure comes into focus—it's Bricker. With a menacing gesture, he raises a finger as if wielding a magic wand. "Have you ever seen twelve million people disappear? Abra . . . cadabra."

The video feed returns to the broadcaster, who is visibly shaken. "While the identities of 'the seven' are unclear, our sources believe the woman shown in the video is one of the abducted scientists, Margot Czarnec—wait, oh God!"

The video feed cuts to a towering twenty-first-century skyline. In the distance, a single projectile comes into view. "This is a video from moments ago in Shanghai, China. Oh God." The projectile flies over the skyline, followed by a blinding flash of light. A colossal dust cloud blankets the sky as far as the eye can see. Buildings detonate with catastrophic force in a devastating chain reaction. The scene unfolds like a nightmarish game of dominos. Caught in the demolition, the camera feed shuts down.

"Shanghai is gone! Oh Lord!" the broadcaster says. Guowei drops to his knees. Carlos crouches next to him.

Adam's heart stops beating. His mind, immersed in a swirl of calculations and dire possibilities, comes to a sudden realization: the destructive power of a typical warhead, capable of a blast radius of up to five kilometers, pales to what he witnesses unfolding on the screen. The top nuclear scientists in the world undoubtedly would increase this yield. But by how much? Based on the magnitude of the destruction, it's clear it isn't an atomic weapon; it's thermonuclear.

"Give me the boy."

Professor Louvet brandishes a semiautomatic pistol. The weapon gleams ominously in his grasp, an extension of his deceit. "You can end the destruction. It doesn't need to go any further," Louvet says. "Just surrender the boy to me."

Adam's mind trembles with disbelief as he confronts the shocking reality. Louvet, revered at the university, an influential nexus between international politics and science, is entangled in dubious dealings with Bricker—an inconceivable notion for Adam to comprehend.

"What have you done?" he manages to ask, the sting of betrayal setting in.

"I don't ask a lot of questions," Louvet says. The decorated scientist points his weapon at whoever moves. "They want him. It can end right now."

The bitter truth dawns upon Adam, choking his spirit. Louvet sold out Margot. Seething, fiery anger foments within him. "Margot . . . how could you?"

With a chilling calmness, Louvet responds, "I believe one day your deductive skills will finally blossom, but right now you're a bit slow." His gaze shifts to Carlos, who slowly reaches to his waist. "Keep those hands in a safe place," he says, pointing his gun at him. "This does not need to get out of control."

Louvet is too smart to clash with seven armored twenty-somethings—unless he has more surprises in his bag. Or unless the stakes are that high.

"There will be more bombs," Louvet continues. "You can help stop it. Bring him to me."

Hala carries Yusef forward. Jacki protests, but Hala remains resolute. "It's the only way. People will die."

"Don't," Guowei says, looking up from his knees. "The destruction is inevitable."

Unflinching, Hala offers Yusef to Louvet.

Adam can't believe his eyes. It's like a game of three-dimensional chess is being played before him, but he's oblivious to it. The world has dramatically altered in five ways in the last five minutes. Nothing makes sense.

"Please, put him right there," Louvet says, pointing to a spot next to the lab bench about three meters away.

Hala breaks the clasp that binds Yusef to her neck and sets him down gently. She tenderly brushes his face. Yusef shivers. "It'll be okay," she whispers to him.

Louvet's malevolent grin stretches across his face. "You made the right—"

Hala lunges at him, knocking his gun from his hand. Louvet shoves her away. Some gasp. Shoes squeak.

Adam lunges toward the bedlam, but he's beaten to the punch. Guowei smashes Louvet in the face with an adrenaline-filled left hook. The sickening crack of his nose precedes the messy fountain of spraying blood. Guowei put all of Shanghai into that blow.

Nigel grabs a fire blanket from a nearby wall-mounted station and wraps it around a shivering Yusef. They hurry out the door. Everyone except Adam.

Adam looks upon Louvet's bloody face with disdain. So many words race through his head, but none are for him. He hustles down the hallway to catch up with the others.

"On ARK's Facebook, there's a post from a few seconds ago," Brandon says. "'Bad choice,' angry-face emoji," he reads. "So, um, yeah, we're pretty well screwed."

Out the doors of the building they go. No ambush awaits them, but it can't be that far behind. The team piles into the Wagon. Carlos jams it into reverse and accelerates away from the scene.

"You said we could trust him!" Jacki yells at Adam. "Now they know right where we are!"

Adam stares down at the rubber floor mats. His mistake weighs on him with crushing intensity and leaves him longing for an escape, a chance to undo the irreversible. Einstein kicked around time travel concepts for years. Going back in time has never been more appealing. He'd dive headfirst into the wormhole. Whether it be five hours, five days, or five years ago, any moment is preferable to the unbearable present.

"There has to be more of them," Carlos says, head on a swivel, checking all his mirrors.

"A new post," Brandon says. "'If you seven want to trade, I'll be waiting with Hugo,'" he reads. "Another one: 'Right where you left him #sweetangel.' What in the world does that mean?"

Carlos swerves onto a two-lane highway, accelerating to top speed.

"Paris," Jacki says, her gaze distant and glassy. "He's going to Paris."

Carlos glances over. "How you figure that?"

"He's talking to me."

"Why's that?"

"Because I know," Jacki replies with a definitive period on her sentence, providing no further explanation. The weight of her information lingers, but no one dares to pry for more specifics.

A blur of trees passes Adam's window. Things have taken a deeply personal turn. ARK knows who they are and plans to strike them with calculated precision, inflicting the most excruciating pain. This was not part of Adam's calculus. But there's no turning back.

Amid their collective uncertainty, Guowei leans to Nigel. "May I borrow your phone?" he asks. "My glasses aren't connecting."

"Sure." Nigel passes his phone. Guowei dials. He waits. And waits. Nothing connects. Guowei's hand shakes as he returns the phone to Nigel.

"Thank you," Guowei says.

"Can someone please tell me what the hell we're going to do?" Nigel asks. "Waiting for cities to get demo'd while we joyride doesn't make a whole lotta sense to me."

"We have what he wants," Jacki says. "We're in control."

"Yeah, you're right. Of course," Nigel says, his voice dripping with sarcasm. "But you know what's strange? For being in control, I feel like I've been doing an awful lot of running. Would've been great if I were a clone of Usain Freaking Bolt."

"We can't keep the kid," Adam says. "He's not safe with us." He doesn't have the appetite to subject Yusef to more trauma.

"He has to stay with us," Hala says. "You heard what Kebe said."

"He said we had to stop ARK," Adam replies, "and if we get to their base—"

"We have to do both. If we lose the kid, we lose," Jacki says.

"This isn't just some kid," Guowei interjects.

"You have their address?" Nigel asks Jacki. "Maybe we can roll up and, you know, kill them all. Disassemble their nuclear bombs while we're at it. Do that real Power Ranger hero stuff."

"You don't gotta do all that," Carlos says slowly, bringing the conversation to a standstill. "Cut the head off the snake and the rest will wither and die."

"I'm gonna need a translation," Nigel says.

Nigel earns a glare from Carlos in the rearview mirror. "Bricker," he says. "You want to end it? You end him. He says he's in Paris. He wants the kid. We use the kid. Get an open look at him and . . . *bang bang.*"

"You can't do that!" Hala says. "He's a child."

"He's not a pawn. This isn't a game," Guowei adds.

"We have to find a place for him," Adam says.

"Why? You got another guy you trust?" Brandon asks, immediately averting his eyes and swallowing, regretting the words as soon as he said them. It was a low blow from someone Adam was starting to consider a friend.

Adam's ordinary anxiety storm swirls into an emotional category-five hurricane. Seeing Yusef thrown into this vortex reminds him of his earliest traumatic memories. Margot was his driving force. And she's gone. His mentor betrayed them in unimaginable ways. His decision let his team down and jeopardized everything. Add to that all the insecurities and doubts he's lived with his entire life. Though Einstein's brain might have been difficult to shut off in other ways, it feels now like Adam's been cursed with a seemingly eternal struggle. He works hard to be a good-natured, well-meaning person. He'd never want anyone else to feel the way he does every day.

Adam isn't counting on more than a wink of sleep for the next few months. He needs to find a purpose to persevere through this hellacious storm—and fast. Because tonight he has nothing to live for and few reasons not to bring it to an end.

Adam takes a deep breath, knowing this thought storm will loop indefinitely. It will drown his consciousness, leaving him to thrash to the surface just to take in a breath. But why?

He looks down.

The gray mark on his wrist flickers orange.

This time, instead of turning off, it glows steadily.

CHAPTER 42
YOLIA

I **N A RURAL HOSPITAL** outside Caracas, the supply
of naloxone was running out. Nurses and doctors
dashed gurneys to whatever opening they could find and
administered lifesaving aid. Carlos moved from patient
to patient. He hadn't had a minute to change out of his
N95 mask, but the hospital was in short supply of them
anyway.

This wasn't anything new. Carlos had seen flurries like
this before. Teen after teen was brought in, they likely were all together, and whatever they were using was
laced with fentanyl. A rage built inside him. He dealt with
the effects of brutal chemicals, but he really wanted to
address the cause: Thiago.

"Doctor Ramirez," a nurse said, handing him a loaded
syringe.

Carlos rushed to inject naloxone into the thigh of a
middle-school-aged boy in a Houston Astros baseball jersey. He tried to ration it the best he could.

With a successful delivery, he hurried to his next patient to inject the rest of the vial, swapping in a new needle. He shouldn't reuse the vial, but it's a corner he had to cut. There's no time.

But then Carlos's heart stopped.

Unresponsive in the bed was his own fourteen-year-old brother, Eddie.

Carlos squeezed every last drop out of the syringe, his hand trembling. He urgently checked his vitals. All he could do was pray. Carlos had to tell many parents that their kids didn't make it, but he couldn't say it to his own mother. As he pressed his brother's carotid artery, the strange gray mark on his wrist glowed orange.

Finally, a pulse.

Overwhelmed with emotions, he ran his hand through Eddie's hair and ripped the worn N95 mask off his face. Leaving the fervor of the emergency room behind, Carlos stepped out into the waiting room, where Mami and his sister, Dani, stood trembling with fear. Without breaking stride, he crushed them with a tight three-way embrace.

"He'll be okay, Mami," Carlos told her. The flow of tears from this family could overflow a river.

Mami pulled back slightly, her calloused hands grasping Carlos's jaw. In her touch, he didn't feel joy or relief but fire.

"I'm going to stop this," Carlos said with a steely gaze. "This man is never going to hurt us again."

"No, baby," Mami said. "You are a good doctor."

"I know," Carlos said.

Riding shotgun in an aging Subaru, Carlos loaded his favorite pistol. He had a job to do. In the driver's seat was his best friend, Vitor, who had been in Carlos's life since he was twelve. Ten years his senior, Vitor was like the big brother Carlos never had. Their bond could never be broken, and they didn't need to share blood to know that was a fact.

Living in a land run by dictators meant navigating rampant, widespread corruption. Though Carlos and Vitor preferred to repair their neighbors' houses on the weekends or build their grassroots efforts to start a true democracy, that day they were prepared to perform a community service of a different kind—addition by subtraction.

Vitor turned a corner, and Carlos spotted the destination—a bodega of worn brick and faded paint. The crack of dawn cast a quiet stillness over the area; no other cars were in sight.

"That's his place," Carlos said. "He opens it up in five minutes. He's never alone."

Vitor shifted the transmission into park. "If it gets hot in there, I want you to let me deal with it. You got too much on the line."

Carlos shook his head. "You know I can't let you do that."

"I don't care what you say, mijo. It's non-negotiable." Vitor glared at Carlos. He handed him another pistol. "Always carry more than one. Just in case."

Carlos tucked the pistol into his waistband.

Together, they scoped out the area. Their car sat about a hundred meters away from the front exit, the back exit another twenty meters beyond that. The tranquility of the area was broken by the passing of two kids on bicycles, and a gentle breeze rustled the leaves from the yellow araguaney trees, carrying food wrappers from a trash can down the street.

Suddenly, a blinged-out Range Rover roared around the corner, blaring hip-hop. It was an ostentatious display that could only belong to one man—the only man who could afford the rims on this machine and relished every opportunity to make it known to all.

Though some drug lords preferred anonymity, Thiago lived without fear. The local police worked for him, and anyone who attempted to get big against him disappeared. No one dared to even ask about them.

The Range Rover pulled into the rear of the corner store, and his two pieces of muscle exited to check out the area. Satisfied with their assessment, Thiago emerged from the driver's side.

"You don't got to do this. It's my fight," Carlos said.

Vitor scoffed. "Now you're talking crazy."

"You don't think I can handle myself?"

"You know that's not what I'm saying," Vitor said with a smirk.

Carlos and Vitor entered the bodega. The shelves were packed floor to ceiling with rows of snacks, beverages, and essentials. The establishment hadn't been swept in a while, and the defunct deli counter was now the home of a cat that policed the rodents. Thiago hadn't been taking care of the place, but he didn't have to. He just had to push his drugs out the back.

One of the bodyguards idled by the register, engrossed in his phone, until their approaching footsteps drew his attention.

"Where's Thiago?" Carlos asked as he strode toward him, his pistol behind his back. Those were fighting words in these parts, but too much adrenaline coursed through his body to be subtle. It was not a day to finesse with a paint-brush; it was a day for a hammer.

The bodyguard stared at him, devoid of any response. He was calculating his odds. Carlos gripped his pistol and wait-ed for him to roll the dice.

In a flash, the bodyguard drew his weapon, but Carlos smashed him with the butt end of his pistol. The blow sent the bodyguard crashing to the ground, unconscious. Star-tled, the store's resident cat scurried away from its counter.

Carlos fired two rounds into the man.

It was a strange feeling. Carlos had removed more bullets from patients than he could count, but those were the first he had put in.

He headed to the storage room door in the back of the bodega. Vitor kicked it in and fired. A body thudded to the ground. Carlos stepped over the second bleeding bodyguard, still clinging to a dwindling thread of life. The geyser of blood from his chest meant a blown artery; he had about another thirty seconds or so. Not worth another bullet.

They entered the dimly lit storage area, thick with the scent of decaying fruit. In the quiet, a grasshopper landed on a metal rack. The smell of moldy food covered up whatever cologne Thiago might have been wearing. Sweat rolled down Carlos's back.

"Where you at?" Carlos yelled, his voice bouncing off the walls. They searched for Thiago. The potential hiding spots were numerous, and he or any other bodyguards on the premises could emerge from the shadows at any moment. Vitor pointed to his ear: a crunch of gravel.

"He's outside," Carlos whispered. Their eyes drifted to the back exit. As Carlos approached the door, his mind was taken back to the hospital bed, his little brother on the verge of death, the faces of countless incapacitated youths, and his mother's face dripping with sweat in the waiting room. Then he thought of the mothers who weren't so lucky.

They reached the door and cautiously peered outside. The blinged-out Range Rover sat alone.

Carlos's neck got itchy, but he paid it no mind. He took a step outside, ready to fire. Vitor followed. Meter by meter, they advanced toward the Range Rover. He had to be there.

"Behind!"

Carlos whirled around, his heart pounding, and found Thiago perched atop the building, a rifle aimed down at him.

"Watch out!" Vitor's warning rattled in his ears.

Bang!

Carlos was knocked into the gravel, consumed in a cloud of dust. He lost his grip on his pistol, helpless to prevent it from slipping away.

Vitor hung in midair before him, a dark hole in his chest. Then his legs gave way.

Carlos scrambled to reach for the other pistol tangled in his waistband. He couldn't get it.

Thiago lined up his kill shot.

But something knocked him off the roof before Thiago could pull the trigger. His body crashed in a bloody heap, his leg likely broken from the fall. He was shot.

Carlos still hadn't pulled the pistol from his waistband. Vitor laid motionless. The shot came from elsewhere. He snapped his head around to look over his shoulder. In his periphery, Papi lowered a semiautomatic silenced handgun.

Rushing over them, Papi asked, "Are you okay?"

Frantic, Carlos administered CPR to Vitor, but it was no use. He hadn't been a doctor long, but knew when a body couldn't be saved. Rage filled him as he wiped the sweat from his brow. "No, Papi. I'm not okay," Carlos said.

Thiago writhed on the ground, wounded and defenseless. Carlos gripped the backup pistol that Vitor had given him and marched over to Thiago. Papi grabbed him. "Don't. Don't give in," he said. Carlos brushed him off, resolute in his decision. There was only one way this story ended.

"I can get the police here," Papi said. "Justice will be done." He scrambled but couldn't stop the inevitable.

Carlos momentarily broke his stride, turning to face Papi. "That man deserves to die, Papi. Right now."

Papi, digesting the weight of Carlos's words, relented. "Okay."

Carlos returned to his task, calmly walking to the thrashing, helpless Thiago. "You don't have the nuts, ese," Thiago told Carlos.

"Ah, okay." Carlos pointed his pistol at him. "*Nos vemos.*"

Another bullet rips through Thiago's neck. It wasn't his. Carlos's head snapped around as Papi lowered his smoking weapon. Thiago's thrashing ceased; he took his final breath.

"Don't give in, my boy," Papi said. "You have too much good inside you."

The job was done. Overwhelmed by a wave of emotions, Carlos broke down. Tears flowed from his eyes. He walked toward Papi and was met with a tight hug. "Thank you," Carlos said.

"Keep your *yolia*. Never forget it," Papi said. "We will fix all of this."

STREETLIGHTS ILLUMINATE the lonely stretch of this three-lane French freeway. In the tranquility of the early morning, Carlos has seen more deer than people, but he's come upon some traffic for the first time in a while. As he eases his foot off the accelerator, he glances down at the script adorning his forearm—a tattoo of the word *yolia*, beautifully stylized with street-art flair. It is one of his most recent additions. Starting from the chest, his canvas begins with indigenous symbols, and as it journeys down his arms, it evolves into more modern Latin designs. The story of his people.

The smooth freeway ride could lull a baby to sleep. Carlos whizzes past a road sign that reads PARIS, 30 KILOMETERS. In the rearview mirror, his teammates catch a rare nap. It's been four hours on the road. He knows his teammates are struggling—physically, mentally, and emotionally—but they've all hung in during this crazy situation, and he gives them props for that. The news of being clones rocked them. They have a lot to live up to—and, in some cases, live down. The revelation that he's Che Guevara was interesting, but Carlos is his own man. Always has been and always will be.

And Guevara would respect that.

The Wagon catches up to a black car crawling in the left lane. Carlos reaches for his turn signal to weave around, but the black car does the same before he can.

"You kidding me?" Carlos checks his mirror, ready to bounce back to the left lane, only to see another black car speed into the space. He angles to pass on the right, but a third black car hits the accelerator, leaving him no room. Behind him, a fourth black car draws nearer.

His neck itches.

"Uh, fellas," Adam says, breaking the silence. The others shake off the light sleep.

The car on the right weaves into their lane. Carlos swerves a little but has no place to go. "What the heck are you doing?" Nigel asks.

"It's a trap!" Carlos says, gripping the wheel, bracing himself for a rough ride. He deftly maneuvers to avoid contact.

"Can you see anything?" Jacki asks.

The car in front slams on its brakes, and Carlos follows suit, rocking everyone in the Wagon.

"Does your taser have that range?" Adam asks Brandon.

"Only one way to find out," Brandon replies.

Carlos passes a freeway exit sign; the next ramp is half a kilometer away. The black cars flanking him swerve into his lane, and Carlos maneuvers to narrowly evade collision.

"Which car?" Brandon asks.

"Take out the rear," Carlos says, focusing on the exit ahead, the path to liberation.

"Why would you want the rear?" Brandon asks.

"Just do what he asks!" Adam says.

The exit lane is visible. They can't miss it. "Now!" Carlos yells, pressure bubbling in his gut.

Guowei and Hala lean out of the line of fire, granting Brandon the space he needs. Stretching over them, he steadies his aim and unleashes his weapon.

Zap!

Unexpectedly, the rear car speeds up, its incapacitated driver slumping forward onto the steering wheel. The horn blares as the vehicle barrels out of control.

"That was a miscalculation," Brandon says.

The rear car closes in on the back fender of the Wagon. It violently veers left and cartwheels over the median.

With the freeway exit imminent, Carlos slams the brakes. The black cars cruise forward, leaving a gap. Gripping the leather steering wheel, he veers right. The Wagon ramps a concrete lip, careens down the exit, and lands on all fours as it plunges into a heavily forested area.

Every sign Carlos passes is blue and official. All in French. "What's that say?" he asks.

"*Le Château de Belvoir*," Jacki says.

"In English."

"The Castle of Belvoir."

They pass a giant yellow diamond-shaped No OUTLET sign—unmistakable and in English, likely for tourists. It's the worst possible sign to see. Carlos's itchy neck confirms it. They were better off riding it out on the freeway.

As the Wagon emerges from the dense forest, a sprawling fifteenth-century French castle comes into view. The stone and brick fortress is seated upon thousands of acres of land. The battlements carve out silhouettes against the sky, and its towering spires spear the heavens. Carlos has only seen such a building in a book.

Suddenly, a beam of light slices through the black emptiness of the sky. A helicopter illuminates the rear window of the Wagon. Despite Carlos's best efforts, it was all for naught. ARK was in the air too.

Jacki nods to Carlos, an unspoken confirmation of what needs to be done. It's time to take a stand.

The Wagon ascends the uphill path toward the imposing château.

Nigel breaks the silence. "There's nowhere else to go."

"Yeah," Jacki says.

"And?" Nigel asks desperately.

Carlos jerks the wheel to the left. He rips a U-turn through a patch of grass until the Wagon skids to a stop, positioning them head-on with hovering helicopters, a convoy of black cars, and a fleet of motorcycles.

"Well, this sucks," Brandon interjects.

Solemn eyes survey the surroundings through the windows, each individual slowly realizing it is about to become their battlefield. "This is it," Adam murmurs, recognizing the moment for all that it is.

Carlos readies his pistol. Besides Jacki, he's not confident any of them will have the instinct to do what is necessary. They will need guidance and a lot of help. "Shoot the snake on sight," he says.

And to hunt that snake, Carlos will have to slither.

Hala tightens the fire blanket around Yusef. Though the blanket is plenty thick, there's no blanket in the world that could stop the young boy from shivering right now.

Carlos had a long drive to think through the options should this situation present itself. His plan is the only one with any chance of working, and he's the only one with what it takes to pull it off.

"He has an army," Guowei says. "Even if he's here, he won't expose himself."

"We're gonna find out," Carlos replies. "Get out there. Hurry up."

"What are you going to do?" Jacki asks incredulously.

"I'm going to end this," Carlos says, filling each syllable with resolve.

"You have to tell us what you're going to do!" Jacki demands. "You can't make unilateral decisions like this without a plan."

"I need you out there," Carlos says calmly. Odd sensations surge through his body like his blood is pumping a special cocktail for the occasion. "Trust me."

CHAPTER 43
WHERE YOU AT?

THE ROAR OF THE HELICOPTER BLADES whips Adam's hair in every direction as he emerges from the passenger side of the Wagon. The others pile out, the silhouette of a dark forest at their backs. Atop a gentle hill ahead of them looms the château, casting an inky shadow over the landscape.

If there's anyone on the team Adam trusts, it's Carlos. It's Adam's nature to always be on the lookout, and Carlos has always beaten him to the punch—and he's undoubtedly thrown more punches in his life. But Carlos's demand to be a lone wolf is equally untimely and unsettling.

Clad in a long raincoat, its collar flapping wildly in the relentless wind, Zed stands before an army of fifty rebels, each armed with a rifle leveled at the Phoenix Elite. His voice cuts like a whip. "Go ahead and drop those bazookas, lightsabers, voodoo dolls, and whatever else you're carrying."

Adam, Brandon, and Guowei oblige, placing their weapons in a pile. This was expected. Even if Adam could get off a shot with his bazooka, there are still too many of them. But they keep their pistols snug in their holster pockets of their tactical suits.

The driver's side door swings open with authority. Carlos exits, clutching something substantial in his hands. He ducks behind the door, using it as a makeshift shield.

"This is really a simple proposition," Zed says, striding forward nonchalantly. "You give me the boy. See, it's easy."

"Don't move!" Carlos yells. "Put your guns down!"

Zed doesn't break stride. "Oh, Che, I admire your fieriness. I know it's in your nature, but if I were you, I'd consider your teammates before you do anything brash."

Carlos kicks his car door closed to reveal a bundle of blankets, the barrel of Carlos's pistol digging into the fabric. Gasps escape the lips of his teammates. A shiver zaps Adam's spine. Even Zed freezes, momentarily taken aback by the sudden escalation.

"Whoa! Hold on!" Jacki yells.

"The hell you doin', man?" Nigel says. "He's just a kid!"

"I will end this right now if you take one more step," Carlos says. His will is steeled. He's gone all in. He isn't turning back.

Zed raises his hands and adopts the facade of a peacekeeper. "Relax, hombre. I know you have problems, but there's no reason to take them out on a little boy."

"Show your face, you coward!" Carlos yells through the crowd, cutting through the charged air. "Where you at, Bricker?"

The once-hostile rebel army now stands in disarray, their weapons drooping as mumbles ripple through their ranks. "Relax. Just give the boy to me," Zed says, trying to de-escalate.

"Back up, asshole," Carlos says, his grip on the gun tightening, the threat of violence palpable. "If he wants him, he can come get him."

Adam's eyes dart between the bundle and the empty Wagon. Where's Hala? Something's not adding up. On his iGlasses, he can see Carlos's heartbeat pumping at 180 beats per minute, but he can't get a read on Yusef through the thick blankets. Fear grips Adam, his hand trembling as he reaches for his pistol. He rests his finger on the trigger but keeps it holstered.

"We can work something out," Zed says.

"Carlos!" Jacki says, stepping toward him.

Adam grabs her arm, an unexplainable nuance in the mystique compelling him to act. "Let him do this," Adam whispers to her. Jacki stares back at him, shocked.

Carlos shakes with rage, digging the gun deeper into the blanket. His voice pierces the silence like a blade. "Where you at?!" he yells. "I will turn this kid into a bloody Picasso."

Zed cracks. "Fine. Fine!" A sudden desperation breaks his once-impervious confidence. "Go get him," he tells his rebel assistant, who promptly retreats to one of the black vehicles.

Carlos locks eyes with the others, unbridled intensity oozing from his every pore.

The assistant returns, leading a mysterious figure over to Zed behind the army of rebels. Is it Bricker? They are similar in height, but their body armor makes it impossible to discern their identity.

Adam's finger dances over the trigger of his concealed weapon. As soon as Bricker shows his face, as unlikely as it is that Adam will hit him, he has to take his shot.

Amidst the crowd of rebels, the assistant emerges with a robot, its neck a long rod and a tablet for a head. Adam has never seen anything like it before. The assistant places the enigmatic machine next to Zed.

"Well, that's different," Brandon says.

"What the hell is that?" Carlos asks. "Where's your hero?"

The assistant adjusts the tablet head, directing it toward the Phoenix Elite. Bricker materializes on the screen, anxiously gathering his bearings in front of his webcam. He's outdoors, somewhere with trees.

"You all are a bit difficult to pin down, eh?" Bricker says, eyeballing the group. "Is that Guowei over there? Please send my condolences to all his family and friends. That bomb had a yield that surpassed even our most optimistic projections." Guowei remains stone-faced. "And it looks like you have my son. Nice of you to keep him warm."

"You won't win this," Jacki says.

Bricker's lips curl into a sinister smile. "Who said anything about winning? It's about survival. If you and your friends choose to be reasonable, we can reach some sort of accord. I have more warheads about to break ground very soon. They are expected to arrive on the doorsteps of your loved ones. I suppose I could allow a reprieve in exchange for your generous cooperation. Perhaps I could save a few seats for you, your families, and friends aboard my ark. Just give me my boy."

"Come take him yourself, you coward," Carlos says.

Adam's phoenix mark blinks orange, as do the marks on the others' wrists. It's a unifying feeling. Their fate will be decided on their terms.

Bricker's eyes narrow with a glint of amusement. "Hmmm, really? Even you, Guowei? If you could have your family back? Keep them safe? You wouldn't do it?"

"You're a sick bastard. That's what you are!" Carlos says.

Bricker shakes off the insult. "I may be many things, but I'm neither sick nor a bastard. At the end of the day, I just want my son. Shouldn't a boy be with his father? Play catch? Teach him math? Show him the way of the world? Isn't that the way it should be, Dr. Ramirez?"

"He's not your son," Jacki says.

"You are very wrong about that," Bricker says. "I made him. I worked very hard to make him." On the tablet screen, a hand brushes dirt from a small tombstone adorned with a decorative cross. It reads HUGO SCHULTé. 2019–2021. SLEEP WELL, MY ANGEL.

"What if I told you I could bring him back for you, Jacki?" Bricker asks. "Would that change your mind?"

Jacki becomes unhinged at the sight, unleashing a maelstrom of ferocity. Ignoring Guowei's failed attempt to restrain her, she launches herself at the army and the robot, propelled by fury. "Get the hell away from him, you piece of shit!"

Bricker turns the camera back to himself. "What would Hugo want you to—"

Jacki decapitates the robot with a flying punch, sending its shattered tablet head skidding along the ground.

Chaos erupts as rebels encircle her. She thrashes them with her elbows and knees, but after knocking out a handful, they tackle her and hold her at gunpoint.

During the commotion, Brandon reaches for his taser in the pile of discarded weapons.

"Don't touch anything!" the rebel captain yells.

Meanwhile, Nigel sprints to Carlos, adjusting his nano-gloves. "Promise me you won't do anything stupid!"

"No," Carlos replies. He tucks his gun under his chin and traces the pattern on the screen of his biker gloves. His compact motorbike ejects from the backpack and unfolds between his legs. The handlebars extend to arm's reach. He places his gun in the convenient holster attached to the instrument display.

Blanketed Yusef in one arm, he cranks the accelerator, and Nigel jumps on the back of the motorbike. Boosters blast the motorbike forward, propelling it into hyperspeed. Carlos weaves to dodge a pair of rebels and zooms toward a fallen log. He ramps it and maneuvers into a narrow opening in the forest.

Thirty rebels on motorcycles give chase. The rebel captain signals the rest on foot to attack.

With Yusef whisked away, Adam redirects his attention to the rebel army. Engaging in a fierce struggle, he wrestles with one rebel, managing to push them away momentarily. However, three more rebels seize him from behind, overpowering him and slamming him to the ground. The odds seem insurmountable.

The rebel captain smashes Brandon in the jaw with a powerful elbow. He goes down hard, his face buried in the grass.

Guowei tosses a rebel across the hood of the Wagon. The rebel captain attacks him. Guowei dodges and puts him in a chokehold. He squeezes, attempting to slide his arm under his chin. The rebel captain breaks free and grapples him. The two mammoths tussle, their bodies tumbling toward the château.

In the field between the château and the Wagon, a rebel points the long silver barrel of his rifle at Jacki's head. "You want me to kill her?"

Observing the unfolding battles around him, Zed surveys the scene with a calculating gaze. "Not yet. I kinda like her. Father wants to give them a little more time to think about things," he says. "Did you count seven?"

"I, uh, I didn't count them."

With a three-barreled pistol in hand, Zed casually walks toward the Wagon.

Meanwhile, with sweat and dirt in his eyes, Adam struggles to reach the unconscious Brandon lying in the grass. Three rebels swarm him. Their combined strength pushes Adam's body to its limits. He feels himself losing ground, his balance slipping away. As he struggles, the rebels overpower him, driving his head into the earth. The men pile their bodies on his and squeeze the air from his lungs.

"You wanna tell us the code to your little toy over there?" The rebel tries to unlock the pattern on his bazooka. *Good luck with all 389,112 possible patterns*, Adam thinks. His concern, however, shifts to whether the bazooka will lock up permanently after too many failed attempts.

As Zed walks past, he addresses the rebels, "You can maim him, torture him, just don't kill him until we get that pattern. The weapons are for me." He leans his head into the open side door of the Wagon.

Beneath the weight of three bodies, Adam strains, aching from the severe pressure, his cheek pressed into the grass. His eyes lock on Zed, and a knot of anxiety coils inside him. Adam can only watch helplessly as Zed circles around the Wagon. His breaths become shallower, each gasp a Herculean effort, an arduous battle against an invisible force. In the face of death, in the eye of his darkest storm, he cannot move.

CHAPTER 44
KHAN

IN THE SHADOW of the Renaissance-era château, Guowei grabs the rebel captain's head and squeezes like a vise grip. The man is not going out easily. Guowei digs deep to tighten the hold, but the man twists away, dislodging his helmet.

In the clear moonlight stands the rebel captain, unmasked. Although he has more facial hair and a buzz cut, he could be Guowei's twin—another clone of Genghis Khan.

The revelation suspends Guowei in a moment of shock. In the delay, the other clone hurries inside the château, and Guowei pursues.

Inside the stone walls, Guowei's doppelganger swings a glistening medieval sword at his head with deadly intent. Guowei hops backward, evading the attack, only centimeters separating the razor-sharp blade from his ear. The clone strikes again, but his wild swing misses its mark, throwing himself off-balance.

A suit of medieval armor on display stands watch in the corner, equipped with weapons. Guowei makes his move for it. Wielding a sword of his own, Guowei grips the hilt and angles for an opening.

In a flash, Guowei's consciousness is transported back to a distant past. All of the modern touches of the setting have been wiped away, his hallucination replacing it all with a world of Dark Age warfare. He and his opponent are suddenly wearing armor crafted from hardened leather and iron, laced together onto a silk backing. Under the protection of iron Yuan helmets, Guowei and the clone, two Mongol warriors, square off mano a mano.

Guowei rolls his shoulder around to loosen his tight muscles and assesses his opponent's possible moves. The potential strikes glow with an ethereal blue light, manifesting the Clone Khan's intent.

With lightning speed, the clone lunges forward with his sword. Guowei swiftly parries the strike. He pushes back against the clone to create space and rolls into a hallway lined with suits of Mongol armor and artifacts. Flames engulf the corridor. He draws strength from them as if his ancestors have returned to the battleground with him.

Unyielding in his pursuit, the clone feints to the left and then twirls, tornado-like, to slash at Guowei. At the last second, Guowei leaps away from the deadly arc of the blade. The clone repositions his feet and swings his sword like a sledgehammer. Guowei holds his sword up to block in time, but the impact rattles his grip. His weapon slips from his hands and clatters to the stone floor.

The clone darts at him. Guowei avoids the thrust but stumbles. A sharp pain shoots through his ankle, but feeling pain means he's still alive. This sword fight needs to turn into a close-quarters brawl. Empty-handed, Guowei charges him. He grabs him with a head-and-arm lock, Jacki's signature move, and judo-throws him. Thunder booms upon impact. An earthquake shakes the ground. The flames shoot higher, and the inferno closes in on them.

Ferocious, Guowei grabs the clone's wrist with both hands and steps over his head. Step by step, he follows his training. Guowei torques the clone's arm into a kimura with a burst of power.

"You're too weak," the clone hisses through gritted teeth, strained with pain. But the clone is entirely at Guowei's mercy. What is he to do with him? As Guowei considers the options, one choice emerges as the clear victor.

Snap!

Guowei breaks the clone's humerus like a twig, and the sickening snap transports him back to reality. The visions of Mongol warriors and flickering flames fade away. Once again, he stands in the cobbled corridor of the vacant medieval castle, clad in his tactical suit.

The clone writhes and cries out in pain. Guowei retrieves his fallen sword. The demolition of Shanghai. The murder of his parents, his brother, and countless others. ARK does not know who they are dealing with.

With two hands firmly around the hilt, Guowei plunges the sword into the clone's leg. He leaves him in a pool of blood and the cacophony of his echoed screams.

CHAPTER 45
SWERVE

NIGEL FIGHTS TO KEEP HIS LUNCH DOWN on the bone-rattling ride through the forest. Little explosions burst around them like they're racing through pyrotechnics. How Carlos navigates these treacherous paths with a four-year-old child perched on his lap is beyond Nigel's comprehension.

Carlos zigzags through lines of trees, a literal trailblazer, as the motorbike shaves back foliage and creates deep furrows in the earth. Nigel steals a nervous glance over his shoulder. The rebels continue their chase, but the terrain and Carlos's driving prevent them from gaining ground.

Suddenly, the motorbike hits a jarring bump, launching them airborne for a heart-stopping moment. Nigel clings to his seat to steady himself.

Carlos leans back, attempting to regain balance. "Shit!"

Miraculously, he lands the bike cleanly. But the blanketed Yusef slips from his grasp. Squeezing his seat between his legs, Nigel desperately lunges to catch any fiber of the fire blanket.

But his fingers grasp only air.

Carlos revs to speed up. He's not turning back.

"You have to turn around!" Nigel yells, his plea swallowed by the wind.

The fire blanket catches a gust, unfurling like a parachute before settling in a heap on the ground. A pair of headrests from the Wagon tumble onto the grass.

Nigel can only stare in disbelief, his mouth agape. "Oh, oh, oh . . . you dog," he says. After all that, it's just a blanket. Carlos played everyone. And playing his own team sold it even more.

Carlos grins as he accelerates toward a massive oak tree. "Grab that tree!"

"What? Why?" Nigel asks, dumbfounded.

"Turn on your gloves."

You are legit crazy, man. Nigel leans off the motorbike. He fully extends his arms, the howling wind jostling him off his seat. His gloved hands slap the tree's rough bark, and his legs clamp tightly around the bike. The laws of physics carry them off the ground like a whirling dervish, trees and leaves spinning in a dizzying blur.

"Let go!" Carlos yells.

Having lost all sense of his current position in the universe, Nigel releases the tree, his eyes squeezed shut. The tires thud to the ground, and the motorbike skids to a stop, providing a momentary respite from the crazy ride. Somehow, Carlos has stuck the landing.

But there is no time to celebrate. The first wave of rebel motorcycles runs over the flattened fire blanket, speeding toward them. "Uh," Nigel utters, his spine tingling as they wait to be massacred in a stampede.

A pair of rockets extends from the sides of the motorbike beneath Nigel's feet. "This might be stupid," Carlos says.

Thirty motorcycles hurtle straight at them. Nigel braces himself for the impending collision. "Anytime," he says.

Carlos launches the rockets at the rebels, and they explode on contact. Trees splinter and crack, snapping under the force of the detonation. Birds scatter in a frenzy as shrapnel soars through the air. The once-roaring motorcycles fall into a hushed silence, their riders swallowed by smoke and complete annihilation.

Carlos revs the engine like a battle cry. He maneuvers the bike into the billowing cloud, disappearing under its veil.

"Where the hell's the boy?" Nigel asks.

CHAPTER 46
WHAT'S INSIDE

UNDER HER INVISIBILITY CLOAK, Hala grips Yusef in one arm and delicately strokes his hairline with the other. Her heart pounds with fear and desperate hope, yearning for the torment to end. The Wagon's keys are in the ignition, and her foot is on the brake. Hala can see everything around her as though it were grainy security camera footage. In this grim reality, she wishes for the world to remain devoid of vivid colors.

Zed prowls the Wagon's perimeter, gun in hand. Hala's ears catch the sound of the trunk opening, but she resists the urge to turn her head and steal a glance. There are noises—rustling, grunts, the tug of fabric, muted murmurs.

In the side mirror, Hala witnesses Adam locked in a desperate struggle with a rebel in the dirt. He mounts the rebel, forcefully pressing his head into the grass. Adam strains to reach the pistol in his front pocket. He's nearly there. The outcome of their fierce skirmish seems of little concern to

Zed, who continues his patrol around the Wagon with an air of indifference.

A subtle shift in Yusef's chest startles Hala. She prays it's not what she thinks it is. Her hand swiftly covers his mouth to muffle any noise, but it is too late.

Yusef sneezes.

Terror seeps in. They've lost their cover. She tightens her grip on Yusef, praying another sneeze isn't imminent.

A deafening gunshot causes a jolt through Hala's spine. The bullet flies through the windshield, leaving a hole and a spiderweb crack. Only her eyes move, but she can't discern the origin of the shot. It may have been a stray. She prays it was a stray. With everything inside her, she tries to remain perfectly silent. A dilemma engulfs her—should she flee? Stay in the car or escape on foot? Amidst the whirlwind of emotions, she knows freezing up is not an option. She has to protect this little boy. Her hormones run rampant. She focuses on taking slow, steady, quiet breaths, and waits.

Through the mirror, she sees the rebels converge on Adam. Suddenly, a figure obstructs her view entirely. The rear door on the driver's side flies open, and the smell of wretched breath closes in on her.

"Where are you at, brother?" Zed hisses. "I know you are in here. Don't worry. I'm here to save you from these evil people."

The driver's side of the Wagon sinks on its suspension. The giant man must have stepped inside the vehicle. The SUV trembles as Zed, grunting and straining, grapples with an unseen force.

Then, like a flash of light, the world in the side mirror returns. Adam grabs Zed by the waist, his muscles bulging.

With an explosion of strength, he drags Zed out of the Wagon and slams the giant onto a heap of injured rebels.

"Go!" Adam yells through the pandemonium.

In a frantic frenzy, Hala turns the key in the ignition. The Wagon roars to life. She shifts into gear and slams her foot down on the accelerator. The wheels spin and slip on the grass. With just a few more excruciating meters, she'll be free and clear, racing toward the beckoning safety of the distant highway.

But in the rearview mirror, Zed hurries to catch the vehicle. Adam tries to grab him, but Zed tosses him away. Rapid gunfire follows, but there is no clear indication that anything found its mark.

Determined, Hala plows ahead, envisioning a path to freedom. A thud bangs on the side panel of the Wagon. In her side mirror, she sees Zed riding a motorcycle. His arm reaches out, gripping the mounted handle along the Wagon's open trunk. The fleeting feeling of hope trades places with paralyzing fear.

The Wagon swerves as she tries to shake Zed off. His body swings wildly, but his iron grip doesn't loosen. When Hala reaches the sanctuary of the paved road and the traction of the asphalt, the vehicle surges forward, leaving the rebels behind.

Overhead, the rebel helicopter hovers low, its lights shining through the windows. Hala's heart sinks as she realizes she will not get away.

She weaves down a one-lane dirt road in the French countryside, a blur of uncertainty and fear. Her eyes dart to the side mirror, where she sees Zed stubbornly clinging to the back of the vehicle. Adjusting his grip, he seizes a headrest from the rear row. He's stepping inside.

Hala's hands tighten around the steering wheel, her mind racing for a way out. In her lap, Yusef stirs. Faced with limited options, Hala removes one of her iGlasses from her eye. She can't think of anything else.

"Hey, buddy," she whispers. "It's medicine. It will help you feel better." She puts the lens in his mouth, praying for its efficacy. Yusef chews hesitantly and swallows.

"I'm sorry," Yusef says.

It's the first time she's heard him speak. She's stunned at the sound of his voice, which carries a weight far beyond his years.

"No. We'll get out of this. It's going to be okay."

Yusef looks up to her with a blank expression. "No. It won't." His raw words cut her. The four-year-old delivers the unvarnished truth that her gut has warned her about. She wants to ease his worry, but she's coming up empty.

The invisibility cloak is torn away, and the world around Hala suddenly blazes into vivid color. The cold barrel of a gun presses against her temple, and her body tenses.

"Hello, Queen." Zed's voice slithers into her ear.

"No! Don't do this."

"That's not your choice to make," Zed says, chillingly calm. He jerks the emergency brake. The Wagon screeches to a halt. Hala slams into the steering wheel.

"I'm so sorry," she whispers, hugging Yusef tightly, rivers of anguish flowing down her trembling face.

Yusef wipes the tears off her cheeks. "Don't cry," he says, fearless in the face of the darkness that engulfs them.

The rebel helicopter descends, and as it lands, its light envelops them in its blinding aura, sealing their fate.

Zed throws the driver's side door open. He smiles disconcertingly and waves at Yusef. "Nice to see you again, brother," he says with unsettling warmth. He extends a hand toward Yusef but stares at Hala with a haunting intensity. "Don't make me scare him," he whispers to her.

Yusef doesn't budge.

"You want to go on a helicopter ride?" Zed says, his tone brimming with false enthusiasm. "It'll be fun."

When Yusef still doesn't move, Zed seizes his arm and wrenches him from Hala's desperate embrace.

"He's a good kid," she says, her soul shattered. She should have done more and fought back, but in her heart she knows she never stood a chance.

A twisted smile curls upon Zed's lips, and his eyes home in on the innocent child. "Yeah, he's perfect," he says before carrying Yusef to the awaiting helicopter.

Hala sends out a message to the team on her iGlasses: I LOST HIM.

CHAPTER 47
VICTORY

ZED BUCKLES YUSEF into his seat, and triumph is shot into his bloodstream. It is a momentous victory. He pats the helicopter pilot on the back. "Can you tell Father the good news?" Zed asks. "And please let him know that we're on our way home. He's waited a long time for this."

"Of course, sir," the pilot says as he types on his phone: @THEREALNOAH THE BOY IS COMING HOME. Zed's eyes gleam with anticipation; their grand plan has no more obstacles.

Seated comfortably within the helicopter, Zed scans a series of tablet screens across this makeshift mobile command center. Each screen, with labels like PARIS, JOHANNESBURG, and CAIRO, displays an underwater view of swaying seaweed or vibrant schools of fish. Zed taps on the PARIS screen and clicks a button marked DEPLOY.

Zed flips one screen to an episode of *Paw Patrol* and hands the tablet to Yusef. "I know you like this." Yusef accepts the tablet, but his attention drifts to the window. Zed tenderly massages Yusef's palm in a circle. "Father will be very excited to meet you," he says. Leaning toward the pilot, Zed asks, "How far away are we from Paris?"

"About 120 kilometers, sir."

"Tell me when we get to 250."

Returning his focus to Paris, Zed runs his fingers across the controls. The text ARK 23 appears at the bottom of the page. With a gentle tap, a comprehensive list of controls springs forth—RUDDER, SPEED, DEPTH, LAUNCH. He toggles the settings, steering a drone submarine. The sleek ten-foot vessel, camouflaged in shades of sea green, glides beneath the Seine River, past rocks, floating algae, and scattered litter.

An explosion lights up the night, jolting Zed from his daydreams.

"They're coming for you."

CHAPTER 48
DO OR DIE

WINGS SPREAD WIDE and jetpack buzzing; Jacki pursues Zed's helicopter, tracing its westbound path through the dark, cloudless night. Controls in each hand, she angles like a hawk, an exhaust trail in her wake.

Jetting after the Wagon put her right where she belongs: in the fray.

The warning beep from her left control interrupts her focus; her battery life hangs precariously at a mere 20 percent, offering a scant five minutes of remaining airtime. The NEED SOLAR RECHARGE pulsations blink in red from the screens on her jetpack's handles.

The moon is a dim lantern in a dark sky. Its feeble light won't provide the juice she needs. But it makes no difference to Jacki. She has made her decision: she will get this boy or go down in flames.

Jacki presses a red button on her right control, igniting a powerful thruster blast that propels her forward with renewed speed, the wind whipping through her hair. She catches a fleeting glimpse of Yusef through the helicopter's window, his eyes following her every move. Zed grips a handle and leans out the sliding door into the night sky. In an instant, he raises his three-barreled pistol and opens fire. Jacki falls back, but with another tap of her control, she bursts forward in a flash of red.

Zed aims and pulls the trigger.

But he's out of bullets. As he scrambles to reload, Yusef smacks the fresh magazine out of Zed's hand, sending it spiraling out of the helicopter.

Beep! Beep! Beep! BATTERY LIFE <1% LAND IMMEDIATELY.

This is her last chance. Jacki triggers another burst of power and propels herself toward the helicopter's landing gear. She stretches her arm to its limit. Her fingertips graze the landing strut. But her jetpack emits a prolonged, feeble beep and abruptly shuts down. Against the relentless pull of gravity, Jacki struggles for a grip.

She doesn't get it.

Jacki's fingers slip off the strut, and she free-falls back to earth. Amidst her thrashing plummet, a glimmer catches her eye—a distant orange glow emerging over the horizon. Desperation grips her as she maneuvers her backpack toward the sunrise, yearning for any sign of life from her screen.

It's not charging.

Messages from Brandon stream down her iGlasses: SHE'S STOPPED. SOMETHING HAPPENED. TURN NOW! JACKI, ARE YOU OKAY? With two blinks, she deactivates the device. Joan of Arc went up in flames for refusing to bend her principles. This is another thing they'll have in common.

Below her is a vast expanse of untamed grasslands in shades of greens, browns, and yellows. She savors the view.

It's beautiful. The mountains and plateaus of Massif Central scrape the sky in the distance, a sight she has flown over more times than she can remember.

She lets go.

She rolls over to admire the stars. Her limbs flail freely, and her hair blows wherever it wants. Closing her eyes, a flood of blurry memories fills her mind. All her ages blend together into one beautiful montage—winning a schoolyard game for her classmates, throwing her judo teacher to attain her black belt, and hopping into the cockpit of a jet as part of le Aéronavale.

In every memory, her parents are always smiling warmly and supporting her along her journey. Their love was constant, unwavering through all the mistakes she made. Jacki could watch this movie over and over again. Is this what it is like to die?

The memories shift, replaced by one face—her Hugo—her fair-skinned, red-headed boy whose smile made his mother the happiest she had ever been. The doctors told her he wouldn't be hers long, but she believed in miracles then. They could fight. Regardless of what happened in the world, the snuggles with her boy would make it all stand still. Her special boy. Her heart and soul.

In joining him in the dirt, Jacki finds a profound peace that washes over her weary soul.

CHAPTER 49
ODDS ARE NOT ON THEIR SIDE

IN THE BACK OF THE MANDELA WAGON, Brandon scrolls around the map on his iGlasses display. The FRANKLIN, HATSHEPSUT, KHAN, MANDELA, GUEVARA, and EINSTEIN markers are all huddled closely together. Still, the solitary D'ARC marker is static in the distance, approximately three kilometers away to the southwest. Unfortunately, no road will take them there, so they have to imagine their own.

Blood rushes to Brandon's head, momentarily disorienting him. Jacki was always mean to him, but he deserved it, and as the Mandela Wagon bumps along the rutty French grassland, he hopes she'll be mean to him again.

"Are you sure it's not there?" Hala asks eagerly.

Brandon's display shows only one HATSHEPSUT marker. He's never seen a second one before, but there hasn't been an instance where two people share the lenses of one person. Just in case he missed it, his eyes retrace the markers scattered across the digital landscape, searching for another one. Finally, he looks at Hala, a glimmer of faith on her face as

Guowei squeezes her hopeful hand. A hope he has to shatter. "I don't see anything."

Eagerness drains from Hala's expression, replaced by a puddle of disappointment. "Can you tell if it's on? Can you tell if it's been on?"

"You can see the iGlasses if they're activated. I'd presume the contact in Yusef's stomach isn't on since it isn't showing up," Brandon replies. "If you waited until . . . well, you know, and then cleaned it off real nice, put it back in your eye—"

"We get it," Guowei interjects.

"It was a good idea, ingenious really," Brandon says, attempting to lift Hala's spirit. "But eating the technology won't help us in this way moving forward."

Having sufficiently let down Hala, Brandon returns to his task. He sifts through his recording of the encounter with Zed and the rebels. There has to be a clue somewhere buried within. He had to have seen something. He scrutinizes each frame, zooming in and out, rewinding and fast-forwarding. He scans Zed's body from head to toe, hoping for a flicker of insight, but can't glean anything from the effort. Frustration creeps in, and he shoos the memories away.

He was no help to the team during the skirmish, and that's certainly no laughing matter. Benjamin Franklin would be deeply disappointed if he knew how useless his DNA had become. Or worse, Brandon imagines, Ben would pen a sharply worded satire about him that he'd title *The Seventh-Best Clone*.

Returning to the GPS display, Brandon zooms out, observing the entire world map.

That's odd. Why are Kebe's iGlasses still on? No longer in Nowhereville, Russia, it appears Kebe's remains were moved to Washington, DC. The US government must have prompted a cleanup.

This sparks an idea.

Brandon dives back into his visual archives, flipping to the conference room. Kebe scurries into the room, and Adam and Guowei wrap a chain around the door. Brandon fast-forwards through the scene, laser-focused on the nonsensical strings of characters that Kebe types into the computer. Kebe looks Brandon in the eye and mouths, "Watch close." He continues to type. Brandon combs through the text in super slow motion:

*Nc5//> PEi.Me/gmsxW<5L% dOKCak3snG*HfK

Among the cascade of seemingly chaotic characters are two slashes, the universal programming indicator for commenting out a piece of code. Intrigue gives way to optimism. This couldn't be an accident. His eyes trace the text, finding nothing that obviously points him in the right direction. Brandon treads cautiously, wary of raising false hopes within the team, but in his gut he knows there is something significant here.

Adam's voice breaks Brandon's concentration. "Turn here!"

At a blinding speed, Carlos careens down a steep incline. "Are you sure?" he asks. Blades of grass whip against the windows, a surreal blur of green as they plunge into the vast emptiness of an open field.

"Yep. That's her last known location," Adam says. He casts a fleeting glance at the rest of the team, silently inviting their input, but nobody has a thought worth contributing. Nigel gnaws his meticulously manicured fingernails.

The sun rises over the hillside, partially blocked by a solitary tree in the distance. Some light filters through the leafy branches. Brandon notices something near the mighty trunk. Perhaps a groundhog or a squirrel. As his eyes sharpen, recognition hits him like a freight train. Brandon thrusts his finger toward a figure prone in the distance.

"She's over there!"

CHAPTER 50
BLEAK REALITY

ADAM CAN FATHOM ONLY ONE explanation for how Jacki got this far away from the château, and it fills him with trepidation. There's only one reason she'd stop moving. What they are going to encounter will undoubtedly be a gruesome sight. But they at least have to make sure.

Sore and numb, despondent but persevering. Inevitability settles upon him. Shanghai was the proof of concept; other cities would be next. But now, they might fall faster and more furiously. The bleak reality is that they must locate the ARK base and have no clue where it might be.

Kebe's final instruction was explicit: protect Yusef. Yet despite the combined efforts of all seven of them, they could not do it. They are resigned to picking up the pieces. A wave of guilt washes over Adam, mingling with his anxiety and exacerbating his distress.

Having traversed five thousand acres of wild grasslands devoid of any sign of a forest, they now direct their attention toward a solitary tree. It stands as an ancient behemoth, its branches freshly broken.

The sight before them elicits a horrified whisper from Adam's lips. On the ground, lying on a branch beneath the tree, is a body, still and prostrate. "Is that her?" Guowei asks.

Without a moment's hesitation, both Adam and Brandon bail out and sprint toward the fallen body. The rest follow suit, abandoning the vehicle to join their desperate run. With each stride, the figure becomes clearer—a red-and-orange phoenix patch adorning the shoulder of their uniform. There lies Jacki, supine on her back.

Jacki's jetpack is busted, and her face is deeply lacerated. Tears shimmer in her eyes, but instead of despair, she admires the fluffy clouds of the coming morning.

"Are you okay?" Adam asks. "Jacki? Jacki?"

Jacki nods feebly. "Yes sir."

Adam traces the path of her plummet, but despite all the broken branches, he can't quite discern the precise trajectory of her descent or how she could have survived the fall. However, he notices something else as he charts her path through the sky. The warm feelings of finding Jacki dissolve in his stomach acid, replaced by a nauseating churn of dread.

A streak of light darts toward Paris.

"No," Guowei whispers.

"What is it?" Nigel asks.

Panic grips Adam's senses, words spitting out of him, "We have to go now!"

Everyone piles into the Wagon. Carlos jams the gas pedal, executing a sharp U-turn.

"How much time do we have?" Nigel asks him.

Adam struggles to compute. "I . . . uh, we . . . I'd guess . . . thirty seconds to get fifty kilometers away from where it explodes. Maybe."

The speedometer on the dash crosses 160 kilometers per hour as the vehicle jolts violently over the uneven terrain. The Wagon drifts onto a paved road with a sharp turn and screeching tires.

An explosion flashes red across the sky. Even from kilometers away, a plume of smoke rises—and it's building.

"The Hiroshima bomb only had a blast radius of a kilometer," Guowei says. "This missile had to strike much farther away than that . . ."

The cloud of devastation chases them like a predator. The earth cracks. Trees vaporize in the accelerating cloud of annihilation.

"Looks like we have a new champ," Brandon says.

Up to 180 kilometers per hour, Carlos deftly navigates through the racing traffic to outwit the impending doom.

"It has to stop. Doesn't it?" Hala asks.

"No," Adam says. Though he's wondered how much he and Einstein have in common, he recognizes they share a fluency in this topic. "Theoretically, there is no limit to the amount of fuel you can put in a thermonuclear bomb. It won't stop until the lithium cools." He glances over his shoulder. The cloud shows no signs of slowing its relentless pursuit. "This might be . . . it."

Like a ravenous vortex, the cloud overtakes trailing cars. Asphalt breaks into shards. The temperature increases by the second.

Carlos stands on the pedal. "Come on, baby."

The monster is coming. No time for last-minute phone calls to loved ones. It will be a quick and painless conclusion.

It is then that the Wagon leaves the ground.

Carlos relinquishes his grip on the steering wheel and presses his palms against the roof. Jacki does the same. Adam squeezes his eyes shut and curls his body into a protective ball as best he can, bracing for the inevitable impact.

Every sound is overwhelmed by an earsplitting whistle. It will all be over soon.

Inertia plays cruel tricks on his body. A sharp thump jolts his lower back. The vehicle violently plunges into a ditch.

With quaking fear, Adam opens his eyes to a sun blotted out by a manmade storm, a grim and desolate canvas of dirty, grayish-brown hues. The whistle fades, the cloud dissipates, and glimmers of sunlight begin to pierce the destruction.

CHAPTER 51
NEXT STEPS

RITZY POOL PARTIES were a staple of the Dillon lifestyle. After jet-setting around the world, breaking quarterly sales records and shattering his lofty projections, Chimdi Dillon loved unwinding with his family. And quite a family it was. Anyone in attendance would have failed a pop quiz about how they were related to everyone else.

Like clockwork, sixteen-year-old Nigel sat on the floor next to an outlet so his phone could charge while he used it. The device served as an essential conduit, feeding his headphones beats from the kings of hip-hop in the Western world. They were the only people who seemed to get him. Only so many folks who looked like him rolled in the dough he had.

Nigel could always read a room, but nobody figured him out—or really ever tried. It didn't help that he loathed small talk and considered it a waste of time. That's why he picked a room with minimal foot traffic. He wasn't a narcissist like some thought, but he wouldn't dispute he was moody. While most teenagers in his situation would have envied being heir to an empire, Nigel found himself more and more conflicted.

Growing up in upper-class South Africa, he faced haters from all angles. People hated him for the color of his skin, and people hated that he didn't sacrifice everything his family worked for to help the less fortunate. Among his extended family, his oom was the only one who understood him.

"What you doin' in here, boy?" Kebe asked. "It's a beautiful day outside, and you're in here playing on your Game Boy. Listenin' to rap music that'll poison your mind."

"Stop it. You got jokes?" Nigel was happy to spar with the old man for a round or two. "You know those people are crazy. You should start worrying about why they didn't make you crazy."

"Oh, they do. They do." Kebe said, taking a seat on the desk. "I was just talking to your daddy. You ready to run all this business?"

Nigel's response was immediate and resolute. "No. I can't. He is going to need to find someone else for all that."

"Sure you can," Kebe said, his confidence surprising Nigel.

"What makes you say that?" he asked, genuinely intrigued by his uncle's perspective.

"Boy, you don't have to do it alone," Kebe said. "You have a team. You just need to trust them."

Nigel smirked, seizing this rare opportunity to engage in a heart-to-heart with his oom. "Oh, if you didn't think those people out there were crazy, you haven't met Dad's team yet," he said, savoring each moment. "Hey, Oom, when am I going to meet your kid . . . what's her name?"

Kebe's smile faltered, betraying a hint of uncertainty. A nervous chuckle escaped him before he responded, "I don't know. Maybe one day. It's hard for all of us to get around."

"Cool, I'd like that. You really think I can run this business, or you pullin' my leg?"

Kebe crouched down, his hand finding its place on Nigel's shoulder. The weight of his touch conveyed a sense of trust and wisdom. "You might be a pain in everyone's ass, mine included, but when push comes to shove, I know that you'll do what it takes."

"You really believe that?" Nigel asked.

Kebe nodded solemnly, his belief unwavering. "I do."

Nigel couldn't hold back the smile. "Now I know you're crazy." Kebe swiped at his new dreads out of revenge. Nigel manufactured pure outrage. "Now I know you didn't just touch the look!" he said, swatting his hand away.

NIGEL INHALES A DEEP BREATH, filling his lungs with the oxygen from a world that might not survive the night. He stretches his weary legs, a painful reminder of the journey thus far. The Phoenix Elite regroups at a rest stop tucked along some surviving trees while others are cracked, uprooted, or scorched down to the trunk. There is no rhyme or reason to the destruction; the winners were seemingly chosen at random. The concrete base of the structures remains, but their roofs have been torn away without a trace. Signs are bent, their steel yielding to the forces. The stop's four snack machines endure, but not much longer, battered by families hoping to secure what might be their last meals.

The baguette machine will be the last one standing. It turns out when the bomb hits, everyone wants the candy.

Dozens of French families scurry around in a state of pure terror. One family, badly injured, tries to break into a half-destroyed vending machine for a melted Twix bar that'll give them enough calories to survive the night. Paranoia runs rampant. Time hangs suspended, even though hours have passed since the devastating attack on Paris.

Amid the madness, the group consumes the first food they've had a chance to grab in hours. Fortunately, they got to the snack machine before the rest of the apocalypse survivors showed up. In the middle of all this craziness, they are the only seven who know the grim truth: that bomb was just the beginning. Carlos offers his bag of peanut M&Ms to Jacki. She grabs a few.

A disheveled woman, her age impossible to discern under all the soot, bleeds from a gash across her forehead and pleads hysterically in rapid-fire French. She's backed by a mob of furious, similarly unkempt people. They aren't the first to mistake them for the military.

Hala steps in front of the group. "Sorry, we are not the police," she repeats in English and French. "We are trying to help." As the de facto press secretary, she gives her teammates a chance to take a breath.

Nigel takes in the pandemonium. Like many moments on this arduous journey, he wonders what Mandela would do in the face of a certain apocalypse. Downing a bag of potato chips is likely not the answer. When his oom said, *I know that you'll do what it takes*, this probably isn't what he had in mind either.

Among the desperate throngs, a family battles one of the vending machines. A young boy with dark curly hair, reminiscent of Yusef, stands by his father, who slams the machine, the kid's cries mingling with the metallic clamor.

Nigel can't watch anymore. He approaches the family and retrieves a Snickers bar from his pocket. He gently hands it to the sobbing child. "You can have this."

The boy's teary eyes widen in awe as if Nigel had bestowed upon him a treasure beyond measure. Nigel offers the boy a high five, his nano-gloved hand connecting with the child's tiny palm. The boy's hand sticks. Jerking back and forth, unable to break free, the boy giggles. Nigel releases his hand. "Are you a superhero?" the boy asks, his voice quivering with innocence and hope.

A pained smile dances upon Nigel's lips. "Nah, I'm not." His words carry away with the breeze.

"Thank you," his father says, extending a hand to shake Nigel's. Nigel obliges and slips a wad of two hundred rands into his hand, Nelson Mandela's face on each. Nigel winks at him and walks away.

CHAPTER 52
PURPOSE

UNDER THE SHELTERING SHADE of one of the rest stop's trees, Adam hunches over, haunting images of a ruined Paris projected on his iGlasses. Watching the terrified people before him does little to assuage his inner turmoil. Hunger gnaws at his empty stomach, but he knows he won't be able to keep down any food. He's lost Margot, Baba, Yusef, and every parent he's ever known. He's not just a prisoner of the past, but also his bleak predictions about the treacherous, impending future. Perhaps it would've been easier to let the nuke swallow him whole.

As his thoughts wander, a memory fragment emerges from the depths of his desolation. Kebe looks him dead in the eye and says, "Adam, you will be the heart of this team. Without you, there will be no team. No mission." Adam's phoenix mark has yet to revert to its natural color and still glows bright orange, flickering occasionally. There must be a reason he's still here.

Suddenly, a file materializes before his weary eyes, the letter *K* in an orange ring above a file name that reads Adam. Intrigued, he opens it and finds a series of edited clips from his visual archive.

He and Guowei pulling Brandon from the dirt pit.

Shoving Nigel out of the way of the car driven by the Italian bomber.

Blasting the abductors with his bazooka as they aimed at a prone Carlos.

Sprinting down the community center hallway to chase down Zed, who had Jacki pinned to the wall, forcing him to flee.

Rushing through the cloud of debris to help Guowei up in the locker room. Suplexing Zed from the Wagon so Hala could escape with Yusef.

The clips transition to a video of Kebe in his office at the training facility. His somber eyes meet the lens of a webcam, his voice trembling with sympathy and conviction. "Adam, I'm recording this just in case you need it. I suspect you may. What storms in here," Kebe points to his head, "and what swirls in here," he points to his gut, "I know it feels like a terrible affliction, but what it is, is a superpower. You see problems, you diagnose problems, you solve problems. People do not see or feel the world like you. What you are is simple: you are irreplaceable. We will not make it without you. I just thought you might like to know that."

Kebe reaches up and fumbles to turn off the camera. The video screen fades to black, plunging Adam into a cascade of emotions.

Tears trickling down his face, Adam wipes away the evidence of his overwhelming despair. The orange mark on his wrist flickers indecisively between gray and orange before settling on orange. He tries to keep it together, but his emotions overflow.

Where did that file come from?

CHAPTER 53
FIREBIRD

ENGROSSED IN HIS TECH, Brandon perches atop a picnic table, unbothered by the hysterical French folks. He fixates on deciphering the intricate code left by Kebe. The supersize energy drink resting by his side longs to be cracked open—perhaps later. He has spent many years hacking for amusement, but now the stakes are high. Something has to be in here. He has to be more important to the team than the guy who lies unconscious in the grass and trips people with his body. His frustration mounts as error messages persistently thwart his progress.

*Nc5//> PEi.Me/gmsxW<5L% dOKCak3snG*HfK

It's staring him in the face.

He grabs a string of the text: PEi.Me/gmsxW. It's a shortened URL.

"That's it!" Brandon says, breaking through the cacophony of screeching tires and slamming car doors. He swiftly enters the URL into the command line as the team wanders over. "Just a second."

The command computes. No errors this time. Some sort of application downloads. Exhilaration charges him, and he can't help but release an exultant *woo!* that he quickly realizes is sorely out of place in his surroundings. He finishes it anyway. "It appears my time at that lowly American technical college has paid off." Loading wheels spin slowest when the anticipation is greatest.

Finally, the loading wheel vanishes, and a messaging app named Firebird loads on his iGlasses. Its icon is the familiar phoenix symbol. A stream of messages populates from an encrypted file labeled Admin, with a circled *K* as its icon. Brandon senses the weight of anticipation among the group. "I'm going to share my view."

"What is it?" Jacki asks.

Brandon hears the question, but is still mid-exploration of the app. "I don't know yet. It looks like some type of bot. Perhaps some advanced AI?" He scrolls through the previous messages, including a deluge of images.

"Oh wow, you think that's the . . . ?" Nigel asks.

Amidst the images, Brandon comes across a photo showcasing a massive aquarium. Adam chimes in eagerly, "Zoom in on the aquarium."

"Why? Do you like fish?" Brandon asks.

"No, there's a reflection."

Brandon zooms in to uncover a chilling sight—a collection of warheads. The weight of their discovery settles upon the team. Carlos whispers a sobering, "Boom boom."

"Is this from Kebe?" Hala asks. Brandon grapples with the thought. Could it be possible?

"I mean, the icon is a *K*," Jacki says.

"Can you ask it a question?" Hala asks.

Brandon snaps out of fairy-tale land. It's a reasonable question. "Let me try." With anticipation hanging, Brandon inputs his query:

B: CAN I ASK YOU A QUESTION?

The screen comes to life, displaying three small blinking dots, silently indicating activity. A response materializes:

K: YES.

B: ARE YOU DR. KEBE?

K: NO. DR. KEBE IS DEAD. HE'S LEFT YOU WITH ME.

Brandon lets out a sigh of relief, earning stares from everyone. "Well, at least we aren't going to have to deal with zombies, am I right? Perhaps Kebe transferred his digital information into a channel of some kind to keep the flow of intelligence available to us. It isn't inconceivable if he had access to an adequate AI platform."

"Ask about the photos," Jacki says.

B: ARE THOSE PICTURES OF THE ARK BASE?

K: YES. WE HAVE A SOURCE INSIDE THAT SENDS PICTURES TO US INTELLIGENCE THROUGH A SECURE CHANNEL. ANY INTELLIGENCE THAT'S BEEN COLLECTED HAS BEEN PUT IN THIS MESSAGE CHAIN.

B: WHERE IS THE BASE?

K: WE DO NOT KNOW, BUT EFFORTS ARE BEING MADE TO TRACE THE SIGNAL OF THE PHONE USED TO CAPTURE THOSE IMAGES.

"If the AI is an administrator for this system, can they turn it on?" Hala asks.

"What do you mean?" Brandon replies.

"If our iGlasses are in this system, and they can send us messages like this, can they turn the system off and on?"

It dawns on Brandon. She's referring to the lens traveling through Yusef's digestive tract.

B: CAN YOU TURN OFF MY IGLASSES?

K: YES, BUT YOU WOULD LOSE CONTACT.

B: CAN YOU TURN ON ALL THE IGLASSES?

With bated breath, he awaits a reply.

K: YES.

B: *PLEASE TURN ON ALL THE IGLASSES. EVERYWHERE.*

The anticipation among the group is palpable as they await the entity's response. Finally, the reply arrives:

K: DONE.

Euphoria hits his body like a drug. Brandon dives into the GPS tab and zooms out from their present location. His eyes widen with exhilaration as he discovers the activation of numerous iGlasses. Beyond the Phoenix Elite members, most of the icons are labeled with numbers, forming clusters primarily in the Washington, DC, area.

One icon with a HATSHEPSUT indicator stands right next to him. Another with the same HATSHEPSUT indicator hovers over New Orleans, Louisiana.

Brandon clenches his fist and pumps it with a burst of triumph.

"We need to get in the air," Jacki says. "We're twelve hours behind."

CHAPTER 54
LIEUTENANT SCHULTÉ

WHEN THE GROUP ARRIVES, there is pure anarchy beyond the busted gate of the Cognac–Châteaubernard Air Base. Jacki's instinct is to hurry in to help. It's unsettling to see undermanned personnel scurrying around like headless chickens. Jets catapult into the sky one after another, their thunderous roars dominating the airspace.

The Wagon stops at a checkpoint booth manned by an overwhelmed French soldier. "This is a restricted area," he says in French, pointing his assault rifle at their vehicle, ready to deny them entry. Jacki leans out the window, making her presence known. The French soldier's weapon lowers as recognition dawns on his face. "Lieutenant Schulté! Please!" He steps aside, allowing the Wagon to drive over the busted gate and into the base.

Capitaine de Corvette barks orders to his shell-shocked officers, dressed in jeans, a T-shirt, and his military-issued hat. "Go! Go! Go!" he says in French. "Find the survivors! Where are my damn pilots?"

"Here, Capitaine," Jacki says, her voice rising above the turmoil.

"Schulté. You're next. The Mirage is prepped and ready." With that, he turns to his next order of business, and there's not a second to waste.

"No, Capitaine," Jacki says, catching de Corvette off guard, his head snapping back. She knows he's not used to arguing, but he's also not accustomed to a nuclear attack on his homeland. "I need the Transall C-160. With respect, Capitaine." Jacki nods toward the bus-like transport aircraft nearby.

"The Transall?" de Corvette says, thoroughly confused. "I need you in a jet."

"I will save many more lives this way," Jacki says. "I need to bring these men and our ground vehicle."

De Corvette's gaze lingers on the members of the Phoenix Elite. He stares her down as if issuing a silent challenge. She doesn't blink. Even in this chaos, her commanding officer had to remember the last order he gave her: to follow through on an order above his pay grade, sending her on a supersonic jet into the unknown. Although not without his warts, de Corvette's memory was unblemished, and she knows he holds his protégé in high regard.

After a tense moment, de Corvette relents. "Okay, Lieutenant. Get your ass up there."

Jacki salutes him. "Yes sir."

Ten minutes later, the hose is disconnected from a fueling truck, and the Wagon drives up the back ramp of the Transall C-160.

Jacki eases herself into the pilot's seat. Her usually composed mind bears a load she's not accustomed to carrying. From a pocket in her tactical suit, she retrieves a picture of Hugo smiling toothlessly before the breath-taking backdrop of the Alps. Though it's been hours since she survived the descent she can't comprehend, her mind and soul remain caught in a disorienting free fall. She spent years building a fortress around herself, seeking simplicity as a means to survive. But somewhere in the sky, her once-impenetrable fortress crumbled into dust. Every breath she takes is because of a miracle, because of her guardian angel. She tucks Hugo's photo into a crack in the dash, a comforting reminder to fight like hell.

Jacki tinkers with knobs and dials, doing her best to navigate the unfamiliar layout of the Transall cockpit. It may not mirror the configuration of her jet, but she knows that every crucial control must be here somewhere.

Brandon's fingers stray to a dial near the copilot seat, triggering a beeping sound. "Whoopsie," he says. "Kinda sensitive, eh?" Jacki corrects his error but chooses not to bury him underneath a pile of insults. Today, she's feeling charitable. With the twists, turns, and taps of her controls, the mighty engine fires up.

"So, you don't think the US will be a bit peeved that we're gonna waltz into their airspace when terrorists are bombing cities?" Brandon asks.

"Let me worry about that," Jacki says.

Ascending into the sky, the Transall rises over the remains of Paris. Rubble blankets the city. No green. No brown. No people. Only dust. The City of Lights, her home, is vanquished. A gigantic, disfigured iron corkscrew lies atop demolished buildings. The leftovers of the Eiffel Tower.

While Brandon soaks in the carnage, Jacki averts her eyes. She won't look at her city in that condition for another second. "Can you give me their coordinates?"

CHAPTER 55
LAMBS TO SLAUGHTER

ADAM AND THE OTHERS secure themselves to a retractable bench, which quivers beneath them as the plane steadily gains altitude. The Wagon creaks before them in the cargo bay but, fortunately, stays firmly planted. As the aircraft soars, new posts from ARK flash across their iGlasses, threatening to cast an even more melancholy shadow over their mission:

WELCOME HOME #REUNIONS CONDOLENCES TO PARIS.

THE FLOOD IS COMING. WE START ANEW. #COUNTDOWN.

Everyone else in the cargo bay is in a daze. The prospect of what they are about to do is settling in. "We might be too late," Adam says. He can barely hear his own voice over the rumble.

Nigel, wrestling with a thought, whips out his phone and unbuckles his seat belt. Whatever is bothering him, he can't take it anymore. The rest of the group watches him, puzzled by his sudden urgency.

"What are you doing?" Carlos asks.

"Just taking care of some business," Nigel replies cryptically as he rises from his seat.

Carlos makes a grab for the phone. A wave of tension ripples through the cargo bay, and Adam fears he may have to separate the two at thirty thousand feet.

Nigel dodges Carlos's hand, but Guowei snatches the phone. After studying the screen himself, he turns it to face the others. It is the webpage for the US Department of Defense.

"Look, we've taken this as far as we can," Nigel says. "We need professionals. It's on their turf! Let them nuke the hell out of it themselves!"

"And what about the boy?" Hala asks.

"He's just one kid!" Nigel says. "We're talking about cities here. Think about it! Let the US deal with their problem!"

"What if they're behind it?" Guowei asks.

Nigel dismisses the notion with a shake of his head. "That's ridiculous," he says. "You're talking about the United States. You don't think we can trust them?"

Hala interjects firmly. "Only trust one another."

"They spend trillions hunting terrorists," Carlos replies, "and they can't find them in their own backyard."

"I mean, it's not like the terrorists, you know, come out and say, hey, we're gonna do some terrorism now," Adam interjects.

"I understand. I'm just sayin'," Carlos says. "They look where they wanna look. I don't trust that."

Nigel shakes his head. "We're talking about the end of the world, and you honestly think we're the best people to handle this situation?"

An uncomfortable silence descends upon them, each grappling with the weight of Nigel's lingering question. It's impossible to know the right way to go. Even though Nigel voiced it, Adam suspects they've all contemplated the same uncertainty.

Guowei breaks the silence, a resolute determination in his voice. "I will see it through to the end. Kebe asked us to do this. Everyone else agrees."

"He said we needed seven for a reason," Hala says. "This is why we're here."

"If this is the end, I'm happy to serve with you all," Adam says. "In a really bizarre way, we're kinda like, uh, brothers and sisters. I've never had . . . well, anyone." He can't remember the last time he spent this much time with the same group of people.

"Don't talk like that," Hala says. "We'll make it. We can end it."

"Oh, it's gonna be the end all right," Carlos says, the comment jabbing Adam in the gut. The last thing he wants to hear is such a grim sentiment, especially from Carlos.

"We're walking dead. Lambs to slaughter," Carlos continues. "You don't put your hand in the beehive and not get stung." He gazes at his own calloused fingers. "But if you know who you are, where you come from, and what you stand for, it don't matter what they're gonna do to you. You gotta take your stand." Carlos stretches his neck a little. A mix of tears and fire swirls in his eyes as he speaks. "A warlord pushing drugs into your little brother's veins. Some wannabe thug taking his shot at your sister behind the school. A whacked-out psycho who wants to blow up the world. It don't matter. You go to war together. Brothers and sisters. Even if they kill your people, you push on. Do your thing. You pay your respects later. We're gonna find those bastards in their hole and blast the shit out of them, not because we might win but because it's the goddamn right thing to do. There's seven of us. We push hard enough, long enough, and we might make it to the queen bee. End her reign."

An odd sensation runs through Adam's body, one he'd imagine would be better served if an enemy were in front of him to fight.

"I thought it was some nonsense crossfire, eh?" Nigel says.

"We got who we wanted," Carlos replies with a penetrating gaze. Nigel grins, acknowledging Carlos's point.

"We might be able to increase our chances . . ." Guowei offers, seeking someone with whom to engage in thoughtful deliberation.

"All right, I'll play," Nigel responds. "Care to share?"

"A strategy," Guowei says. "If a rook guards the king, you lure the rook away, distract it from its defensive responsibilities."

"You gonna use your pawns, Grand Master?" Carlos asks.

"Of course, it all begins with strong pawn structure," Guowei grins.

"So, what are you proposing?" Nigel asks.

"A trade," Guowei says, his grin widening. "Something of value. A sacrifice. And they walk right in." He locks eyes with Carlos as if silently conveying a shared understanding.

Adam's gaze sweeps across the cargo bay, searching for inspiration among the surrounding objects. Even if one of them can get in, sneaking the other six into a secured base will be challenging.

Adam's eyes land on Hala's hijab, adorned with a crown, and then to the Wagon. A spark of something takes hold in his mind. "What if we all drive right in?"

Adam, Guowei, Hala, and Carlos bounce ideas off one another. They unbuckle and explore the cargo bay, considering items that might be useful. It's the first time they've had a chance to think. Adam relishes the electric energy among the group.

But Nigel takes all of it in from the outside. Caught up in some thought, he zones out, staring aimlessly. As the group delves deeper into their discussions, Adam wonders whether they have all seven after all.

CHAPTER 56
ROLE PLAYERS

THE STARLIT SKY stretches before them, a serene backdrop to their long journey. The Atlantic Ocean is wide. Brandon pulls his gaze from the endless horizon to his pilot, Jacki, her profile bathed in the soft glow of moonlight. He can't help but notice the picture of the boy she propped up on the instrument panel.

Jacki's guarded nature seems to have been pushed ajar. Maybe she hit her head when she fell from that cloud? Brandon has flirted terribly, so for now he decides to be a regular human person—as regular as he can manage.

"He's a cutie," Brandon says.

"Thanks," Jacki says. "He was." Brandon's heart sinks. Was that a sensitive topic? After a brief pause, Jacki turns toward him and adds, "He is."

Just then, Adam pokes his head between Jacki and Brandon. He excitedly passes a folded sheet of paper to Brandon. "Check this out."

Brandon unfolds the sheet of paper. It's a rough pencil diagram of a cover that sits atop the Mandela Wagon. "It's . . . brilliant," he says, unable to contain his admiration. "Was this Guowei's idea or . . . ?"

"You think we can do this?"

"I'm Benjamin Franklin. I'll build you a freakin' zoo if you want me to."

Over the next few hours, the cargo bay of the Transall becomes a bustling hub of activity. The Phoenix Elite work tirelessly on the construction of the supersize contraption. Screwdrivers, socket sets, nuts, and bolts are strewn about the cargo bay in disorganized madness. Any tool the French military had on hand for repairs finds a place on the floor. Brandon sifts through it all for just the right piece. He doesn't know what that piece is yet, but he'll know it when he sees it.

Meanwhile, Adam scavenges whatever he can from the Wagon. If it's not welded to the frame, it becomes a candidate for the growing junk pile on the floor. Seats, rearview mirrors, and even the spare tire are relinquished to their new purpose. "Hey," he says to Brandon, nodding toward a six-foot aluminum ladder hooked to the cargo bay wall. The glimmer of inspiration in Adam's eye is contagious, and Brandon's mind races with possibilities.

Hala hands Brandon her crown. She unlocks the pattern, and the flowing cloak flutters from it. She explains the process of achieving invisibility. As he spreads the fabric out, aiming to find the perfect center line, he pauses to ask, "Is it okay if I make some modifications?"

"Whatever it takes," Hala says. "I was once a forgotten queen. Now I guess I have no choice but to be seen."

With a pair of scissors in hand, Brandon pauses. "So I can cut it or . . . ?"

"Yep," Hala says. "Snip, snip away."

With a wave of apprehension, Brandon positions the scissors, his hand trembling slightly. "This has to be worth a cool five billion," he says before cutting into the fabric.

Carlos and Nigel grab hold of the corners, stretching the fabric taut. Guowei, armed with a tape measure, assesses the dimensions. "Roughly four meters by five," he says, allowing the tape measure to roll shut.

Brandon ruminates silently through calculations and conversions until he reaches a point of surrender. "So in feet that's . . . ?"

After hours of diligent labor and unwavering focus, the cargo bay stands empty, as if the Wagon had vanished into thin air. A sense of accomplishment washes over the group.

"It's beautiful," Adam says.

"Did we do the fabric proud, old lady?" Guowei asks.

"Oh yes. I don't think they'll see us coming," Hala says. "If it's good for my people, it's good for me. Is that what a queen would say?"

"Depends," Carlos says. "But in your case, I think it hits the mark."

Brandon pops his head triumphantly from the sunroof of the invisible Wagon. "Booyah! I like what I saw today. And I really like what I don't see today."

Suddenly, the airplane jolts violently, and a heartbeat later, jubilance transforms into frantic scrambles. The once-solid ground gives way beneath Brandon's feet. Gravity plays tricks on his senses, spinning his world into disarray. Panic gushes through his veins, a cold grip tightening around his thoughts, making it difficult to find solid ground amidst the swirling chaos.

A sharp bank to the left sends the team spiraling into the invisible shield of the Wagon, which slips from Brandon's grasp and slams against the rigid hull of the cargo bay with a crunch.

Carlos leans toward the cockpit. "What's going on?!"

CHAPTER 57
UNDER FIRE

***W**HAT ISN'T GOING ON?* The blip streaks across her monitor like a comet.

With a map of the United States on a dashboard monitor, Jacki crosses the threshold into US airspace through the Gulf of Mexico. She stretches her shoulders and cracks her knuckles, preparing for the upcoming performance. It's showtime.

Jacki takes evasive maneuvers through the swampy forest, triaging like a medic in a war zone. Bullets ricochet off the rugged exterior of the aircraft.

"Under fire!" Jacki shouts. She banks left between a pair of cypress trees and dives low. They're going to need more appropriate ammo to pierce the Transall. The aircraft leaves the sea behind and glides over Louisiana's bayous, kilometers upon kilometers of marshlands and swamp forests. Jacki adjusts the altitude, maneuvering the massive machine low enough to make out the intricate details of the landscape below, determined to stay beneath the radar.

The Transall C-160 zips over a fishing boat, whose workers startle at its colossal shadow and thunderous noise. "Bonjour, mon ami," Jacki murmurs.

A missile blazes by, missing them by mere meters and disappearing into the marshland below. The water erupts like a geyser.

That's more appropriate ammo.

Barely keeping his balance, Brandon flops into the cockpit. "Who would've guessed the US would be protective of their airspace?" he says. "Oh yeah, me."

Jacki doesn't bat an eye. "You can dodge the radar but can't dodge the eyes. I'm surprised we got this far inland. I should be able to get us on the ground in a minute or two." She banks hard to the right, pushes the yoke forward to dive low, and initiates the landing gear.

A boom rings in her ears. The entire plane shudders under the impact of a massive force. Buttons across her dashboard beep wildly and light up like a slot machine.

"Buckle up!" she yells to the back.

CHAPTER 58
TURBULENCE

HALA CLUTCHES THE FABRIC of the foldout seats, her knuckles burning white as she tries to anchor herself amidst the tumult. A bitter wind howls through the gaping hole in the side of the aircraft. Leftover tools and debris become projectiles, succumbing to the suctioning jaws of a beast whose deafening howl threatens to drown out all thought.

Nigel's clasp fails him, and he plunges toward the hole. He flails for anything. He misses.

Fear grips Hala, but there's no time to think. She lets go of her seat and slides toward Nigel. Her knee slams against the Wagon's front tire, but she wraps her legs around it and extends her arm blindly back into the treacherous vortex. Nigel grabs her hand, jostling her body, threatening to dislodge her from her tenuous position.

Adam's voice booms above the tempest. "We have to seal the hole! Guowei!"

Guowei struggles against the powerful vortex and crawls toward his sticky-foam crossbow on the opposite side of the plane. Each gust of turbulence pushes the weapon further away. With a stretch, he narrowly pinches it between his fingers and inches it back.

Hala's knee weakens, her grip loosening, and Nigel edges perilously closer to the gaping hole. She tries to tighten her hold. She can't. Only the interlocking of her ankles prevents her from being torn away. The aircraft suddenly descends. A heavy pressure settles in Hala's head. Her arms go numb as the sensation spreads. Her vision blurs.

The plane stabilizes, giving everyone a chance to gather themselves. Hala desperately tries to improve her grip. If she can pull her knee behind the tire, she can stabilize herself. Bad idea. Her left foot slips, leaving only her right ankle wedged around the wheel, the last line of defense preventing her and Nigel from plummeting out of the plane. Nigel's shoes dangle from the edge of oblivion. Her foot wavers.

And then, as if by some unseen force, she feels buoyed, supported. Glancing downward, she sees Carlos beneath the car, clutching her foot within the crook of his arm, his body wrapped around the tire.

Hala pulls with everything she has, but the minutes she's held on are wearing on her. Her muscles scream in protest as if they are being ripped off the bone—and Nigel's grip is getting slippery. She tries activating the glove on Nigel's hand with her pattern. It doesn't work. He looks at her with hopeless eyes; he knows the end is near.

Nigel's grip slips through her fingers.

His legs slide out of the hole.

A tortured cry escapes Hala's lips, and she closes her eyes in sheer terror, unwilling to witness her teammate fall from the plane. Her racing mind doesn't let her offer even a hasty prayer. She is consumed by the fear that a similar fate awaits her.

But when Hala summons the courage to reopen her eyes, there he is. Nigel's lower half still dangles from the hole, but his right arm is fused to the fuselage with sticky foam.

Gasping for air, the sticky-foam crossbow in his hands, Guowei lays his head on the cabin floor.

The brief rest is broken by a massive thud.

CHAPTER 59
HOLD IT TOGETHER

RIVULETS OF SWEAT trace paths down Jacki's face, navigating the tension cracked in her forehead. *Hold it together, hold it together.* She's not sure whether she's referring to the plane or herself. She struggles with the controls. The pressure is getting to her. Her moves aren't crisp. Her reflexes are delayed.

"I need you, boy," Jacki whispers, glancing at Hugo's picture on the dash.

The landing gear is ready. All she needs is a flat stretch of earth—any flat stretch of earth. But with kilometers of marshland ahead of her, Jacki realizes that a water landing might be their only option. That choice would render their ground vehicle useless.

A giant cypress tree rises quickly into view. Jacki yanks the yoke back, and the plane shudders under the strain, avoiding the imposing trunk by centimeters.

A glimmer of hope emerges on the horizon—a small parcel of farmland.

A wheel of the smoking Transall bounces off the grass. Jacki's concentration is absolute as she battles to maintain control, holding the yoke steady. They touch down and barrel toward the farmhouse ahead. Jacki shifts as much as she can, but she can only hope it will be enough. The flaps strain against the wind. The plane slows down some, but the farmhouse and anyone inside will be demolished at this speed.

She wrenches the controls as far to the left as possible, willing the plane to defy fate. By the slimmest of margins, the wing skirts past the farmhouse and plows into the cornfield behind it. The cabin floor vibrates as it jolts through the uneven, rutty terrain until, finally, coming to a complete stop.

Jacki and Brandon hurry into the cargo bay. "They have eyes on us," she says. "We have to move."

A huddle forms around Nigel, who is stuck to the floor caked under a layer of Guowei's white foam. Helpless, he looks at Jacki and Brandon. "I'm gonna be a minute."

Guowei jabs a section of the foam with a crowbar, but it doesn't budge.

Carlos taps Adam's bazooka. "Any ideas?"

"Yeah, that won't work," Adam says. "We need something strong enough to break that compound."

Jacki's eyes dart around the cargo bay for a solution amid the deafening roar of military jets overhead. They cannot afford to waste any time. They have seconds, not minutes, before the US military's ground forces close in on their position.

"Your glove!" Guowei shouts. "If it can bash through concrete, it's our best chance. Let me see it."

"You mind using the left?" Nigel asks. "My right is occupied at the moment."

"I'm left-handed," Guowei says.

"Now, I'm just letting you borrow it," Nigel says. Guowei takes off his glove and holds it for Nigel to unlock it.

As he pulls it on, Guowei stretches his index finger to activate the hard mode. He drops to one knee to position himself and throws a thunderous hammer fist onto the hardened foam. The metal paneling rattles, and a crack spirals from the point of contact.

"Wow," Brandon says. "Maybe he should have the super gloves and you get the glue shooter."

"No, those are mine," Nigel smiles. "I ain't trading." Another smash from Guowei, and the foam shatters. Nigel pulls his arm free, but his other glove is coated with the stubborn substance.

"Hurry! We have to move!" Jacki swings the passenger door of the Wagon open, her eyes searching for an escape route through the farmland.

"Jacki," Brandon says, holding out a cardboard box in his outstretched hands.

"We don't have time to do this right now," Jacki snaps incredulously.

"I wanted to give you something."

Jacki peers in the box to find her busted jetpack, with zigzags of soldering and duct tape holding it all together. Despite its rugged appearance, the screens on the handles illuminate with vibrant colors, signaling a full charge. "When did you . . . ?"

"It was a long flight," he says, a flicker of mischief dancing in his eyes. "You belong in the air."

Jacki's heart unexpectedly swells with appreciation, a genuine smile breaking through the tension on her face. "Thank you," she says. "Now get your ass in the Wagon."

"Yes ma'am."

CHAPTER 60
SACRIFICE

AS THE WAGON ZIPS along the Louisiana interstate, cutting through the forested heart of New Orleans toward Yusef's location, Adam monitors their journey using the GPS map on his iGlasses. Carlos hugs the shoulder and maintains a cautious speed, but the conspicuous ladder and wire frame attached to the roof draw the attention of passing drivers. In his brainstorming of the device, Adam overlooked the logistics of transporting it. Sensing the need to evade prying eyes, they take the next exit to try their luck on the backroads.

"Got something big," Brandon says. "I fed Firebird Yusef's coordinates, and it sent this back."

The new photo of the compound loads onto Adam's iGlasses, an overhead image of a nondescript compound on a few acres of land near the mouth of the Mississippi River. The building has a footprint three or four times larger than a typical family home adjacent to a gigantic garage.

ARK hiding in plain sight.

A new ARK post on Adam's display pops up, momentarily distracting him: Los Angeles. Tokyo. More to come. #findyourark. He swiftly discards the message. They have one job to do.

"It was my assumption that the base will have some sort of security perimeter, if not multiple layers on the outside," Guowei says.

"The aerial images support that," Jacki replies. "I see a gate about twenty meters from the building."

Adam squints, attempting to decipher a minute detail near the building's entrance. Is it a computer entry of some kind? A thumbprint or retina scanner? He clicks through a few photos and zooms in. "Look near the door . . ." he says. "I don't know . . . what is that?"

"It looks like these guys are stuck back in 2014 with their number-pad entry lock," Brandon says. "Poor saps."

"If we make a sacrifice, they will have to open those gates. That will be our opening," Guowei says.

Hala, caught off guard, asks, "Wait, who agreed that'd we be making a sacrifice?"

Guowei nods solemnly. "If we are all going to get in, we must lure ARK out. It has to be a good reason."

"So what do we have to give them?" Hala asks.

"That's the question," Guowei says. "Nobody keeps all the pieces on their board. We won't win without losing something."

Deep within, Adam feels a sense of kinship with these individuals—these are his brothers and sisters. "Me," he says. "It has to be me."

"What? No," Hala says. He doesn't flinch. "No, you can't be serious. It's not going to be any of us. We will win or lose together."

Locking eyes with Guowei, Adam senses an unspoken understanding between them. "Then we won't win," Guowei says. "We have to offer them something they want to achieve a more advantageous position. Splitting up will improve our chances. The deeper we can get someone in, the better. It's our best move."

"Whoa, who's making that call?" Carlos asks. "You really think our smartest move is giving them our Einstein?"

"Yeah, when you say it out loud, it sounds like a terrible idea," Brandon replies.

"Give them Franklin," Carlos says.

"Wait! What?"

"He's like Diet Einstein," Carlos says with a smirk. "He would be useful to them."

"That's a good point," Jacki adds, sharing a sideways smile with Carlos.

"Or we tease Einstein and give 'em Franklin," Carlos continues.

"Hey, hey, hey, people. I'm right here," Brandon interjects.

"Ah, the good ol' bait and switch," Nigel says. "I can dig that.

"Benjamin Franklin would be a truly extraordinary asset!" Brandon says animatedly, like he's been blasted with a concoction of turkey spirit and lightning. "I won't stand idly by and allow you to besmirch his name on American soil."

"So you agree he'd be a worthy sacrifice?" Jacki asks.

"Hey! I—" Brandon begins. "I suppose that's the position I just argued."

"It has to be me," Adam says. "Bricker came for me years ago; he might want me now. And even if they don't need me now, they want my bazooka. If it needs to be one of us . . . if one of us has to surrender . . ." Adam considers the swirling swarm of thoughts that overwhelm him minute to minute, but this swarm ends with Margot's face. "I'm glad it's me. It's why I'm here. I'm not afraid of what they'll do to me. I've got one shot left, and I'll take it if I can."

"You don't have to do this," Hala replies. "There has to be another way."

"You have some nuts on you, *mijo*," Carlos says.

"I don't know about that," Adam says. "I've got nothing to lose. I've lost everything already. Except for you all. And this is the only way I might not." The Wagon falls into an eerie silence. Adam finds it difficult to imagine a life without these people. When the week began, it wasn't an outcome he would have predicted.

The finality of Jacki's voice breaks the silence. "Well then, it's settled."

Jacki navigates Carlos to a bridge spanning the mighty Mississippi River, kilometers upstream from its convergence with the Gulf of Mexico. They pass a sign that welcomes visitors to PHOENIX, LOUISIANA—POPULATION 23,515.

"You're kiddin'," Carlos says.

"Ironic," Jacki replies.

Phoenix? Adam supposes Bricker is either sentimental or truly infatuated with burning the world to the ground. It certainly isn't an accident.

Two white churches bookend the dirt road down the center of this small town, and there is not a restaurant or gas station in sight. The paved road toward their destination stretches into a lush swamp forest. Zooming in with his iGlasses, Adam can see the heavy-duty gate and detects the heat signals of likely guards.

Beyond the gate sits an unassuming log cabin. "Wait here," Jacki says as the Wagon creeps to a stop.

CHAPTER 61
RIGHTEOUS MAN

AS TWO FIGURES ENTER the command center, a screen transitions from the map to Bricker's live stream. His smile widens with uncontainable delight. The color-coordinated bookshelf behind him has never looked brighter. He can't contain his joy as his life's work comes to fruition. The world will soon be a better place.

The wall of high-resolution security screens surrounds this central monitor, where red circles pulsate around targets on a world map. Shanghai and Paris flash red, and the cities up next flash blue. It's all a reminder that brighter days are ahead for all. Miniature drone submarines blink from the depths of all the world's oceans, and six more are poised and ready in the Gulf of Mexico.

Zed holds Yusef's hand, guiding him closer to the screen. "My boy!" Bricker says. "Your father has missed you dearly. You wouldn't believe how hard I've tried to find you all these years." Yusef gazes up at the screen but remains silent.

"He's a shy one," Zed says. He playfully tousles his hair, knocking Yusef off-balance.

Bricker scrutinizes Yusef's appearance. Did he do it? Is this who he thinks it is? Will he turn the page to humanity's next chapter with the Son of God by his side, under his tutelage? Will the boy grow to appreciate his efforts to make the world a better place? He finds it hard to throttle his excitement.

"We'll soon see if you've been worth all this trouble," Bricker tells Yusef. It's a loaded sentiment he does not expect Yusef to understand. "And then we will shoot off some fireworks. Do you like surprises? You see that cabinet with a green sticker on it?" Yusef doesn't move. "Come here. Don't be afraid of Daddy."

Zed nudges Yusef forward. "Don't you like presents?" Bricker asks.

Timidly, Yusef reaches for the knob on the green cabinet. Within, he finds the small flat present wrapped in plain red paper and adorned with a green bow.

"Go ahead, open it" Bricker encourages him. Yusef rips the paper. It's a book: *The Story of Noah's Ark*. On the cover, pairs of smiling cartoon animals pile aboard a large wooden boat. "Do you know that story?" Bricker asks. "Noah was a righteous man."

"Father," Zed interjects, staring into a security monitor. A motorbike has pulled up to the main security gate of the compound. Its riders then speed away, vanishing into the trees. Suddenly, a massive explosion rocks the earth around them.

"They're here," Zed says.

"Dammit!" Bricker smashes his fist into his desk. Yusef trembles with fear. Bricker notices and adjusts his tone.

"The bad guys are here. We have to hurry our little experiment with you." He opens his messaging app: @ARK911 IT'S TIME—JB.

Bricker changes a screen to the drone subs underwater, a sight that always makes him smile. "You wanna see some fishies?" he asks Yusef.

A new post: @THEREALNOAH ABOUT TEN MINUTES.

Bricker changes another screen to a computer interface with only one button: LAUNCH ALL. He guides the cursor over it. "If you do a good job. I'll let you push the button."

CHAPTER 62
STEALTHINESS

BRANDON PINCHES THE LUXURY LEATHER steering wheel of the Mandela Wagon as he maneuvers through the imposing gates. The spacious paved area before the cabin has enough room for a semi-truck to execute a U-turn. Brandon's years of running track have paid off, granting him such finesse in gently easing the accelerator, nudging forward inch by inch. He thinks quiet thoughts: James Bond squinting under the tender embrace of the morning sun. Jason Bourne feeling a baby's breath ruffle his arm hair. John Wick reaching Zen in a yoga routine. Jack Reacher stirring from a well-deserved afternoon nap.

A thundering fleet of motorcycles erupts from the gate. They zip off the pavement and onto the marshy soil, chasing down Adam and Carlos. By Brandon's hip, Nigel maneuvers the invisibility screen as he stands through the sunroof. The winds of the bikes' whizzing velocity ripple through the screen, sputtering water on it as they go, threatening to blow their cover. At that moment, Brandon realizes he is exhaling too sharply through his nose, the stiff breeze jostling his nose hairs, threatening to shatter their concealed presence.

Guowei's hushed voice brushes against his ear. "Quicker, quicker."

Brandon presses the accelerator without his trademark finesse, and he jars the Mandela Wagon. Nigel teeters from the sudden acceleration.

"Not like that," Guowei says.

A rebel sniper aims from his perch on the highest branches of a water tupelo. His rifle points indiscriminately in their direction before he raises a walkie to his helmet. The hefty gates begin to crank shut. They have to make it through, and they're only halfway there.

A soft whooshing sound pulses rhythmically. Where is it coming from? Brandon inspects the surroundings, searching for the source of the mysterious noise.

Nigel ducks into the Wagon. "Bro, turn off the wipers!" he whispers urgently.

Oh God. Brandon must have inadvertently triggered them. He grabs the handle, but he clicks on his turn signal. *Eek!* Wrong handle. With gritted teeth, he swiftly resets everything.

The gates snap shut behind them. They made it. Brandon's heart pounds, his relief mingling with a lingering unease.

The treetop sniper peers through his scope in their direction. But can he see them? He mechanically peers around the area. The stoic sentinel displays no signs of alarm. Eventually, the man diverts his attention, shifting his focus in another direction.

Now all they can do is wait. And not turn on the windshield wipers.

CHAPTER 63
ASHES

*T*HEY BIT.

Adam and Carlos tear through a bayou hiking trail on his motorbike. The marshland sputters water as the tires struggle for traction. Bullets slice through the air and pummel the trees around them. The rebels are in pursuit, a lot of them. Precisely what Adam was hoping to see.

On his iGlasses map, the FRANKLIN, MANDELA, HATSHEPSUT, and KHAN markers move past the gate. Also precisely what he was hoping to see.

Carlos cranks into another gear and weaves around a puddle. "Where you wanna land, *mijo*?" he shouts over the engine's roar.

Adam has never jumped off a moving motorbike before. The bogs around him all look similarly soft and squishy. The rebels gain ground, and decision time is imminent. "I mean, I don't know—"

Before he can finish his sentence, a stray bullet strikes his back and knocks him from the motorbike. He lands against jagged rocks. Disoriented, he comes to a complete stop face down in a puddle, his torso ablaze with pain. That could've gone better. A parade of revving engines whooshes by. Clutching his throbbing elbow, Adam rolls over to see a trio of rebels standing over him.

He scrambles for his bazooka, but it's ripped off his shoulder. "This is the one Z really wanted," one of them says, pressing a heavy boot into Adam's back.

They cuff him. Adam doesn't resist—it's all part of the plan.

After a short jeep ride back to the ARK base, six rebels escort Adam through the gate and toward the building. He hopes his battered body will hold up, because cooperation is his ticket to infiltrating the facility as deeply as possible. But the worst, he's sure, is yet to come.

"Pretty cool," says the rebel whose shoulder Adam's bazooka now adorns.

They march Adam to what initially appears to be the wooden front door of the cabin, but his iGlasses pick up on eight inches of steel reinforcement and an intricate electronic system concealed beneath the facade. A message from Hala appears on his iGlasses: GOOD LUCK. WE WILL COME HELP SOON. Adam doesn't dare look for any sign of the Wagon on his way. His GPS indicates his teammates are nearby, but if his eyes wander in that direction, it might attract rebel attention. With tunnel vision on the entry, the card reader and number pad from the surveillance photographs are within his sight.

A rebel pats himself down and locates his swipe card. "I swear I'm gonna lose this thing." With the ID card in view, Adam angles his head to get a better look, hoping his quick glance is enough. The rebel waves his ID across a scanner and then moves to input a passcode that has six blank lines. Adam strains his neck, yearning for a better angle to see the code. But another rebel seizes him by the hair before he can and yanks his scalp back. "What are you lookin' at?" They twist his neck, turning his head away. He struggles against the grip, fighting to catch the last digit. He can't.

Pangs of anxiety shoot through his gut. However long he was going to be inside on his own will now stretch even further.

The reader accepts the code. The automatic door swings open, and a shadowy interior looms. Adam is led by rebels across the hardwood floors of a cozy family sitting room and a welcoming scent of pine. Adam desperately tries to capture every cubic meter of his surroundings, hopeful that the live stream of his unauthorized tour will provide vital intelligence for the team. Sections of the wooden paneling have been slid open, exposing three hallways—one to the left, one to the right, and one straight ahead. The rebels steer him down the middle corridor, which he suspects leads to the expansive garage behind the cabin. Along the hallway, windows look out over the bayou and its forest of bald cypresses.

Traversing the worn wooden floor of the hallway, Adam notices fresh motorcycle scuff marks leading directly into a bare wall fashioned with rectangular wood molding. Extremely odd. A rebel taps a camouflaged button along the trim, causing the entire wall to slide into the floor to reveal an enormous freight elevator. Now the tracks make more sense.

The rebels toss Adam inside, and he stumbles to the ground. They drop his bazooka at his feet. One rebel steps inside to press a button but steps out. It looks like Adam will make the descent alone.

The doors close, and the elevator cranks to life.

But they left him alone with his bazooka. He rolls over to his stomach and struggles to stand up, the handcuffs making the simple task a balancing act. Eventually, he makes it to his feet. Despite possibly being able to unlock his weapon, it quickly becomes obvious he can't physically pick it up to use it. Unlocking it is what they are after, and he can't risk falling into a trap, especially with the elevator potentially stopping at any moment.

On his iGlasses, the D'ARC and GUEVARA markers move along the map while all the others remain static. If they've been captured, or worse, his fate is all but sealed.

Descending through seemingly endless layers of sediment, the elevator finally grinds to a halt in front of a door embedded in the earth. Adam breathes in the chillier, musty air, every nerve ending crackling with apprehension.

The door opens with a creak and a ding. A giant waits for him on the other side. With his three-barreled pistol in hand, Zed steps onto the elevator with an eerie calmness. "Going down?" Zed asks, as if they were at the mall. Together, they quietly descend farther, the chains of the freight elevator groaning foot by foot.

Zed holsters his pistol and bends over to pick up the bazooka. His fingers trace its sleek design, indulging in the tactile sensation of the carbon-fiber casing. He fiddles with the screen lock. "Quite a toy, isn't it?" he asks.

"It's incredibly dangerous."

Zed playfully aims the bazooka at Adam, his intentions veiled in menace. "To be honest," he says, removing his ski glasses to peer through the weapon's sight, "this is the only reason I want you alive. Kaboom." He mimics the recoil of the bazooka, and an uneasy huff escapes Adam's lips. "I can't wait for you to unlock it for me."

With his ski glasses off, Zed's side profile and soulful gray eyes are familiar. Why does Adam recognize him? He hastily activates the facial recognition feature on his iGlasses, but the result is inconclusive.

The elevator shudders to a halt.

The second level is an underground weapons silo and sprawling laboratory. A putridity of rotting meat stings Adam's nostrils; above him hangs an overflowing aquarium littered with thousands of dead fish. The living feast on the dead. The sight disgusts him, but he suspects that's the point.

Adam's breath snags as he beholds the rows upon rows of thermonuclear bombs before him. Millions of lives. Unimaginable destruction. All within eyesight.

As Adam takes in the scene, his eyes are drawn to the nearby cranes, their mechanical arms lowering submarines onto flatbed trucks affixed with metal guardrails and covered with tarps to conceal their lethal payload. The submarine, once a symbol of exploration and adventure, has long been perverted into an instrument of warfare, and ARK is taking it to another level. These subs are prepared for their sinister purpose. The juxtaposition of their innocent origins and ominous transformation is a testament to the literal and figurative depths humanity can sink to get what it wants.

"Pretty impressive, ain't it?" Zed says. In a disconcerting gesture of courtesy, Zed motions for Adam to proceed. "After you." As Zed extends his arm, the sleeve of his trench coat slides up, exposing a glimpse of skin.

Zed has a phoenix mark.

CHAPTER 64
LIFT OFF

THE SPRAY OF BULLETS showers Carlos in tree bark. He grits his teeth and plows his motorbike through swampy water. They've chased him for minutes, but he hasn't ceded one centimeter of ground. Bullets ricochet off his suit and rip new holes in the fabric; the fire is heavy and relentless. Sweat cascades down his face, melding with the suffocating humidity of the swamp. Fear and determination clash, and tear at his resolve. If his ticket out of here didn't make it, it must be for good reason—he'll have to find his own way.

But then he spots her, perched within the dense foliage—Jacki, arms open, her wings spread wide like a majestic bird preparing for flight. Carlos deactivates his bike, which folds into its backpack form, and springboards off a fallen tree. He crashes into her, causing her to stagger back, and bear hugs her around her waist.

"You good?" she asks.

"Go!" he shouts, clutching the straps of her jetpack.

As the sound of approaching jeeps and motorcycles grows louder, Jacki blasts off into the sky. The takeoff jars Carlos, and he almost loses his grip instantly. His feet dangle in the sky.

A wave of bullets whizzes past them.

He adjusts his fingers, stabilizing his clench. "Good lookin' out, sister."

"Hold on," she says. Jacki flies higher with a tap of her red button. They soar above the rebel forces and chart a direct course back to the cabin.

CHAPTER 65
ON THE DOORSTEP

BRANDON IS THRILLED that his construction has held up. He watches the treetop sniper perched above through the windshield from the driver's seat. The man peers through binoculars like he's trying to spot trouble miles away, oblivious to the action a few feet below.

Inside the gates and just outside ARK's log cabin, Nigel carefully positions the ladder. Standing through the sunroof, he balances the weight of it and the invisibility screen atop the Mandela Wagon. Then he ducks back inside.

Brandon opens the driver door, wincing at the mouse squeak of its hinges. They should've lubed it up when they had the chance. Hala, Guowei, and Nigel follow him, weapons in hand. They step onto the solid pavement, their shoes making a hushed melody with each delicate footfall. The treetop sniper swings his rifle toward them. He must have heard something.

Their cover is blown.

A blinding flash of crackling white light finds its mark on the sniper's chest. His body crumples gracelessly from the tree and lands with a thud on the soft soil. Triumph surges through Brandon, and he celebrates by blowing on the tip of his taser like it's the barrel of a smoking pistol.

Scurrying past the sniper's incapacitated body, the Phoenix Elite reaches the front door of the log cabin. Guowei shoots a wad of sticky foam onto the security camera's lens while Nigel and Hala keep a watchful eye, pistols at the ready. Meanwhile, Brandon focuses on the card reader, feeling the weight of the task at hand.

He retrieves the small tablet from his pocket. A high-resolution cropped image of the rebel's security badge from Adam's visual stream is on the screen. With trepidation, Brandon waves the barcode from the fabricated card over the laser scanner.

The first try doesn't read it.

Sweat beads on Brandon's palms as he repeats the motion, this time a bit slower. The reader's display changes: SCAN ACCEPTED. ENTER PASSCODE.

"Eight-two-four-nine-eight . . ." Brandon mutters to himself.

"I thought it was nine-*nine*," Guowei says.

Now Brandon is puzzled. "I thought for sure there were two eights."

The rumble of engines reverberates across the bayou.

"Get it together, y'all," Nigel says. "They are going to be back here soon."

"No, it was a nine," Hala interjects. "I just rewatched the video."

"Wait, which nine are we talking about?!" Brandon asks as he slowly loses his grasp on the number system.

"The second nine," Hala says.

"That second eight needs to be a nine," Guowei adds.

"How many eights are there?" Brandon asks. But at this point, what even is an eight? Is eight a number at all, or just a nebulous abstraction? He can feel his pulse throbbing in his temples, certain his blood has never flowed faster in his life.

"It's a nine. Push it," Hala says.

"Hurry the hell up!" Nigel yells.

Brandon punches a nine. "And the last number is . . . ?" he trails off, angling for a suggestion.

"A ten percent chance," Guowei says. Brandon picks six. The screen changes: INCORRECT PASSCODE. RE-SWIPE ID. An "oh God" escapes his lips.

Engines roar, and the noise intensifies as it draws nearer. Brandon rekeys the number pad for what must be the umpteenth time. The pattern has become second nature: eight-two-four-nine-nine . . . but then what?

Nigel loses his patience. "What if y'all got one of those first numbers wrong? What if the password changes?" he asks, leading to a heavy silence. Nigel activates his nano-gloves, his right one still caked in white foam. "I can get us in that door. We are wasting all our time right here."

Brandon knows he's not wrong, but bashing in the door immediately announces their arrival. "Have I tried an eight?" he asks.

"Yes! You just did," Guowei replies.

"All that's left is three, zero, or seven," Hala says.

"Are we still feeling good about that second nine?" Brandon asks, searching for any glimmer of confidence. "On a scale of—"

The rumble builds like encroaching thunder, signaling the rebel's imminent arrival. "They're coming!" Nigel shouts. "Hurry your ass up, or I'm smashing a hole through this wall."

Jeeps emerge from the murky swamp, storming the entry gate. Resigned to the impending failure, Brandon punches the final number—zero.

Passcode Accepted. The latch on the door pops. "Yes!" Hala exclaims as she yanks the door open.

In disbelief, Brandon mutters, "I am the smartest man alive." His brief reverie is shattered by gunfire peppering the cabin's facade. Guowei answers with suppressive fire with his pistol before joining the others inside.

"Seal the door," Nigel says. Guowei trades his pistol for his crossbow as the heavy door slams shut, cutting off the outside world.

On his iGlasses, Brandon grabs an attachment from the Firebird chat thread—an electrical grid outline of the ARK facility and a real-time facility heat map that charts the movement of people inside. With a quick analysis, he identifies three hallways leading from the entryway; all the heat readings point to the right. He motions to the team, and they move swiftly down the sleek hallway with windowed doors on either side. It appears they've stumbled upon rebel dormitories.

"Open this map." Brandon sends it out to the others.

"We'll find the boy," Guowei says. "You two—"

Bang bang!

Guowei is shot in the chest, knocking him back into the wall. He winces, but his armor absorbs the impact. Brandon examines the hall for the source of the gunfire. His iGlasses pick up a pulse from behind a door ten feet down the corridor. "On your left," he says.

Hala returns fire, and bullets fly through the door in both directions. The barrage subsides, and the hall falls into a silence. In the dark dormitory, the rebel lies on the floor with his rifle, dead.

"We have to split up," Hala says. "You two find Adam. We'll find the boy."

Parting from Guowei and Hala, Brandon is guided by the peaking electrical output of the facility, tracing the signal along the school-like wing of the cinder-block building. It leads him to an intersection where a locked door stands before him. "It has to be here."

Nigel smashes through the knob with his nano-gloves. Gun in hand, he kicks the door open. Inside is an empty control room adorned with wall-mounted computers. "Bada bing," Brandon says.

"How do you know these are the right ones?" Nigel asks.

Brandon scrambles to a nearby monitor. "As long as they're on the same network, they're all the right one." He boots the machine up, only to be met with a password prompt. Nigel peers over Brandon's shoulder, the anticipation mounting. "Give me a minute." An ordinary password prompt might be a barrier to a mere mortal, but Brandon has no qualms. He cracks his knuckles.

Nervously, his eyes dart between the screen and the shifting heat map on his iGlasses. A cluster of dots converge as one and start moving through the facility in their direction, three hallways away. It's not an immediate danger, but there's an unsettling vibe as it steadily closes in. "You better move quick," Nigel says.

"Come to Daddy," Brandon taunts the machine. Its feeble resistance won't be a barrier for long, but will it be long enough?

"We don't have time to mess with this. We're supposed to be finding Adam, and Adam isn't in here. Our team could be dying out there."

"This is the only way to stop their missiles," Brandon replies. The decision is clear to him. As much as he'd enjoy not dying, there are seven of them, and these nukes will kill millions if unleashed.

The rebels turn down the first hallway on the heat map, their pace quickening.

"We gotta deal with this first," Nigel says.

"I just need a little more—" Brandon begins, only to hear Nigel leave the room. *Yep, that's not what we talked about.*

With a final click, Brandon successfully infiltrates the guts of the ARK command center application. He gains access to the locations and command of the missiles, but there's no obvious way to bring everything offline.

The rebels turn down the second hallway—the shortest hallway.

Brandon clicks on a missile labeled ATHENS, scheduled to launch. As he delves deeper into the options, he can't figure out how to deactivate it, so he changes the launch date to the year 2222. He should be able to figure it out by then.

Dozens of missiles require his attention. He clicks to BEIJING and hears a rustling outside the door. Is Nigel back?

He glances at his heat map, and a sinking feeling strangles him.

The control room door swings open. Three rebels enter, their rifles aimed directly at him. The room plunges into a smothering silence, broken only by the pounding of Brandon's heart.

CHAPTER 66
RETURN OF THE MONGOLS

WITH HALA BY HIS SIDE, Guowei closes in on a remote heat signal. Through his iGlasses, most heat signals on the map are clustered, but this one is alone and smaller than the rest. In his mind, there's only one person it can be, and Kebe asked him to protect him.

They arrive at the garage door across from the camouflaged freight elevator—the same door Adam saw during his live stream. They cautiously explore the area. The heat signal overlaps with a dead end before them. "It says it's right here," Guowei says in disbelief. "What are we missing?"

Hala looks to the ceiling. "We are in the right place, unless . . ."

"It's underground," they simultaneously conclude.

"Wasn't this the elevator Adam went down?" Guowei says, his fingertips gliding along the rough grain of the weathered wooden molding, searching for any clue. And then one panel feels different from the others. It's smooth and plastic. He presses it, and the elevator comes to life with a low hum.

They exchange a fleeting glance, silently acknowledging the dangers that lie ahead. The doors to the elevator slide open, and a massive armed rebel steps off, armed to the teeth. Another massive armed rebel joins them from the hallway behind them. They are surrounded.

"Stay close," Guowei whispers to Hala. He fires two quick blasts from his crossbow. The rebels raise their guns, but their barrels are covered with wads of sticky foam. The rebels discard the weapons and charge the pair, knocking the crossbow from Guowei's grasp. Guowei smashes one with a crushing left hand, sending their helmet spinning. Hala executes a jumping soccer-style kick to the other's head. The rebels wobble, then discard their damaged helmets.

It's like Guowei is looking in a hall of mirrors. They are both Genghis Khan clones.

The first clone lunges at them. Guowei grabs his wrist before the clone can swing, and with a half turn of his body, he steers the clone's face into the floor. Hala fires her pistol at the second clone, but her shots ricochet off his bulky armor. The clone disarms her with a roundhouse kick but is met with a foot in the face from Guowei.

Guowei wrestles with the first clone. Their strength is nearly identical. Thoughts of his loved ones—his father, mother, and brother—flash through his mind, and a familiar fire rises from deep inside.

Suddenly, he blacks out, and when he comes to, he and Hala are in full Mongol armor. The wooden walls of the ARK base have become the weathered stone of an ancient temple.

With swift brutality, Guowei slams the first clone against the wall, grabs him by the jaw, and bashes his head into the rigid stonework.

The other clone shoves Hala into the wall while Guowei grapples with the first clone. The free clone drives his knee into Guowei's kidneys, sending him to the floor, and punches him in the jaw, rattling his skull.

The clone draws a dagger from his utility belt. Prone on the floor of this ancient stone temple, Guowei's options dwindle to nothingness. Checkmate is imminent. He raises his hands to protect his face. The dagger-wielding clone lunges forward.

In an instant, Hala kicks the man in the head, and he crumples. She unleashes a flurry of kicks at his brother as well.

Guowei's consciousness slips away, plunging him into an abyss of darkness. When his senses gradually return, he finds Hala extending her hand to him. She's back in her tactical gear, the ancient Mongol armor nowhere to be found, and they are in the wooden elevator wing of the ARK base.

He's back in reality. It's a pleasant sight.

She pulls him to his feet, but their respite is brief. Six more identical Genghis Khan clones enter the hallway, armed and poised for battle.

CHAPTER 67
EVERYTHING

ZED WALKS ADAM through a line of thermonuclear warheads, twirling the bazooka with a cowboy's casual swagger. Adam searches the space for any object that might help him escape his handcuffs. On his iGlasses, a YouTube video of a marine shows how to pick them with a hairpin. Conceptually, Adam gets it, but he needs the right tool.

A glass tank embedded in the floor mirrors the aquarium suspended above. Inside the glass tank are captive scientists, bony in their faces, despair in their eyes. Among them, Adam finds no sign of Margot. "How could you?" he asks with trembling lips.

"We had some disobedience," Zed says nonchalantly. "It won't take long until they understand why we do what we do. A little tank time helps them think more clearly."

Adam's eyes dart around a cluttered workstation, where supplies and tools lie in disarray. He spots a ring of hex keys among the mess—the perfect shim. Adam moves discreetly toward the table. His fingertips graze the cool metal of one key, but Zed abruptly redirects him toward a small room. "This way," he says.

The shelves in the room are filled with guns, with boxes of ammo stacked along the wall. Zed places the bazooka atop a chipped mahogany desk adorned only with an old globe, then digs through its drawers.

"Where'd you get that tattoo?" Adam asks.

Zed remains silent, consumed by his search. Adam persists. His words are desperate to gain even a fraction of an advantage. "The one on your wrist," he continues. Any second he can buy is a victory. Zed pauses but continues to ignore him. He resumes his frantic rummaging. "It looks a lot like mine." Zed slams a drawer closed and moves on to another. "A bird rising from ashes."

"I'm just a big fan," Zed finally responds dismissively. "Had it done this morning. You are my hero."

"You should know there's only one more charge in that gun." Adam nods to the bazooka on the desk, hoping to sow a seed of doubt in Zed's mind.

Unfazed, Zed responds with a twisted smirk. "Fortunately, nuclear energy is a strength of ours."

"It's actually plasma."

"Same difference," Zed replies with a dismissive wave.

"Well, not really . . ."

Finally, Zed finds what he's been looking for: a handcuff key. "We don't use these often. Not a lot of visitors," he says. "We'll have to shoot all your friends if they don't cooperate. Maybe test the bazooka on them." A creepy grin spreads across his face as he relishes the thought. He strides over to Adam and presses his three-barreled pistol to his head. "I'll uncuff you. You'll unlock the device and—"

With as much torque as he can muster, Adam smacks Zed across the jaw with his uncuffed hand, sending his ski glasses flying. Zed falls into a heap, clutching his wounded mouth, blood oozing between his fingers.

Adam grabs the bazooka and bolts from the office. Every muscle fiber strains as he races back to the glass tank of imprisoned scientists.

"Where are the controls?!" he yells as he stops above a sea of eager eyes. But the thick glass barrier muffles the scientists' responses. Adam strains to catch their words, deciphering nothing. Undeterred, he repeats his plea, stealing a fleeting glance over his shoulder for any sign of Zed. One of the scientists points down a hallway on the opposite side of the room.

Adam sprints in that direction, his footsteps echoing through the dim, rocky corridor. Any rebels awaiting him certainly will hear him coming, but there's no time. Zed is surely after him, but the big man won't be able to keep his pace. Adam grips his bazooka, readying himself for whatever lies ahead.

Guided by his iGlasses, he follows a heat reading from the tunnel's end. He reaches a state-of-the-art biology lab—spotless white walls, buffed floors, and equipment that would make Nobel laureates blush. He crosses the lab to a set of small glassed-in holding rooms with thick steel doors. ID readers and fingerprint scanners ensure that only authorized personnel have access.

The first room is empty, with no reading on his heat map. Inside the second room is a person curled in a corner. A gaunt woman rests her head on the wall. Her blazer fits loose on her shoulders, and a familiar silver watch dangles from her wrist.

It's Margot.

Silently, she mouths his name, her words dissolving into the thick glass barrier. Adam presses his hand against the cold surface. The light at the end of his tunnel, his reason for enduring. She's here. She's still here. He made it.

I haven't lost everything.

Tears fill his eyes. She speaks to him, but the soundproof space blocks out all the noise—and Adam is a terrible lip reader.

Adam smashes the steel door with the butt of his bazooka. He rams his shoulder into the glass again and again and again. Margot, her hands pressed against the window, provides silent encouragement. Kick after kick, swing after swing, Adam pours every ounce of his strength into it, but he isn't even making a dent.

His frustration reaches a fever pitch. He knows he has one last option. Adam aims his bazooka. It's his last shot. He'd prefer to save it for Bricker, but he'll need to figure that out later.

"Back up!" he yells to Margot.

She's looking not at him but past him, pure terror on her face.

A club crashes down on Adam's skull, a brutal impact that rattles his brain. Black spots swarm his vision, and his body fails, crumpling from the force. He struggles to claw his way back to consciousness, pushing through the overpowering fog, only to find a pair of size sixteen boots and the screen lock of his bazooka thrust in his face.

"Unlock it," Zed says.

A defiant resolve clenches Adam's jaw as he musters the strength to reply, "You'll have to kill me."

Zed rips off his ski cap, wiping his face with it before casually discarding the garment. His edges are fuzzy, but Adam's disorientation gradually steadies. As Zed turns his gaze back to Adam, the flickering light reveals his face in chilling detail for the first time.

Looking down upon Adam is a spitting image of Abraham Lincoln.

"I destroy my enemies when I make them my friends," Zed says, offering Adam his right hand and scratching the corner of his eye with the gun in his left. The gray phoenix mark on his wrist is as clear as day. "Join me, brother—"

Adam kicks Zed square in the jaw. The three-barreled pistol flies from his hands.

Adam scrambles to his feet and charges him, adrenaline propelling through him like a particle collider. He is not leaving this lab without Margot. He rams his shoulder into Zed's stomach, driving him into the concrete wall but bashing his own head in the process. The world spins in disorienting disarray, threatening to devour his senses. He shakes it off.

He sidesteps Zed's lunge and throws a haymaker into his jaw, a punch he had saved for the abductors. Zed rolls with it, absorbing the impact. He just took his best shot. Adam is caught flat-footed. Zed counters and rocks him in the temple. The onslaught escalates to a merciless barrage of strikes to his liver and stomach. The sickening crack of a rib makes his body shudder.

Zed grabs Adam around the neck and yanks his head into his ruthless knee. A concussion vibrates through his skull, his vision slipping in and out. Zed hurls Adam against a table of chemistry glassware like he's a bag of garbage. He writhes in a lake of glass shards.

Reality is setting in: he's not leaving this lab alive.

Zed's silhouette looms over Adam's broken body, casting a shadow that devours the remnants of his strength and will. Straddling him with twisted satisfaction, Zed pummels Adam, his clenched fist a merciless piston. Blood erupts from Adam's face like a geyser, pain throbbing throughout his face. His senses fade away with each strike. His thoughts slow.

And slow.

Until they end.

CHAPTER 68
END OF TIME

UNABLE TO BEAR the horror unfolding, Margot turns away, her heart plummeting into an abyss of despair. The first semblance of hope she's felt in days has been cruelly extinguished, leaving only a scene of unimaginable carnage in its wake. She tracks the seconds with her watch, desperate to count Adam's respiratory rate from his breathing chest. But there's nothing to count. For him to come all this way for this is ghastly. Margot had thought she had already been through hell, but she was only standing at its gates.

The welcoming spirit that once defined Adam's face is now a grotesque tableau of swollen flesh. His lifeless body lies twitching in a pool of his own blood. It is the final sign that his nervous and muscular systems are turning off.

As the tall monster rises to his feet, stretching his bruised fingers, Margot collapses into a ball, her form wracked with tremors. What's left in her dehydrated body streams down her face. The tall monster wags a finger at her, motioning for her to come closer, but she doesn't move a muscle. A mass of pressure radiates through her organs as if her body is shutting down. Not a moment too soon.

The tall monster taps the control panel on her door, his bloodied thumb leaving streaks on its surface. He sets his sights on Margot with diabolical intent, his lips moistened by a lascivious lick. As the monster reaches toward the fingerprint scanner, there's an astonishing movement behind him.

Behind him, a bloody mass wobbles to its feet.

CHAPTER 69
ZOMBIE

THIS AIN'T OVER YET. Through bloodied lips and swollen eyes, Adam manages to mutter, "Where are you going?" His body is overwhelmed with pain; there's no sense in taking inventory of the injuries. Whatever Zed has left to throw at him cannot make it worse.

Stunned and annoyed, Zed walks up to him and delivers a powerful punch square in Adam's face. The force of the blow sends Adam reeling backward; the wall is the only thing keeping him upright. His body loosens upon impact, and he shakes off the grip of rigor mortis. He finds the energy to put his hands up, assuming a fighter's stance.

As long as he has a heartbeat, he's not going anywhere.

Zed stares him down, loading up his next strike. "If I'm being honest, for an Einstein"—Adam flings a wild punch, but Zed dodges it effortlessly and pops Adam in the jaw—"you are one dimwitted fool."

With a quarter turn, Adam slips Zed's next punch, sending his fist into the concrete wall. The bones in his hand crunch. Apparently, that wall is stronger than Adam's skull.

Seizing the moment, Adam slides behind Zed and wraps the handcuffs around his neck. He jumps on his back, pulling with all his might until his back is on the ground, the choking big man falling on top of him. The muscle fibers in Adam's arm part. Zed gasps, desperately trying to pull the handcuffs away, but he can't.

Adam isn't letting go. He can't let go. He won't let go.

Out of options, Zed rolls to his stomach and slides a hand through the choke. He gulps in a couple of clean breaths. Sapped of energy, Adam spots the bazooka a couple of body lengths away. He drops his hold and goes for it.

As Zed scrambles to his feet, Adam reverses course, plants his foot and shatters the cartilage of Zed's nose with his shin, knocking him unconscious instantly.

"Emancipate that, asshole," Adam says, taking in a full, victorious breath of air. He unlocks his bazooka and levels it at the fallen Zed, preparing for a final, decisive shot.

But what about Margot?

He motions for her to move away and aims his bazooka to free her. But he can't pull the trigger. With such little control of the blast, he can't risk it.

His gaze falls upon Zed's three-barreled pistol, loose on the lab floor. Adam grabs it and fires round after round at the glass until a crack spirals from the center. Adam presses his back against the weakened glass, lines up his elbow, and smashes a hole through the window, shattering it to bits.

He reaches his hand out for Margot—and she grabs it. It feels so good. He made it. Tears well up in his eyes, caked with blood.

Adam aims at the unconscious Zed. Though he just bashed him with every body part he has, there's a different feeling about pulling the trigger—even at the guy who just about killed him. Adam closes his eyes and squeezes.

It's out of bullets.

He flings the gun away in exchange for Margot's hand. "We have to hurry," Adam says. "They will be after us."

They run back to the central lab and the gigantic aquarium, an oddly valuable landmark. Adam fumbles with the elevator controls. It requires some sort of scan, but he doesn't have the credentials.

"There's another way," Margot says. She leads him through a few hallways to a wooden door. "It runs parallel to the elevator. I've seen some enter this way. They'd go here when the elevators are transporting the trucks."

Adam kicks the door in. Inside, a rickety iron stairwell winds upward through the earth, a seemingly infinite helix of steps.

"How much time do we have?" Margot asks, beginning their ascent.

"None," Adam says. "Are there just the two levels?"

"I'm only aware of two. There may be more. What do you need to do?"

Adam's mind races, contemplating the weighty objectives: save Yusef, disable or destroy the nukes, end Bricker, find my teammates, and escape—oh yeah, and save the other scientists. Rather than get into the weeds, he tells her, "We have to stop them."

"Okay," Margot says. Her eyes search his face for more specifics, but he offers none. "Let's do it," she continues.

"Are you okay?" It occurs to him he probably should have asked this before they were running up a hundred stairs.

"Better than I've been in a while," Margot replies. "But you look much worse than I do." She hasn't lost her sense of humor.

They finally reach the next level and another door; this one is unlocked. Adam takes a moment to steady himself, drawing a deep breath to prepare for the unknown on the other side. He turns the handle and swings the door open.

Standing before him is an army of rebels. Their guns are leveled directly between their eyes, ready to unleash a deadly payload.

CHAPTER 70
THE PHOENIX

ON THE COLD STONE FLOOR, Adam, Margot, Guowei, Hala, Brandon, and Nigel kneel at gunpoint in the ARK command center, their hands behind their heads and their weapons in a pile before them. Jacki and Carlos are their only hope, but Adam doesn't see them on the security monitors. Chances are they've met a similar fate, or worse. When the world comes crashing down, this is where the button is pushed. They've traveled around the world to get here, only to become helpless spectators to the impending massacre.

A rebel guard steps aside, granting Zed entrance into the command center. He has cleaned himself up from his encounter with Adam, though his nose remains swollen and crooked. Cradled in his arms is Yusef, seemingly unharmed but devoid of expression. His eyes widen when he sees Hala. The guards notice, and one steps forward to point their rifle in her face.

Suddenly, every monitor in the command center snaps to black before a mosaic of Bricker in his office library appears. "This is where the magic happens," he says. "I admire your tenacity, your bravery. Kebe always had good taste. He prepared you well, just not well enough. Nevertheless, I must admit you've got something worth saving."

Rebel guards wrestle Jacki and Carlos into the room, forcing them to their knees in line with the rest. The clatter of their backpacks hitting the pile echoes like the shattering of Adam's hope.

"Oh good, now it's a party," Bricker says. "Can you go get my cake?"

Zed cracks a smile. "I ate it," he says.

"With the press of a button, I will wipe out 10 percent of the world's population," Bricker says, "and it's the 10 percent that needs to go first. Frankly, I'm putting them out of their misery. As they look down at us from their ivory towers in their cesspool cities, they do not realize that their structures and their minds are rotting from the inside. The world as you know it is over. Dams burst, ice caps melt, and the flood engulfs. But ARK will shepherd new life through the waters of this broken world. I'm offering you the chance of a lifetime. Be part of the solution and exterminate the problem. You all have special skills and qualities that can help usher in a new age. Join our big, happy family."

"You're a monster," Margot blurts. "Nobody wants your pathetic, sad—"A rebel jams his gun into her head.

"We aren't unlocking the weapons," Adam says.

"We'll see about that," Bricker replies. "But honestly, you all intrigue me more than your toys. My son might disagree."

"I do." Zed says without moving a muscle.

Bricker smiles before continuing. "I'm one of the few people who truly can appreciate how much work it has taken for you to get here today. About twenty years—it's nothing to sneeze at. I'd hate to see such a significant investment go to waste. You're Albert Einstein, for heaven's sake! Do you realize how long it would take me to make another one like you? You all are very valuable cattle. Your best days are still ahead of you."

Adam remains resolute, his body relaxed, and his spirit surprisingly at ease. "You'll have to kill us," he says. If he's going to die, he's ready.

"I might. And it would be a pity. I hope you recognize that what's before you is inevitable. You might not know it yet, but there's much worse to come to this world if I'm unsuccessful." Bricker glances at the others. "This is my best and final offer. Join us. Otherwise, we'll unfortunately have to drop a bomb on you. Come on, don't be shy."

Adam hasn't come this far to submit, and his teammates haven't either.

But then Nigel stands.

The thoughts of his teammates fly through Adam's iGlasses as messages: WHAT IS HE DOING? ARE YOU KIDDING ME? HAS HE BEEN PLAYING US THE WHOLE TIME? I KNEW SOMETHING WASN'T RIGHT WITH HIM. Adam himself struggles to articulate a coherent thought.

Carlos tries to look Nigel in the eye, but Nigel doesn't bother. Instead, he walks over to Zed and stands with the rebels behind him. "Don't hate," Nigel says. "It's a business decision."

"You're fake, man," Carlos shakes his head. Nigel just looks at the floor. Adam's mind whirls in disbelief, struggling to reconcile the teammate he thought he knew with the reality before him. Carlos sensed it from the minute he met him, but Adam didn't. He can't fathom that Nigel has been a fraud this whole time. It doesn't compute.

Bricker interrupts the tense silence. "That's a good start," he says, his voice flush with satisfaction. "Nigel, I'm honestly surprised your team was able to find us and make as much progress as they did. Others have tried. But it's you seven who made it. If I might ask, who do you think has been the most valuable?"

Nigel inhales deeply as if steeling himself to the weight of his decision. "Clearly, there's someone," Bricker continues.

"I mean, if there's one," Nigel says, "it's probably Jacki. She led us well."

"How am I not surprised?" Bricker says. Did Nigel just spare Jacki or put a bullseye on her? "Joan of Arc in the flesh. A warrior and one heck of a mother," Bricker continues. "It's a pity she doesn't see the value of being Joan of this ARK." He turns to Nigel. "So she's the greatest threat?"

Nigel hesitates, seemingly torn between loyalties. "Yeah, sure," he finally concedes. Jacki stares a hole through him. Two guards switch their attention over to her. "But the only reason we got here was Kebe," Nigel adds.

"Kebe . . . a good man," Bricker says. "Just worked for the wrong people." An automatic steel door opens, and a uniformed rebel with a stethoscope wrapped around their neck rolls a hospital gurney into the room. Other rebels follow, pushing beeping medical equipment. "Oh, good. I'm glad you are all here for this."

Lying on the hospital gurney is an old man, intubated and unresponsive.

The man in the bed is Bricker.

"Don't be startled," Bricker continues. "You are looking at a marvel of medicine and artificial intelligence. Though my body has failed me, my consciousness is here." Bricker gestures to his computer screen. "For now. Soon, it will return where it belongs when my body is up for it. My oldest son and I have been looking forward to the reunion for some time. We are excited to usher in a new age, walking side by side."

Carlos can't help but chuckle. "So that's you?" He nods to Bricker's body on the gurney. "Your crumpled-ass body."

"My brain still works just fine," Bricker replies.

"You're crazy, bro," Carlos says. A message from Carlos pops up on Adam's iGlasses: KILL THE BODY, KILL THE MIND. His chirp proves effective, extracting valuable information.

"A man can only do so much," Bricker says. "They have limitations, but fathers—well, fathers can lead generations. And perhaps I might indulge myself and live vicariously through my sons." Zed carries Yusef to the gurney and sets him on the ground. "I know you all met my boy, Yusef. He's a special kid. I've waited for this day since the moment I made him."

Yusef's eyes lock with Hala's, desperation scarring his face. "He's just a boy!" she says desperately. She lunges forward, but a brutal force slams her back onto her knees. Three guards point their guns at her. Yusef turns away.

"That is a really bad idea," Bricker says. "I want you to be alive to see this. If this won't convince you to be a believer in our mission, nothing will."

Zed crouches down next to Yusef. "You see that man?" He gestures to Bricker's body. "He really needs your help." Zed guides Yusef's gaze toward Bricker's screen, a silent plea for compliance.

Bricker smiles down at Yusef. "I'm really sick, and I need you if I'm going to feel better. I want you to heal me. Make me walk."

Yusef looks around, unsure what to do.

The Phoenix Elite watches him helplessly. It all becomes clear to Adam. If Yusef somehow heals Bricker, and Bricker raises him as his son, the consequences could be far more dire than anyone could have ever imagined. The magnitude of it all is suffocating.

"Be the man you're supposed to be," Bricker says.

"He could be hundreds of people," Adam spits out before a rebel jams a rifle into his neck.

Yusef concentrates and raises his hands like a magician. He wiggles his fingers, directing his energy toward Bricker's lifeless body.

But nothing happens. Yusef drops his hands. "I can't," he says.

Zed cocks his three-barreled pistol. Every impulse in Adam's body urges him to stop it. Fresh blood pumps into his muscles, priming him to act.

"Don't disappoint me, son," Bricker says, disappointed and threatening. "Heal me."

Yusef raises his hands again, hopelessness in his eyes. He clenches his jaw and channels all his determination, but again nothing changes.

"Heal me. Make a good choice. Heal me!" Bricker quivers with desperation.

Zed points his gun at Yusef. "Do it."

Before there's time to think, Nigel throws a left hook into Zed's cheek and dives for Yusef. The rebels open fire on Nigel as he shields Yusef with his body.

Chaos explodes.

Jacki snaps a rebel's elbow, grabs a gun, and mows down five others.

With a pair of guns, Carlos rampages through the crowd. He dives onto Nigel, sliding in the blood pooling under him. Carlos reaches for a pulse as he fires on another rebel.

Recovering from Nigel's punch, Zed aims and shoots Hala, Guowei, and Brandon with a single trigger pull.

Application windows open on various screens across the command center. Desperate, Bricker opens up the LAUNCH ALL button. He clicks it. Each drone icon on the map flashes a bloody shade of red, and a five-minute timer activates.

Jacki tackles Bricker's physical body, knocking over the gurney and all the apparatuses. She beats the hell out of him until she is tossed aside by Zed.

Adam attacks Zed, who connects with a short uppercut that sends Adam to the ground.

Brandon hurries to a keyboard. The submarine icons on the map start blinking. His fingers fly across the keys.

Guowei hurries to pull Yusef out from under Nigel. He's still alive. Urgently, he ushers him over to Margot. "Go!" he yells.

The mayhem plays out in front of Hala, who lies against the wall with her hand on her neck. Her fingers are covered in blood. A gunshot caught her up high.

A rebel rushes over to crush Guowei with the butt end of a pistol.

Hala springs to her feet, launching herself toward the rebel. With an elbow strike to his chest, she momentarily stuns him, and as the rebel swings back, she kicks the pistol out of their hand and sends it skittering toward Adam, who lies prone on the ground.

Zed, towering over Adam, punches him mercilessly. Adam grabs the pistol and fires, missing Zed's head but blasting the cartilage of his ear clean across the room. Doubled over in pain, Zed flees.

Jacki grabs Bricker's body from behind, locking in a rear naked choke. She kicks away tubes and wires connected to him. She squeezes whatever life is left inside out of him. Bricker's image on the monitor flickers until it vanishes, leaving only the silent library behind.

With the countdown clock ticking away, Brandon feverishly taps at the keyboard. DEACTIVATED flashes across the screen. "I got it!" he yells, whipping out his tasers to join the fray.

A red light blinks from the screens. "Brandon!" Adam shouts. Brandon incapacitates a rebel with his taser before scrambling back to investigate. "What the hell is that?"

Brandon zooms in on the map. "I . . . I don't . . . ," and then a sudden fear grips his voice, "Oh God, it's here! We have to get out!"

Guns spray bullets everywhere. Enemies fall. Guowei helps Carlos to his feet. Adam ushers everyone out the door.

Everyone except one.

"What about Nigel?" Hala asks.

"He's gone," Carlos says.

Jacki kicks open the door to the staircase. Adam watches as everyone races to the top, heading for safety. High above,

Margot lugs Yusef in her arms. However, Adam knows that his mission isn't complete. He runs in the opposite direction, down the staircase.

A level below, Adam arrives at the tank of scientists. He steadies his bazooka. With a resounding *kaboom!* the base quakes, and the warheads teeter precariously on the edge of destruction. His blast opens a hole through which the scientists flee. In the aftershock, the gigantic fish tank overhead shatters, releasing a deluge of water and fish, both alive and very much dead. Adam's clothes are drenched in the monsoon, but his focus remains unyielding. "We have to go!" he shouts above the cacophony.

The door to the freight elevator opens, and the scientists flood inside, with Adam in the rear, ensuring everyone is safely loaded in.

Now they are at the mercy of the speed of this elevator.

It begins its ascent, carrying them from the madness below. All Adam can do now is close his eyes. He did what he came here to do. Margot will be safe; his friends will make sure of that. If enduring his arduous existence on this earth was meant for that sole purpose, it was all worth it.

Finally, the doors open. The wood-lined corridor stretches out before them. A path to safety. With the scientists leading the way, Adam feels the base tremble beneath them. The front door is in sight, covered in foam but blasted off its hinges by rockets. A sign of success. His friends have made it out.

The scientists scurry through the door one at a time, their desperation driving them forward. Adam is almost there, only five strides from the doorway.

An earth-shattering explosion rocks the world, engulfing the base in a cataclysmic blast. The force propels Adam through the air, his body weightless, thrown like debris. As he hurtles through the air, he catches a glimpse of a vibrant wave of light passing over him before he collides face-first with the coarse bark of a sturdy mangrove tree.

Cheek on the ground, he looks back to the cabin to see it leap from the earth before being swallowed by a sinkhole. He glances over to see Margot huddled with his teammates. They have won.

The dust settles, and Carlos runs to him, shouting, "*Mijo!*" He swiftly conducts a frenetic triage inspection of him. Adam winces as searing pain blazes through his ribs, yet it's accompanied by a novel sensation of euphoria. It's never felt better to crash land into a marsh.

"I'm good," Adam says.

"My man!" Carlos helps him to his feet and joins the others. Deep breaths mingle with the scent of blood, and utter exhaustion permeates the air.

Hala wipes away her tears with trembling hands as she hugs Yusef. "I can't believe he did that," she says, choking on her emotions.

With the chaos of the skirmish behind them, the full weight of Nigel's sacrifice sets in. Seven people walked into this ordeal together, but now only six walk out.

"He did the right thing," Jacki says, her hand finding Hala's shoulder. "I didn't know he had that in him."

"Big ol' nuts on that boy," Carlos adds. "I guess Mandela might've been in there after all."

Wet eyes are everywhere, including Yusef, who likely felt the jolt of every bullet that struck Nigel's body. Adam locks eyes with the boy. "The man that saved you was named Nigel. Nigel Dillon."

Yusef pushes away from Hala and runs away. "Hey, kid!" Brandon says, but it's no use. They'll have to chase him. Carlos is the first to his feet.

Yusef stops at the edge of the sinkhole where the cabin once stood, now just a pile of scraps five meters below grade. He waits and waits. The smoldering embers gradually fizzle out amidst the wreckage.

"Look, mijo, he's gone." Carlos puts his hand on Yusef's head. "I'm very sorry." Carlos's sorrowful eyes search the faces of the others, silently pleading for guidance.

"Just let him," Jacki says.

Hala steps from the group and, with a gentle touch, rubs Yusef's back as he stares into the gaping void. But when she reaches for his hand to guide him away from the death, Yusef recoils, yanking his hand away. "No," he snaps.

The sound of rustling breaks through the hushed stillness. It gets louder and louder, more insistent with each passing moment.

Something stirs in the cabin wreckage. A bloodied hand pushes aside a broken plank.

It can't be.

Nigel pulls himself awkwardly from beneath the rubble, as astonished by his survival as his teammates are. A miracle unfolds before their eyes. All eyes shift to Yusef.

Climbing up the steep edge of the sinkhole, Nigel reaches out, his hand trembling with exhaustion and exhilaration. Carlos clasps it and pulls him up the final step.

"Does my face look all right?" Nigel asks.

"As ugly as ever," Carlos says, jerking Nigel into a tight embrace. At long last, they've become brothers. "Your fingernails look good, though."

Nigel turns his attention to Yusef, whose eyes shimmer with unshed tears of joy. Jovial, he scoops the child into his arm. "Hey, kid."

On Nigel's wrist, his gray phoenix flickers but remains orange.

EPILOGUE

THE CLEANUP EFFORTS HAVE BEGUN. Concrete and dust still cover the land where Paris once stood, and the corkscrew remnant of the Eiffel Tower reminds the world of what's been lost and the work ahead. But helping hands across Europe have brought equipment to remove the destruction. One thing is certain: in the face of the tragedy, like their brothers and sisters in Shanghai, France will rebuild.

Jacki steps across the debris. She pauses, absorbing the magnitude of the devastation. Her eyes trace the countless hands toiling tirelessly to mend the broken fragments of their beloved city. Disasters wrought from the worst in people can bring out the best in people. Shoulder to shoulder, once strangers but now united by tragedy, her neighbors work hand in hand and forge bonds that transcend the wreckage before them.

Jacki crosses the wreckage to what was once a sixteenth-century Catholic cathedral, shards of colorful plate glass crunching underfoot. A section of the wall still stands defiantly. Behind it is a gathering of hundreds of people, all captivated by a bishop's rousing sermon. Despite there being no pews and barely a building, today's church service goes on as scheduled.

Jacki slips into the back. She greets the family next to her with a smile. After three years away, she has returned.

SUPERHEROES CHASE each other across the sky, a flurry of movements that defy gravity. Their swift movements, a ballet of power and agility, accompany a symphony of zaps and blasts.

Kids sure do love their action figures.

And Hala loves watching them embark on their missions to save the world. She and her large family crack up at the impromptu performances, fueled by boundless creativity and youthful exuberance.

Hala's father played the gift giver with his unexpected presents. All the cousins got one—Yusef got two—and the toys look just like Hala and Guowei. Even though her father complains about how suspicious it is that Facebook sends him the perfect ads at just the right time, he can't help but click on them, which, in this case, led him down the rabbit hole to a make-your-own-action-figure website.

In the mix with his new Egyptian family, Yusef is doing exactly what he should be—just being a kid.

HARD AT WORK with family elders, Guowei is finishing the mrouzia under the careful supervision of Hala's sitto. After a taste, Sitto delicately sprinkles a handful of spices into the batch and gestures for him to stir it. He is far from mastering Arabic, but thankfully Sitto is very expressive with her hands.

Within earshot of the authentic joy, Guowei pokes his head from the kitchen window to catch a glimpse. Hala's cheeks radiate as she relishes the show with her sister just a stone's throw away. It's a vantage point he can grow accustomed to.

"I'm not sure what she expects," Guowei says to Hala.

"Well, you must not be doing too bad, *habibi*," Hala hollers back. "You're still in the kitchen!"

Suddenly, Sitto affectionately pinches Guowei's cheek, accompanied by a playful slap on the other side. "Inshallah," she mutters under her breath.

Hala points Guowei over to Yusef. With a flurry of whimsical sound effects, Yusef leaps toward another boy like he's a superhero himself. He does a lopsided somersault, eliciting an infectious belly laugh from the surrounding crowd. Guowei cracks up with her.

He's happened upon a new home.

THE MAP ON BRANDON'S iGLASSES gives him turn-by-turn directions for his walk through the labyrinthine office complex of the MIT campus. Maybe he will come across the Minotaur after all. Sporting a neat ponytail that tames his unruly hair, he's dressed in a freshly pressed shirt and slacks, ready for the job interview of a life-time—an opportunity tailor-made for a Benjamin Franklin. The campus laundromat still doesn't accept crypto, but fortunately he found a dry cleaner that does.

Brandon hesitates outside Room 1776, its door ajar, reluctant to disrupt the woman diligently engrossed in her work. He raps his knuckles against the door with a soft cadence. "Are you Henrietta?" he asks.

The lady looks up from her work. "Ah yes, Mr. Freeman, please shut the door."

THE WORN STONE PATH to Carlos's mother's humble abode is a testament to the countless people she has welcomed over the years. The front door, a portal of warmth and hospitality, perpetually open, invites friends and family into its embrace.

Carlos admires the plants in Mami's small garden. As he crosses the threshold, he is greeted by the uproar of a surprise party. It isn't much of a surprise—he saw everyone's cars parked along the street—but he feels the sentiment all the same. The entire community somehow always fits in his mother's living room.

Mami charges through the crowd, arms outstretched, her eyes brimming with uncontainable joy. She pulls him into a fierce embrace.

His little brother, Eddie, flaunts his phone around the room. It's playing the video of Carlos's heroic handiwork in the streets of Rome captured by a bystander. "Kaboom!" he shouts as Adam's bazooka fires. "It's at two million views!"

Carlos hugs his sister, smooshing their cheeks together. "You're crazy," she says.

Carlos can't help but break into a sheepish grin. "I know, I know."

Extraordinary pride gleams across the faces around the room. That was their boy out there saving the world. "Thank you all for coming," he says.

Mami grabs him by the head and plants a kiss on his cheek. "They need you back at the hospital. People have been waiting for you."

"There are other doctors there, Mami," he says. "They are good doctors." Brushing his thoughts aside, she dismisses this notion with a wave. "Fine, I'll get over there. But I want to make a few stops on my way."

Worry flashes across his mother's eyes. "Now don't you go running around with those bombs anymore," she says.

"I love you, Mami."

"No bombs!"

G OLD-PLATED CHAIRS with silky blue upholstery encircle a long oval table hewn from a single slab of granite. An entire wall of windows overlooks Johannesburg from a breathtaking vantage point. The modern skyscrapers light up the foreground, and the picturesque savanna hills roll in the back. Its beauty extends as far as the eye can see.

Executives wear suit jackets embroidered with the Dillon Exotics logo, for today is the day that Chief Executive Officer Chimdi Dillon is to appoint his son the company's new president, the crowning of a new prince. If there was a silver lining to being a clone of Mandela, Nigel might be able to avoid the graying horseshoe atop his father's grinning head—he'd take the smile, though.

"The keys are yours, my son," Chimdi says, handing Nigel a set of decorative Dillon Exotics keys. They pose for a photo op before his father pulls him in for a full-fledged hug, which prompts applause from the ten other guests.

Nigel has had second thoughts about this ascension his whole life. Recent events have only made it cloudier, but ultimately it is the right move.

"Thank you all for believing in me all this time," Nigel says. "I'm happy to take on this role, but I want to emphasize"—he eyes his father—"I'll be doing some things a little differently."

DILIGENTLY FOCUSED in the École Polytechnique chemistry lab, Adam undertakes nanomaterial synthesis by subjecting aluminum oxide to intense heat via a Bunsen burner. Goggles on, he directs a laser beam onto the flask and notes any observed structural, optical, and thermal properties of the material. Despite hours of dedicated work, precise control over the laser sensitization process eludes him. His dissertation, "Synthesis and Characterization of Laser-Responsive Nanomaterials for Quantum Applications in Fusion Energy," seemed promising. Yet the practical execution proves to be more resistant than anticipated, with the experiments stubbornly resisting his attempts to uncover its elusive secrets.

An envelope lands on the lab bench beside him. It's from OXFORD UNIVERSITY'S POSTDOCTORAL SCIENCE DEPARTMENT and addressed to him. He looks up to find Margot. "I've been waiting in the hall for hours, hoping to surprise you when you left," she says. "But this will have to do."

Adam rests his goggles on his messy hair. "I'm sorry. I had no idea."

A warm smile graces Margot's lips as she places a basket of plastic-wrapped cookies on the table. "I know. Because then it wouldn't have been much of a surprise, now would it, Einstein?" Her eyes twinkle with affection. "Your coffee's gotten cold." She uses tongs to take the flask off the mesh screen above the lit Bunsen burner and holds his Styrofoam coffee cup over it.

Adam unbundles the cookies, marveling at their home-made perfection—thick, crispy, and studded with chocolate chips. "You really didn't have to do this."

Satisfied with the extra heat, Margot turns off the burner and sets down Adam's coffee before settling on a lab stool across from him. "You know, after you finish saving the world, you don't have to jump right into your dissertation."

"It's good for me to stay busy."

Margot reaches for his hand. "You know there are other ways to stay busy?" He looks into her eyes and sees everything he's ever wanted.

Margot wears a black halter dress with lace around the edge. The neckline gracefully frames her collarbones, leaving her shoulders tantalizingly bare. Her trademark watch must be waiting at home. In its place is a slender bracelet that twists like a strand of DNA. She always wears that watch, and now he can see something he couldn't before.

On her wrist is the same phoenix mark he has on his.

Adam's voice quivers, unable to hide his astonishment. "Have you had that the whole time?" They've been going to school together for years. How hasn't he noticed?

Margot's gaze lingers on his wrist. "Yes, I kind of hate it. That's why I always wear my watch. And you might laugh, but I'm convinced it glows when I'm in the lab. Like it knows how much radiation I'm absorbing or something—and I'd rather not be reminded of such things."

Adam turns his wrist, his mark emanating a warm, orange glow. "You mean like this?"

Margot's icy-blue eyes widen in surprise.

Who is she?

"Well, let's worry about that insanity later. You've got mail."

"Oh, I, uh, there's no rush," Adam says. "I don't think I want to go to England. Too many . . . British people," he smiles. "I know exactly where I want to be."

A faint blush spreads across Margot's cheeks. "You, sir, need a cookie." She picks one up, bringing it to his lips. He takes a bite, and the gooey chocolate erupts on his tongue.

Adam reaches for a cookie to feed her in return, but as he stretches his fingers for one, a sudden vibration jolts his attention away. His phone is buzzing.

It's a group text from Brandon: !?!

THERE HAS BEEN NO ACTIVITY on the ARK social media feed for the last six months—until today. A solitary hyperlink has emerged. Clicking it loads a video posted on a file-sharing site from the dark web.

A haunting shadow dances on a rocky wall. The video, captured by an unsteady handheld camera, ventures deeper into a cavernous void, the atmosphere laden with an ominous sense of foreboding.

"Four score and seventeen years ago," says an eerily familiar voice, "a single man moved the world with his pen. Germany began a revolution the likes of which the world had never seen before."

As the camera moves forth, it reaches a dimly lit clearing. The shot focuses on an army materializing from the shadows, gathering figures built like titans. In perfect unison, they raise their arms in a salute.

"And we'll do it again."

The camera zooms in on their vacant eyes and the small black mustaches above their lips.

The story of Adam Eberhardt and the Phoenix Elite is just getting started. Stay tuned for Book 2 in the series, *The Phoenix Elite: Civil War,* which will be released in 2025.

As indie authors, reviews are integral to our efforts to reach new readers. If you enjoyed *The Phoenix Elite: Sacred Blood,* please consider leaving a review at your point of purchase and on Goodreads. Thank you for reading every last word!

C.T. Clark is a high school teacher turned author who is following the advice he's long given his students: "Dream, learn, grind." Having already penned an award-winning Amazon Studios screenplay, *The Phoenix Elite: Sacred Blood* is a passion project ten years in the making and his debut novel. C.T. resides in Central Ohio with his wife, six kids, and several guinea pigs. You can get plugged into C.T.'s internal world at http://www.ctclarkbooks.com

ACKNOWLEDGEMENTS

I had a great deal of maturing to do to give these characters the story they deserved. The core aspects of this story were written as a screenplay in 2012, but if I had published it then, so much would be missing. I had to develop individually, emotionally, culturally, and spiritually to write the story how it needed to be written. I still have a long way to go, but I hope I've done it justice.

As this crazy world has spun over the past twelve years, I saw aspects of my "fiction" bleed into reality in ways I didn't expect. This compelled me to revisit it in a new light. I decided to bring it back as a novel, primarily because of my desire to control the end product and write exactly what I wanted to. Several considerations must be taken into account in screenwriting. Countless fingers pull apart the story in the process, and what's left in the end often is so far from the author's original intent that it is not recognizable. But to realize it as a novel meant I had to really learn how to write.

I'd like to thank Michael C and Alexandra O, two of my earliest editors. I sent them what I thought was a novel—and after devoting nine months to writing it, I convinced myself as much. They endured it, saw through the writing and missteps, found my story anyway, and encouraged me to keep at it, seeing the potential in the ideas. After another six months of rewriting, I sent something entirely different to my third editor, Michael M. Few times in my professional and creative life have I found the synchronicity I've enjoyed with Michael. Not only has he really improved my writing and the delivery of the story, but he really got the tone I was after and knew the characters as well as me. Getting this novel across the finish line in this condition is a testament to his help.

I would also like to thank my loving wife, MacKenzie. We've had an interesting life so far. Writing such a thing would be impossible without her support and inspiration.

A significant impetus for writing was to give my eldest child, Logan, something to read. He had already read through a great deal of popular young adult literature, and I was interested in bridging his reading into adulthood. Each day in the summer was a challenge to give him another handful of pages to read. He kept wanting more and, thankfully, still does. The books (yes, this is the first in a five-part series) have become a fun conversation piece we can pick up occasionally. Thank you for reading, buddy!

And then, obviously, I need to acknowledge this book is impossible without my tumultuous, often circuitous, route to Jesus. The Christian allegory and commentary on modern American Christianity you may have picked up on are not accidental. While I am a broken person—not above reproach by any means—understand these aspects of the story were included with great veneration and a genuine hope there are better days ahead for the Christian culture that has gone astray. While I'm not qualified to deliver a sermon, I've been fortunate to witness the work of God come through several miracles throughout my life. Miracles that my degree in mathematics cannot explain any other way. I hope you see them, too. This does require that you pay attention to notice when they happen.